Sweat

Sweat

A novel by
Mark Gilleo

THE
STORY PLANT

The Story Plant
The Aronica-Miller Publishing Project, LLC
P.O. Box 4331
Stamford, CT 06907

Jacket design by Barbara Aronica Buck

Print ISBN-13: 978-1-61188-051-9
E-book ISBN-13: 978-1-61188-052-6

Visit our website at www.thestoryplant.com

For information, address The Story Plant.

First Story Plant Printing: August 2012

Printed in The United States of America

Acknowledgments

Acknowledgments can be tricky. There is always the risk of forgetting someone. I tried to keep this in mind when I was writing the acknowledgement section for my first novel, *Love Thy Neighbor*. Then I promptly forgot someone I had no excuse for omitting. So with that oversight in mind, I would like to thank my good friend, Tim Davis. Tim helped with both this manuscript and the last, and went as far as to try to teach me some proofreading symbols in his editing efforts. He is a better teacher than I am a student. So thank you Tim, and this time around you get top billing.

For this book, I would once again like to thank my A-team of readers: Jim Singleton, Fabio Assmann, Tim Davis, Michele Gates, Don Gilleo, Claire Everett and Sue Fine. I would also like to thank a couple of other people for their opinions, help, support, and in at least one case, a potential idea for a future book. So for their various input, contribution and support, I would like to thank Sharon Mitchell, Marlo Ivey, Cornelia Newbold, Amy Ganz and Jim Mockus. I would also like to thank Lou Aronica and The Story Plant.

And last, but certainly not least, I would like to thank my family and friends, in particular my wife, Ivette.

Prologue

Morphine made the Sunday paper more palatable. For as long as Jake could remember, coffee had been the chosen accompaniment for the Lord's Day morning ritual. Mass, a thick paper, the Sunday ads, and a pot of good drip coffee. But when a yellow hue in the eyes indicates liver failure, and when the kidneys are relying on a dialysis machine to do their work, routines have a way of changing. Sure, caffeine was the still the champ of the legal morning kick, but it did little to ease bone-deep pain.

The story began in the lower left corner on the front page of *The Washington Post* and snaked through several columns between pages eight and ten. Jake, dressed in jeans and a dark blue Georgetown University t-shirt, his Sunday's best gathering dust in the closet, took a sip of water. He cleared his throat and read aloud with smooth clarity and muted animation, taking cues from the professional voices on the audio books that were strewn about the corner table in the bedroom. The article was a human-interest story, a journalist's rendition of the facts, pieces of a case pulled together from observations, known habits, and evidence:

Sometime before ten in the evening on May 3rd, Kazu Ito, advanced placement high-school student, broke from his statuesque pose overlooking his college-level calculus text and stood from his chair. He interlocked his fingers and stretched toward the ceiling, exhaling in a squeal that finished with a small roar. He grabbed his iPod off the corner of his desk, pulled his Seattle Seahawks hooded sweatshirt over his black head of hair, and left the lights on in his room as he shut the door.

Kazu stepped off the front porch and stared at the light shining through the trees and fog in the strip of woods between his house and the gas station mini-mart on Route 18. It was time for his evening study-break. Straight A's didn't come easy, and Kazu powered his cerebral engine with Mountain Dew and Skittles.

The son of Japanese parents working for a local Sharp Electronics research facility, studying was a way of life. He didn't have the verve of an immigrant's son trying to pull himself from a third-world background. His father was an engineer, his mother the daughter of one. They had moved from Tokyo, hardly a city teeming with flies and raw sewage. No, Kazu didn't have to study to climb the social ladder. He had to study because his parents were Japanese and they demanded that he did. It was that simple.

The mini-mart with two pumps in the front parking lot was off the beaten track, two miles from the center of town and the strip malls and supermarkets that sprung up during the years following the high-tech boom in the great Northwest.

Luke "Pops" Wilson greeted everyone who came into his establishment with the same smile, a modest flash of dentures and reborn Christianity. At sixty-five, his face weathered by the passage of life and years of wild youth, Pops was now a man of peace. When the young man entered the store from the fog and darkness and asked to use the john, Pops smiled and pointed to the single door on the far side of the establishment he had owned for over three decades. As his only patron in the last hour weaved his way past the coffee machine, the hot-dog roller, and the long aisle of candy and chips, Pops looked out the front window at an empty lot.

He turned on the small radio he kept on the counter and

checked the clock on the wall. In twenty minutes he would hit the lights, count the day's cash, and put it in the safe in the small office in the back of the single story building. Tomorrow he would start over at the crack of dawn and thank the good Lord for his job and the ability to serve the public with petrol and snacks for the road.

Pops heard the door to the bathroom shut and looked up. By the time the flash of darkness moving behind the far aisle registered, it was too late. The blast from the sawed-off double-barreled shotgun sent him into the cigarette and chewing tobacco display, nicotine vices raining down on his body as it crashed to the floor. Sprawled on the tiles, Pops fought for consciousness as the backside of a dark sweatshirt dug through the register and shoved wads of cash into its pockets. When Pops opened his eyes again, he was alone. With waning strength, he squirmed across the floor and pushed the silent alarm button under the counter with the toe of his boot. Gasping, he pulled the phone off the counter by its cord. The call to 911 was the last one Pops would ever make.

Kazu Ito walked into the mini-mart with his hood on and his iPod blaring. He bee-lined it for the cold sodas in the refrigerator in the back of the store and stopped at the magazine rack on his way to the register to check out AutoWeek's Import Car of the Year. Mountain Dew and Skittles in hand, music playing beneath his hood, Kazu never saw the police officer high on adrenaline and hell-bent on blind justice. He never heard the word "freeze."

The mini-mart, thirty years without incident, claimed its second victim in ten minutes. By the time the ambulance and police back-up arrived on the scene, the sawed-off shotgun left by the original robber was resting firmly in Kazu's rapidly cooling hands and the store's surveillance tape had magically disappeared.

Jake stopped reading as the boney hand of his lone audience landed on his arm. He looked over at the gaunt face next to him and watched her chest rise and fall in shallow breaths. He read the last paragraph of the article to himself and folded the paper in his lap.

Kazu Ito was dead. That was the only fact that really mattered, the only fact that had a family in the Seattle suburb of South Renton screaming for justice and weeping for consolation. The rest of the story was a distraction. The Kazu Ito incident was the third killing of an innocent Asian in the Seattle region by law enforcement in just under a year. But before he rested in peace, Kazu would reach out from the great beyond to jumpstart the biggest news story of the year.

And Jake's life would hang in the balance.

Chapter 1

The half-paved road made a wide turn around a stand of palm trees and abruptly ended at a closed metal gate fifty yards ahead. The black four-door sedan with tinted windows rounded the curve and hit its brakes, a cloud of dirt washing over the freshly waxed vehicle. The trailing white ten-seater van steered its way through the wave of dust, bounced through a rut in the road, and lurched to a final halt, brakes screeching.

Senator John Day primped himself in the backseat of the car. He straightened the collar of his shirt, checked his fly, and decided for the second time that he looked dapper enough for the camera and the occasion.

"Are we ready to do this thing?" the senator asked, not looking for an answer. His Chief of Staff nodded from the driver's seat as he put the car into park.

Senator Day stepped from the car and stared down the towering fence line with as much stoicism as his jet-lagged mind could muster. His tall lean frame hunched forward and he pressed his hands into the small of his back. "My back is killing me."

Peter Winthrop, American businessman-turned-tour-guide, rose from his side of the car. "Eighteen hours on a plane isn't good for anyone except a chiropractor and his accountant."

Peter took a deep breath of the saltwater-laden air, and stared at the sprawling compound of buildings and warehouses in front of them. "What do you think?" he asked, looking over the roof of the vehicle.

"Christ, Peter. It looks like a prison camp." The senator ran his fingers through his straight salt-and-pepper hair and contemplated the task at hand.

"It is a prison camp," Peter responded with a smile, hitting the senator on the shoulder as he made his way around the trunk of the car. "But it's *our* prison camp."

The door to the white van slid open and a four-man filming crew poured from the vehicle into the blistering afternoon sun. A blurry layer of haze and heat hovered over the ground, the warmth of the earth radiating up the pants legs of the politician from Massachusetts.

"Where is our host?" Senator Day asked.

"I thought we'd be met at the entrance," Peter answered. "Let me see what I can do."

"Please. I didn't just travel halfway around the world to stand in the heat."

Peter walked past the closed gate of the ten-acre facility, his tanned skin relishing in the tropical sun. He peeked into the unmanned guard booth and picked up a gray phone on a wooden post near the massive chain-link fence. Peter frowned at the phone, a telecommunications relic without a dial, and put it to his ear. A faint ring teased the limits of his hearing, and he pressed the phone harder to the side of his head.

Across the dirt entrance to the facility, the senator's filming entourage stared at their destination, mouths gaping, eyes bulging. The pudgy cameraman with a perfectly trimmed goatee squinted behind his designer sunglasses. "Good God," he said.

"'Good God' what?" the senator snapped from a distance.

"Sir, I think that is razor wire," the cameraman quipped, pointing his finger to the large rolls of flesh-slicing metal that topped the fence for as far as the eye could see. "I'm not so sure…"

Senator Day growled. "You are getting paid to film and keep your mouth shut. You'll do exactly as you are told. You'll film what I tell you to film. No razor wire, no gates, no security guards, no guns. Keep it clean." The senator paused and then continued. "No, scratch that. I don't want clean, I want fucking *charming*. Think Disneyland."

A glint of disdain simmered in the cameraman's eyes.

"Well, get moving," the senator snapped. He always felt better when he was giving orders.

The cameraman turned toward his director's assistant, his soundman, and the college intern who did most of the heavy work. "Let's get the equipment out of the van. We can start filming an opening sequence with the company sign in the background." The senator nodded at the cameraman and smiled. The freshly painted *Chang Industries* sign was sandwiched between a set of soaring palm trees, the white lettering on the blue background melting perfectly into the tropical sea in the distance.

The college intern, the lone wheel in his mind beginning to turn, mumbled to the bohemian director-in-training. "Is that fence to keep people in or to keep people out?" The entourage, hands full of camera equipment, paused briefly and looked back up at the fence.

No one answered.

The senator's chief aide and head of public relations, Scott Ryder, a Columbia grad with a Tom Cruise smile, stood next to his boss as Senator Day rubbed his chin, one elbow on the roof of the car.

"Sir, quite frankly the cameraman isn't the only one concerned. I have my reservations as well."

"Scott, your opinion is noted."

"Senator, if someone should decide to check out this facility, to verify our little show, it could prove, shall we say, problematic." The senator's aide, still looking impeccable after twenty-four hours on the road, shifted his weight from foot to foot as if he had to take a leak.

"That's what I have you for, to ensure that things don't become problematic."

"Sir, with all due respect, there could be ramifications..."

"Thank you," the senator said sternly, looking down his nose at his aide. "I'll notify you when your opinion is needed again."

Peter Winthrop leaned on the post next to the fence and finished his conversation before hanging up the phone. He turned his broad shoulders toward the senator and approached the hood of the car with a smile. He loosened his royal blue tie and spoke with his usual car salesman tone.

"The owner apologizes for keeping us waiting. Someone will open the gate momentarily. The guard at the front gatehouse is making his afternoon patrol of the perimeter. He should have been here to let us in."

"Patrolling the perimeter?"

"I'm sure it's just an expression."

Senator Day turned at the waist and looked around. Scott was sulking near the trunk, shuffling through his electronic organizer and the senator's schedule for the upcoming week. Across the makeshift movie studio at the entrance to Chang Industries, the cameraman arranged the angle of the video camera on a tripod and assessed the lighting. He ordered his crew around like a basketball coach without a whiteboard, fingers pointing left, arms darting right.

The senator leaned toward Peter and spoke quietly. "Peter, this place isn't exactly as advertised."

"Since when is advertising accurate?"

"This is not a joke."

"Everything is fine, Senator. You wanted a garment manufacturing facility. I give you Chang Industries. I've been doing business with the Chang family for years. It has been a mutually beneficial and financially rewarding relationship. This place is ours for the filming. Just look around. Fabulous sunsets, views of the ocean, palm trees, and not a cloud in the sky."

"Nothing is perfect," the senator said. A bead of sweat ran down his brow, past the distinguished crows-feet stretching from the corner of his grey eyes.

"Relax, Senator. After we film, I'll see to it that you get a massage. Maybe get two girls to work on you. Clothing optional."

The senator paused. "No one underage."

"Of course," Peter answered, smiling.

A brief, audible buzz interrupted the conversation. The front gate to the facility chugged with a rattle of loose metal, then began to slide open without further protest.

Lee Chang and a well-built Chinese employee made their way across the open dirt lot between the gate and the main building. Senator Day's eyes passed over the manager of the facility and settled on the enormous employee with the ponytail and powerful swagger. The senator muttered under his breath. "Look at this guy. The Mountain of Shanghai."

Peter grunted in response.

Lee Chang stepped through the still-moving gate and greeted Peter with a handshake and a pat on the shoulder. "Good to see you again, Peter," Lee said in near perfect English. "Sorry to keep you waiting. One of my guards should have been here to let you in." Lee's red silk button-down shirt flapped lightly in the wind. His jet-black hair was freshly combed, a thin moustache stretched over his lip.

"I hear he was patrolling the perimeter," the senator said.

"Lee," Peter interrupted, pulling his host by the elbow. "It's a great honor for me to introduce Senator John Day from Massachusetts."

"Senator Day, it's a pleasure to meet you. Welcome to Saipan, Commonwealth of the Northern Mariana Islands."

"Thank you for allowing us to visit your facilities."

"The pleasure is mine, Senator. Anything you need, just ask. Anything at all." Lee Chang stepped aside and his oversized companion cast a shadow on the senator's torso. "I would like to introduce my assistant and a longtime associate of the Chang family, Chow Ying. He arrived last month to help me out here at Chang Industries."

"Exactly what does he help with, moving furniture?" the senator asked, smiling and extending his hand.

More handshakes followed as the senator's chief-of-staff and the camera crew were introduced. Behind his calm exterior, the senator's penetrating grey eyes were measuring everything in his vision. Next to him, Peter Winthrop also calculated the possibilities of the scenario. While Lee Chang was playing the role of gracious host, all sides knew it was a wad of cash in a brown envelope that was the main motivation behind the welcoming committee.

The senator looked around at the afternoon sky and spoke. "It would be great if we could get a tour and pick our spots for filming."

"Of course, Senator. This way please."

Lee Chang sugarcoated the tour of the facilities as he walked, the live performance of a rehearsal perfected earlier in the day. He kept his visitors moving, answering the senator's questions as the cameraman took notes and the entourage lugged equipment and whispered among themselves.

"Chang Industries is truly a global success story," Lee Chang said, his hands sweeping in a grand gesture away from his body. "Our workers are the epitome of the success of globalization. The standard of living and wages we supply our workers will deliver them and their families from the poverty of some of the poorest countries in the region." Lee paused for effect. "And, as you all know, everything produced here on Saipan is officially made in the U.S.A."

"Everyone wins," the senator said aloud.

"Everyone wins," Lee Chang repeated.

"Could you tell us more about your employees?" Peter asked, knowing the response before it was given.

"Our girls are very well cared for," Lee said. "We run the cleanest facility on the island. As you are about to see."

Lee Chang briefly glanced around the property for his missing guard and then continued his tour. "There are three main buildings here at Chang Industries, in addition to several smaller structures where we store chemicals, tools, excess material. The building on the left houses an infirmary and an office on the first floor. My personal residence is above the infirmary on the top two floors. My home is not very large, but it is more than adequate for my simple tastes. The building in the middle is the workshop floor. Two warehouses are located in the back of the workshop at the rear of the building. On a busy day we have over a hundred workers in here, making everything from winter parkas to khaki shorts."

As the group approached the front doors of the workshop floor, Lee Chang continued. "The large building to the right is the seamstresses' living quarters, which I will show you momentarily."

The cameraman asked the entourage to hold their position in front of the building. He snapped several still frame shots and filmed a minute of footage with the senator and his chief-of-staff surrounded by Lee Chang, Peter Winthrop, and the large Chang Industries employee.

Lee Chang led the smile-brigade until the cameraman dutifully said, "cut." The light on the video camera clicked off, and Lee Chang forged ahead. "As I mentioned, the building we are about to enter is the main floor of the manufacturing facility. Twenty-five thousand square feet of efficiency."

The tour of Chang Industries took just over two hours. They filmed inside the main doors to the facilities and next to the entrance to a scrubbed and sterilized warehouse. Long tables stretched from one end of the work floor to the other, the hard benches made from mismatched planks of wood tidily tucked under the tables, out of sight. Flower bouquets stood at the end of each row of workbenches.

"Can we film in the seamstresses' quarters?" the senator asked.

"Of course. Of course," Lee Chang answered.

The crowd walked through the double doors of the seamstresses' quarters, past a pile of neatly stacked shoes and slippers near the entrance. Lee Chang led them to the first room on the right. The movie set was built and waiting for the camera.

"This room is typical of the housing here at Chang Industries. Each worker has her own bed, TV, air conditioning, and desk. There is a shared bathroom at the end of the hall that was remodeled last summer."

Peter took his turn giving orders. "Film this room. Be sure to get the TV and the air-conditioning." He turned toward the senator and winked. "This room is better than most college dorms, and we pay twenty grand a year for our kids to have that privilege."

The camera crew set their equipment in the hall and filmed directly into the room. "Where are the workers now?" the cameraman asked, earning him a scowl from the senator.

"I arranged for the workers to have the afternoon off in the city. I thought it would expedite your filming efforts."

The cameraman knew he was being lied to. What he didn't know was that upstairs, packed eight to a room, a hundred seamstresses from a dozen Southeast Asian countries were huddled behind locked doors. Sweating through another tropical afternoon, they took turns rubbing each other's backs, putting hand lotion on their calloused knuckles, nursing various ailments that came with carpal tunnel syndrome and the occasional on-the-job beating. They didn't know who their visitors were, or why they had spent most of the day cleaning a hole-in-the-wall sweatshop. But they would know when their visitors left. They would be back at their machines before the front gate closed.

Filming concluded with shots on a knoll behind the main manufacturing area, the slight elevation allowing the camera to focus over the barbed wire fence for an unobstructed view of a brilliant sunset over the waters of the Pacific. With the proper angle, proper lighting, and proper focus, the cameraman followed his orders to perfection. The fifteen thousand dollars he and his men had received for immortalizing lies in the lens of his camera wouldn't weigh on his conscience. He didn't have one. Fifteen grand for eighteen hours in a plane, a few hours of camera work, and two days in the sun. It was easy money.

The senator's filming entourage milled about near the main gate, whispers floating between them. Lee Chang eyed the group as he walked past. "I'm afraid I'm not going to be able to join you and the senator for dinner this evening, Peter," Lee said flatly, approaching Peter from the side. "I have some urgent business that needs my attention."

"I'm sorry to hear that," Peter replied. "Maybe you and I can get together on my way back from Hong Kong next week?"

"It's possible. I have some business trips planned, but if you let me know your schedule, I'll see what I can do," Lee Chang answered. "Meanwhile, I've taken the liberty of reserving your favorite table at The Palm. I assume that is acceptable for you and the senator."

"That's fine. Thank you for the trouble."

"No trouble at all. And if you like, Chow Ying can drive you over and see to it that you make it back to the hotel safely," Lee Chang offered, gesturing toward the large Chinese man who hadn't strayed far since their arrival. "He's very reliable. And not only does he drive but he's big enough to keep you out of trouble, should you find any," he added with a laugh.

The senator looked at his all-star aide. "Scott, take the night off."

The senator's chief-of-staff looked around. In Washington, he would have protested for the opportunity to stay awake for another twenty-four hours in the name of career advancement. But looking around, he saw no one to impress. And he couldn't imagine any restaurant on the island with a who's who reservation list.

"Yes, sir. I'll grab a beer in the hotel bar and hit the hay. Getting up early to go waterskiing tomorrow."

The senator rubbed his hands together. "Well, then, that's settled."

Ten minutes later, with the white van packed, Lee Chang, Peter Winthrop, and Senator Day waved the senator's public relations filming entourage goodnight.

As the van pulled away in a small cloud of dust, the senator inspected the main guard booth and the now present guard. Lee Chang took Peter by the arm and stepped away. The sweatshop boss dropped his voice to a whisper and looked over Peter's shoulder as he spoke, "Interested in the usual companionship?"

Peter, in turn, looked over at the senator who looked back and nodded in approval to the conversation he couldn't hear but fully understood. "Is Wei Ling available?" Peter asked as if ordering his favorite wine from the menu.

"Yes, of course. Wei is available. Shall I find a companion for the senator as well?"

"Yes, the senator would enjoy some company. Someone with a good command of English. I don't think he wants to spend the evening playing charades," Peter responded.

"No, I'm sure he wouldn't." Lee Chang smiled, nodded, and barked at Chow Ying in Chinese. The large subordinate walked across the front lot of Chang Industries, down the side of the main building, and vanished into the seamstresses' two-story living quarters. The CEO, senator, and sweatshop ruler went upstairs to wait.

Traditional Chinese furnishings cluttered Lee Chang's living room.

"Nice piece," the senator said, running his hands across a large black cabinet with twelve rows and columns of square drawers.

Peter spoke. "It's an antique herbal medicine cabinet. The Chinese characters written on the front of each drawer indicate the contents."

"Tattooed reminders of a former life," the senator said with poetic license.

Lee Chang stepped over and pulled open one of the drawers. "And now it holds my DVD collection."

"Modernization never stops," Peter added.

The three men found their way to the living room and Peter and Senator Day sat on the sofa. Lee took a seat on a comfortable wooden chair, small cylindrical pillows made from the finest Chinese silk supporting his arms.

The middle-aged woman who entered the room to serve tea didn't speak. She had standing orders not to interrupt when her boss's guests were wearing suits. The senator watched the woman skillfully pour tea from a blue and white ceramic teapot. He wondered if the woman was Lee Chang's lover. Peter knew Lee's taste ran much younger.

The intercom came to life on the wall near the door and Chow Ying announced that the ladies were ready. A brief exchange followed in rapid-fire Chinese before Lee Chang ended the conversation abruptly, flipping the intercom switch off.

"Gentlemen, if you are ready, the car is waiting."

The senator took the front seat next to Chow Ying. Peter gladly sat in the back seat, squeezing in between the two beautiful Asian women. As he got comfortable in the rear of the car, Wei Ling whispered in his ear, her lips tickling his lobe. Peter smiled as his lover's breath blew on his neck.

Shi Shi Wong, the senator's date for the evening, looked up at the seamstresses' quarters as the car began to move. She spotted several faces pressed against the glass of a second floor window and fought the urge to wave.

By the time the black Lincoln exited the gate of Chang Industries, Peter had one arm around each lady. He kept them close enough to feel their bodies move with every bump in the road. He leaned his torso into theirs with every turn of the car.

Peter Winthrop's favorite table at The Palm was in an isolated corner next to a small balcony overlooking intimidating cliffs thirty yards from the back of the restaurant. A steady breeze pushed through the open French doors that led to the balcony, blowing out the candle in the center of the table as they arrived.

Peter asked for recommendations from the chef and ordered for everyone. They had spicy barbecued shrimp for an appetizer, followed by a salad with freshly sliced squid that the senator refused to eat. For the main course, the party of four shared a large red snapper served in a garlic and lemon-based Thai sauce. Copious amounts of wine accompanied every dish.

Chow Ying waited subserviently in the parking lot for over three hours. He fetched two cups of coffee from the back door of the kitchen and drank them in the Lincoln with the driver's side doors open. With his second cup of coffee, he asked the waiter how much longer he thought the Winthrop party was going to be.

"Another hour at the most," came the reply.

On the trip back to the hotel, the honorable senator from Massachusetts threw his honorability out the window and sat in the backseat with the ladies. Flirtatious groping ensued, the senator's hands moving like ivy on human walls. His Rolex came to rest on Wei Ling's shoulder. His Harvard class ring continued to caress the bare skin on Shi Shi Wong's neck.

Peter made conversation with Chow Ying as the driver forced himself not to look in the rearview mirror. Peter, never bashful, glanced at Wei Ling on the opposite side of the backseat, their eyes meeting with a twinkle, her lips turning up in a smile for her lover. Peter smiled back.

Wei Ling was beautiful, and a sweetheart, and intriguing enough for Peter to find an excuse to stop in Saipan when he was on business in Asia. He usually brought her a gift, nothing too flashy, but something meaningful enough to keep her compliant in the sack. A dress, lingerie, earrings. He liked Wei Ling, a simple fact tempered by the realism that he was a CEO and she was a third-world seamstress. Pure attraction couldn't bridge some gaps. But Lee Chang was proud of the fact that Peter had taken a fancy to Wei Ling. It was good business. She was a company asset. He wished he could put her on the corporate balance sheet.

Chow Ying dropped the party of four off at the Ritz, an eight-story oasis overlooking the finest stretch of white sand and blue water on the island. He gave Wei Ling and her sweatshop roommate-turned-prostitute-without-pay a brief command in Chinese and followed with a formal handshake to the senator and Peter. He waited for the four to vanish through the revolving door of the hotel and then pulled the Lincoln into the far corner of the parking lot.

The senator and Peter weaved slightly across the lobby of the hotel. Wei Ling and Shi Shi Wong followed several paces behind. The concierge and hotel manager, jaws dropping momentarily, engaged in a seemingly urgent conversation and didn't look up until the elevator doors had closed.

Chapter 2

The memorial service was held at St. Michael's, a stone and masonry masterpiece that stood at the intersection of Pennsylvania Avenue and Twenty-Third Street in the District. The main vestibule of the church sat three hundred comfortably, four hundred if the parishioners were willing to get friendly. Christmas and Easter had the sinners lined out the door, but on a Saturday morning for a funeral, the pews were less than a quarter full. Father McKenna, who had baptized Jake twenty-four years before, just feet from where the padre now stood, opened the Bible and read a verse from Corinthians.

Jake Patrick slouched and wiped tears from his eyes, shoulder-to-shoulder with his relatives in the front row of pews. Three uncles, their spouses, eleven cousins, and old friends of the family Jake had known since birth had all made the trek from Portland. Distant friends and relatives in both geography and support. With a nod from Father McKenna, Jake stepped forward and delivered the main eulogy, a speech he wrote and rewrote two dozen times before he came up with something good enough for his deceased mother. Uncle Steve followed with a few words of his own, and when he finished laying praise on his sister of forty-eight years, there wasn't a dry eye in the house.

His mother would have appreciated the sentiment, if she hadn't been so pragmatic. But before Susan Patrick had passed, she'd let it be known that the funeral wasn't for her—it was for those she was leaving behind. She was in good hands. "The rest of you still have time to serve," she loved to say. The last time Jake heard his mother utter those words with her magical smile and a wink, he had managed to laugh. They laughed together amidst the plethora of medical equipment that had filled his mother's living room—beeping and pumping and hissing—straining to prolong her life.

Yes, his mother would have appreciated the friends, family, and co-workers who came to pay their last respects. The good thing about dying slowly, if there is any redeeming quality in prolonged agony, was the opportunity it gave everyone to say goodbye. It was a morbid reality and an opportunity that perhaps only the loved ones of someone lost suddenly can truly appreciate. Real tragedy struck without warning.

The crowd came to pay their respects, the goodbyes long since expressed. And less for a single exception, there were no surprises, no unexpected faces in the multi-colored streams of light formed by the sun forcing its way through the arching stained-glass windows.

Six pallbearers were more than enough to lift the casket, the container far outweighing its contents. Jake didn't see his father until he was exiting the church, one sixth of the weight of the casket resting on his left shoulder. Their eyes met, his father nodded, and for a second Jake thought he saw a tear on the cheek of the man he hadn't seen in over six years.

The procession followed the hearse and its police motorcycle escort through Saturday morning traffic to King James Memorial off Sixteenth Street. Jake's mother had agreed with the selection of her final resting place, a stone's throw from Rock Creek Park and the National Zoo. It was nice—as far as cemeteries go—and if that helped to ease the grief of those she was leaving behind, then fine. Personally, she didn't care where they put her. Her credo was, "Love me when I'm alive, not when I'm dead."

Most did.

The ashes-to-ashes, dust-to-dust ceremony at the plot of freshly dug earth was short. Hands caressed the casket in a final unfulfilling gesture of intimacy, roses placed on the white cloth that draped the middle of the coffin like an untied belt. Jake made his way to the casket, gave his mother a symbolic final kiss goodbye, and then broke down sobbing for the only person in the world he really loved.

The post funeral gathering was held at Uncle Steve's; Jake's only relative who didn't require a long-distance phone call. The familiar faces from the first several rows of pews at St. Michael's now filled the tight, outdated kitchen with its cracked Formica countertops and worn linoleum floor. The women tried unsuccessfully to evict the men who stood around the small kitchen table inhaling chips and dip, circling like vultures waiting for a more substantial carcass. Jake's mother's favorite jazz CD played in the living room, loud enough to hear throughout the small first floor of the brick row house.

Uncle Steve, fifty, bald, and feisty, passed out cold Miller Genuine Drafts to anyone who would join him in a pre-noon drink. Mrs. Nelson from two doors down moved her sixty-eight-year-old body like the former salsa dancer that she was, and transformed the dining room table from a bachelor pad pile of magazines and newspapers to a place where people could sit down and eat. Smokers were banished to the back porch by Father McKenna, who was the first to take Uncle Steve up on his offer for a late morning beer.

The doorbell rang and Uncle Steve, bald head glistening from the heat of the kitchen, shuffled toward the front foyer, beverage in hand. A curtain hung over the oval window in the antique door, offering only a silhouette of the tardy guest. Steve peeked behind the curtain, yanked the tarnished brass knob, and opened the door. Cold stares spoke volumes as the silent collision of the past and present soured the already somber atmosphere.

"It's been a long time Peter," Uncle Steve said.

"Yes it has, Steven."

The two men stood face-to-face through the half-opened door and Uncle Steve made no effort to invite the guest into the house.

"Jake mentioned he saw you at the memorial service. Awfully nice of you to come."

"I didn't know that Susan had passed. I got a phone call in Hong Kong and caught the next plane out as soon as I heard," Peter replied honestly.

"Still the world traveler, eh?"

"Some things never change."

"You said it, not me," Steve replied with bite.

Miles Davis filled the void in conversation.

"Still in the roofing business?" Peter asked.

"When my body lets me. Bad back, worse knees. Some mornings I can barely get out of bed."

"Looks like your liver is still working," Peter retorted, gesturing in the direction of the bottle in Steve's hand.

For a brief second it was just like old times, two brothers-in-law taking jabs at one another. But time has a way of making strangers out of even brothers, and another moment of awkward silence fell on the two.

"Could we not do this today?" Peter asked. "I just stopped by to say that I'm sorry for your loss. I know you and Susan were close."

"Yes we were, but not as close as your son was to his mother."

"May I come in?"

Steve considered the request but didn't move. It was a battle of wills between Uncle Steve, a blue-collar roofer with dirt under his nails, and Peter Winthrop, *GQ* magazine cover model with manicured nails.

"Just for a minute. I won't stay long."

"You never did," Steve replied. He took a swig of his beer, fully opened the door with his left hand, and motioned his ex-brother-in-law into his home.

Peter advanced slowly through the living room, past an old upright piano littered with pictures of people he knew a lifetime before. Uncle Steve followed behind, observing Peter as he took in the ghosts of his past. Peter nodded to an elderly couple on the couch. The white haired husband and wife nodded back at the well-dressed stranger.

Peter stopped at the entrance to the kitchen. Jake was at the back door, talking to a vaguely familiar face whose name Peter had long since forgotten. The crowd ripping through the hors d'oeuvres and working on food preparations took notice of the intruder, held their breaths, and exited the room as if someone had discovered a bomb in the refrigerator.

Jake felt the vacuum created around him and turned toward the far doorway to the kitchen. As the whispers grew in the next room, father and son stood at opposite sides of the kitchen like heavyweights in their respective corners of the ring before a fight. Uncle Steve stepped back to give the two some privacy, while remaining close enough to intervene if they needed a referee.

"Hi son," Peter offered first.

"Hi Dad," Jake replied. It felt normal to call him Dad, but it was a title he used without any emotional attachment.

"How are you holding up?" Peter asked, out of his element in the role of a father.

"Been better."

"Yeah, I guess so. Sorry to hear about your mother."

"I'm sorry too," Jake replied. He wondered if his father was as uncomfortable as he was.

A long pause interrupted the stalling conversation.

"I wish there was something I could have done."

"You could have stopped by and visited her. She was your wife at one point. And the mother of your only child."

"I didn't think she wanted to see me."

"She was dying, Dad. She wasn't in the mood for a fight."

"Well if she wasn't in the mood for a fight, then I'm sure she didn't want to see me."

Jake forced a small, brief smile. "Mom didn't share your problems with me and she never uttered a bad word about you when I was around. She didn't walk around singing your praises, but she never badmouthed you either."

"She was a good woman."

"The best."

"You're right. I should have come to see her." Peter didn't believe his own words, but hoped they would provide some comfort to his son.

The resemblance between father and son was unmistakable. The broad shoulders, the brown hair, the chiseled face. The smile. The walk. Jake was casually mesmerized, staring into the paternal mirror at what he expected to look like in another thirty years. He hoped he looked as good as the man in front of him when he reached his fifties. Genetics are a strange thing, he thought. And while he looked at his father, he felt nothing. Jake didn't hold a grudge because his father was an alcoholic, workaholic, or womanizer. He may have been all of the above, but Jake didn't know. And it is hard to be upset about something you don't know or can't remember. He wasn't angry, hurt or disappointed—he wasn't close enough to the man in front of him to have any of those emotions. Everything happens for a reason and Jake tried to leave the past in the past, a skill he learned from his mother. All Jake knew was that he could expect a hundred dollars for Christmas and another hundred for his birthday. The money arrived in generic cards, usually a week or two late, his father's signature probably forged by a secretary.

But Jake did know that his father was successful, and if he hadn't already known, the thousand-dollar suit his father was wearing would have been a clue. He knew his father ran a company or two and lived in a house with a pool. But the talk of private jets, beach houses in the Caribbean, and a garage full of German and Italian sports cars was hearsay. He knew his father had paid child support when his mother had requested it, but she had done her best to keep his money out of her life and the life of her son.

Peter looked at Jake, and as his son had looked at him and seen his own reflection, Peter saw images of himself as a young man. He remembered his son as an infant and had spotty recollections of his son's pre-teen years, but he had missed most of the major milestones. He never met his son's dates, never went on vacation together, missed his son's all-star dominance as the pitcher of the year for the high school city champions, and passed on an invitation to his son's college graduation in favor of a week in Fiji with some floozy whose name he had long since forgotten.

For the first time in his life he felt a fleeting moment of remorse. Then it was gone. Peter Winthrop was a user, always had been. It was a by-product of his upbringing and the neverending chase for more money, more toys, and more women. People were objects, to be used as objects and discarded once their usefulness was exhausted. He didn't set out to act the way he acted, it was just the way he was. Like a leg-humping dog that is never reprimanded, he didn't know any better. When he was younger, no one ever told him there was another way. As he got older, no one dared to.

He knew he was a shitty father, as his own father had been to him. There was nothing he could do to make amends for the past, and he didn't even bother to hope to repair the relationship with his only child. All he could wish for was that his son would have a child of his own and break the vicious cycle of poor fathers that ran through the Winthrop family tree.

"Can I get you something to drink?" Jake asked, breaking the silence.

"No thanks. I have to get going."

"Are you sure? You're welcome to stay," Jake said, assuming the role of the adult.

"No, I'm sure," Peter replied. He reached into his wallet and pulled out a business card. He plucked a Waterford pen from his breast pocket and scribbled some numbers. "If there is anything you need, I'm a phone call away. Anything at all. You can reach me at any of those numbers, day or night."

Jake stared at the card pinched between his father's thumb and index finger. Behind his father's shoulder, Uncle Steve looked on at the business-like exchange of information between a father and son acting like complete strangers.

Jake accepted the card, slipped it into his jacket pocket and said, "Thanks."

As always, Peter concluded the business deal with a handshake. A hug was out of the question for both of them.

"Maybe we can catch a Redskins game this season? I have box seats," Peter said, his mind already out the door.

"Yeah, maybe," Jake replied. He knew better than to wait by the phone.

Uncle Steve followed Jake and his father to the door. Peter smiled to the room of strangers, raised his hand slightly in a half-attempt at a wave, and exited the house. He hopped into his two-seater German roadster and drove out of the lower-middle-class neighborhood. He felt better as he worked his way home, back to a residential area with a population in a much higher tax bracket. His kind of people.

***

The Day residence was a meticulously restored townhouse on the corner of P and Thirty-Fourth Streets in Georgetown. The renovated home with a historic lineage had been on the market for over a year when the senator and his better half offered $6.5 million. Papers were signed the following week and by the end of the month, the Days moved in. The garage stored a Mercedes S-class sedan and a Lexus SUV. A distant cousin of the senator's wife, a Georgetown University graduate student, rented the small apartment on the second floor of the carriage house overlooking the heated pool.

Mrs. Day was cooking spaghetti, one of her many "specialties," none of which challenged the professionally accessorized kitchen. She hired a chef with an impressive résumé who came twice a week to give the appliances a thorough running through. He made whatever was requested and ad-libbed a few other gourmet meals that he left covered in plastic wrap in the refrigerator. The ever-changing dietary whims of the senator's wife kept the chef on his toes. She wasn't picky by nature, and it wasn't her fault that she was bossy and oversensitive. It was the third-trimester hormones.

The senator got out of the car and waved to his personal driver. Briefcase in hand, he stepped through the iron gate that enclosed the short brick walkway and made his way to the door. He passed through the small study, throwing his briefcase, the day's *Washington Post*, and a stack of mail he brought home from work on the leather club chair in the corner. He followed his nose to the kitchen.

"Smells great."

"You might want to wait until you taste it before you throw out too many compliments," she replied.

The senator kissed her on the cheek and touched her protruding stomach.

"Any action today?" he asked, hand just above her stretched navel.

"No, he's been quiet. Must not be in the mood to treat his mother's bladder like a soccer ball."

The senator bent over and put his ear on the top of the protruding mound. It was six weeks before the due date.

When dinner was finished, the senator cleared the table. The maid would take care of the dirty dishes and the laundry in the morning. Mrs. Day waddled upstairs for a shower.

The honorable senator from Massachusetts grabbed the paper and the mail off the chair in the study. He poured a double bourbon in a glass of the finest Austrian crystal and slipped out of his black Italian leather shoes. He flipped through the stack of mail he brought home and sorted the envelopes into three piles. The "must reads" went on his lap, a few letters from his constituents went on the corner of his desk, and the remainder went into the wastebasket.

He sipped his bourbon, read the paper, and opened his mail with CNN on in the background. He looked at the last piece of mail in his hands, an eight by eleven inch envelope with no return address. His full name and title was written in impeccable penmanship across the front.

He reached for his letter opener; a gold-plated blade with a bald eagle mounted on the end, and cut the top off the envelope. The neatly typed letter was short and to the point. It was also completely unnecessary. The photographs told him all he needed to know. A nice shot of his hand on the upper thigh of a beautiful Asian woman in the quiet corner of a classy restaurant. Another picture of the senator leaving the restaurant, his hand on his female companion's ass.

The rules were clear. The price for silence was one hundred thousand dollars.

Senator Day picked up the phone.

From a mobile bed on the fifth floor of George Washington Hospital, the senator's chief-of-staff tugged at the cord of the wall-mounted phone. His swollen knee screamed with pain. A tube ran from the IV stand to a vein in the crook of his right arm. The skin was raw, irritated. The adhesive used to keep the needle in place was a constant source of annoyance. Even more annoying was being out of the political loop, away from the schmoozing necessary to get things done. He had been in the hospital for over a week, and it was now nearly three since he had felt his ACL snap, an out-of-control water ski twisting his leg to an unnatural angle.

"Scott? How's the knee?"

"Senator... The knee is fine, as long as I don't move and the Oxycontin bottle still rattles when I shake it. The staph infection, well, that's a different story."

"Jesus."

"He hasn't been listening," Scott replied, trying to lighten the mood.

"Any word on when you'll be released?"

"Not yet. MRSA is a bit of a wild card. At least the doctors have stopped talking about the possibility of losing the leg."

"I'll take that as good news."

"My leg seems to think so."

The senator paused and then continued. "Business question for you. What do you know about international wire transfers?"

Scott took a pensive breath. "Wire transfers? From what angle? Got a bill in the works I haven't heard about? The legislative director hasn't mentioned anything."

"No, it's of a more personal nature. Hypothetically speaking, is it possible to do an anonymous wire transfer?"

"How hypothetical are we talking?"

"A hundred grand of hypothetical."

Scott sat up in his bed and grimaced. "Well, the current statute flags the IRS for any wire transfer over ten thousand dollars. Meaning that if you wire an amount ten grand or over, you have to fill out paperwork that goes to the IRS. In theory, anyway."

"So if you wanted to do a wire transfer without notifying the IRS, you could send, say, nine thousand nine hundred ninety-nine?"

"They call that smurfing. It was a practice popularized by drug dealers in the eighties and now used by myriad elements of the regulation-avoiding public. I would stay away from nine thousand nine hundred ninety-nine. It's an overly suspicious number."

"So maybe eight grand here, nine grand there."

"That's what I would do," Scott said. "From different accounts."

The senator considered the advice before his chief aide continued. "There's another option I can think of."

"I'm still here."

"I might know someone in banking who could arrange to do the wire transfer without the paperwork."

Senator Day thought aloud. "How much would that cost me?"

"Monetarily…nothing. Politically, it would be a debt. We wouldn't get it for free."

The senator loved it when his chief-of-staff used the word "we." As far as he was concerned, it was a term of endearment. Good help was hard to find.

The senator didn't think long. "Make the call and see what your contact says."

"I'll get back to you later this evening."

"And Scott…keep this quiet. No one finds out. I mean no one. Especially the staff."

"Yes, sir."

The senator read the letter and the explicit directions again. He drained his glass, filled another, and tilted the bottom toward the ceiling. Images of former presidential candidate Senator Hart with a blonde on his lap, sitting on a yacht appropriately named *Monkey Business*, flashed in his mind.

The sound of his wife's footsteps on the floor above shook him from his momentary daze. He stuffed the pictures into his briefcase and reread the letter. One hundred thousand dollars to a bank account in

Hong Kong. For a senator with ambition, a hundred grand seemed like a reasonable sum to pay to keep his career on track. Hiding a six-figure payout to a Hong Kong bank was easy. His wife didn't keep track of the money. As long as the credit cards weren't declined at Saks Fifth Avenue and the checks didn't bounce, she would never notice. Calming the sea of revenge brewing in the senator's head was more difficult. He would pay the money, and then he would see to it that the owner of the bank account in Hong Kong understood that John Day was not a person who could be squeezed without repercussions. He was a senator, a Harvard Man, and a member of one of the most influential families in the history of the Northeast. He had power, wanted more, and nothing was going to stand in the way of his ambitious plan to one day reside at 1600 Pennsylvania Avenue.

Chapter 3

Jake got out of his car and eyed the mailbox at the end of the driveway. It was only a ten second walk across a small patch of grass that masqueraded as a front lawn, but it was a trip that was growing more painful by the day. Jake reached the end of the yard, shoved his hand in the standard issue black box with its red flag, and pulled out the day's torment. He carried the thick stack of mail across the grass, past the "For Sale" sign that he and the real estate agent had pushed into the soft ground a week ago, and up the four stairs of the front porch.

The days were numbered for the house where he had grown up. The sadness he felt added to the burden he now faced. For the majority of his life the house had been a source of good memories—the normal stuff of childhood and the teenage years. Birthday parties, holiday gatherings, pictures on prom night. He got his first kiss on the very porch where he now stood, the same porch where his mother had sat him down and broke the news of her cancer.

He fumbled for the key to the deadbolt, balancing the stack of mail in the crook of one elbow. He stepped across the threshold of the foyer, threw his wallet and keys on the small table resting at the foot of the stairs, and made his way through the living room. The mail went on the coffee table, next to the disaster area of bills that already waited for his attention.

He changed clothes in the laundry room off the back of the house, grabbed the last beer bottle from the fridge, and made his way to the sofa. He sipped the cold suds and stared at the pile of mail.

The stack of envelopes stared back.

His mother's medical treatment, which ultimately failed, had cost a fortune. It was a fortune she didn't have. Health insurance covered the initial diagnosis and treatment, but when she reached the maximum lifetime limit of the policy, the debt outpaced the ability to pay by roughly the speed of light. When the house sold, if it sold, it would bring in enough money to cover almost half her debt. The rest was unrecoverable. It was a deal his mother had agreed to, giving up everything she had worked for in exchange for more time with the only thing that mattered. The collectors were already on the hunt, and Jake hadn't answered the home phone in three days.

With *Who Wants to be a Millionaire* on the TV, Jake dug through the stack of mail and pulled out a half-dozen, late-arriving condolence cards. He flipped through the stamped envelopes and answered the questions on the game show playing in the background without looking up. He set aside the bills for the gas, electricity, water, and phone without opening them. The bill from Georgetown University Hospital loomed large on the corner of the table, and Jake reached for the envelope cautiously as if it were booby-trapped. It seemed heavy to the touch. Jake sighed, opening the multiple-page invoice slowly, squinting as if it would ease the pain of the six-figure debt announced within. Three hundred twenty-two thousand dollars and change. Jake thought about the sum, shook his head, and reached for his beer.

He had five hundred twenty-seven dollars in his personal bank account, another forty in his wallet, and a ten-year-old Subaru station wagon in the driveway with a full tank of gas. The balance of the medical bill was out of his league. Way out of his league.

They had survived the last six months of his mother's life on loans taken out against the equity of the sixty-year-old home. Jake wasn't responsible for whatever balance the sale of the house wouldn't cover, but he would be left with nothing, his mother's life insurance policy long since cashed out. But he would need to come up with money for the bills and the monthly mortgage until the house sold. Not to mention whatever money he needed to live. Uncle Steve offered to help, but Jake couldn't force himself to take money from an out-of-work roofer who was barely getting by.

The only thing certain about the future was that he would be facing it alone. He was looking for work and an apartment near the university, but things were slow on the job front. Before his mother had passed and reality set in, he had made a pact with himself to hold out for what he had taken to calling "meaningful employment." No more working until two o'clock in the morning in the service industry. The race between dead-broke and waiting tables was one he wasn't sure he'd win. After an eighteen-month hiatus, rejoining the Masters program in English Literature at American University was the only real plan he had. Three months of summer vacation and then ten months of serious studying until graduation.

He needed cash. School loans would come in September and provide enough to make it through the fall semester, but that was still three months away. If he limited himself to frozen TV dinners and skipped lunch, he would be broke in two weeks. He could forget about paying the mortgage for July. The prospect of a long hot summer made him sweat. He had exchanged the burden of taking care of his mother with the burden of taking care of himself. He wasn't sure which was worse.

The refrigerator was barren and the thought of having a few more beers leached into Jake's brain. Ten minutes later, he made the responsible decision to get drunk. It had been a long time since he had sucked down dollar drafts for Happy Hour at McFadden's. And if he drank enough tonight, his stomach wouldn't be in the mood for food tomorrow. With the money he would save by not eating tomorrow, he could afford a beer or two. It had been a year and a half since he had tied one on. He could use the temporary break from himself and his life.

He made some calls looking for drinking recruits, pounded out a few text messages, and then made the eight-block walk to the bar.

***

Jake showed his ID to the doorman and walked un-accosted through empty space to a stool at the bar. Georgetown, George Washington, and American University were on summer vacation, and the pub business in downtown D.C. was feeling the usual summer pinch. For certain bars, the influx in summer tourists just couldn't make up for the weekly binge-drinking student crowd.

Jake ordered a draft—each glass was selling for seventy-five cents until eight-thirty. He had already saved a quarter from the usual one-dollar Happy Hour price. He downed his beer, called over the bartender, and saved another twenty-five cents.

Maroon 5 played on the sound system and echoed off the walls of the empty bar. Jake realized it was the first time he had ever breathed clean air in the maze-like, three-story establishment. McFadden's was relatively new, a modern steel and concrete watering hole in the midst of some of the nation's oldest bars—joints with missing mortar and cracked walls. McFadden did what most bars trying to simulate old age did—they put in wood-paneled walls, threw antiques around the room like a blind interior decorator and, for a finishing touch, turned down the lights. Jake had once been a Thursday night regular, right after his evening class on nineteenth century authors. He looked around the bar and missed being a student, missed the carefree lifestyle that was now a distant memory.

"I'm Matt," the bartender said, introducing himself. The bartender knew the first rule to pulling in the tips, in the absence of a perky set, was to establish rapport.

"Jake. Nice to meet you."

"From around here?"

"Born and raised."

"Not many of those around."

"No, not too many real Washingtonians left," Jake answered. "It's quiet in here tonight."

"It's summer. Most of our customers are GW students. It'll pick up a little later. It's still early, my friend."

Jake looked down at his watch. Five minutes after eight. Twenty-five minutes until the seventy-five-cent drafts bumped up to a full dollar. He ordered another.

"Drinking alone this evening?"

"Depends if anyone feels like coming to look for me. We'll see."

"No shame in downing a few by yourself," the bartender answered. He was in the wrong profession to point out any of the AA telltale signs of alcoholism.

"Yeah, well, it's been a bad year," Jake said, without elaborating. He wasn't going to share his life story with a bartender. Drinking by himself was one thing; weeping into his beer with his head on the bartender's shoulder was something else entirely. A man does have his limits.

The bartender didn't press for details. When a customer says, "It's been a bad day," he tended to ask. When a customer says, "It's been a bad year," he didn't want to know. He brought Jake his third beer in twenty minutes.

"Redskins fan?"

"Absolutely. Hard to grow up around here and not be one."

The two fell into football chatter, the kind of serious emotional banter that is the glue of the male social infrastructure.

"Snyder ruined the team," Jake said. "A billionaire businessman with no more football knowledge than you or I."

"He did do one thing right."

"What's that?"

"Hired the hottest cheerleaders in the league."

"Unfortunately they can't catch for shit."

The conversation continued through the return and departure of Joe Gibbs, stupid draft picks, free agency, the upcoming schedule, and predictions for the playoffs.

"No one looks better on paper than the Redskins in April."

"Amen to that," the bartender answered, pouring a beer for another patron at the far end of the bar.

The quiet mood of the bar was broken with the entrance of eight twenty-something ladies in a bachelorette party. The group of well-accessorized and fully primped females filled the gap around the stools between Jake and the bar's only other patron. A brunette from the group ordered eight lemon drop shooters, and the young ladies threw them back with synchronized gusto.

The bartender looked at Jake with a raised eyebrow and a smile. "Looks like you have some drinking competition."

Jake laughed a little and tried to eye the females without staring.

Matt, the bartending matchmaker, jumped in. "Ladies, let me introduce you to my good friend Jake."

The group gave Jake a cautious once over.

The bachelorette was wearing a t-shirt with a scavenger-hunt list of items she needed to collect, or tasks she needed to accomplish before the end of the evening. The list ran the gamut: from scoring a kiss, to unbuttoning a guy's shirt using only her teeth, to getting a guy to hand over his underwear. Lacking an alternative male audience, the women moved in on their prey.

"Hi, I'm Kate," said the drink-ordering cute brunette with

shoulder-length hair. She pulled her friend-of-honor closer so that Jake and the bachelorette stood face-to-face. "This is Paula. She is getting married next week."

"I figured as much," Jake replied, lightly flicking the bachelorette's ridiculous looking tiara with his finger.

"You wanna help us out with her scavenger list?"

"Sure he does," the bartender answered for Jake before he had a chance to think about it.

Jake scanned the list on the girl's shirt. A kiss he could do. A public spanking was within the realm of possibility if he kept drinking.

"What about your boxers?" Kate asked.

Jake looked up and tried to remember what he was wearing under his khaki cargo shorts. He turned away, pulled up his t-shirt, and pulled out the top of his boxers. A reasonably new pair with a conservative dark green checked pattern. He turned back toward the ladies who tugged at his waist to get a look at the goods up for negotiation.

"I'll tell you what. Let me have another beer or two and I'll think about giving you my boxers."

The ladies cheered. Paula the bachelorette grabbed Jake's beer off the bar and pushed it toward his lips. He drank as fast as he could, beer trickling from the corners of his mouth. He wiped the beer from his face and swiped at the drips on the front of his shirt. He apologized for his lack of manners to the heart-breaking brunette with mesmerizing brown eyes.

"If you give me your phone number, I'll give your friend my boxers," Jake said, backed by the confidence of four beers.

"Deal."

"I'll be right back," Jake said hopping off the stool and heading toward the restrooms in the back of the bar, beyond the pool table.

"Where are you going?" Kate asked.

"To take off my boxers."

"No, no, no. You have to take them off in front of us. Right, ladies?" Kate said. More cheers and one "hell yeah" shot from the group.

Jake moved back to his stool. "I'm not drunk enough for that."

"No boxers, no number," Kate taunted.

Jake's reinforcements rolled through the door halfway through his next beer. Tim and Aaron divided the sea of eight ladies who encircled

Jake and were taking turns pulling at the waist of his knee-length shorts.

"What do we have going on here?" Aaron asked, dressed in a suit and fresh from another day of summer employment at a Washington think-tank that analyzed world migration.

"Hey guys," Jake answered. He turned toward the women and made introductions. "Ladies, meet Tim and Aaron."

The women surrounded the new recruits and began tugging at the belts of the complete strangers. There was something magical about inebriated girls out on the town for a bachelorette party.

While Aaron entertained the ladies with his well-rehearsed pick-up lines and shovels of bullshit, Tim, wearing old Birkenstocks and a t-shirt, pulled Jake aside. "We bought tickets for Europe this morning. It's still not too late to go." Judging by his attire, Tim was already in boarding-pass mode.

"Not going to make it. Cash is a little tight at the moment."

"I can loan you the money. I'll hit my parents up for it. I'll tell them my car needs some work. They live in Colorado. They'll never know. It's going to be the trip of a lifetime. Six guys, hitting the highlights of Europe. French, Spanish, and Italian women."

"Those are the highlights of Europe?"

"Is there anything else?"

"I'd love to go. If something changes, you'll be the first to know."

"It'd be good for you. Take your mind off things."

"I'd love to, but I can't."

"Suit yourself. But if you aren't going to go, at least let me buy you a beer," Tim said, motioning toward the bartender.

The evening turned into a blur. The guys crashed the bachelorette party and led them on a pub-crawl up Connecticut Avenue past DuPont Circle. They stood back and watched the ladies get nine of the ten items on the bachelorette scavenger list. Then they added another ten X-rated tasks on the back of her t-shirt in permanent marker.

In the middle of the action, with an early nineties disco remake pumping in the background, Jake magically took off his boxers without removing his shorts, a feat no one at the packed bar had ever seen before. The drinking lasted until just after midnight, when a member of the bachelorette's party didn't return from a trip to the restroom. A waitress approached the group and asked if they knew a redhead in a black skirt. Tim and Aaron helped drag the semi-conscious, kamika-ze-loving girl from the tile floor and put her in a cab.

In the midst of the commotion, Jake and Kate made their exit. No one noticed their departure until they were in a taxi of their own, making out in the back seat.

***

Lee Chang made his daily call to the bank, and with the afternoon wire transfer settlement, the money poured in. He transferred the money to a bank in Shanghai under a different name and closed the account in Hong Kong. He moved the money to two other accounts, which he also closed behind him with zero balances. By the time his cousin withdrew the funds from a bank in Beijing, the person at the end of the money trail was a gray mist.

Like taking candy from a baby.

Lee Chang took out two more pictures and smiled. Certainly a man who is willing to pay one hundred thousand dollars would be willing to pay five hundred thousand, he thought. Maybe even a cool million.

Chapter 4

Jake woke up before Kate, his bare ass facing the ceiling uncovered. He looked over at the girl he had met the night before and was thankful she looked as good as he had thought with alcohol surging through his veins. He fought the natural male desire to quietly slink out of the apartment, but had no idea where he had left his clothes. The sun was up, but it was still too early for someone with a hangover to try getting vertical. For the last year, he had been trained to wake up at dawn to care for his mother, and he was still re-learning how to sleep in. He put his head under the pillow and fell back into a fitful sleep.

When he opened his eyes again, Kate was sitting on the bed wearing only a t-shirt, her back against the headboard.

"Good morning, Jake," she said sheepishly, flipping through the latest issue of *Cosmopolitan*.

"Good morning," he answered, pulling himself slowly into a seated position next to her.

Both of them wanted to say something mature. Kate took a first stab at it.

"Jake, you know I've never slept with someone on the first date before."

"Technically it wasn't a date," Jake replied.

So much for maturity.

"You know what I mean. I'm not the type of girl who goes around having one-night stands," Kate said.

"Well believe it or not, neither do I," Jake replied honestly. He leaned over and kissed her on the cheek. It seemed like the right thing to do.

Kate went to the fridge and returned with two glasses of orange juice.

"Do you need some aspirin?" she asked.

"No, I'll suffer through the pain. It'll remind me why I don't drink."

They sat on the bed and talked, Jake still naked beneath the bed sheet wrapped around his waist.

"So you're a medical student?"

"Third year at GW."

"Med school sounds like a lot of studying."

"The first few years were hard. It gets easier. Or maybe you just get used to it."

"I'm starting back to school in the fall. I took a couple of semesters off."

"For fun?"

Jake stumbled. "No, definitely not for fun. My mom recently passed after a long battle with cancer. I spent most of the last year and half taking care of her. I guess you can say I learned a little about nursing and oncology."

Kate listened to Jake without interrupting and when he was finished, she spoke. "I'm sorry for your loss. And though you may not want to hear it, I'm sure the experience will make you a stronger person."

Jake shrugged his shoulders and smiled. "Thanks." Feeling a somber mood seeping into the room, he stood for the first time, still clutching the sheet against his groin. He tried not to blush and wasn't sure if he succeeded.

"It's a little late to be bashful. I pretty much saw it all last night," Kate said. "Besides, I'm going to be a doctor; I've seen a few naked bodies."

"As true as that may be, I'm the only one standing here without clothes."

Kate stood and took off her t-shirt, joining Jake in his natural state.

"Now what do you have to say?" the cute brunette asked with a combination of conviction and sarcasm.

Jake turned a deeper shade of red. Kate enjoyed the moment and his embarrassment.

"Have you seen my shorts?" he asked.

"They are in the living room, on the floor in front of the sofa."

Jake waddled through the bedroom door and Kate smiled at the half-moon that peeked out from under the sheet. He found his shorts on the floor, his shirt on the counter in the kitchen, and his belt near the balcony door. The evening must have been more interesting than he remembered. He dressed and sat down on the Italian leather sofa to put on his shoes. Nice apartment, he thought. Granite counter tops, crown molding, and large windows that ran from the floor to the ceiling.

Kate came out from the bedroom back in her t-shirt, running shorts completing the outfit.

"So can I have your number?" Jake asked. "I did forfeit my boxers after all."

Kate laughed. Nice teeth, great smile, he thought.

They exchanged numbers and Kate finished the conversation with, "You'd better call."

"I will," Jake answered, doing a final check of his personal inventory—phone, keys, wallet. Preparing for his walk of shame, he took a quick peek into his wallet and cringed at the emptiness. "Where are we?"

"What?"

"What's your address?"

"1750 P Street. The Commodore."

It was a fifteen-block walk home, but he wasn't about to ask for money for a cab. He gave Kate another kiss, this time on the mouth, bad breath and all.

Kate shut the door and smiled. She liked him. He was charming. He was strong and serious, yet shy and sweet. He had potential.

Her parents were going to hate him.

***

The nausea came on like a locomotive. Wei Ling flung herself from her perch on the top bunk and landed on the thin carpet with a light thud. She doubled over, grabbed her stomach with both hands, and stomped her way to the community bathroom at the end of the hall. The tight confines of the sleeping quarters assured that Wei Ling's departure didn't go unnoticed by her three roommates. But it was five in the morning, sleep was at a premium, and the alarm wasn't set to start screaming for another half an hour.

Shi Shi Wong slept in the bunk under Wei Ling and the light

aluminum frame of the two-story bed made every movement of either occupant a shared one. Through a half-closed eye, Shi Shi watched Wei Ling bend over and dart from the room. It wasn't uncommon behavior. The food served by the sweatshop kitchen haunted all the ladies from time to time. Shi Shi tossed and turned for twenty minutes before slipping on her bright green flip-flops and going to check on her bunkmate.

Wei Ling was curled in the fetal position, clutching her stomach on the floor in front of the toilet in the first stall. The remains of last night's sesame noodles painted the floor between her body and the intended porcelain target. The longest strands of her hair mixed with the nastiness on the dirty tile floor. Shi Shi pulled her bunkmate up by the armpits and half-walked, half-dragged her friend to the shower stalls on the opposite end on the room. She fetched a wet hand towel and pressed the cool cloth to Wei Ling's face and neck.

The foreman in charge of the morning headcount came up two seamstresses short in workgroup B. He demanded an explanation, and when no one volunteered information, he started swinging. When he reached the third girl, he closed his hand and landed a full-speed punch to the side of her head, sending her ninety-pound frame flying off the wooden seat onto the floor. Chinese curses flowed from the foreman's mouth and he ordered everyone to get to work before stomping off in the direction of the seamstresses' quarters. Every girl knew what was next.

Wei Ling was sweating profusely, and Shi Shi Wong was trying to coax her out of bed when the foreman stormed through the door.

"It's six-thirty, you lazy pieces of shit. Get your asses to work."

Shi Shi looked up and risked her face. "She's sick. She needs to see a doctor."

The foreman looked at Wei Ling and back to Shi Shi. "You have five minutes to report to your work area," he said without sympathy.

On cue, Wei Ling sent a shower of vomit onto the foreman's opened-toe sandals. The foreman's need to cleanse himself overpowered his urge to use the girls as punching bags, and he limped to the shower to wash his foot. He yelled over his shoulder down the hall to Shi Shi. "Take her to the main building, have Chow Ying call the doctor, and get to work. You have four minutes."

***

The large room on the first floor of the administrative building served as Chang Industries' doctor's office, sickbay, and hospital. The four-bed room was well equipped. It had to be. Employees who were injured or too sick to work cost the company money. There was no time to be sick, not on Chang Industries' dime.

The doctor strolled in, black bag in hand, thirty minutes after he received the call on his boat. Wei Ling was on the bed in the far corner, half asleep. She had thrown up two more times after blasting the foreman's foot and was feeling as bad as she looked.

The doctor was American and competent. He had graduated from NYU before attending UCLA medical school. He was in his mid-forties, with sharp looks and a serious, but kind, bedside manner. He lived on Saipan as the physician for both Chang Industries and the local hospital. He could have worked anywhere, but after his first month on the island, he found himself unable to leave. The snorkeling, fishing, and sunsets were addictive. Living near the beach had spoiled him. He vowed never to return to the rush of a big city. He had spent twenty years of his life in downtown New York and LA. and had endured enough smog and congestion to last a lifetime.

The doctor asked Wei Ling a few questions and Lee Chang needlessly translated them into English. Wei Ling answered honestly. He took her pulse and blood pressure, and felt the glands on her neck. He tapped her stomach and asked what she had eaten in the last twenty-four hours.

"Are any of the other girls ill?" the doctor asked Lee Chang.

Lee Chang looked at Chow Ying and re-asked the doctor's question.

"Not that I know of," Chow Ying answered. "Everyone else reported to work on time."

Lee Chang and his new main henchman watched the doctor finish the cursory examination in silence.

The doctor went to the huge storage room and unlocked the door. He turned on the light and dug through the shelves of medical equipment and medication. Wei Ling could hear the soft clanking of glass and the squeaking of the metal shelves. The doctor reappeared with a small box, sat down on the stool at the side of Wei Ling's bed, and told her what to do.

The initial pregnancy test read positive. A second test was administered and the results came up negative. The doctor drew blood and marked the small glass vial with Wei Ling's name. He would take the blood to the hospital and settle the "pregnant, not-pregnant" confusion once and for all. His instincts told him the girl was pregnant. The blood test would confirm what Wei Ling already knew. She was as regular as clockwork and had missed her period by ten days and counting. There was nothing to do but pray for a miracle.

The doctor told Wei Ling to get some sleep and ordered a day of rest. Lee Chang agreed to one day. She was expected back at work tomorrow.

Lee Chang and Chow Ying finished wolfing down a lunch of stir-fried rice when the doctor called back with the official prognosis. Wei Ling was pregnant.

Lee Chang went ballistic.

Chang Industries' seamstresses were kept on a tight leash. They were forbidden to fall in love, much less become pregnant. Trips off the company grounds were limited to groups of four, with a company-sponsored chaperone. But the workers were creative, a blind eye could be bought with the right favors, and once in a great while a seamstress showed up pregnant.

Lee Chang would handle it as he always did. There would be a dock in pay and the seamstress would have an abortion whether she wanted one or not. The cost of the abortion would be added to the seamstress's overall debt to the Chang family.

Lee Chang and Chow Ying stormed into the infirmary. With a level of anger reserved for the most blatant company infractions, Lee Chang approached the side of the bed and violently shook Wei Ling from her light sleep.

"Who is the father?"

"What?" Wei Ling answered, still groggy.

"Who is the father?"

Wei Ling didn't answer.

Lee Chang slapped her on the face, his thumb catching the corner of her mouth, drawing blood. An immediate red impression of four fingers appeared on her otherwise unblemished skin.

"You should know, you sent me," Wei Ling said, breaking into tears.

"Peter Winthrop? Is Mr. Winthrop the only man you have been with? If it's one of the company guards, you had better tell me now. I'll find out eventually anyway."

Wei Ling looked up at Lee Chang's face. A vein pulsed visible in his forehead. Her hatred for him was justified, and yet somehow she felt sorry for him. He was more than just cruel. He ruled with an iron fist because he wasn't smart enough to rule with his head. He was a bastard, but he was also pathetic, hopelessly lost in a family of brilliant business-men and politicians.

"I didn't sleep with Mr. Winthrop," she said, tears of shame rolling down her face. "I slept with the other American."

"Senator Day?" Lee asked, looking first at Wei Ling and then at Chow Ying.

The word "senator" caught Wei Ling by surprise. She looked at Lee Chang's face, his anger now mixed with excitement.

"I only knew his name was John."

Lee Chang's heart beat faster. His throat became dry and he felt faint. He was delirious with possibilities. He may have been the low-man on the family totem pole, but he was cunning enough to see the opportunity lying in the bed in front of him.

Lee Chang's personality thawed, and Wei Ling heard him speak with compassion for the first time in her two years on the island. "It's okay," he said, touching the crying girl's head. Wei Ling flinched and then pushed herself to the far side of the mattress.

"Get some rest," Lee Chang continued. "Everything will be fine."

Lee Chang stepped outside, pulled out a cigarette with shaking hands, and lit up. Chow Ying followed his boss through the door and pulled out his own almond-flavored brand of domestic Chinese smokes.

The child of a U.S. Senator! Lee Chang couldn't believe his luck. What an opportunity! To hell with blackmail for money. He had much bigger plans. The girl was his ticket off the island.

Chapter 5

Jake flipped the business card through his fingers with the skill of a street magician. He batted the pros and cons of what he was considering back and forth in his head like a tennis ball going over the net at Wimbledon. He shut his eyes and opened them a minute later, no wiser. He looked up and said a prayer both to God and his mother, asking for guidance. He waited another minute, still looking upward, but received no heavenly intervention. No parting clouds. No rays of light. He picked up his phone and called the number.

No answer.

He left a message on his father's voicemail and hung up. *The ball's in your court*, he thought. He didn't expect a call back. He had stopped waiting by the phone when he was seven. "Expect nothing and you won't be surprised when you receive nothing," he had learned. Defense mechanisms come in many forms.

The phone was still in Jake's hand when it rang. For the first time in two decades, his father had returned his call. He looked up at the ceiling, and for a moment he thought he felt his mother's presence. Miracles do happen.

"Hi, Dad."

His father mustered up his friendliest greeting and before the conversation could stall, Jake laid his request on the table. "Say, any chance of getting a job at your company for the summer?"

Peter Winthrop managed not to choke on the request. Without his normal, careful consideration, he answered. "Sure. How does tomorrow suit you?"

***

The weekly Monday morning call was not a highlight for either Lee Chang or his father, the great C.F. Chang. Their conversation steered clear of friendly banter, family chitchat, and gossip, and when Lee did venture off topic, his father quickly brought him back to business. What was the weekly output of the facility per employee? What orders were next to be filled? How many units were shipped? Lee Chang had learned to answer the questions with precision. He knew the numbers of the business under his control. It was the one thing he absolutely had to know. He didn't plan on being banished to Saipan forever. He once believed that knowing his corner of the family business was his best chance off the island. But no longer. Wei Ling and her not-so-immaculate conception were going to expedite his return to favorable-son status.

C.F. Chang was the patriarch of the family and one of the most well-connected men in China. He prided himself on knowing everything that could affect his many businesses. He paid good money to smart people at home and abroad to keep him informed, and had no tolerance for surprises. With a billion dollars a year generated in manufacturing, defense, communications, and utilities, he couldn't afford to be asleep behind the wheel. So between his own ambition, and that of those he hired, he never slept.

The head of the family empire was not interested in listening to his son's big announcement, and he grew impatient as Lee explained the visit from the U.S. Senator weeks ago. C.F. Chang already knew about the senator's trip to the island, and he didn't want to have the facts rehashed through his son's warped perception. Confident his son couldn't possibly tell him anything he wasn't already aware of, C.F. Chang nearly missed the single biggest surprise of his adult life.

Lee Chang held his breath as his father digested the news. A thousand miles away, C.F. Chang stared into the picture of his own father hanging on the far wall of his office in Beijing. Then he spoke. "Keep this quiet and keep that girl healthy."

Lee Chang smiled. For once, he and his father were on the same page.

***

Jake took his turn going through the revolving door and walked across the lobby to the information desk. Peter Winthrop kept his one hundred fifty employees busy on the top two floors of International Plaza at the corner of Thirteenth and K streets. It was as nice an office as there was in Washington, sharing two blocks in either direction with a dozen of the most prestigious law firms in the country.

The wood-paneled elevators with their brass fixtures opened on the fourteenth floor and Jake stepped into his father's world for the first time. An attractive blonde sat at the reception desk, under a formidable "Winthrop Enterprises" sign. She smiled eagerly as Jake approached.

"I'm Jake Patrick. I am here for my first day of work," he said without pride or pretension.

"Yes, Mr. Patrick. Your father is expecting you," the blue-eyed babe answered with a level of professionalism foreign to Jake. Another blonde receptionist was summoned and the son of the president and CEO followed his new, and equally attractive, host down the wide hall. The office was immaculate. No cheap carpeting, no cramped cubicles. Every seat had a view and everything was in its place. It looked like a place where serious people did real work.

Jake was handed off again, this time to an older receptionist who rose from her chair to greet Jake with yet another ear-to-ear smile. Dark blonde hair fell to her shoulders, a model's face with green eyes rested on a toned body. Sure, she was older, but Jake had little doubt that she had been a hottie in her day.

"Hi Jake, I'm Marilyn Ford, your father's personal assistant."

"Nice to meet you, Marilyn."

"Your father had to step out of the office on urgent business. He should be back in the afternoon. Until then, I am here to help you get settled. Your office is this way."

"I don't need an office. A desk would be fine."

"Well, I guess you are getting both—an office with a desk," Marilyn answered without room for negotiation. "You'll like it. It has a nice view of McPherson Square."

Marilyn opened the desk drawer and grabbed a key ring that would make any janitor weak-kneed with envy. A bell attached to the key chain rang with every move she made, as if the sound of the jingling keys alone wasn't loud enough to wake the dead.

"Quite a set of keys," Jake said innocently.

"Somebody has to keep duplicates around here," Marilyn answered. "People lose them and I'm the key master."

Marilyn backtracked halfway through the office floor that Jake had just covered, took a left and headed toward an isolated corner. The description of the office she gave Jake as they walked didn't do the room justice. Jake stood at the doorway and watched Marilyn switch on the lights and open the blinds. Sun burst into the room transforming an already brilliant office into a masterpiece.

"Good God," Jake said.

"Does this mean you like it?"

"It'll do," he answered poker-faced. It was far nicer than anything he imagined. The wooden bookcases, handmade desk, and deep leather chairs were overkill for Jake's ambition. He was looking for a part-time job, not an extended stay in the oval office.

"I thought you might find it acceptable," Marilyn answered.

"Are you sure this is okay? There must be a few people in the company eyeing this office."

"Of course there are. But until you leave, they are going to continue eyeing it from a distance."

Marilyn reached for the desk and picked up a piece of neatly typed paper. "Here are some phone numbers for you. The security desk on the first floor, the main reception desk, and some contact names in our legal, finance, and international departments. Numbers change around here from time to time, so you may get an updated list a couple of times a year. Feel free to move around, meet people, and ask questions. I also have your new email address, user ID, and password. The head of our IT team got here early this morning just for you. I will take you around to formally introduce you to everyone after you get settled in."

Jake's small briefcase from Staples wouldn't take long to unpack. The office was large enough to live in, and the leather binder that held his schedule wouldn't fill a tenth of the desk space.

"I was sorry to hear about your mother," Marilyn said.

Jake paused, surprised by the condolences. "Thank you."

"She was a sweet woman," Marilyn added, staring out the window at the park below.

"I didn't know you knew her."

"I've been your father's secretary for over twenty-five years," Marilyn replied. "I've met just about everyone in your family. I attended your parents's wedding."

"I didn't know that."

"I wouldn't expect you to. I even changed you once, though I'm quite sure you were too young to remember. Your father brought you into work and when you soiled your diapers, my job duties were expanded to cover the crisis. I didn't mind. You were a little angel."

"I still am," Jake replied, trying to cover his embarrassment.

Marilyn smiled. "Well, I'll leave you to get settled. Stop by if you need anything. I'll check in with you in an hour or so and give you the complete tour. The men's room is just beyond the reception desk, on the left-hand side."

"Thank you," Jake answered to Marilyn's departing backside.

"My pleasure," she replied.

Jake tried not to stare as Marilyn walked away. A definite former hottie.

Peter showed up at work a little after four. Winthrop Enterprises in its entirety snapped to attention as if there were a buzzer on every desk that shocked the employees to life when the boss arrived. Jake noticed the increase in work effort, no small feat for a group that seemed plenty busy already. The more daring employees offered a "good afternoon" to the CEO. The good-looking female employees received a response.

Jake was at his desk in the corner suite alternating glances between the spread of documents on the desk and the crowd that was gathering in Franklin Park across the street. Welcome to Washington. There was never a shortage of protesters, or things to protest, and it looked like the group in the park was preparing to set up camp.

Jake flipped through Winthrop Enterprises' financial statements and marketing propaganda for the past year. Page by page he learned more about his father and his father's business than he had ever known. He moved back to the first page of the executive summary and looked at the picture of his father, showing his best used-car-salesman grin, standing in front of a huge Winthrop Enterprise sign in some unknown location.

"Glad to see you made it, son."

Jake looked up at his father who was wearing the same grin as in the picture. It was a smile Jake himself was known for. With straight white teeth resting between two symmetrical dimples, Jake flashed an identical smile back. The fruit doesn't fall far from the tree.

"Yeah, I made it. You shouldn't be surprised. I said I would be here at the start of business and I always keep my word."

"Of course you do. Just like your mother. The woman never made a promise she didn't keep. Do you have dinner plans tonight?"

Jake wondered if his father was capable of a real conversation. He wondered if they were going to continue talking as if they had been on speaking terms for the last six years. "Not really. Whatever falls out of the refrigerator, I guess."

Peter looked at Jake and hoped his son wasn't speaking literally.

"Son, if you are having problems, I can advance you your first paycheck."

Jake shook his head. He could use the money, but there was no reason to make himself look like a complete bum. "I'll pass on the advance, but I will take you up on dinner."

"Fair enough. We will be having a nice meal with Senator Day from Massachusetts."

"Oh," Jake answered, wanting to take back his acceptance to dinner. A meal with his father was daunting enough. Dinner with a senator wasn't going to make an evening getting to know Dad any easier.

"We'll talk a little business, a little politics. It should be interesting."

"Okay, sure." Jake looked down at his slacks, shirt, and tie. "Am I dressed well enough?" He looked like any other twenty-four year old in an office.

"You look fine. I have an extra jacket if you need to borrow one. Marilyn will bring it to you."

"Thanks."

"My driver will pick us up in front of the building around six-thirty."

"I'll be ready."

***

The maitre d' stood at attention behind the podium, every white hair on his post-retirement head perfectly combed and slicked back. He checked the seating chart, looked over the waiting patrons, and smiled at the small well-dressed crowd standing near the door. Peter tipped the doorman a twenty, walked past two waiting middle-aged couples, and approached the maitre d'. Jake excused himself to everyone in earshot and followed in his father's presumptuous wake.

"Mr. Winthrop. Good evening, sir. How are you this evening?" The maitre d' recognized a hundred customers by sight and knew half of them by name. Mr. Winthrop was an erratic regular. Twice a week sometimes, once a month when he was occupied with business or pleasure. But he was unforgettable.

"Good evening, Albert. How is the wife?"

"She is well, thank you." It was a lie the maitre d' told a half dozen times a day. Customers didn't want to hear about his ill wife before sitting down to fifty-dollar plate of linguini with fresh sea scallops.

"Your table is ready, sir. The senator is waiting."

"Has he been here long?" Peter asked.

"Five minutes. He was early as usual."

"Let's hope he's as enthusiastic and punctual at work. You and I are paying his salary."

Albert laughed. "Sir, somehow I doubt that he is."

Jake watched his father with interest. He was complex. A hard-ass and a charmer at the same time. Jake was getting a crash course in the type of education most kids learn through observation over a lifetime.

"Albert, this is my son, Jake."

Jake stepped from the shadows of his father and extended his hand. "Nice to meet you."

"Good looking young man, Mr. Winthrop," Albert said shaking Jake's hand and looking at his father. Peter took the compliment for his son to mean that he, too, looked good.

The senator stood as Peter and Jake approached the table. The senator's guest, a blonde firecracker no older than Jake, put her lipstick back in her purse and tried to stand, balancing precariously on a pair of four inch heels.

"Senator, pleasure to see you again."

"Peter, please call me John."

Round robin introductions followed and the senator offered Jake the seat next to his dinner guest, Dana. The senator explained how Dana was helping out in his office on the Hill until his Columbia University alumni aide, a victim of a waterskiing accident in Saipan, recovered. Dana glowed as if she had just been introduced onstage at a beauty competition. Jake thought of Kate and wondered what she was doing this evening.

Dinner lasted three hours. Jake was bored after the first ten minutes. He read the paper, followed politics, and listened to NPR. He knew what was going on in the world, but he was lost in the incessant name dropping of Senator X, Congressman Y, and Special Committee Z. Senator Day and Peter Winthrop were engaged in an unspoken battle of who could talk the longest without being interrupted. It was neck-and-neck heading into dessert.

Jake's main entertainment for the evening was the senator's office assistant. A short conversation with the young blonde told Jake all he needed to know.

"What are those?" Dana had asked pointing to the capers on Jake's plate.

"Raisins," Jake had answered.

"Nasty."

The girl was eye candy, perhaps a senate office toy, nothing less, but certainly nothing more. She was a disaster at conversation and in dire need of table etiquette. Jake was mesmerized, though not by her looks, which had probably caused a few geezers on The Hill to order oysters for lunch. She was a study in human behavior, and in wasted real estate between the human ears. She reapplied lipstick after every course, fidgeted in her chair endlessly, and twice Jake saw her lift one cheek and casually pull at what he hoped was a wedgie.

"Jake, the senator and I have some more business to discuss. We're going to head over to the Presidential Club on Fourteenth Street for cigars and brandy. My driver will take you and Dana home." It wasn't a question or a request, and Jake didn't care. He was looking forward to falling asleep on the sofa in front of ESPN's SportsCenter.

"That's fine. I'm tired. It's been a long day."

"That's what the working world will do to you," his father answered. His father looked at the senator and the blonde bimbo who was chewing a piece of gum with vigor. "I forgot to mention, Jake started working for me today at Winthrop Enterprises."

"That's great. Good for you. If you feel like getting an early start on a political career, I can always pull a few strings for you," the senator said with a wink. "Good looking young man like yourself could go far in politics."

"Thank you, Senator. I appreciate the offer. I'll let you know if things don't work out where I am," Jake said, winking back.

Peter paid the check and the four stood and pushed in the high-back wood chairs. The restaurant was still full, families and dates stuffing their faces with the best Italian food in the city. The waiters, cooks, and busboys wouldn't get off for hours. For at least two of the patrons, the heartburn from overeating would last well past closing.

As Peter and the senator walked out the door, a platonic couple in matching his and her suits watched through the window of the restaurant as the two men got into the politician's car.

"Now what?" the woman asked, her red hair glowing under the recessed ceiling lights that ran along the front of the restaurant.

"For today, we let him go," her date said before cursing under his breath.

Chapter 6

Half a world away, the good doctor's morning routine rarely changed. He was up at dawn, downed two cups of coffee with the morning paper, and was out the door with a banana in hand forty minutes later.

It was a half-mile walk to the beach and another quarter of a mile to the small marina where he rented a boat slip for a hundred dollars a month. The walk took a little over ten minutes, no slower than driving his red Jeep convertible down the winding roads. When the weather didn't cooperate, the doctor used the time on his boat to clean his fishing equipment and tidy up the cabin, which was immaculate most of the time anyway.

It was a brilliant summer day on Saipan and the doctor walked down the beach at a leisurely pace, eating his banana in slow bites and greeting familiar faces of expats who, like himself, couldn't force themselves to leave the island. He could see *The Sea Nurse* from a point on the beach where the currents from the south headed further out to sea. The twenty-five-foot, twin-engine boat was among the largest in the marina. She was a beauty and the good doctor loved her more than he loved any woman in his life. Sure, the boat was more expensive to take care of than any woman, but it also gave him a lot less shit.

He climbed on board and checked the moorings, pulling firmly on every line. He unlocked the door to the cabin and stepped down the three stairs into the small but comfortable one-room suite. He changed into his swimsuit and grabbed his mask, snorkel, and fins off the floor before heading back into the light of the world outside. He untied the boat and started the engine with a single turn of the key.

The Sea Nurse never let him down.

It was a fifteen-minute ride to his favorite spot off the coast where he alternated days between snorkeling and spear fishing, depending on whether he wanted to catch the night's dinner. The Cortez Reef area was one of the most beautiful on the island. Its status as a protected marine-life zone kept most of the tourist boats away. The restriction on boats in the protected area made it nearly impossible to get a permit, and the few who were lucky enough to have one tried to influence local powers to keep others from getting theirs.

The doctor spit in his mask and washed it around like fine wine in a glass. He jumped overboard and forced the water from his snorkel with one mighty blast. He checked his watch and set the bezel on his Rolex Submarine for forty minutes. He had to be at work in an hour. He held his breath and went under.

***

The two men on the stolen speedboat looked at the map again. The compass read due north and, according to their best guess, the Cortez Reef was nearby. They putted along carefully, trying to maintain an equal distance between the boat and the shore. The one thing they didn't want to do was get lost. The driver knew boats. The navigator knew neither boats nor how to read a map. The chance of getting truly lost at sea was near zero, but running out of gas was a possibility. Their possession of the boat, and the dead body of its owner lying in the small hull, would be impossible to explain. The fewer people they had to interact with on the island, the better.

They had arrived the night before, stayed in a cheap hotel, and paid with cash. They had walked out of the hotel lobby down the street and caught a cab in front of the Hyatt. It was easier to be anonymous among the crowd at a hotel with three hundred rooms. But the major hotel chains asked for identification and that was something the men weren't willing to flash around. Catching a cab from the busy hotel would at least provide another step of mystery for the police, should it be needed.

The good doctor swam without incident for thirty minutes. There was surprisingly little activity in the reef for a day with ideal weather conditions. He saw the usual assortment of reef inhabitants—triggerfish, clown fish, sea urchins, and crustacean representatives from every family. No octopi, no reef sharks, no moray eels. It was odd not to see the bigger fish, but every day was different, and the good doctor knew that no matter what he saw, a bad day spent on and below the water's surface in a life-size aquarium was better than a great day on land.

The speedboat on the water above cut directly between the good doctor and *The Sea Nurse*. Tourists. As required, the doctor had marked his diving spot. On the surface of the water, four orange buoys bobbed on the calm sea. Not even a quiet corner of Saipan was insulated from the occasional asshole. The good doctor was willing to give twenty-to-one odds that the boat ignoring his safety was being driven by Americans or Australians—the two most offensive tourist nationalities on God's green earth.

The doctor surfaced for air in the wake of the speedboat's pass. He kicked his legs hard and propelled his body out of the water just enough to see the boat turn around. He waved his hands frantically in the air as the boat completed its turn and made a beeline for his position. He removed his mask and snorkel and waved them above his head, yelling at the top of his lungs. The driver of the speedboat glared ahead, pushed the accelerator forward, and gave no indication he was going to steer clear. The doctor wasn't about to wait to see if the boat would change course. Without his snorkel or mask, he took a deep breath and dove. It was a hundred yards to *The Sea Nurse*, and he was going for it in one breath.

The good doctor heard the boat make one pass and then another. His lungs were on fire and his eyes burned as he headed toward the submersed white outline of the hull of *The Sea Nurse*. Twenty yards away, he knew he wasn't going to make it. He stopped himself three feet below the surface and swiveled his head to the left and right. He saw nothing. He heard the muffled sound of the motor somewhere above and made a judgment decision. One more quick breath. He broke the surface of the water for the most oxygen-deprived breath of his life and gasped for air. The thud of the speeding boat against the side of the physician's skull was the last sound the good doctor ever heard.

***

Peter Winthrop's car pulled up to the curb and picked up his passengers. A large black man in a dark black suit got out from behind the wheel, introduced himself as Shawn, and shut the door behind his patrons as they settled in the back seat. Ten minutes later, Dana got out of the car, hit her head on the doorframe, and stumbled on her high heels.

"Cute girl," the driver said to Jake in the back seat as they both watched Dana walk toward her apartment building's entrance.

"You didn't have to sit through dinner with her."

"That bad?"

"Let's just say that she was fine when she was chewing her food."

The driver laughed. "Where to?"

"Twenty-Seventh Street NW. Two blocks from Nell's Café." The small restaurant was a mainstay for quick cheap meals and Jake was sure the driver knew where it was. "Have you been driving for my father long?"

"Off and on for a few years. Your father is one of a handful of regulars."

"You see a lot of these black sedans for hire here in D.C."

"Yes, you do. My company runs over fifty, but I would put the total number for the city around two thousand."

"A lot of congressmen?" Jake asked.

"Yeah, sure. And a lot of lawyers, diplomats. Your father is the rare businessman."

"What do you think of him?

"Who?"

"My father," Jake answered. "And you can tell me how you really feel. I don't know him that well to be honest, and I'm sort of trying to figure him out."

"I don't know if I can answer that question."

"Sure you can."

"Then let me rephrase it. I don't know if I should answer that question."

"I'll make it easy on you. I'll go first. My father ran out on my mother and me when I was too little to remember. From what I have seen, he is a both a schmoozer and a bully."

The light at the intersection of Twenty-Fourth Street turned yellow, then red, and the car pulled to a halt. The driver looked over his shoulder at Jake in the back seat.

"Your father expects me to show up on time and drive him wherever he wants to go, without spilling his coffee on him or his newspaper. That is my official answer."

"What is your unofficial answer, off the record?"

"Persistent, aren't you?" the driver said with a smile.

"I'm just looking for some clues. I'm getting the idea of who my father is when I am around him, but you never know."

"Okay, Jake. Off the record, your father is the moodiest person I have ever driven. You know, these days they have all these medical terms—bi-polar, manic-depressive, chemically unbalanced, whatever. Some people are just mean and nasty until they need something, and then they are sweet as pie. Now, mind you, I'm just the driver, so our relationship consists of him sitting in the back seat and me driving. But I hear him on the phone, and drive him with his business acquaintances. This isn't a limo, there's no privacy window, so I hear it all. He can be nasty or sweet. And I know most of the time which it's going to be before he even gets in the car."

"Thanks for saying so."

"I didn't say anything, if you know what I mean."

"I hear you."

The car pulled up to the front of Jake's mother's house. The light from the kitchen cast a faint yellow hue into the living room.

"I'll see you around, Shawn."

"Take my card, Jake. If you ever need a ride, give me a ring."

"Only if I can charge it to my Dad's account."

"Hey, he's your father. That's between you and him. I just drive the car."

***

The Presidential Club was *the* place for Washington's elite to quench their thirst. Groups of large leather chairs huddled around small marble-top tables, the thick burgundy carpet reaching up to grasp the bottom of the table legs. Cigars and glasses of brandy kept each other company on the tables as the power circles drew and redrew their political lines in the sand.

Senator Day made his way through the room, nodding at colleagues, acknowledging familiar faces through the dim light and thick cigar smoke. The Presidential Club was Washington's version of Las Vegas. What happened in the expensive lounge stayed in the lounge. It wasn't called a club by accident. Wives of members were permitted but frowned upon. Lovers were a different story. Call girls made the occasional guest appearance.

Senator Day directed Peter to a table near the rear of the club, and a waiter with a small humidor appeared as the two sunk into their respective leather chairs. Peter selected two Dominican cigars wrapped with tobacco grown from the finest Cuban seeds and handed one to the senator. The waiter placed a cigar cutter and a box of oversized matches on the table before disappearing in search of the senator's favorite brandy, stored on the private shelf behind the full bar.

"How is business, Peter?" the senator asked. Peter understood that dinner with Jake and the senator's blonde aide was merely a preamble to the discussion at the club. A meal for the sake of a meal before real conversation could take place.

"Very well, Senator. Thank you for asking. If all goes well, I may have some upcoming business in Brazil."

"Brazil?"

"Yes. Have you been?"

"No, I'm afraid not."

"The women are beautiful."

"I'm sure they are." Inside, the senator cringed at the thought of another international tryst.

Peter continued. "The Brazilians understand the balance between work and life's other pleasures. They don't let one interfere with the other."

"An admirable quality."

"Indeed."

The senator inhaled as he ran his nose along the length of the cigar. He reached for the cutter on the table, snipped off half an inch, and put the unlit cigar to his lips.

"How did your filming efforts turn out?"

"Very professional. We completed editing last week. All told, our trip produced thirty solid minutes of footage."

"When is the film scheduled for its big screen release?"

Senator Day squirmed slightly in his chair. His thoughts turned

toward the photographs he had received in the mail and the wire transfers that vanished without a trace into a bank in Hong Kong. The senator lied. "I'm planning to work it into the schedule this month with the
Special Committee on Overseas Labor. We are at a critical juncture and
need to make our recommendation to the Senate."

"I'm sure your constituents will be pleased with your
recommendation."

The senator flashed his best smile. He knew all too well how deep
Peter kept his hand in Congress's pocket. His guest understood that the
senator had a vested interest in the garment industry. Peter personally knew many of the businessmen with manufacturing interests in the
senator's home state—businessmen with thick briefcases and thicker
wallets that pushed, coerced, and bullied for status quo and the ability to
overlook a little human suffering in the name of making money.

"I would love to see the footage from Saipan," Peter said.

If you only knew what I know, the senator thought. That tape and
those photos could ruin my life.

The senator lied again. "That can be arranged."

"Please let me know. Of course, I'd also be happy to testify before
the committee in any way that you see fit."

Now there is an idea. "That may be very well received, Peter," the
senator said, his mind churning.

"I'm at your disposal."

Peter took a sip of his brandy and a pull from his cigar. The senator
looked around the room to keep tabs on the night's list of who's who.

"How is your chief-of-staff?"

"Scott? Took a few weeks before they could even do surgery due to
swelling and internal hemorrhaging. He was scheduled to be back at
work this week, but that was before he developed a staph infection. The
doctors aren't saying when he will be released. In the meantime, the rest
of my staff is floundering to cover for him. Twenty employees who can't
get out of each other's way."

"Waterskiing can be dangerous."

"Everything can be dangerous," the senator answered. The senator saw his segue into the heart of the topic he was looking to broach.
"By the way, I wanted to thank you and Lee Chang for your assistance
with my aide. Lee was most helpful in coordinating the medical care on

Saipan. Under the circumstances, I felt somewhat responsible for my employee's injury."

"Lee Chang knows Saipan very well."

"Yes, he seemed to be very well-connected. A very interesting man."

There was a slight change in the nuance of the conversation, a mild shift in mannerisms Peter immediately recognized. "In what way, Senator?"

"I understand Lee comes from a very successful family."

"Yes, he does."

"So why Saipan? Running a sweatshop seems like, how should I put it...an underachievement."

Both men jogged for position.

"The Chang family has manufacturing interests in a half-dozen Asian countries," Peter said, pausing briefly to sip his brandy. "But Chang Industries on Saipan is the most profitable."

"Lee has brothers, no?"

Peter knew the senator had been doing his homework. "The Chang family has a proud lineage in China going back too many generations to count. Lee has two elder brothers who are successfully running other business interests of the family."

"In China?"

"Yes, on the mainland."

"In Hong Kong?"

"No," Peter answered.

"So only Lee resides outside of the country?"

Peter didn't respond. Years of doing business with snakes taught him never to divulge all his information at once. The truth was simple. After Lee was caught with the underage daughter of a high-powered politician in the Chinese Ministry of Trade, Lee's father had been forced to make a decision. And C.F. Chang chose money over his youngest son.

"Yes, Lee is the only son working outside of China on a full-time basis," Peter finally answered, his mind filtering every word of the conversation, trying to gauge where the senator was going.

"What about money?"

Peter smelled blood. "I'm sorry, Senator?"

"Does Lee share in his family's fortune?"

"I imagine he is well taken care of."

Peter thought about the senator's question and stored it in his memory bank. "Is there a problem?"

"No. No problem at all. I'm just gathering background information. I know I asked some questions about Chang Industries before our trip, but I wanted some more information on our host. I need to be prepared for the Senate Committee. You know how it is with politicians. Any imaginable question could come up."

"I understand, Senator."

"Of course you do, Peter. That is why you have your office right here in D.C., close enough to hear the whispers circulating the halls on Capitol Hill."

"I'm not hiding my intentions, Senator. I'm into money, politics, and women. Usually in that order."

"Please, there is no need to get defensive. I'm just saying that you could have your office anywhere, but you choose to keep it in D.C. Very prudent. Keep an eye on legislation that will affect your business. Very smart."

"Senator, my home is D.C., but the world is my office."

The senator had asked enough questions for one evening. He reached to the table and raised his glass. "To continued success."

The two powerhouses clinked their glasses and sipped their drinks. They finished their cigars and brandy, dousing themselves in alcohol, thick smoke, and suspicion.

Chapter 7

The stainless steel handcuff dug into Wei Ling's left wrist, leaving a purple bruise in the shape of a bracelet like a punk-rock fashion statement. Her backside was sore from lying hours on end, the only alternative she had to standing directly next to the bed. A bedpan in need of attention rested on the floor under the mattress, just beyond the outstretched toes of her bare feet. She was trapped in a world so narrow it made a cell in the solitary confinement block seem like a suite at the Four Seasons.

The middle-aged lady who took care of Lee Chang visited Wei Ling three times a day. She brought soup and rice for breakfast, noodles with a plate of steamed vegetables for lunch, and a full meal in the early evening. It was a balanced diet, and better than the food from the sweatshop kitchen served to the able-bodied seamstresses. Wei Ling's food was coming directly from Lee Chang's personal refrigerator. No bruised fruit. No vegetables on the verge of spoiling. Every dish contained real chunks of chicken, pork, or beef, a vast culinary improvement over the usual unidentifiable meat particles. Everything had its positive side, and for Wei Ling the food was the only thing she had to look forward to.

Food aside, Wei Ling knew she was in trouble. No one with your best interest in mind locks you in a storage room and chains you to a bed. The good doctor hadn't come since the morning she was diagnosed as pregnant, and Wei Ling wasn't holding her breath waiting for his next visit. With the bloated body of the doctor sitting on a slab in the morgue, skull caved-in, she was right to assume he wouldn't be stopping by anytime soon.

Wei Ling wanted an abortion. She didn't care that it would cost her five hundred dollars in penalty money to the Changs. The baby would bring shame to her own family, and her family's honor had led her to Saipan in the first place. The honor of working overseas. Honor and a little cash to help her struggling family in Southern China's Guangzhou region. Coming home with a baby, worse still a half-breed, was not an option. Her family would disown her, and she wasn't from a place in society where a single mother would be met with open arms. She knew the path. Her family would disown her, she would be deemed unemployable, and she would end up on the street.

Having the baby wasn't an option.

Lee Chang promised her daily that an abortion was on the way, per company policy. Two other girls had become pregnant since Wei Ling's arrival at Club Paradise, and the doctor had acted quickly, under the orders of Lee Chang. So she waited for her fate in the recently transformed storage room, one arm cuffed to the metal bed frame. She was a prisoner, and like all prisoners, her life choices were limited. Worse, she was alone.

The seamstresses' quarters, for all its rules, regulations, and downright mean spiritedness, was a hell of a lot better than where she found herself now. And she missed her friends. Shi Shi Wong and the other hundred seamstresses were her family. Misery loves company, and in the seamstresses' quarters, they all helped each other to get by.

Her current isolation took away her only mental outlet. The handcuff on her wrist took away her physical ones. She never thought she would say it, but all she wanted was to have an abortion and be allowed back to work. She wasn't asking for much, but Wei Ling had a growing suspicion she would never see the inside of the seamstresses' quarters again.

***

Shi Shi Wong looked for her slippers in the piles of footwear scattered on the floor and stacked into four-foot-high bookshelves near the back door of the seamstresses' quarters. She wedged her feet into her green-trimmed flip-flops and slipped out the unlocked door into the rainy night.

The grounds were off limits after lights-out, a nightly ritual marked with a five-second alarm blast at eleven-thirty sharp. The doors to the seamstresses' quarters were locked some nights and open others, depending if the guards remembered to bolt them, which in turn was dependent upon the nightly poker game and how much the night guards drank.

But the locks were the least of Shi Shi's worries. The guards kept an eye, albeit an inebriated one, on the property, and any girl on the grounds after hours was guaranteed a beating. No whips or batons—just a good old-fashioned, barehanded roughing up with a few kicks thrown in for emphasis. A beating bad enough to remind the guilty party and her co-workers of the rules. A beating just short of an injury that would prevent her from working. It was a fine line, and the guards needed to look no further than Lee Chang to see how it was done with precision.

Shi Shi stooped as she walked behind the seamstresses' dorm and stopped at the corner. A lone guard stood at the front gate, his silhouette visible under the dim overhead light. Shi Shi crouched down, held her breath, and listened. The light pattering of rain on the puddles of mud that had formed on the dirt ground was the only audible sound. She looked around in the darkness between the buildings, stood, and covered the distance between the seamstresses' quarters and the factory in short, quick strides. She moved quietly among the fabric sheds behind the factory that held rolls of cotton, nylon, and hi-tech concoctions with fancy names like Rip-Proof Synthetic and Moisture-X.

Shi Shi stopped and repeated her crouch-and-listen routine.

Nothing.

With a final short sprint from the darkness, Shi Shi touched the side of the infirmary wall, crouching under the security lights just beneath Lee Chang's residence. She wiped at the wet glass with the sleeve of her sweatshirt and peered through the window into the empty infirmary. "Where are you?" she said to herself in her native tongue.

She shuffled among empty boxes, garbage cans, and crates of discarded swatches of unused fabric. A dull yellow glow emitted from the next window on the first floor, the weak light drowning in the rain as it reached the end of its spectrum. A TV blared from Lee Chang's residence above, the sound of screaming soccer fans broadcast live from China overpowering the sound of rain hitting the fabric sheds' tin roofs. Shi Shi stepped up on two old crates and looked in the window next to the infirmary. The rain on her face and the textured sliding windows didn't prevent her from immediately recognizing the body of her bunk-mate of two years. She tapped on the window and Wei Ling sat straight up, pain shooting down her arm to her elbow. She looked through the glass, saw Shi Shi's face, and began to sob.

Wei Ling tugged at the bed, moving the heavy frame and mattresses inch by inch until she could reach the bottom of the window. She put the pain of her left wrist out of her mind and stretched with her free hand, turning the lock and teasing herself with freedom. Shi Shi, still standing on the crates, pushed the window open, rain splattering into the room. She grabbed Wei Ling's outstretched arm and embraced it.

"Wei, are you ok? We've been worried about you."

"I knew you would come looking for me," Wei Ling said, tears streaming from her eyes. "I'm pregnant," she said before the sobbing spell escalated.

"From that night?"

"Yes. The American."

"Wei. I'm so sorry."

"Lee Chang keeps telling me that the doctor is coming to take me to the hospital, but I've been chained to this bed for a week now."

"The doctor is dead."

"Dead?"

"They found his body on the beach earlier in the week."

"Are you sure?"

"Putani, the new girl from Thailand, is sleeping with one of the guards. He told her. He thought it was funny."

"You have to get me out of here. That crazy Lee Chang is going to kill me."

"It's okay. If he wanted you dead, you'd be gone by now. I'll think of something, but I can't get you out tonight. I'll talk to some of the girls and see if they can help."

"Make it quick."

"What about Peter?" Shi Shi asked. "He will come looking for you sooner or later."

"I hope so."

"I'll be back tomorrow or the next day. As soon as I can get out without getting caught."

"Hurry."

"Take care."

Shi Shi kissed Wei Ling's hand as Wei Ling caressed her face with her fingertips. The meeting through the window ended suddenly, the crate supporting Shi Shi's small frame creaking once before giving way with a violent crash. Shi Shi's arm was ripped out of the window and a muffled cry slipped out.

"Shi Shi?" Wei Ling repeated several times with no reply. She stretched to shut the window, her flesh cutting against the handcuff. Wei Ling sat down on the bed and continued to cry.

Hopeful tears combined with hopeless ones.

***

Shi Shi's weight crashing through the crate brought the night guards out of their poker shed, whiskey and beer bottles in hand. Not detectives to begin with, their observation skills were further numbed by alcohol, their ambition robbed by greed and the chance to take money from each other through five card stud, deuces wild.

Shi Shi hid behind the building that housed the sweatshop floor and waited for the three guards to finish their half-hearted search of the back of the facility. When the cussing started again in the shed, Shi Shi limped across the small patch of wet ground to the seamstresses' quarters and opened the door.

She limped down the hall, blood and mud trailing behind her. Her ankle was already starting to swell, a faint blue ring forming around the outside of the bone. She grimaced when she walked, the pain telling her something was broken.

Her roommates heard Shi Shi before she reached the room—the panting sound of the injured girl dragging one leg behind her. "Shi Shi!" her roommates said, turning on the small light next to the door.

"Shhhhhhhh, the guards are outside," Shi Shi responded, flopping her butt onto the mattress of the lower bunk bed. Blood ran down her leg from her knee to her foot, a deep gash that everyone agreed would need stitches.

The roommates, dressed in light shorts and t-shirts as sleeping apparel, hurriedly tended to the wound with soap, water, and a stream of small Band-Aids. It was all they had.

"Did you find Wei Ling?"

"Yes. She's in the storage room of the infirmary. They have her chained to a bed. She's pregnant."

Curses flew out in Chinese, English, and Thai.

"She's in serious trouble. Lee Chang keeps telling her the doctor is coming and that they will take her to the hospital to get an abortion. But we know the doctor is dead."

Shi Shi told the girls what she knew. It was a story no one wanted to hear. It could have just as easily been one of them. They had all been used as a tool to drum up business for Chang Industries. They would have to help her. She was family. And she would do it for any of them.

***

Lee Chang took his morning walk around the grounds with a cup of black tea. He spot-checked the fence out of habit, looking for holes or places where the fence had been pulled back. No one had tried to break into Chang Industries since a group of thieves had stolen a shipment of silk nearly two years earlier. The police were subsequently put on the payroll, and patrols of the road leading to Chang Industries increased enough to thwart any further crime from outsiders. He walked behind the building, checked the security of the sheds, and headed toward the sweatshop floor to see if everyone was in place. Heading back to his apartment for his morning shower, Lee Chang passed the broken crate under the window. He took two steps before the green-trimmed sandal registered in his mind. He set his cup of tea on the top of an empty blue plastic barrel and reached into the broken remains of the crate. He looked up at the window to the storage room and his heart skipped a beat. He slapped the bottom of the sandal against the palm of his open hand. "Son of a bitch." He looked at the sandal closely, knocked off some dirt, and squinted at the faded Chinese characters. Lee Chang read the characters to himself, and then aloud with one addition, "Shi Shi fucking Wong."

Shi Shi had her head down, sewing through her fifth jacket in the bottom half of the hour. A breakneck pace. Beneath her sweatpants, her leg was swollen, her cuts bleeding into the tissue that encased the lower leg like a soft-sided cast. She ignored her leg as best she could, putting the energy from the pain into her work. She thought about herself and then thought about Wei Ling.

She never saw the baton or the hand holding it. Lee Chang dragged her from her seat by her hair, Shi Shi's screams bringing the work floor to a halt. When Shi Shi found her feet, Lee Chang punched her in the face until she lost her balance. It was the vicious beginning to a permanent vacation.

Chapter 8

The ladies packed into the bathroom, the only forum in the seam-stresses's living quarters large enough for a mass audience. The bar-racks-style living quarters were a squat two stories—twelve rooms on each floor, four girls in each room. With girls standing in the showers and draped on the sinks, most of the seamstresses were present and accounted for. Wei Ling and Shi Shi Wong's roommates, twin sisters from Thailand with unpronounceable names, laid out their plan and asked for volunteers. The punishment for being caught was going to be severe. Physical abuse, fines they couldn't afford to pay, and the contin-ued suspension of privileges that began when Wei Ling moved into the infirmary.

The women nodded. They understood.

The girls returned to their rooms and began quietly and method-ically looking through their belongings for anything made of paper. The writing tablets were first to go, followed by napkins, paper towels, torn pieces of tissue boxes. Nothing was considered too outrageous and nothing was turned down. Old letters from family members, envelopes, the borders from old newspapers. They were all ripped into manageable pieces.

The girls stayed up all night. With cramping hands and watering eyes, they wrote identical sentences on every piece of paper. They shared the pens and the half dozen short golf pencils someone had brought back from a trip into town. Eyeliner worked well, and was in plentiful supply. They finished twenty minutes before the morning wake-up call, split the piles of paper among themselves, and waited for an opportuni-ty. They didn't have to wait long.

***

The emergency shipment of khaki shorts was nothing short of a catalogue order from God. The summer fashion season was in full swing and the popularity of the knee-length, double-pocket, Army-drab-green shorts was a surprise hit at the Republic Outfitters. Every store on the East Coast was sold out and the backorders were growing at an outstanding rate. A rush order for twenty thousand pairs sent the busy sweatshop floor into a pace of delirium rarely seen. The fabric was scheduled to arrive the following morning and the ladies were told to prepare for serious work. They had two days to complete the order. Twenty thousand pairs of shorts. Ten thousand pairs a day. Sleep was optional, dictated by Lee Chang.

The smell of oiled machinery and the acrid stench of dye filled every corner of the vast sweatshop floor. Dust hung in the air, tiny particles of fabric sent into motion by the relentless crisp snipping of scissors powered by calloused hands. Each worker hunched over her identical workspace—a sewing machine, a single drawer, and a two-square-foot chunk of smooth tabletop that was barely enough room to sew a pair of pants. Heads down, they silently ran fabric under the bobbing needles of their machines, the non-stop mechanical hum as constant as the summer heat. It was tedious, carpal-tunnel-syndrome-inducing work. Conversation was limited to work-related topics, and there wasn't much to discuss when you are sewing fabric at a pace of one pair of shorts every five minutes.

The girls worked in teams, the sweatshop floor divided into different groups. The seamstresses were the majority of the floor's workforce, but everyone took turns learning the ropes and honing their skills in three other areas: inspection, packing, and fabric preparation. The seamstresses passed the shorts to the finishing group who added the zippers, buttons and appropriate tags. Once they were completed, the goods went through inspection and were then packed according to the customers' specifications. Chang Industries' lone female henchwoman oversaw the activities in the inspection room. She grabbed a pair of shorts from the finished stack at random, yelling as necessary when she found a defect. Once the goods passed through her station, the strongest of the seamstress workforce folded and packed the goods.

Starting first thing in the morning, the girls in packing took on another responsibility. Each pair of shorts was packaged with a piece of paper. Careful not to draw the attention of the foreman, the packing team removed the pieces of paper hidden in their own pockets, socks, and sleeves, and stuffed a note into every pair of shorts that came through their hands. Beneath the plastic bag in the dirty trashcan in the bathroom, other seamstresses stashed additional notes for the girls in packing to replenish their supplies. For one full shift, the routine was the same. A note in the pocket, the shorts folded, and then placed in boxes according to their size.

The group functioned well as a team. Chang Industries, if nothing else, ran efficiently. And the girls were counting on that efficiency to get the shorts off the island before the shit hit the fan.

Chapter 9

Jake picked up the ten-foot yellow moving van from a sketchy rental lot near New York Avenue. It took one trip to move the bed, a sofa, and the dining room table set. On his second trip, he wrestled with his bike, a couple hundred books, and miscellaneous household items that hadn't been used since the funeral.

Kate met him at his new apartment near Cleveland Park to help him move and unpack. The one-bedroom apartment was on the fourth floor of the oldest building on the block, and the lack of an elevator became a serious issue with the weight of the sofa in his arms. The narrow staircase and tighter hallways added to the nightmare of moving. Jake felt guilty for having his girlfriend of four weeks help him move the sofa, but he was a gentleman and gave her the light side of the load.

She wasn't his first choice of moving partners. His friends were in Europe and Uncle Steve was on crutches. Besides, Kate had volunteered for moving duty, and she didn't complain. It was another check in favor of his girlfriend in the "pros column" of his mental pros-and-cons list.

By noon, the three-room rental started to look like an apartment. Jake didn't need much to get by and it showed. He rearranged the sofa and the TV in the living room while Kate unpacked the dishes in the kitchen. He gave her free range to put things where she saw fit. The kitchen wasn't his forte, and as long as he could find a plate, a bowl, and a glass, he was fine.

Finished, Jake and Kate sat at the small dining room table and looked around.

"It looks good," Kate said, pleased with herself and her interior decorating skills.

"It'll do," Jake replied. "All I have to do is hang a few pictures and get a bookcase or two."

"I need to get home and take a shower," Kate said, standing and wiping the hair from her face. "We have to be at my parents's by three. I'll pick you up at your mom's house in an hour."

Kate left and Jake watched her walk down the squeaky staircase and its many turns. She was a good woman. He was nervous about meeting her parents, but he couldn't avoid them much longer without raising suspicions. They had only been together a month, albeit a passionate one, but her family was close-knit and they lived nearby. Besides, it was the Fourth of July and the plan was for a backyard barbecue. Jake reasoned there were few things less stressful than a cookout with burgers and hotdogs.

He threw some food in the goldfish bowl, and the two identical black bubble heads with fan-like fins fought over the flakes like it was their last supper. He grabbed his keys and locked the door on his way out. He had just enough time to return the van, get back to his mother's house, and take a shower.

***

Kate's Lexus pulled up to the guardhouse.

"Miss Sorrentino," the unfriendly guard said with authority.

"Hi, Max," Kate answered.

Jake leaned forward and waved, the guard unimpressed with Kate's passenger and guest.

"Quite a party your parents are having today."

"They do it every year. You're welcome to stop by after you get off work."

"Thank you, but I have to get home. I'm taking the kids to see the fireworks."

"Well the invitation is there if you change your mind. You can bring your kids."

"Have a good evening, Miss Sorrentino."

The entrance to the private community was nothing more than a guard booth with a flimsy gate, but it made the residents feel better. As the car pushed forward, estates peeked through the heavily wooded street. The farther they drove, the larger the houses became. Jake grew nervous. He was in millionaire country—congressmen, football players, internet company cash-outs. They lived here, and they lived well.

"Nice homes," Jake said.

"Yeah I guess they are," Kate answered as if it were an original thought. Jake wasn't sure whether to believe her naivety.

They passed a modest house on the right and Jake commented, "That one seems a bit out of place, it only has a two-car garage."

"That is the Crowe Estate. They have about thirty acres. When I was in junior high school Mrs. Crowe taught me how to ride horses," Kate responded. "And that is not the main house. That's the guest quarters."

So this is how the other half lives, Jake thought. He realized what half he had been living in, and he wanted to switch teams.

The Sorrentino residence was at the end of the country lane. Twenty acres of rolling hills overlooking the Potomac River. It was beautiful land, and the house accentuated its splendor. Kate pulled her Lexus in front of the verifiable mansion and parked between the large fountain and the stone entrance. A dozen cars were parked in and around the long driveway, a mix of autobahn-certified German autos and other high-end imports.

Kate stopped at the step to the front door and looked at Jake. "Relax. You look a little nervous."

"That's probably because I am."

Kate didn't bother to share that she too was nervous for other reasons. With the exception of Ricky Groves in the sixth grade, her parents had disapproved of every boyfriend she ever had. The reasons varied, but were all the same: they simply weren't good enough for the Sorrentinos' only daughter. Not from the right lineage, not the right breed, not the right stuff. Not good-looking enough. Not smart enough. If you looked for a reason not to like someone, it was easy to find one. And her parents looked hard.

Kate pushed open the large wooden front door and invited Jake into her world.

Initial introductions with Mr. and Mrs. Sorrentino went down in the kitchen, and Jake answered the standard questions well enough to earn an invitation backstage, to the barbecue festivities in full swing in the backyard. Kate's parents eyed the couple through the glass wall, and her father cringed when his daughter's hand reached for Jake's.

Jake followed Kate across the multi-tiered cedar deck and down the walk to the edge of the pool. The huge brick barbecue pit in the corner pumped smoke into the air, the six-foot gas-powered grill large enough to feed an army. Jake eyed the food on display. Not a hot dog in sight. Freshly cut tuna and swordfish cooked slowly on the right hand side of the grill. Filet mignon and shrimp on bamboo skewers took up residence on the other half of the metal grate. Nachos and dip were absent, replaced with crackers, heart of palm, and black caviar.

Sundresses and blue blazers ruled the scene and Jake felt grossly underdressed in his polo shirt and knee-length shorts. He reminded himself to have a word with Kate. Next time he wanted a little more detail of what he was getting himself into. Small groups mingled around glass-top tables talking about vacations in Tuscany, the real estate market in Honolulu, and bank accounts in New Zealand that were paying eight percent interest. He had never been to a tie-only barbecue, and if the first fifteen minutes were any indication, he would live comfortably not having to attend another.

Kate's father cornered Jake on his way back from the bathroom. Kate was on the deck, her ear being bent by an elderly aunt who had already repeated herself twice. Mr. Sorrentino seized the opportunity to lay down the rules, *mano a mano,* as only a father can do.

"Kate tells me that you are in grad school at American University."

"Yes sir. I am getting my Masters in English Literature."

"What do you do with a degree in English Literature?"

"I don't know yet. Maybe teach. Maybe get involved with a non-profit in D.C."

It wasn't the answer Mr. Sorrentino was hoping for. He hated to hear anyone say, "I don't know" when it pertained to their future. He was equally offended by the term "non-profit."

"What does your father do?"

"He's in international business…importing, exporting."

"Sales?" Mr. Sorrentino said in more of a statement than a question.

"No, he is the CEO and President."

"Based in Washington?"

"Incorporated in Delaware, headquartered in D.C. The company has offices on both coasts and facilities overseas."

"Tell me about your family."

Jake balked. It was a question he didn't like.

"I have a small family. Most of them live in the Portland area. I have an uncle in town."

"Any chance you will follow in your father's footsteps?"

"In business?"

"Yes."

"I don't know," Jake answered.

Mr. Sorrentino swallowed at the resurfacing of his least favorite expression. He hated to think about his daughter dating anyone, but especially a young man without a plan. Change your mind later, but for God's sake have some idea what you want to do with yourself.

"I'm working at his company this summer."

"Learning the ropes?"

"Yes, I guess so."

With the word "guess," Mr. Sorrentino had heard enough. Jake needed some direction. Something definitive. One of the problems with young kids these days. Mr. Sorrentino feared for the future of the country.

Jake just wanted to get away from his girlfriend's father. Mr. Sorrentino asked questions with a stare so intense it was as if he were making inquiries directly to your soul. His gaze burned through Jake's eyes and penetrated his skin. Every question was loaded. Jake didn't like the man.

"May I ask about your profession, Mr. Sorrentino?"

"Sure, Jake. I'm mostly retired now. My business interests lie in real estate, construction, waste removal, imported produce, restaurants."

"How is the waste removal business?"

"There is never a shortage of waste, Jake. Never met a person who didn't produce any, and the population keeps growing."

"True enough."

Jake chalked up Mr. Sorrentino's condescending attitude to natural arrogance and an overbearing nature when it came to his daughter. Jake wanted nothing more than to tell Mr. Sorrentino a couple of things. First and foremost was that, indeed, he was giving it to Mr. Sorrentino's only daughter and enjoying it immensely, thank you very much.

He wondered if the details about caring for his mother over the last eighteen months would wipe the smug look off Mr. Sorrentino's face. The all-nighters, the trips to the doctors, learning how to give injections with the skill of a seasoned nurse. Do that for a year and a half and see if you come out of it with a life plan. Life changes and having a plan guarantees nothing. Jake knew the words would be lost on Kate's father. He was a hard-ass, and a scary one at that.

"It was good speaking with you, Jake," Mr. Sorrentino said. "And let us conclude this conversation on a constructive, positive note."

"Please," Jake answered.

"There are two things I will not tolerate as a father to my daughter. Number one is infidelity. If I catch you cheating on my daughter, I will cut your balls off and feed them to the dogs. Number two—if I catch you lying to me or my daughter, the same thing will happen to your tongue. Understood?"

Jake looked at the madman in front of him. "Sounds pretty straight forward to me," he answered. "But remember this, Mr. Sorrentino: for every man who cheats there is a woman cheating as well. And for every man who lies there are at least an equal number of women lying. Men just can't hide it as well. The chance of me breaking Kate's heart is equal to the chance that she will break mine."

"Just so we know where we stand," Mr. Sorrentino answered as if he hadn't heard Jake's short soapbox sermon.

Kate knocked on the glass door and her father changed from Dr. Jekyll to Mr. Hyde.

"How are my two favorite guys?" she asked, opening the door.

"Just getting to know one another, right Jake?" Mr. Sorrentino said.

"Right."

"Dad, if you don't mind, I want to steal Jake from you. Aunt Theresa wants to meet him."

"He's all yours," Mr. Sorrentino said with a sadistic twinkle in his eye aimed in Jake's direction. With Kate's father in mind, Jake chalked one up in the "cons column."

Jake and Kate stepped outside. His uneasiness didn't go unnoticed. They may not have been dating long, but both were already good at knowing what the other was thinking.

"Kate, we need to talk."

"Sure, Jake. But first I want you to meet Aunt Theresa." A quick smile and light handshake later, Aunt Theresa turned to Kate. "Very handsome."

"I know," Kate said, pulling Jake away.

Hand-in-hand they turned from Aunt Theresa straight into a human wall. Three broad-shouldered men stood abreast, creating a barrier that would require a less-than-subtle change in direction.

"Hi, Tony," Kate said, looking upward.

"Introduce us to your new friend," Tony said, standing between two massive sides of beef known as the Castello brothers.

"Tony, this is Jake. Jake this is Tony. He's a friend of the family and a business associate of my father."

"Nice to meet you, Jake," Tony said, squeezing Jake's hand until the bones in his knuckles rubbed each other.

"And these other two guys are Eddie and Mike Castello," Kate said. "People call them brothers, but they are really cousins. My aunt raised both of them."

"As far as you are concerned, we are brothers," Mike said, shaking Jake's hand with a reasonable grip. Eddie stuck out his tree trunk arm and grunted something only Mike understood. They may have been cousins, but they had the mannerisms of two people who were raised under the same roof. A house where the family didn't speak.

"For what it is worth, you don't look like brothers," Jake said.

"That's because they're not," Tony added, as if he had solved a mystery.

"Well, I guess that's why."

"Jake, I expect you to treat Kate right. She is like my kid sister."

"Of course," Jake answered.

"Don't worry about Tony," Kate said. "He is a big teddy bear on the inside."

And a grizzly on the outside, Jake thought. "Nice meeting you all. We'll see you around." God I hope not. At least not when it is dark.

Jake stepped to the side and let the trio-of-trouble walk by. Kate led Jake through the yard by his hand, directing him to the gazebo. She sat him down and looked into his eyes. "What is it?"

"I'm not sure how to tell you this."

"Just say it. You can tell me anything."

Jake's stomach turned with a combination of early relationship infatuation and fear. "Don't take this the wrong way, but your father is crazy."

Kate laughed. Jake wasn't the first boyfriend she had brought home who had voiced concerns over her father. "He is just a little overbearing."

"Oh, Kate, he's more than a little overbearing. And Tony… the guy nearly broke my hand."

"They are just trying to be protective. They are harmless."

"Harmless?"

"Jake, my mother and father have a saying. 'Sometimes it takes an insane act by a sane person to prove a point.' Don't worry about my father. He gets a little crazy when it comes to his daughter. He is just showing that he loves me."

"Kate, I understand your father loves you, but let me tell you about our little conversation. Your father said, and I quote, that he would 'cut off my balls and my tongue if I cheated on you or lied to you.'"

"I'm sure he meant it figuratively," Kate said, gently rubbing Jake's thigh.

"How the hell could he mean that figuratively? He said he would cut my balls off and feed them to the dogs."

"See, there you go," Kate said with a satisfied look on her face. "I told you he was speaking figuratively."

"'There you go' what?" Jake asked.

"We don't have any dogs."

Chapter 10

Marilyn walked into the office Monday morning to a full voice-mail box. Even when the CEO and president of Winthrop Enterprises wasn't out of town, Peter Winthrop didn't answer his own calls unless they came directly to his private cell phone—a number he didn't give out to just anyone. You had to be royalty, or close enough to royalty that you could arrange a meeting with them. Marilyn was Peter's assistant and switchboard. She did her job with perfection, trained to perfection over the last twenty plus years. She was very well compensated for standing guard as the final barrier to communication between the outside world and her boss.

The frantic urgency of the messages left on Peter Winthrop's phone was unusual, and Marilyn wrote down the number with haste. She listened to the messages a second time and decided a return call was in her best interest. Her boss was outside Rio, scoping out a potential factory to sell to a Japanese investor, but she knew he would call. He liked his morning update, the more detail the better. And if she could solve a problem without wasting her boss's time, that was fine too. That's what she was paid to do.

With the name and number of an employee from Republic Out-fitters scribbled on the paper in her hand, she hit the numbers on her phone. She checked the clock on the wall, and after two rings, was surprised to hear a human voice this early in the morning.

"Good morning. Republic Outfitters, Amy Grant speaking."

"Good morning. This is Marilyn Ford, personal assistant to Peter Winthrop. I am returning several calls that were left for Mr. Winthrop over the weekend. Is there something I can help you with?"

"Good morning, Marilyn. Thank you for getting back to us. We have a bit of an issue with the rush order of shorts we received from our manufacturer in Asia."

"Could you please hold for a moment?

"Yes."

Marilyn opened her desk drawer and pulled out a file on active projects. Republic Outfitters was third from the front. She read the file quickly and returned to the phone. "Twenty thousand pairs of shorts. Rush-ordered. Chang Industries, correct?"

"That's right," the unlucky employee from Republic Outfitters answered from the company's quiet headquarters in Maine.

"Rest assured that if there are problems with the quality of the product, we will handle it immediately at no cost to you."

Amy Grant, corporate firefighter for the Republic Outfitters' director of logistics, fumbled for words and went back to her original request. "I really need to speak with Mr. Winthrop directly," she said forcefully.

"Mr. Winthrop will be out of the office for a few days. I assure you I keep all of his affairs in the strictest of confidence."

"Still...."

"I understand your concern, but please understand mine. I have worked directly for Mr. Winthrop for over two decades and everything he knows, I know."

"Well we have a bit of an unusual situation with the rush order of shorts."

"As you have said."

"You might have to see this to believe it. Do you have a fax number where you can be reached?"

Marilyn gave her the fax number, again promised to handle the situation, whatever it was, and hung up.

Amy Grant, black spiked hair to go with her pierced eyebrow, took several minutes cutting, pasting, taping, and copying. She had been working on the company emergency all weekend with her boss, trying to find the right people to talk to. When they found the first note, everyone assumed it was a hoax. When the number of notes passed two dozen, Republic Outfitter's quality control group checked the contact person for the contract on the emergency order of shorts. Surprisingly, they found the same name in the contract as in the notes. Peter Winthrop.

Amy finished honing her kindergarten cut-and-paste skills and looked at her handiwork. She placed the stack of paper face down, and fat fingered the final number on the fax machine before hitting send.

Marilyn impatiently waited by her personal all-in-one fax, copier, and scanner. Peter was due to call any minute, and she would feel better knowing what the emergency from Maine was all about.

Jake walked in the office, gave Marilyn a wave and a "good morning," and continued on to his office, briefcase bulging with files and newspapers. Twenty minutes later, Marilyn contacted Amy Grant at Republic Outfitters to tell her she was still waiting. The spike-haired employee insisted she had sent the fax, and checked the confirmation ticket that the fax machine generated automatically. She confirmed the number with Marilyn, who reconfirmed that the sender had sent the fax to the wrong number. The first page of the fax came in, inching its way from the slit in the top of the machine. The page was a photocopy of smaller pieces of paper, pushed together in an odd collage—a Picasso masterpiece made from scraps of paper, a plain sheet of office paper serving as the canvas.

Marilyn looked at the first page and then the next. She glanced at the machine and its small display window. There were five pages in total, but she didn't wait to see them all before picking up the phone. Her demeanor was noticeably more serious.

"Where did this come from?" Marilyn asked.

"That's just it. They came in the order of shorts we just received. We do a cursory examination on a sample number of shorts as they come in and the inspector found the first note. Then he found another."

"How many did you find all together? I see the fax is five pages long."

"Oh that's just the tip of the iceberg. There are hundreds of notes so far, and still more keep coming. I don't have a clue what the total number is, but it looks like it is in the thousands."

"Isn't that wonderful," Marilyn muttered.

"What would you like us to do?"

"Check all the shorts and any other merchandise you get from Chang Industries. Keep all the notes. Mr. Winthrop will see to it that you are compensated for the extra work."

"But what about the notes?"

"I will handle it and get back to you."

Marilyn hung up the phone, looked around helplessly, and began to cry.

When Peter called, Marilyn grabbed her keys, unlocked her boss's door and went into the privacy of his office. She came out a full hour later, eyes watering, sniffling like a kid with allergies in the middle of spring. It was only nine o'clock in the morning, and already it looked like the beginning of the second worst day of her life.

***

Jake fetched a cup of coffee from the main lounge on the far side of the floor and returned to his office to check his email. There was plenty to do at Winthrop Enterprises, if Jake felt like working. As the president's son, no one was busting his balls. He did have daily meetings with the international trade team, a group of ten serious professionals who kept track of the movement of goods across the globe. They were masters of importing, exporting, and international trade law. They knew custom officials by name in fifty countries and had bought, sold, imported, and exported just about every item known to man. The group of international trade specialists at Winthrop Enterprises was like the prison inmate who could get anything for anyone, for a fee. They danced the edge of legality, toes just inside the line, but willing to cross it if the money was right.

Jake liked the international group. They opened his eyes to a whole new world. He had done a short, two-day rotation in accounting and finance, but found the people even more boring than their stereotypes. Even the marketing group, which as far as Jake could tell didn't actually do any marketing, was surprisingly quiet. But international trade was interesting, and the group humored him and his questions. Sure Jake knew he was the president's son and the employees were probably following orders—showing Jake the ropes, entertaining him.

But Jake wasn't loafing on the job either. He was working hard to learn something so different from English Literature that at times the trade group members seemed like they were speaking a foreign language. The international trade team may have had to accept him with open arms, but if Jake had any say in the matter, they were going to absolutely *love* him before long. Diligence served with a smile.

A megaphone blared outside the window and Jake stood from the piles of paper at his desk and checked on the action in Franklin Park across the street. It was early, before the heat really set in, and there was already a loose-knit group forming in the one-square block park.

He was learning to love his office and his front row seat to the live entertainment played out across the street. The organizers of today's gathering either had no agenda or weren't well prepared. There was no indication that the religious freaks or abortion nuts were going to spend the day praying for the sinners' souls. The group didn't look like the normal vets either, who formed regularly to bitch about poor treatment, a complaint that was probably true. They sure as hell weren't tree-huggers from the West Coast converging on the city. The most organized faction in the park was still the homeless camped out in their normal spots on the park bench, behind the hedges, and on the heating grates fed by the subway system below—prime real-estate in the winter that the homeless marked with their belongings year-round.

Jake looked away from the window and his eyes fell on the tray of his fax machine. Another random junk fax. Someone had his number. He took one step on the plush beige carpet, reached down, and picked up the piece of paper that would forever change his life. Pandora's Box on an eight-by-eleven inch sheet of paper.

***

Marilyn sat at her desk, shoulders slumped, eyes puffy, a small trash-can full of tissues next to her chair. The morning went down the crapper with the phone call from Republic Outfitters, and Marilyn now looked ten years older than she had when she got off the subway. The wrinkles were showing, the small veins pronounced, the first layer of make-up wiped away one tissue and tear at a time.

Jake approached Marilyn's desk like a defensive lineman on the blind side of a quarterback.

"I need to speak with my father," Jake said with bite.

"I just spoke with him. He's on the road and can't be reached until tomorrow."

"Then you and I need to talk."

"Can it wait, Jake? It has been a rough morning."

"No, Marilyn. It can't wait." Jake held up the fax. Marilyn looked at the unmistakable piece of paper she had neglected to look for in the midst of her morning emotional breakdown. Fresh tears welled up in her eyes.

"Grab your bag and let's go," Jake said.

"Where are we going?"

"Out of the office."

Marilyn snagged her purse from the back of her chair and snatched her cell phone off the desk. She ripped a handful of Kleenex from the box in rapid succession and shoved them in the pocket of her white cotton blazer. The receptionist and several Winthrop Enterprise regulars gave Jake and Marilyn suspicious looks as they waited silently for the elevator. The whispers grew as soon as the elevator doors shut.

A block from Winthrop Enterprises, *Good Morning Sunshine* served breakfast, usually coffee and toast, to a paper-reading clientele in suits. Marilyn and Jake were the only couple in the joint—all the other patrons were enjoying their morning dates with *The Washington Post*. A few *Wall Street Journals* were on the counter, read and folded.

Jake ignored the "wait to be seated" peg-lettered sign standing near the door and led Marilyn to a table near the window.

"Two coffees and one order of waffles," Jake said to the lone forty-something waiter who took the order with a nod. The twenty-seat wannabe diner was library quiet.

"What the hell is this?" Jake asked, whispering forcefully, placing the fax on the table.

"How did you get this?"

"It was on my fax machine."

"Oh, dear God," Marilyn said. "Of all the fax machines in the company."

"Who is Wei Ling?"

"She's a girl your father knows."

"And she is pregnant?"

"That's what it says."

"It also says that she is being held against her will. Just what the hell does that mean?"

"I don't know."

"Does my father know?"

"Yes. I told him this morning."

"What did he say?"

"He told me he was going to make some calls," Marilyn answered. "But I got the feeling there was more to it."

"So who is the girl?" Jake asked again.

"She works in a factory in Saipan that your father does business with."

"A girlfriend?"

"Jake, your father doesn't have girlfriends."

"Is it his baby?"

Marilyn tried to answer, but the tears suddenly streaming down her cheeks magically prevented it. Jake waited. Women cry for different reasons, and Jake wasn't in the mood to soothe anyone's tears.

"Jake, I'm sure this Wei Ling girl is, shall we say, a romantic interest of your father. Not a girlfriend, mind you. More like a play toy."

"And she is pregnant."

"We don't know," Marilyn said almost incomprehensibly through a new round of tears.

"You seem to be taking this hard."

"There is something you need to know, Jake. Something that may come as a surprise."

With that simple sentence, all remaining hints of composure drained from Marilyn. She sobbed openly and every customer in the restaurant looked over.

Jake waited again. He was good at waiting. Almost as good as he was at measuring people. Whatever Marilyn was about to say, Jake knew it was going to be good.

It was a gross underestimation.

"I used to be one of your father's girlfriends. I know from personal experience how this girl feels."

"I'm sorry," was all he could muster.

"No, Jake. I'm the one who is sorry."

Marilyn then burst into a full-fledged fit of inconsolable hysteria, an outburst of emotions normally reserved for national catastrophes and the death of a boy's first dog. Two customers raised their hands and asked the waiter for the bill. The waiter delivered the checks, picked up two cups of coffee, and brought them to Jake's table.

"Is everything all right?" the waiter asked. Jake nodded and gave him a hushing gesture with his hands. "Please," the waiter added, glancing around at the customers to indicate that the crying was ruining business.

Marilyn excused herself to go to the bathroom and the waiter came back with the order of waffles. Jake slapped some butter on the two-tiered stack and poured a healthy dose of syrup into the dimples. Marilyn returned, wiped her cheeks again with a wad of Kleenex, and took a sip of her coffee.

"I had an affair with your father, Jake. Twenty-five years ago."

Jake quickly did the math in his head and a stern look washed over his face. The smile, the kind eyes, the cheerful personality were no longer part of his character.

"I'm listening."

"I was young, your father was charming. We spent a lot of time together. One thing led to another."

"Did my mother know?"

"She eventually found out, and then promptly threw your father out of the house. You were one, and just beginning to walk."

"I always thought he left us."

"Well he did, in a way. And it was my fault…" The tears were back with a vengeance and Jake just stared at her while she bawled. He eschewed all sympathy from his heart and pushed his warm, uneaten pile of waffles to the edge of the table.

Marilyn, speaking through huffs, continued. "There is something else. I became pregnant after you were born. At your father's request, I had an abortion. I've regretted that decision every day since. Every day."

Jake didn't know what to say. She was now talking about herself, and Jake finally understood the reason for her tears. Marilyn was a victim. A victim of his father and a victim in her own mind.

"We need to do something."

"Jake, let your father handle it."

"What's he going to do?"

"Handle it."

"I want to contact the girl."

"Forget it, Jake."

"I can't."

"Jake, your father is someone who likes things his way. He will handle this, whether you want him to or not."

"I'm going to see if there is something I can do."

"Like what Jake? Get on a plane to Saipan? Your father is a big boy, with a lot of friends."

"Marilyn, did you read this fax? This girl is begging for help. She has gone through extreme measures to get this to us. We can't sit here and do nothing. And after what you have been through? Doing nothing is not a choice."

"Jake, I can't help you. Winthrop Enterprises is my life. I have equity in the company. It is the only thing I know. I am a forty-five-year-old executive assistant who has only had one employer."

"Fine. Forget the girl then. I won't. My father doesn't scare me."

"That is because you don't know him." Marilyn took another drink of her coffee and Jake gestured for the check. Silence filled the void as Jake threw a twenty on the table. "I may know someone who can help you," Marilyn conceded quietly, staring out the window.

"Who?"

"His name is Al."

"What does he do?"

"All I can say is that he may be able to help."

"Give me his number."

"I can't. I'll arrange for a meeting. That's the best I can do."

"Fine. The sooner the better."

***

Jake headed back to Winthrop Enterprises with Marilyn in tow, three paces behind. They exited the elevator and casually strolled through the whispers and stares before Jake locked himself in his office. He swiveled the monitor on his computer slightly and tapped into the single greatest source of information in the internet age: Google.com. He typed in the search words "Saipan" and "police department," moved his cursor to the SEARCH button and hit ENTER. After a few clicks of the mouse, he was staring at the Department of Public Safety for the Island of Saipan. He jotted down the phone number and clicked through some other pages from the search results.

Jake read about Saipan, supplemental information to a history lesson from Mr. Jennings in eighth grade. A tropical island paradise where the U.S. dollar was the official currency and the U.S. Postal Service delivered the mail. Who knew?

The call to Saipan's Department of Public Safety's switchboard went through without a hitch.

"Saipan Department of Public Safety. Is this an emergency?" the female voice asked in a slow voice.

"No, this is an inquiry."

"I'm sorry, but no one is available at the moment to handle inquiries. I can patch you through to voice-mail if it is not an emergency. Someone will get back to you as soon as they can."

"Please. Put me in touch with the man in charge," Jake said with fake authority, not knowing the minute size of the Saipan police force.

As Jake waited to be connected, he found himself looking around the office nervously.

"You have reached the voicemail of Captain Talua. I'm sorry that I'm unavailable to take your call. If you leave a detailed message, I will get back to you as soon as I am able." A long beep followed and Jake prepared himself for his speech.

"Yes," Jake stammered. "My name is Jake Patrick and I wanted to ask the police to check on the whereabouts and well-being of a Saipan resident. The resident's name is Wei Ling… I have reason to believe she may be in trouble." Jake left his name for the second time and then repeated his work number twice slowly. *That should get the ball rolling*, he thought to himself. Just an inquiry to see if the notes stashed into the pockets of the imported shorts were a scam. If Marilyn wouldn't help, fine. He had no problem doing the right thing.

***

Captain Talua, a hefty man in his early fifties with a dark complexion and shallow wrinkles around the corners of his eyes, opened the blinds to his small office and looked out the window, taking in the depressing landscape across the police impound lot. A lone impounded truck, towed in a year before and never claimed, rested in the seashell-filled lot beside the skeletal remains of three police cruisers. Recent budget cuts on the island hit the police department hard. Fewer funds meant fewer officers and less equipment. The island was currently policing its seventy thousand residents with a fleet of five cars, most of them in need of repair. The cars in the growing graveyard behind the building were being cannibalized one part at a time to keep the current fleet on the road.

Captain Talua poured coffee into his favorite mug, brown stains stretching over the edge, dripping until they reached the emblem on the front, the University of Hawaii's official crest. His son went to UH, and every time he looked at the mug, it reminded him that his son would make something of himself. Get off the islands. See the world. The mug also reminded the captain that a tuition check was due in another month.

Armed with a cup of java and a view of paradise, Captain Talua pressed the button next to the blinking red light on his phone. The first call was from the local loony, Karliya Momali, a main figure on the streets of Saipan's main city, Garapan. Every morning Ms. Momali led an invisible tour group to all the island hotspots. It was the same routine rain or shine—the beach in the morning, the tourist trap souvenir shops in the afternoon, after-tour drinks down at *Breakers* for dinner. Captain Talua listened to the message from Ms. Momali informing the captain that a member of her make-believe tour entourage had gone missing. She would be waiting by the phone for the captain to call her back. Captain Talua knew Ms. Momali's memory wouldn't last as long as the message.

The second voicemail was from the captain's brother-in-law, a pain in the ass of such proportions that the captain had more than once considered divorcing the love of his life just to get away from him. His brother-in-law was calling to see if he could press charges against his neighbor. A coconut had fallen from the neighbor's tree, which straddled their property line, and hit one his free roaming chickens. The captain deleted the message as his brother-in-law explained in detail how the chicken was now walking in circles and may have to be put down. The captain shook his head. The things you should know before you say, "I do."

The third message was Jake's and the captain listened to the voicemail in its entirety. On the second pass, Captain Talua wrote down the girl's name, and on the third try, he managed to catch Jake's name and number. *Wei Ling*, he said to himself, followed by a surly grunt.

He pushed his rolling chair around his desk with his feet and pulled a file from a stack on the corner table near the window. No sirens went off in the captain's head. No warning bells of suspicion rang in his ears. The phone calls were not uncommon. They usually came from family members looking to make contact with a relative who was incommunicado. Saipan averaged two murders a year, and in his fifteen years as captain of the police force on the island, every killing had been committed by spouse, family member, or a boyfriend. Sure, there were accidents, people on the run passing through the island, lost causes looking for a place to be lost. But when the captain got a call looking for an Asian woman, he always checked the Chang Industries list first.

The captain opened the file and flipped the piece of paper with his scribble on it next to the file. He looked down the list, looked back at the name on the piece of paper, and checked the list again. Employee number one hundred eighty-seven. Wei Ling. Seamstress. Chang Industries.

As I thought, the captain said to himself.

The captain looked at the folder and reminded himself that he needed an updated list of the girls at Chang Industries. It was summer and time for the arrival of a new shipment of hard-working sewing princesses. He made a note to stop by and see Lee Chang. He could pick up a new list and see if the Chang Industries coffers were in the mood to contribute to the captain's family education fund.

Captain Talua went to the john for his morning constitution, and then returned the call to Jake's office. He left a short message stating that the girl in question was present, accounted for, and in good health.

Chapter 11

C.F. Chang ordered Chow Ying back to Beijing with a ten-second phone call that lacked explanation. The Mountain of Shanghai worked directly for Lee Chang, but everyone worked for C.F., also called "laoban," loosely translated as "boss" in Chinese. And when C.F. Chang called, you went, no questions asked. Chow Ying closed his mobile phone, packed a single leather bag he had bought in Hong Kong a decade before, and grabbed his passport. Chow Ying, all two hundred thirty pounds of chiseled muscle, sat in the airport until a seat was available on a connecting flight through Seoul, and boarded the last plane out for the day.

Ten hours later Chow Ying checked into the top floor of the five-story Emerald River Hotel, twenty minutes from Tiananmen Square in downtown Beijing. He slept for a few hours in bed, got up for a glass of water and went back to sleep on the small sofa, legs hanging over the sweeping arm of the worn furniture. He woke from his slumber, took a shower, and tied a slightly stained hotel towel around his waist when he finished. He wiped the moisture from the mirror with his bare hand, leaving a streaking smudge in the glass, and looked at his reflection. He wondered what had happened to the carefree boy who once enjoyed school, sports, and his friends.

He checked the time and called down to the front desk to order a taxi. The young lady at the front desk answered in rough Chinese that the taxi would be there in five minutes. Chow Ying answered in an equally gruff tone, "I'll be down in four."

The humidity in Beijing was stifling, sucking dryness from the air and everything in its grasp. A shiny coat of fresh moisture immediately replaced the sweat that Chow Ying wiped from the back of his neck.

He slipped on a light pair of cotton pants, a lighter-weight shirt, and reached for his eight-inch hunting knife resting in its leather sheath on top of the TV cabinet. C.F. Chang could be demanding, but Chow Ying had yet to attend a meeting with laoban that wasn't professional. He threw his knife back on the sofa as he left the room.

The hall was empty when Chow Ying pulled the door shut and rattled the handle to make sure it was locked. He swaggered toward the elevator at the end of the long corridor with its communist red carpet and outdated lamps mounted sparingly on the walls. He thought about what he was going to have for dinner. Chow Ying was primitive. He operated on sleep, food, and gambling. He would take a woman too, if one found her way into his reach.

The elevator door opened with a quiet "ding" and Chow Ying joined two other male guests in the six-by-six foot lift. The door shut and the elevator dropped with an initial, prolonged chug.

Then all hell broke loose.

The man behind Chow Ying reached up and wrapped his arm around the thick neck of his target as the second man hit the stop button on the elevator. The lift lurched to a halt abruptly, causing Chow Ying and his attackers to momentarily lose their balance. The glimmer of a massive knife blade reflected in the mirror trim of the elevator control panel provided all the warning Chow Ying needed. The two would-be assassins didn't have a prayer.

When the elevator stopped on the second floor, Chow Ying casually stepped out, brushed himself off, and straightened his disheveled shirt. With the pulse of a surgeon about to perform an operation, he walked the three flights of stairs back up to his room to collect his meager belongings.

The female half of the young Chinese couple standing arm-in-arm in the lobby shrieked when the elevator door opened. Two male bodies were propped against the walls in opposite corners of the elevator, their arms resting in their laps like a warped rendition of Buddha in his meditative pose. The Mountain of Shanghai had a sense of humor. The knife, the intended weapon of the attackers, rested on the floor between the two bodies, spotlessly clean. There were no cuts on the victims, no blood. The injuries were internal and fatal; a fact confirmed twenty minutes later by the ambulance personnel who arrived to find that the bodies had been moved from the crime scene to a quiet corner of the small lobby.

There was only one elevator, and the guests needed it.

***

It was late evening when Peter took off his suit jacket and put it on a hanger dangling from the coat rack in the corner of his office. Thoughts of Wei Ling danced in his head, and he sighed the sigh of a man in trouble. He needed to do something. And nothing gave him better ideas than his regal friend, Chivas. He pulled the half-empty bottle of scotch from the small bar in the built-in bookshelves that lined one side of his office. He grabbed the Rolodex on the edge of the desk and leaned back in his chair, flipping through pages, corners tattered from wear. He flipped past the number for the head of the Trade Administration, the number for Clinton's office in Harlem, and the home address of the president of FedEx, Fred W. Smith. His Rolodex had girth and the index cards were full.

He was organized the old-fashioned way. In Peter's mind, paper was an invention that didn't need improvement. Computers broke down, got viruses, needed power. They were great when they worked perfectly, but when they didn't, they were as good as a rock sitting on the desk, taunting the user. Of course, Peter knew how to use computers, but short of a fire, nothing was going to stop his Rolodex from giving out numbers when he needed them. He stored a handful of contacts in his cell phone, programming the small Samsung a duty that Marilyn handled effortlessly. Thumbing the small device with his thick fingers was wasted time. That's what secretaries were for.

The black phone on the oriental antique table in Lee Chang's residence rang once before his part-time cook, part-time housekeeper picked up. She walked to his office at the far corner of the house and announced the caller. A minute passed before Lee Chang picked up the phone.

"Lee Chang, this is Peter Winthrop."

"Good evening, Peter. How are you? I trust your clients got the shorts you ordered last week. It kept us pretty busy for a few days."

"Yes, I understand they got the shorts on time."

"What can I do for you? I hope it is not another rush order. We did what we could with that order but another one will put us behind on other business."

"No, nothing of the sort." Peter had bigger things on his mind than helping a retailer fill their shelves. "I'm coming to town in a week and wanted to arrange the usual companionship, with your permission of course. I wanted to take Wei Ling on a boat trip for the weekend."

Lee Chang swallowed hard and said the first thing that came to mind. "Actually Mr. Winthrop, Wei Ling returned to her hometown in China two days ago. She won't be coming back. Family problems," he added with definitiveness. "I can get you another girl, or girls."

The chess game began and Peter was ready to put Lee Chang into check. "Do you have a forwarding address for Wei Ling? I would like to send her something."

"Let me look around and see if I can locate it for you. I understand your desire to keep in touch with her."

"Please, let me know when you find her address. I will call before I leave next week and let you know the specifics of my itinerary."

"Fine," Lee answered nervously before hanging up with a stream of goodbyes. He thought about the girl tied to the bed one floor under his feet. The goose that was about to lay the golden egg. It was time for the goose to have breakfast.

***

Peter put the pieces together in his mind. Wei Ling was pregnant and the odds were good that she was still in Saipan. Peter considered all the possibilities. "*Lee Chang*," Peter said aloud. "*What are you up to?*" Inside, he knew the answer. The question was what to do about it.

The CEO sipped his scotch and thought in silence, his Rolodex still on the desk, opened to the "C" section of names. He flipped the Rolodex from Lee Chang to Lee Chang's father. Peter hadn't spoken to C.F. Chang in months, since the last negotiation between a textile company in South Carolina that was looking to manufacture bulletproof vests overseas. But C.F. Chang and Peter Winthrop kept tabs on each other, the senior Chang with his fleet of special interest bribes and lobbyists, and Peter Winthrop with more personal intelligence gathering via trips to Beijing and Shanghai.

Peter dialed the number and was connected to C.F. Chang's personal line.

The Chang patriarch answered the phone with a traditional Chinese greeting and Peter replied in kind before breaking into English.

"Mr. Chang, this is Peter Winthrop calling from Washington, D.C. How are you this morning?" The effort to recognize that C.F. Chang was just starting his day halfway around the world did not go unnoticed.

"Mr. Winthrop, it has been too long. How is your evening in D.C.?"

"Fine, fine," Peter replied. "How are your sons?"

"They are very well," C.F. Chang responded. He knew that Peter didn't have any real family to ask about, so he did the next best thing. "How's business?"

"It's shaping up to be a very profitable year."

"I'm sure it is."

"I apologize for calling so early, but I'm afraid I have a serious matter to discuss."

"Please, Mr. Winthrop. What is it?"

"I want to inquire about an employee of yours at Chang Industries in Saipan."

C.F. Chang's heart rate increased. His shirt felt tight around his neck.

"Have you spoken with my son? I'm sure Lee can assist you far more easily than I can."

"Yes, Mr. Chang, indeed I have. Unfortunately, he was unable to help. I understand Lee runs things on Saipan, but I think you might be able to assist with this particular employee."

"I can certainly look into it."

"The employee I'm inquiring about is named Wei Ling," Peter said with measured pace. He could almost hear C.F. Chang's heart through the phone.

"The name doesn't ring a bell."

"Well, this girl, Wei Ling, is unique."

C.F. Chang swallowed harder.

Peter continued, winging it sentence-by-sentence as the words came to mind. "I have gotten to know Wei over the last two years during my visits to the island. She is very sharp. Good business sense. I wanted to look into the possibility of having her come to the U.S. I wanted to see about employing her at my company here in D.C. She could help with many of the Asian transactions our firm handles. I didn't mention any of this to your son, as I thought it was appropriate to discuss the specifics with you first."

"Mr. Winthrop, as you know, my family has manufacturing interests throughout Southeast Asia. I couldn't possibly know all the girls by name. But with all due respect, I question the ability of one of the seamstresses to help your firm. Though I can't speak specifically to the one you mentioned, most of the girls are uneducated."

"Just the same. I would like to pursue this opportunity, if possible, and with your blessing. As I mentioned, she is very sharp and has a surprisingly good command of English. She learned almost everything from tapes, talking to the other seamstresses, and of course from TV on Saipan. Only one of my current staff here in D.C. speaks Chinese."

"I can see your interest. Perhaps I could introduce someone else who can meet your needs."

"Thank you for the kind offer. But I would like to look into the possibility with Wei Ling first. Your son did mention that she had recently returned to China to deal with a family matter. He is not expecting her back and doesn't know how to reach her."

"I will ask my son to look harder."

"Please do. In any case, I would like to contact her."

The silence on the end of the line told Peter all he needed to know.

***

Chow Ying moved across town and checked into a dive hotel in a district where he used to run with the other creatures of the night. Mahjong, drinks, and street fights. It was a good time in his life, the education of the street forced upon him by a bus crash that killed his parents. He felt refreshed to be back in the old neighborhood. The same streets where he had spent his formative years running numbers, fencing bootlegged CDs, and skirting with the law in a country where they handed out the death penalty like breath mints at a garlic restaurant.

He walked down the street in the Hua neighborhood and a feeling of homesickness washed over him. Some of the shops he remembered were still there, some refurbished, some long since leveled. The sun peeked down the alleys and through the shirts and pants that hung on clotheslines running between neighboring buildings.

Two blocks past the small park where the local senior citizens were having tea after their morning Tai Chi, Chow Ying shoved five yuan into a public pay phone.

"Chang Industries," the pleasant voice answered on the other end.

"I need to talk to laoban," Chow Ying barked.

"Who is calling?"

"The person he just tried to have killed."

"Just a moment," the secretary answered without batting an eye.

"This is C.F. Chang," the voice said, answering the phone immediately.

"The men you sent are dead."

C.F. Chang was still digesting the call from Peter Winthrop and didn't expect to hear from his current caller, ever.

"I don't know what you are talking about, Chow Ying."

"The time for games is over. I found your card in the pocket of the untrained knife handler."

C.F. Chang didn't like being called a liar with such directness. There were rules for saving face, guidelines for politeness, even when the evidence clearly indicated he was lying. Chow Ying was Chinese and he should have known better.

"He was, in fact, highly trained," C.F. Chang answered. "As was his partner. It seems I have underestimated you."

"I'm still breathing."

"Yes. Yes you are," C.F. Chang said, considering his options. "Then perhaps we can make a deal."

It was the chance Chow Ying was looking for. He knew if C.F. Chang wanted him dead, it was only a matter of time. He could run, but not far or fast enough. Eventually C.F. Chang would find him. And next time it would be ten men, not two, with guns, not knives. Revenge would come in its sweet time, but for now, survival was the only thing Chow Ying had on his mind.

"What kind of deal?"

"Pack your bags and get your passport. You are going to America. There is something I need you to take care of."

Chow Ying didn't think about the offer. He had no choice. Run and be killed, or bide his time and play the game.

Chapter 12

Jake's car chugged down his father's street, jerking and misfiring past well-hidden million dollar homes. The Subaru had seen better days, and the car was giving its fourth owner every indication that he would be the last. The clutch slipped with every downshift, the brakes squeaked profusely, and its latest ailment added danger to annoyance— an intermittent stall that hit without warning. "Old Betsy" was dying a slow death, like a two-pack-a-day smoker.

The gate was open at 25 Follin Lane and Jake made it halfway up the steep driveway before the Subaru gave out. He put the car into first, turned the key, and announced his arrival to the high-class enclave with a backfire that rattled the double-pane windows. Betsy lurched up the driveway and Jake parked in front of the garage, its closed doors the only thing separating the old Subaru from his father's new Porsche 911 Turbo convertible.

Jake shut the door to his car with an authoritative hip-check and made his way alongside the perfectly manicured yard in the middle of the large circular driveway. He rang the doorbell and waited anxiously. He was seven the last time he had visited his father's house, and the residence he remembered was nothing like the one where he now stood. He looked up at the slate roof three stories above and peeked through the small windows that ran vertically next to the door.

The door opened suddenly and Jake, startled, stumbled to the edge of the porch and teetered precariously over a row of rare roses.

"Good evening, Jake," said the Hispanic women with a kind face and a warm smile. "Your father is expecting you. My name is Camila, but everyone calls me Camille. It is a pleasure to finally meet you."

"Nice to meet you, too."

"Your father has told me a lot about you."

"Well, I doubt that, but thank you just the same." Camille smiled again and her face radiated. She liked the young man. If first impressions were any indication, the son was not like the father.

"Please come in."

Jake stepped into the grand foyer and looked around. The thirty-foot cathedral ceiling was nicely framed by handcrafted wood moldings and adorned with a sparkling crystal chandelier. The dark marble floor stretched to the edge of Jake's view in two directions. A huge grandfather clock rested against an interior brick wall, its pendulum giving off an audible echo as it reached its double-sided apex.

"Can I take your belongings?" Camille asked, gesturing to the brown bag in Jake's left hand.

"No, I got it, thanks. It's just a bottle of wine. I didn't want to come over empty handed. Not sure if it is a good bottle or not, but the guy at *Norm's Beer and Wine* recommended it."

"I am sure it is fine. Please follow me."

The kitchen was in the back of the house, if that is what you could call the eighteen-thousand-square-foot monstrosity Jake's father shared with his two servants. Jake placed the bottle of wine on the island counter and held the brown bag in his hand, not knowing where to look for a trashcan. Camille grabbed the bag and led Jake to the sunken greatroom to the left of the kitchen.

"Please have a seat. Your father will be with you in a minute."

"Thank you."

"You certainly look like your father, you know."

"So I've been hearing a lot recently."

"You don't think so?"

"No, I guess I do take after him in the looks department."

"How about the other departments?" Camille asked with another brilliant smile.

Jake looked at Camille's face and melted just a little. If he were twenty years older, and hadn't met Kate, he would have asked her on a date.

"We will see," Jake answered.

"Can I get you anything, while you wait?"

"No, I'm fine thank you."

"Very well. I'll be in the kitchen should you change your mind. I hope you're hungry," she said before vanishing, not waiting for a response.

Jake looked around the room. It was emergency room sterile. The cushions on the sofa were wrinkle-free. The magazines on the coffee table were aligned as if someone had used a ruler. The massive plasma television on the wall was off, its screen glistening. Four different remote controls for various electronic gadgets were arranged according to size on the end table. It was a bachelor pad with anal-retentive maids. There were no signs of a woman's touch anywhere. Jake wondered what the rest of the house looked like. It must take a lot of furniture to fill a pad this large, he thought. He figured his father needed one servant just to keep up with the dust.

Jake finished looking around the living room and went back to find Camille. He sat down at the breakfast counter and checked out the cookbooks on the shelf to the left while Camille milled about like someone on a mission.

"How do you like working for my father?"

"I like it. He travels a lot, so I have more free time than most full-time domestic help."

"Is he a tyrant?"

"He treats me well. He helped my cousin get a job cleaning in his office building. Her name is Reina. She is cute. You would like her."

Jake figured Camille's answer was a standard, off-the-shelf reply. He knew his father was no angel. "Reina, heh?"

"It means 'queen' in Spanish."

"I'll keep my eye out for her."

"She has already seen you. She told me you were handsome. I must agree."

Jake tried to steer the subject of the conversation away from himself. "So working for my father is okay?"

"I can't complain. He has always been fair with me."

As if on cue, Peter walked into the room with the same intent-to-impress presence that he always carried. The fact that his son was the lone member of the audience didn't change the show.

A handshake, an offer of a drink, and a tour of the house. Jake took it all in. The tour, the showmanship, the bragging. By the fifth bathroom, each with its own bidet, Jake started to wonder why he had come. But years of curiosity had their claws deep into his skin. He was determined to see where the night was going to take him. Hopefully he would learn something. Something about his father, and maybe something about himself.

For the host, drinks preceded dinner, interrupted the main course, and book-ended dessert. Jake drank three microbrews before he started declining more beer, mixed drinks, and the hard stuff. He accepted a second helping of spiced grouper and rice to help put a dike in the flow of alcohol entering his bloodstream. His father liked his sauce, and Jake noticed he held his liquor well. It was not a trait he wanted to emulate.

"Would you like anything else?" Camille asked, clearing the dessert dishes. "Coffee, perhaps?"

"That would be great. Black please," Jake answered before his father could insist on another drink of a stronger nature.

"Would you be so kind as to fetch my single malt and a glass?" Jake's father asked his faithful servant.

"Certainly."

"My son and I will be on the deck."

"Yes, Mr. Winthrop."

The sliding door glided open and Jake and his father stepped onto the expansive wood deck. As was with the rest of the house, the yard was immaculate. Lights surrounded the pool, their reflection shimmering on the water slightly, the surface rippled by a light breeze. There was a rock garden beyond the pool and a screened gazebo on the left where the lighting from the yard met the darkness of the summer sky. A huge wooden fence enclosed the two and a half acres Peter proudly claimed as his backyard.

"Nice yard."

"It should be. It cost a fortune. There is an Asian garden that winds around the Gazebo and stretches to the back of the lot. I tried to have the architect design it after a famous garden in Kumamoto, Japan. There is a pond with carp that cost three grand apiece, and a grove of imported Japanese Maples that cost half that amount. The lighting and fence cost another eighty thousand."

"It is nice," Jake said again, unimpressed with the running total of money spent.

"How do you like work so far?" Jake's father asked.

"It's good. It has been educational. I've learned a lot." Jake laughed at himself and the stream of safe answers.

"You have been doing a great job. You have a good sense of business acumen. A good head on your shoulders. I have been impressed."

"Thanks, Dad."

"Have you given any thought to what you are going to do after graduation, career-wise?"

"Not really. Right now I'm still working on easing back into society. The last year has been rough. Kind of been out of the loop in a lot of regards, if you know what I mean."

"Sure. Sure," Peter said in a deep, soothing voice. "If you are interested, I would be happy to have you join Winthrop Enterprises. I would love to teach you everything I know. Prepare you for maybe taking the business over one day. I can't run the show forever."

Jake didn't respond. He'd only been working at his father's company for a few weeks and a lifetime commitment was more than a little daunting. But he did enjoy working at the company. He certainly enjoyed the steady paycheck of nine hundred dollars a week, after taxes. Not executive money, but not starving student money either. For all intents and purposes, he was an intern pulling in fifty grand a year. He hoped no one else in the office knew how much he was making.

"We'll have to see about that. I'm not saying 'no,' but give it some time and let's see where it goes."

"I understand, son. I just want you to know that I'm here for you. And I would be flattered if you chose to follow in your old man's footsteps."

"Thanks. I appreciate it. I really do."

Camille reappeared and delivered a cup of coffee to Jake and a glass and bottle of Talisker to his father. The light conversation continued until Jake worked up the guts to ask a poignant question.

"So, Dad. Tell me about your side of the family. I never really heard much about that half of my gene pool."

"It is a pool in dire need of a lifeguard, son."

Jake laughed. His father could be as funny as a stand-up comic.

"I think everyone feels that way about their own family," Jake said, sounding older and wiser than his age.

"I guess they do. What do you want to know?"

"I don't know. Anything really. Start at the beginning, if that's easier for you."

Jake listened as the story unfolded and his father held his attention raptly. Peter Winthrop could flat out tell a story. The liquor only greased the wheels of obvious exaggeration, making the story that much better. Even the depressing, dirty laundry of a family he never knew came to cheerful life through his father's voice. But Jake knew where the truth ended and where the exaggerations began. He had the same gift. The ability to draw the crowd in and keep their attention. He used his story-telling skill far more sparingly than his father did, but he recognized the gift and, for the first time, realized it was something he was born with. Maybe the fruit doesn't fall far from the tree, he thought. It may roll a little when it hits the ground, but gravity can only carry it so far.

The early years of Peter Winthrop's existence on this earth seemed pleasant enough. But when his father's story reached the fifth grade, Jake regretted having asked for Winthrop History 101. By the time his father hit puberty, which coincided with his father's third drink on the deck, Jake wanted to plug his ears.

Peter Winthrop was the youngest of six children and the only son in the family born to a feisty French lady and a hard-working Southern Baptist. When Peter was five, his father, Peter Winthrop, Sr., did what every man on his side of the family had done since they emerged from a packed ship hull in the early 1800s—he skipped town. No note, no phone call. He didn't claim he was going out for cigarettes. He didn't run away with a secret lover. He just decided that, after half a dozen children, marriage and fatherhood wasn't for him. He simply woke up one Saturday morning, had breakfast with his family for the last time, took a shower, got dressed, and walked out the front door without saying a word.

As the only male in a family of six women, life was tough for young Peter Winthrop, Jr. The balance of the sexes his father had maintained in the house crumbled with his departure. First the rules changed, and then the game. Where it was once acceptable to leave the toilet seat up, forgetting to drop the seat now earned him unbearable payback. Dirty shoes in the house were confiscated, and Peter had vivid memories of being driven to tears by humiliation and the scorching heat of the street on his bare feet. Clothes left on the floor were thrown on the front porch. Peter's mother had lost control of her life when her husband left.

To overcompensate, she took complete control of her house. As the son of the man who had just sealed her fate as a single mother of six, Peter Winthrop, Jr. was going to be taught a lesson.

Between the ages of five to fifteen, life was one nightmare after another. It was more than just growing up without a father—there were plenty of families in the neighborhood who had lost fathers in the war and still raised children who grew into healthy adults. What took place at 311 Edison Avenue was anything but normal. The house quickly turned into a part-time beauty salon, flower shop, and fashion show. Five older sisters, their girlfriends, and a mother who was light years ahead in the feminist movement was the recipe for a painful existence for a young boy growing up in the fifties in the South.

At eight years old, he knew more about women, their bodily functions, and their views on men than most people three times his age. When his oldest sister learned to sew and took up dressmaking with the hopes of selling her wares, things took a turn for the worse. Peter Jr., too small to fight five sisters and their friends, was the unlucky fashion model of choice. He learned about skirts, dresses, hems and pleats. And that was just the beginning.

When his two middle sisters decided to try their hand at beautician school, the fun really began. Blush, liner, mascara, lipstick. He had tried them all, forced through physical restraint when necessary.

On Halloween, the sisters merged their talents in a transformation of one young Peter Winthrop into the youngest cross-dresser in the entire city of Columbia, if not the entire state of South Carolina. He loved his family for what they were—the only family he had. And hated every last one of them for what they did.

Peter Winthrop, Sr. reappeared at the house on Edison Avenue ten years after his mysterious, silent departure. Peter Winthrop, Jr. was the only one home, and according to his mother's strict rule of absolutely no guests if she was not there, when his father knocked on the door, Peter Jr. refused to let him in. It didn't matter that the guest was his father, or that he had lived in the house for fifteen years. His mother was adamant. Unless Jesus Christ showed up and specifically needed to use the phone or the bathroom, there were to be no guests. Peter Winthrop, Sr. responded, through the door, that he understood. He stood nonchalantly on the rapidly dilapidating porch he had built himself, and waited for his son to get dressed and join him outside. Peter Winthrop, Sr. peaked through the window into the house and was aghast at the hanging stockings, dresses by the dozens wedged onto store-quality racks, and enough cosmetics to cover a busload of prostitutes.

Peter Winthrop, Jr. and Peter Winthrop, Sr. had their last conversation as estranged father and son while strolling down the main drag of Columbia, South Carolina, a few blocks from what later became known as the entertainment district referred to as "Five Points." Peter Winthrop, Sr. offered no apology and no explanation. The father looked at this son, recalled the brief glimpse he had gotten at the inside of the house, and left his son with a singular piece of what he considered useful advice.

"Son, don't you dare grow up to be queer."

It was the only advice the son could remember receiving from his father, and he took it to heart. The possibility that growing up with a bunch of women could, in fact, make him queer was something he hadn't considered. People weren't coming out of the closet on a regular basis in the fifties, and to spot a real queer, in person, was quite a novelty.

Peter Winthrop, Jr. wasn't taking any chances. With his father's warning fresh on his mind, Peter Winthrop, Jr. walked into the football coach's office at Joyce Kilmer High School on Monday morning and told him he was ready to play.

"Have you ever played before?" Coach Dietz, an overweight former high school star, asked with suspicion.

"No, sir," replied the future CEO of Winthrop Enterprises.

"What position are you interested in playing?"

"I don't care. I just want to hit people," Peter answered. It sounded like the manliest thing he could think of. And proving he was a man was the only reason he was there. He was sure there were no queers on the football team. And if there were, the straight players were sure to beat any less-than-manly tendencies right out of them.

The coach looked over the fifteen-year-old and made some mental calculations. Six foot, maybe six=one, one hundred and eighty pounds, give or take a nickel.

"Are you fast?"

"Fast enough, I guess."

"Practice is at four this afternoon. Let's suit you up and see what you can do. That's four sharp. Don't be late."

Peter, decked out in a Kilmer High School white practice uniform, took the field to the type of taunts reserved for new inmates at the state penitentiary in Charleston. The ridicule lasted exactly one play. Peter, much to his own surprise, could hit like a runaway freight train. When Tucker McGee, all-state tailback two years running, came around the corner on the first play of practice, Peter laid him out cold. Smelling salts eventually brought him around, but ol' "lightning feet McGee" watched the rest of practice from the sidelines.

While the players ran after-practice laps around the field, the coaches smiled and huddled on the sideline. When Peter finished his second lap, the coaches called him over and told him that he was their new starting outside linebacker. Peter didn't know the names of all the positions or where he was supposed to line up on any given play, but Coach Dietz didn't care.

The coach's advice was simple. "Cover a player when we tell you to. If we don't specifically tell you to cover someone, you are free to knock the snot out of anyone wearing the opposing team's jersey."

For the four-month football season, Peter Winthrop did exactly as he was told. With every hit, he made it clear that if you came near his side of the field you were going to go home bruised, battered, or broken. He led the team in tackles, sacks and interceptions. And more importantly, he ended the season believing that he had knocked any hiding refuge of queer right out of his body. To make sure, he fucked his way through half the cheerleading squad.

Jake listened to his father and felt sorry for him. While he couldn't condone his father's behavior, the explanation of his own childhood certainly helped Jake understand where he was coming from. But times change, and Jake couldn't help but get the feeling his father was still trying to prove something. He was still the football player who ruled through intimidation. He was still trying to fuck his way through the cheerleading squad. He was still fifteen, and at that age, Jake had nearly ten years on him.

Jake had one more question to ask, but wasn't sure if he had the energy to hear either a lie or the truth. He also knew there would never be a better time. "Dad, can I ask a tough question?"

"Sure, son," Peter answered, his mind still reliving his youth.

"I found a fax at work about a girl named Wei Ling. I was wondering if you know her."

"Aaaah, the fax. Yes, son, I know her. We dated in the past, and I guess she felt like she could turn to me for help. She got herself into a bit of trouble it seems."

"And the baby?"

"I don't know if she is even really pregnant, son. And at any rate, the child wasn't mine. I don't know, maybe she thought if she applied pressure, the baby would be her ticket to a better life. It's hard to say. It's hard to figure out how some people think."

"Where is she now?"

"She's home in China. Don't worry. I've done my best to make sure she is properly cared for."

"That's it?"

"That's all I know."

Jake picked up a cookie off the plate that Camille had placed on the table and chewed slowly. He wasn't hungry, but the cookie put an end to the conversation.

The evening concluded uneventfully. Jake was wired from three cups of the strongest coffee he had consumed in recent memory, compliments of the Latin American kitchen miracle worker. His father was still going strong, well into double digits on the drink scale. Not a slur, not a stumble. The father said goodbye to his son on the front steps of the house, and for a moment, Jake thought he was about to hear a long overdue apology. But instead of an 'I'm-sorry-for-being-a-shitty-father' response, Peter offered him what he could. "Let me know if you want to take the Porsche for a spin sometime."

Jake looked him in the eyes and said "Goodnight". For the first time since he was old enough to rationalize, Jake realized he was a better man for not having had his father in his life. His mother had made the right decision by evicting him. He wasn't really fit to be a father or a role model. Some people are and some people aren't. And sometimes life is just that simple.

As Jake made his way back to his car his father had the last word. "Think about what I said about someday taking over my company. I think it would be great."

Jake rolled the old Subaru station wagon down the driveway in neutral and dropped the clutch as he hit the street. The car bucked once and let out another backfire that woke every sleeping neighbor on the street.

Chapter 13

China Air Flight 43 touched down at JFK International Airport with a screech, the jumbo jet's tires leaving a streak of rubber on the heavily scarred blacktop of Runway 13. Chow Ying followed the herd to immigration and customs, a process measured at JFK in lunar movement, not minutes or hours. He endured the scrutinizing stare of the immigration officer and answered precisely one question—that he was here on business—before America's first line of defense against undesirable foreign elements turned him loose on the Big Apple.

The taxi turned left onto Grand Street from Broadway, past a stretch of pavement marked by narrow sidewalks made even narrower by hawkers selling their fake Gucci bags and Tag Heuer watches. From Grand Street the taxi turned right down Mott, cutting through the Northern end of Little Italy and the ever-expanding Chinatown. New York's Chinatown, home to the largest Chinese population outside of the mainland, was a microcosm of east meets west, in the biggest melting pot on the face of the earth. Chow Ying stepped from the taxi and looked down the block in both directions. The sounds and smells wafting through the air were as familiar as the worn shoes on his feet.

Under the evening light of the city, couples walked to dinner as shopkeepers shuttered their vegetable stands and meat counters for the night. A young man on a moped darted off on the beginning of a delivery run. Chow Ying stood under the neon light of a nearby barbershop sign and pulled the number from his shirt pocket. He tapped the arm of an Asian passerby, a man of equal age but considerably less stature. "Do you know where this address is?" he asked in Mandarin Chinese, the official language of China.

The man responded in Cantonese, a dialect Chow Ying did not

speak, and the dialogue ended as abruptly as it had begun.

An elderly woman with a bagful of winter cabbage, broccoli, and carrots, gave Chow Ying precise directions in Mandarin with a heavy Beijing accent. Chow Ying said thank you in their shared local dialect, and the old woman with numerous wrinkles and far fewer teeth, smiled and patted Chow Ying on his back.

A dark red door and a single light marked the inconspicuous entrance of 234 Centre Street. The old brick building took up a quarter of the block. The windows were dark, the façade unwelcoming, and the crumbling mortar that held the structure together was straining to keep it all in one piece.

Chow Ying pushed the small black button and waited. An audible buzz accompanied the automatic lock release, and Chow Ying stepped into the foyer of the dark building. Despite his sketchy past and criminal inclinations, Chow Ying had never been behind bars. Until now. The cage that kept unwanted guests from entering, and prevented unsanctioned exits to those inside, was a three-sided cell that formed a u-shape against the brick wall and the front door. A security camera attached to the ceiling in the corner watched his every move. Chow Ying was unfazed. Someone knew he was there. He pulled out a cigarette and lighter, and polluted himself while he waited.

He heard the voice from the shadows before he saw his host.

"Who's there?" the voice asked in a calm, almost peaceful tone.

"Chow Ying. C.F. Chang sent me. He gave me this address and told me someone would meet me here."

A small hand pulled on the chain dangling from the underside of the lamp, and a dull light stretched meekly across the room. A lone desk sat in the middle of the otherwise barren first floor. Mr. Wu yanked opened the top desk drawer, pulled out a key, and made his way across the room to release Chow Ying from his temporary confinement.

"My name is Wu. Follow me."

Chow Ying trailed the small man across the room and down a flight of stairs so narrow that he had to turn sideways to traverse. At the bottom of the stairs were two identical black doors, and Mr. Wu knocked lightly on the one to the left. The door opened, and the buzz of people and machines in motion washed away the silence of the old brick building.

Like the dialect of the old woman who gave him directions on the street, the familiar hum of sewing machines was a sweet reminder of home. Eighty seamstresses, voluntary illegal slaves, packed the basement of 234 Centre Street. Imitation designer bags were their specialty, sold on the street by equally illegal vendors. Imported cheap labor and iron-fisting an army of street vendors had made Mr. Wu a Chinatown legend.

Chow Ying continued behind Mr. Wu across the floor, past a line of girls bent over their machines, backs hunched, eyes squinting. One seamstress paused to look up at the source of the shadow on her workstation as Chow Ying passed and was immediately reprimanded. Chow Ying smiled. Employee relations at its best.

Chow Ying entered Mr. Wu's small cluttered office and took a seat without waiting for an offer. Chow Ying wasn't here to play games. Mr. Wu was no one to him, a co-worker at best, both ultimately employed by C.F. Chang. This was business, but there was no need for formalities. Mr. Wu didn't offer any niceties and Chow Ying didn't expect any. Certainly not after the cage at the front entrance.

"Here is everything you need," Mr. Wu said, handing Chow a small nylon bag with a thick waist strap.

Chow Ying opened the bag and examined the essentials for a life on the move. An untraceable revolver, bought from the black market on the mean streets of the Bronx. Ten grand in cash peaked from under the gun, mostly hundreds, but with a smattering of smaller bills. The last item Chow Ying pulled out was a sleek silver Nokia cell phone with a charge cord.

"Where am I going?" Chow Ying asked.

"Washington. You have a reservation on the Amtrak Metroliner to D.C. tomorrow morning. Here is your ticket. Just in case, the ticket is under the name Zao Gun. Amtrak security is non-existent, they don't ask for identification for ticket holders unless you are buying the ticket at the window. There is no security check. Once you reach D.C, you are on your own. Here is a name and address. C.F. Chang implied you wouldn't need any further explanation."

Chow Ying looked at the piece of paper, said nothing, and put it in the bag with the money and the phone. He took the gun and shoved it in the waist of his pants, pulling his shirt over the small bulge.

"One more thing," Mr. Wu asked.

"What?"

"Laoban asked me to keep your passport until you get back."

Chow Ying smiled. "Sorry old man, but you should have asked for it before you gave me the gun. The passport stays with me."

Mr. Wu looked at Chow Ying, considered the statement and its source, and nodded. "Very well."

Chapter 14

Jake's Subaru stalled at the intersection of Constitution Avenue and Fourteenth Street, and nearly conked out again at a red light in the 1800 block. He made the prudent mental note to take the car to the mechanic as soon as his next paycheck arrived. He pulled a u-turn across the double yellow lines in the middle of the road, a perfectly legal driving maneuver in the nation's capital, and putted his way into an empty space left by a vacating van. It was four blocks to the intersection of Twenty-Second Street, an easy hoof.

Jake took his time strolling down the wide sidewalk under the old elm trees that gave more than ample shade but did little to alleviate the city's brutal humidity. It was going to be another scorcher and the humidity was already stifling, clinging like an electric blanket on a summer night. The nation's capital was built on a swamp, millions of tons of earth poured into wetlands to create half of the city. And despite the paved roads and grandiose architecture, the water remained in the ground like a hidden ghost, invisible piping insuring a never-ending supply of moisture to the local climate.

Summer tour buses clogged the road, unloading kids on summer vacation and foreign visitors from the far corners of the globe. A group of Australian tourists stopped Jake and asked if he would take a picture of them in front of the bronze Einstein statue that went undiscovered by most tourists.

"Thank you," a young boy in the group said as Jake returned the camera.

"You're welcome," Jake replied, patting the boy on the head.

Traffic snarled at the intersection of Constitution and Twenty-Second, and it wasn't the result of driver error. The Department of

Transportation had cleverly designed the intersection in such a fashion that Route 66, a major highway, dumped directly onto an already congested twenty-five mph street. For added confusion, and to test driver reaction time, a stoplight rested at the foot of a very short off-ramp.

Well here I am, Jake thought, checking his watch.

He sat down on a dark green park bench with its wrought iron legs and stretched one arm along the back as if making a move on an imaginary date. He checked his watch again. He was right on time. *Here I am. Where are you?*

The light turned red and Jake's attention turned toward the homeless man in the median who went to work on the cars stopped in traffic. He approached the window of every vehicle, holding a sign that simply, and quite needlessly, read "Homeless."

"No shit, Sherlock," Jake whispered to himself.

Jake let the morning sun wash down on his face as he watched the cycles of the cars stopping and the homeless man making his silent pitch. It was an amazing study in sociology. People in suits, in air-conditioned cars, with the windows up, and the radio on. People with breakfast in their stomachs and a three dollar drive-thru super soy latte resting in the cup holder. The privileged going face-to-face with the unfortunate.

The homeless man seemed oblivious to his own plight. He was dressed in jeans and a t-shirt, both of which were old, but neither of which were dirty, torn, or tattered. He held his head high and looked the drivers in the eyes. In ten minutes he successfully panhandled his way, through pity or determination, to two dollars and twenty-three cents.

Jake was ready to give up. He looked over his shoulder at the wide stretch of grass and a group of people his own age playing Frisbee football. It was a beautiful morning, even if he was being stood up on his blind date. It had only taken a few weeks of work to realize that sitting on a park bench was better than being in the office. Jake turned back to the homeless man just in time to catch his sociology lab rat heading right for him.

"Follow me, Jake," was all he said as he passed in front of the bench, the stench of *eau de homeless* trailing behind him.

Jake sprang to his feet, mouth gaping, and fell into position two paces back. The unshaven man in jeans, t-shirt, and worn sneakers walked fast, back straight as a board, a posture rarely seen in the slouching

Generation X and seemingly spineless Generation Y. He walked with an unmistakable purpose, and given the direction they were heading, Jake surmised the only possible destination was the Potomac River.

Jake followed his leader into the shadows near the riverbank, the concrete arch of the bottom of the Roosevelt Bridge forming the homeless man's roof. He shared the barren ground and man-made retaining wall of the river with two other address-lacking tenants. Boxes, plastic, garbage bags, and winter clothes were stacked neatly in piles, wrapped with bungee cords of various colors and lengths.

"Please have a seat, Jake," the homeless man said, gesturing to an old chair with a torn wicker seat and cut-off legs. Jake took the offer and sat down, his knees nearly straight, his feet out in front of him. It felt like a beach lounge chair, without the sand, and it was surprisingly comfortable. The view wasn't bad either. Kennedy Center to the right, the Tidal Basin in the distance to the left.

Al Korgaokar, homeless person extraordinaire, emptied his morning's change into a small hip-hugger bag and zipped it shut. One of the straps on the bag was torn, repaired with a mix of string and rubber bands. Al pulled a red milk crate from his shelf, a crawl space in the upper reaches of the "apartment" where the ground met the bridge structure above. He flipped the crate upside down and sat down next to Jake.

"My name is Al Korgaokar," he said, enunciating every syllable carefully. The measured, almost insultingly slow pronunciation was the product of forty-eight years of people butchering his name.

"You can call me Al," he said trailing off into the first verse of the Paul Simon song. Jake's first thought was that Al could have been an extra in *One Flew over the Cuckoo's Nest*. His second thought was if Al was a singer by trade, he needed no further explanation for his homelessness.

Al Korgaokar didn't act homeless, even among the packrat existence of his living room. Deep blue eyes flashed both a warmth and brilliance, mixed with a certain inexplicable flightiness. His reddish-brown hair reached just below his earlobes and ran around his neck in a perfect line—a cut given by a local homeless man who specialized in hairstyles for his peers. "The Hairman," as the homeless barber was known, charged fifty cents or a cup of decent booze, per cut. The man with the scissors and toothless grin never went back to the shelter broke or sober.

"Or you can call me 'K,'" Al continued. "A lot of my friends here on the street like that one."

"I'll go with Al. I'm Jake Patrick, but I guess you already know that."

"Yeah. Knew the name was Jake. Jake the Snake—an average quarterback with a great name." Al dug through his belongings for something he didn't find and looked up. "So, Jake, what can I do for you? What's your problem?"

"Actually, I don't have a problem."

"Sure you do. You wouldn't be here otherwise."

"Well, it is not really *my* problem," Jake said.

"Even if it wasn't your problem before, it is now. You just learned the first rule of politics. Don't care. If you don't care, it won't be your problem."

Jake shrugged his shoulders and nodded simultaneously in a sign of complete confusion. "I'm here because Marilyn said you might be able to help."

"Jake, Jake, Jake. Keep up. I'm not a psychic and you're not famous, at least not yet. I already know why you are here. You gotta stay one step ahead—that is the first rule of survival."

"I was answering your question."

"Some questions are rhetorical. And your answer wasn't an answer to the question I asked."

Jake wanted to leave, but knew he would regret it. "So you know Marilyn?" he asked dubiously.

"I know what you're thinking. How in God's name does Marilyn know a homeless guy?"

"Well, yeah, I guess that is as good a place to start as any."

"How about a more tactical question? Something like…how in the world did she contact me?"

Jake didn't have the energy to keep up. "Okay. I'll bite. How did she contact you?"

"Like the rest of the world."

"Which is…?"

"She called."

"She called?"

"Jake the snake, for heaven's sake," Al responded, laughing at his own rhyme before turning to the right and digging through a box of what any normal homeowner would call crap. He pulled out an article from the *New York Times*.

The below-the-fold headline read: *Thirty Percent of Tokyo Homeless are Homeowners*. Al handed the article to Jake. Jake glanced at the headline and put the paper in his lap.

"What's wrong? Don't believe everything you read?" Al asked.

"No."

"Maybe you're smarter than you look after all."

"So you're a homeowner?"

"Yes. I'm a homeowner. Don't I look like one? Own a car, too. Homelessness is nothing more than a state of mind."

"Never looked at it that way."

"Most people wouldn't."

"Can I ask a question?"

"Shoot. I've got nothing pressing," Al said, inhaling deeply as he stretched his arms out to embrace his environment.

"If you're a homeowner and you are choosing to be homeless, why don't you just lend your house to someone who doesn't want to live on the street? Let someone live there who needs it?"

"I do, Jake. My brother lives there. He is more needy than anyone I've ever met."

Al stared at Jake, sizing up the young man. Jake looked around at Al's belongings, his life on display.

"So Marilyn called you?"

"I have a phone line with an answering machine. I check it every few days from the phone booth at Potomac Point Park."

"Why?"

"You never know who may try to get in touch with you," Al said, more lucid than a minute ago. "So, back to the first question. How can I help you?"

"Your first question was actually 'what's your problem?'"

"Touché, Jake. Touché."

"I need help finding a girl."

"Hey, buddy, don't we all. And if you think it is hard now, try angry, unemployed, and homeless. Those are not three qualities the ladies are looking for."

Jake laughed. Al didn't.

"Who is the girl?"

"Her name is Wei Ling and she is Chinese."

"Ling?"

"Yes"

"Well, there aren't too many of those. Why don't we look for a John Anderson in Chicago while we're at it?"

"She is from China, but she was working in the garment industry in Saipan."

"The garment industry in Saipan?"

"Yes."

"We call those sweatshops here in the real world."

"I'm sorry?"

"You say 'garment industry' and I say 'sweatshop.' Let me educate you. Girls from poor Asian countries pay a couple thousand dollars, money they don't have, to work in these sweatshops for pennies a day. Saipan is sweatshop-central U.S.A."

"I didn't think we had sweatshops in the U.S."

"Most people don't…and as long as the price is right on their khaki pants in the Sunday advertisements, most Americans don't care."

While Jake thought about the statement, Al continued. "Saipan is actually very interesting. It straddles a political fence. Saipan is a giant international employment loophole. Companies operating on the island don't need to adhere to the intricacies of United States employment law. Workers are paid well below the minimum salary their stateside counterparts receive, and it is all perfectly legal. As a United States territory, Saipan gives companies, domestic and foreign, an opportunity to manufacture goods that are officially 'Made in the U.S.A.' These companies corner the market on cheap labor and U.S. businesses pay no import tariffs because the goods aren't technically 'imported.'"

Jake's head was spinning. The heat and a homeless man giving him a speech on international labor gave him vertigo.

"What do you want with the girl?" Al asked.

"Marilyn didn't tell you?"

"I'm not asking Marilyn, I'm asking you."

"I think the girl is in trouble." Jake pulled out the fax and tried to hand it to Al. Al looked at it for a split second, and left it in Jake's hand without reading it.

"So what does this have to do with you?"

"Nothing, I guess. I just want to help. I want to know who she is."

"Jake, Jake, Jake. If you knew who she was, what would you do?"

"I don't know. Find out if the fax is for real. Find out who is running the company, who is keeping her against her will. Write some letters."

"Write some letters?"

"Yeah."

"You go to school, Jake?"

"Yes."

"What did you study?"

"I'm getting my Masters in English Literature."

"No wonder you want to write a letter."

"The pen is mightier than the sword," Jake snapped.

"Oh Jake, now you are singing my song. I love banter. Shall we take a minute to flex our mental prowess? *Get your facts first, and then you can distort them as much as you please.*"

"What?"

"Mark Twain. I thought we were exchanging quotes."

"No thanks."

"You lose. So, who the hell are you going to write a letter to?"

"I don't know. This is Washington—there has to be some group willing to raise a little hell. There is a protest every week in this town."

"Forget the letter, Jake. Why don't you just talk to your father?"

"How did you know about my father?"

Al looked at Jake but didn't answer the question. "Why don't you just talk to him?"

"I already did. He said he took care of it, but I don't believe him. I even called the Saipan Police Department and they said everything checked out."

"So why don't you believe them?"

"I don't know about the Saipan Police, but I could tell my father was lying."

"And if they were both lying?"

"I don't know."

"Wrong answer."

Jake was getting perturbed. "Then what is the right answer, Al?"

Al stumbled with the rebuttal. "What are you going to do to help this girl?"

"Whatever I can."

"Well Jake, there are a million tragedies played out every day in this world. If there aren't a hundred dead bodies no one cares. You may not be able to help this girl, Jake. Just so you know. Some things are beyond our control as humans."

"Well, I'd feel better about myself knowing I tried."

"Maybe, maybe not. Failure has a flavor all its own, and you aren't going to see it as a pizza topping any time soon."

"Probably tastes like giving up," Jake answered.

Al rubbed his three-day-old stubble. "Okay, Jake. I'll see what I can find out. Give me a couple of days."

Al dug through a small pile of street throwaway goodies and pulled out a cloth environmentally-friendly shopping bag with a faded picture of the earth on the side. Al stuffed a pair of shoes, a few newspapers, and a sweatshirt into the bag. He stood and smiled at Jake, his reddish-brown hair and blue eyes alive. "I have somewhere I need to be, Jake. Gotta run. Come back in a few days."

"How long is a few days?" Jake asked, looking for a specific day and time. "Does that mean Wednesday? Thursday…?"

"A couple of days, Jake. It's not like I'm going anywhere. I don't move to the winter house until November," Al said, laughing.

Al walked away, leaving his front door open and his guest standing in his living room.

Jake asked a parting question. "No offense, but how are *you* going to find out about a girl halfway around the world?"

"Jake, I have my ways. I wasn't always homeless you know."

"Yeah, I know. You're a homeowner."

"A homeowner who used to work in intelligence."

"Intelligence?"

"Yeah, intelligence, Jake. That's how I met your father," Al said walking away. "Come back in a couple of days," he added over his shoulder, his voice echoing under the bridge.

Chapter 15

Chow Ying walked from Union Station to Chinatown, a fifteen minute stroll through what used to be some of the meanest streets in D.C. Gone were the open-air crack markets and shooting galleries, the hookers and the pimps. A prolonged police crackdown in the late-Nineties eventually took its toll on the local dealers. Those who didn't end up behind bars, or dead, simply migrated across town, one rundown block at a time, until they reached southeast D.C. or Anacostia. The crackdown on dealers had been good for the neighborhoods but hell on the crack consumers who had to follow their fixes across the city.

Chow Ying glided through barren lots and boarded up buildings that melted together, a ghost town on the verge of transformation into half-million-dollar condos. He walked without a care, map in hand, cigarette dangling from his lips. He ignored the group of young men who heckled him from a slow-moving, low-ride Cadillac with tinted windows and gold-framed license plates. Chow Ying was on a mission. It was a simple one. Do whatever it takes to stay alive long enough to figure out how he was going to stay alive.

D.C.'s Chinatown was shrinking by the day. Construction of the city's main sports venue, the Verizon Center, opened the floodgates of development hell on Chinatown and its quiet existence as a ten-square-block neighborhood north of the Capitol. Development led to higher land values, higher taxes, skyrocketing rent. One by one, half the Chinese businesses were bought out, moved, or just disappeared. Starbucks, CVS, and a conglomeration of franchised watering holes moved in, all with signs in English and Chinese to keep the right atmosphere. Burgers and fries were going head-to-head with kung pao chicken and hot and sour soup, the winner to be decided later.

But a healthy handful of restaurants and other Chinese establishments survived, and Chow Ying knew that even a shrinking Chinatown
was his best bet for lying low in a city he didn't know. He checked his
map, turned the corner at Seventh Street, and walked half a block. He
stopped walking at the bottom of the steps beneath an unprofessionally
crafted sign with Chinese characters. He made his way up, pushed open
the door to the four-story, ten-room crash pad formally known as the
Peking Palace, and asked for a luxury suite just for kicks.

The old Asian man behind the counter, dressed in a sweaty cotton
tank top and matching white shorts, smiled and handed him the key
to Room 312. "The stairs are in the back, just follow the hall," the old
man said, pointing with a boney finger attached to a bonier arm. "The
gourmet buffet breakfast starts at seven o'clock," the old man added, just
to show that he, too, had a sense of humor.

Chow Ying threw his bag on the only chair in the room, a leftover
piece from an old dining room set bought at a yard sale. He punched
the button on the window air-conditioning unit and a cool stream of air
steadied out. Relief. He pulled out the piece of paper he had received
from Mr. Wu and looked at the name and address. It was nothing more
than ink on paper. He had no feelings for what he was going to do. He
didn't have time to get emotional. Time was ticking. C.F. Chang didn't
ask you to do something at your leisure. You were always on the clock.

***

Chow Ying milled about for half the day among the lawyers and
lobbyists in the 1300 block of K Street. Winthrop Enterprises was in an
area of D.C. that wasn't on the tourist map, and the large Chinese with
a ponytail stood out like a Hawaiian shirt at a black tie formal. Beyond
the lobbyists and lawyers in suits, there just wasn't much to see on K
Street during the day in the business part of the District. The Mountain
of Shanghai, sweating like a cook at an open-pit BBQ, bought a bottle
of water from a local convenience store where the mainstay of its sales
seemed to be lottery tickets to attorneys in expensive cars. Chow Ying
bought five dollars' worth and slipped the tickets into his front pocket.
You never know.

He watched every face that came and went from the address of the
building written on the piece of paper in his pocket. Peter Winthrop

had neither come nor gone. Chow Ying was good with faces. He had spent an evening with the CEO and Senator Day as their chauffeur when they were on Saipan. And though no one was asking, he didn't care for either Peter Winthrop or the senator the Chang family had in its sights. They were foreign exploiters, which in Chow Ying's mind was greatly different from homegrown, full-blooded Chinese exploiters. There was no doubt in his mind he would remember his target on sight. He was equally sure Peter Winthrop would recognize him. Everyone did.

The bus stop, with its backless bench, was the only seat on the block with a direct view of the door to the building that housed Winthrop Enterprises. Chow Ying watched the buses come and go, their arrivals and departures, the occasional summer skirt the only break in the monotony of the task at hand.

Wilting under the heat, Chow Ying sprang to his feet when his mark came out the door. He stared hard and wiped the sweat from his brow. The familiar man in the suit stopped, dug around in his bag for his cell phone, turned his back toward Chow Ying and made a call.

Eight hours in the sun were just about to pay off. He sized up his target as he walked—right size, right build, same measured movements and air of self-confidence. How he loved the hunt. Chow Ying picked up the pace, moving briskly through the crowds on the opposite side of the street, his eyes fixed over his right shoulder as he weaved between the suits.

When the light turned green, Chow Ying crossed the street with the afternoon crowds. As he passed the UPS truck picking up deliveries, Chow Ying grabbed the knife from the small of his back and moved it to the front of his body, still under his shirt. Thirty yards away and closing. *Just a quick stab, angled upward beneath the rib cage, combined with a twist of the neck and the deal would be done.* By the time the blood was pumping out of Peter Winthrop and the crowds on the sidewalk broke into hysteria, Chow Ying would be gone. He would be out of town in less than an hour, and out of the country by midnight.

When Jake clapped his mobile phone closed and turned, Chow Ying was fewer than fifteen feet away, hand tight on the knife. The Mountain of Shanghai looked at Jake's face through the crowd and slammed on the brakes to his emotions. Jake, oblivious, turned and walked in the direction of the subway.

Salt from sweat burning his eyes, Chow Ying again wiped his brow and followed Jake as he slipped below the surface of the Washington sidewalk. *That has got to be his son*, he thought as the escalator inched its way into the shadows. Twenty steps below stood his newly acquired target, one hand on the handrail, the other hand on the sports page. Maybe the young man would lead him to his father, Chow Ying thought, his expression blank. He was on automatic pilot. A patient hunter looking for the right opportunity and willing to track his prey as far as he had to.

Chow Ying grabbed a subway map on his way out of the Cleveland Park Metro station. He walked with one eye on the map and one eye on Jake while weaving through a throng of senior citizens strolling in front of their assisted living complex.

The conceptual layout of D.C. was easy. Letter streets ran east and west in alphabetical order. Number streets ran north and south ascending in both directions as you leave the Capitol. Combine that simple plan with a few hundred memorials and museums to mark the landscape, and one had to really put some effort into getting completely lost. One-way streets and circles wreaked havoc on driving, but walking the city was a breeze.

Jake stopped at the convenience store to pick up a pack of condoms. Chow Ying waited outside, smoked a cigarette, and tried to get his bearings. It was an old habit. Walking was the one form of transportation always available, and Chow Ying kept the compass in his head as accurate as possible. When trouble reared its ugly head, he wanted to know which direction to run. He took a look at the sun, then the block numbers on Connecticut Avenue, and made a rough assumption that he was three miles west of his temporary abode at Peking Palace. He was accurate within a quarter mile.

Jake made a second stop at a Thai restaurant called Otong's for an order of Pad Thai from the street-side carryout window. Chow Ying stepped into the McDonalds two doors down for a less opulent double cheeseburger and large Coke to go, keeping Jake in sight through the glass.

Chow Ying trailed the young Peter Winthrop back to his apartment at a distance far enough to go unnoticed. Jake, unaware of the danger he just led to his door, entered his apartment building without looking back. The Mountain of Shanghai, ketchup in the corner of his mouth, committed the address to memory.

Chapter 16

The Hart Senate Building was built on one of the highest pieces of ground in D.C., the altitude giving the third floor office of Senator Day a sweeping view of the capitol and the national mall that ran two miles southwest to the Lincoln Memorial. It was a room with a view, and one the senator had jockeyed position to get for two terms. Competition for perks was intense, and there was no shortage of battles to fight to improve one's position within the elite of the elite. Senators aren't usually elected by mistake, but when it does happen, the constituents tend to notice by the end of the first term. Three inaugurations was the standing record.

Senator Day's page shuffled around the office, making coffee and planning his work schedule, wedging personal agendas between whatever the senator had on his plate for the day. The senator's Ivy League all-star aide, still recovering from his water skiing injuries incurred in the west Pacific, was sorely missed. The page, a recent grad named Doug, was now teamed with Dana and four other full-time helpers. They had one task among them—caring for the self-admitted brashest senator on the Hill.

Senator Day was on the speakerphone when Dana slipped into the room and delivered the envelope. With lips colored fire-engine red, she mouthed the words "he said it was important," before walking out. The senator nodded, gave a slight wave, and watched the tightest ass in the Hart Senate Building sway its way out of the room. The perfect office assistant.

Senator Day opened the envelope without trepidation, still engrossed in a conversation over a proposal to build a high-level biore-search center in downtown Boston. A future incubation and study mecca for the most deadly pathogens and viruses known to man, many of which the human species itself created. The highly contested topic was gaining momentum on both sides of the political coin. Local Massachusetts politicians were focusing on the prestige and jobs the center would bring. Everyone else with an IQ above the water temperature on Cape Cod was estimating the potential death toll should a mishap occur in the state's most populated area. As it was with most decisions, it was coming down to the important issue—money. The senator was weighing the proposals, and presently having his ear chewed off by the Mayor of Hopkinton, a small town west of Boston that was also bidding for the project.

The senator pulled the contents from the envelope and read it slowly, continuing his conversation on the bioresearch center, pausing between sentences. Yes, he understood the ramifications of a biological agent being released into downtown Boston. Yes, he understood the potential death toll could be in the tens of thousands. Yes, he could only hope that if such a calamity occurred it would claim his ex-wife as a victim. When the senator reached the second paragraph of the letter, his chest tightened, and he cut the conversation short. "I will have to get back to you, Mayor."

The senator felt light-headed as he staggered out of his personal office. The reception room was smaller than his office with two short hallways running in either direction. The senator could hear members of his staff at work as he approached the front desk. His face pale, he asked his faithful Senate page and unfaithful office entertainment a simple question. "Where did this envelope come from?"

Both employees looked at the senator with concern. Identifying shock doesn't require formal medical training. The senator stared at his dumbfounded dynamic duo and asked the question again, this time with enough force to arouse the rest of the staff in the adjacent rooms from their chairs. Dana looked around the reception office as if she didn't understand the question, which may have, in fact, been the case.

Doug the Page, wearing a stunning pink bow tie, answered. "Someone dropped it off about ten minutes ago. An Asian man. Very polite. Very well-spoken."

"Did you get a name?"

"No, he didn't leave one."

The senator asked for a description of the delivery person, someone doing his best to give the senator an early morning coronary. Doug the Page and Dana the Bimbo gave matching descriptions of an unremarkable Asian figure. Senator Day, face now turning crimson, walked back to his office and slammed the door behind him hard enough to put a crack in the small transom above the frame. Staring at the letter, fuming with anger, Senator Day picked up the phone.

Two floors below, Walter Payton, a seasoned veteran of the Capitol Police force, looked down at the blinking red light. A direct line ran from every Senate office in the building to the main security booth, and when the red light flashed, per protocol, everything else became less of a priority. Walter Payton raised his hand trying to silence the madness going on around him and picked up the phone.

"This is Senator Day, I'm ordering a security shutdown."

"Good morning, Senator. This is Walter Payton of the Capitol Police. What is the situation, exactly?"

"I'm requesting the immediate apprehension of a suspicious person on the premises. Consider the suspect armed and dangerous," the senator added with authority, almost delirious.

"Are you injured, sir?"

"No."

"Is anyone on your staff injured?"

"No."

"Was anything stolen or vandalized?"

"No. No crime has been committed...and I was hoping we could avoid one."

Most of the calls to the "bat phone" were lame, emergencies only in title, urgent only to an elite group whose lives ran as smoothly as the Tokyo subway system. The adrenaline the red light had stirred in Officer Payton was already subsiding. "Could you provide a description of the suspect?" the uniformed officer asked, almost bored.

"An Asian man, approximately five-foot-six."

Walter Payton looked down the crowded entrance hall and scratched his head. "An Asian man, you say?"

"Yes, goddamn it, an Asian man. Did I stutter?!" Senator Day screamed, saliva dripping from the corner of his mouth as he leaned over his desk and yelled into his phone.

Walter Payton peered out of his steel and Plexiglas security booth at the sea of black heads surrounding him. The newly formed group calling themselves Asian Welfare and Rights Equality (AWARE) was packed into the hall, five abreast. It had taken the busload of bag-toting citizens nearly an hour to go through security, and the main hallway on the first floor of the Hart Senate Building was now buzzing like a standing-room only sushi buffet. Senator Hamilton from the state of Washington scrambled to lead the group to an open committee room, trying desperately to appease his constituents. Showing full support for the oppressed minority was a PR opportunity no elected official dared to miss.

The AWARE group was on a mission, and Kazu Ito was their poster boy. The murder of a young straight-A student, who was then framed by the police, had galvanized the Asian rim population in the Seattle suburb. They had had enough. Trumped-up moving violations by the police at four times the rate of the white population had been the tip of the iceberg. Then came Kazu, the latest of three innocent lives snuffed out in their prime.

Not even a cross-country bus trip with a toilet that overflowed twice between Minneapolis and Chicago would prevent Kazu Ito's father from having time on the Hill. But being herded like cattle into the cramped hall, going through repeated security checks, and being forced to stand for hours was making the bus ride, stink and all, seem pleasant by comparison. The AWARE group had passed impatient. Waiting for an empty committee room only further emboldened them and strengthened their push for greater protection of their equal rights.

Senator John Day, in a rage, was about to throw gasoline on the AWARE fire, and then fart for good measure.

Walter Payton looked at the scene in the hall and shook his head ever so slightly, the phone still in his ear. "All right, Senator. I can hold them, but you better hurry."

Senator Day grabbed Doug the Page by the arm and headed for the first floor. Dana followed as fast as her three-inch heels would allow, her ankles on the verge of snapping as she swayed and bounced her way to forward momentum.

Senator Day roared out of the elevator, turned the corner, and came to a screeching halt, mouth open. Five-dozen jet-black heads turned toward the senator as Officer Payton stuck out his hand, pointed, and announced to the hall. "There he is."

Senator Hamilton, grabbing the opportunity to make the news for doing something positive, stopped berating Officer Payton who remained in the comfortable confines of his bulletproof glass booth.

It was a small riot in terms of people involved and duration, but a riot nonetheless. Senator Hamilton, sixty-two and in need of all the voting support he could get, tried to simultaneously calm the AWARE group while dishing out a tongue-lashing the likes of which Senator Day hadn't received since he burned down a neighbor's horse barn when he was twelve. Senator Hamilton articulated his threats with grace, the overtures for impeachment with eloquence. He deftly redirected the real mission of the AWARE group, confidently guaranteeing that the newly labeled "most racist senator in modern U.S. politics" would never be re-elected. The senator from Washington, milking the chance to be a hero to his constituents, worked toward a climax. He huffed and puffed, postured and postulated. But before he could deliver the punch line to his impromptu speech, Senator Day, the target of his ire, simply turned and walked away.

The senator from Massachusetts returned to his office, his page and Dana behind him, both less impressed with their fearless leader than they had been when they arrived earlier in the day.

Pausing on his way to his office, he looked at Dana and his page and raised a finger, "Not a word to anyone about an Asian man or a letter. Not a word."

The senator found his way behind his desk and sat in a daze, alternating between re-reading the letter and downing Jack Daniels, straight up. Just when he thought things were back on track. Being blackmailed for money was one thing. This was something else entirely. The cluster-fuck in the hall downstairs merely made the sting of the letter more poignant. Senator Day called his chief aide at home and checked on the progress of the wire-transfer-hide-and-seek he was playing with a trail of banks in China. No news. The senator cussed into the phone. He had let himself believe that the danger had passed. He had paid the money for the original blackmail and waited. He now realized the silence he had been enjoying was merely a lull in the storm.

***

The AWARE group set up camp outside the Hart Senate Building and made three calls to the local media. As the news trucks converged on the scene with cameras rolling, Senator Day sent his staff home with a week off, unplugged the phone, and barricaded himself in his office.

He picked up the letter again and read it slowly. It was simple. Unless he wanted to hear about an illegitimate child fathered by a senator with a sweatshop seamstress on the news, Senator Day was to follow the directions to the smallest detail. The letter wasn't demanding money. It was requesting something far more difficult to obtain, far more challenging; something that required a far greater degree of cunning. He wished he could just write a check.

There was an upcoming recommendation by the Special Senate Committee on Overseas Labor regarding the exportation of jobs to third world countries and the establishment of an international minimum wage for American companies doing business overseas. As a show of good faith, and as a measure of Senator Day's resolve as Chairman of the Special Committee, the letter was demanding a unanimous, unequivocal position against a proposed bill that would limit what the letter's composer referred to as "free trade" and "globalization." The letter was a test. And standing between the senator and success were three colleagues on the Special Committee who didn't share his desire for further internationalization of the great American corporate machine.

Senator Day had work to do.

***

The senator cringed at the television set in the oak cabinet across the room. He reeked of bourbon, a stench that went beyond his personal space and pervaded every corner of his office. One of the senator's shoes was under his desk, the other shoved toe-first into the thin gap beneath the leather sofa and the carpet. His tie was on the shelf under the window. A swig remained at the bottom of the bottle of Jack on his desk. Outside it was dark, and the only indication of time was that the sun went down somewhere near nine o'clock at the beginning of official summer. The senator's head pounded, an appropriate feeling to go with one of the worst days of his silver-spoon life.

The fiasco with the Asian equality group was turning into a night-mare. Kazu Ito's father, the leader of AWARE, wasted no time in milk-ing the press coverage for everything it was worth. The group's own handheld video recorder had caught most of hallway humiliation from earlier in the day. The quality of the tape was poor, the audio scratchy, the hand of the cameraman shaky, but it all came together with great cinematic appeal. And the AWARE group mainlined it straight into the capital's news veins. The timing was perfect. They had been stopped as suspicious visitors in the halls of the Senate, the very halls where their elected officials worked and breathed. Plans to bring their organization and the plight of their Asian brethren to light couldn't have been better orchestrated. It was time to shine. Kazu Ito's death was going primetime.

The eleven o'clock evening news opened with the crowd outside the Hart Senate Building. In his office, the senator's eyes were still glued to the screen. The crowd outside, which had surged to over two hundred thanks to calls from Kazu Ito's father to every Asian organization in the D.C. phone book, had dwindled to fewer than twenty. Most of the AWARE group was now back at the hotel in L'Enfant Plaza, strategiz-ing their plan for tomorrow. The group knew that protesting at night defeated the purpose. There was no traffic to block, no passers-by to incite.

The news crews finished their last clips for the night and were clos-ing up shop. In the confines of his foxhole, Senator Day pulled himself together with a cup of coffee and a wet towel across his face. He put his shoes on, first trying the left shoe on his right foot, and then making the switch.

He turned off his office lights, teasing the final remains of AWARE protesters and news crews who had been watching his office from the ground like a crowd waiting for a jumper on a ledge. Senator Day, hat on his head, strolled to the elevators on the opposite side of the building, body swaying down the long corridor. A lone senate page passed and gave his best "Good night, Senator," salutation, before stifling a laugh. The senator didn't acknowledge the snicker. He was making his first attempt to move past the day's misadventure. The longer he dwelled on it, the longer it would be news. You don't make it to the Senate without thick skin, a silver tongue, spells of temporary amnesia, and multiple personalities.

Senator Day rode the elevator to the basement and walked to the underground sidewalk that ran like a maze throughout the Capitol complex and its surrounding buildings. The senator eyed the small train that ran parallel to the underground walkway, a toy used to shuttle voting senators to the Capitol in comfort. The train was serious business when it was in use, but parked in the hall without any passengers it looked like an enlarged version of a child's amusement park ride. It was not a perk limited to the Senate; the House had its own choo-choo too, bought and maintained with taxpayers' money, of course.

The senator took three underground tunnels and exited a small door on the north side of the Capitol Building. He stepped into the empty street and hailed a cab. Twenty minutes later, he paid his tab in the alley that ran behind his Georgetown home and walked across the backyard and into his house.

The honorable senator sat completely motionless on the foot of the bed, his wife asleep with her head under the pillow. He held his own head in his hands. The image he spent his life trying to portray now dangerously teetering on the cliff of disaster—a cliff named Wei Ling. The years of education, proper upbringing, and the sacrifice of the family lineage that came before him climaxed in one thought that the senator said aloud. "Fuck."

It was the best he could do.

For the first time since his car had broken down in South Central L.A., the senator was scared. But politics were on his side. He was from Massachusetts, historically one of the friendliest states to morally questionable acts by their governing representatives. His mind raced between desperation and hope, ego and humility. His life was on the line—his wife, his job, his ambition. "Nice job, John," the senator said to himself. "Two and a half decades of hard work, thrown out the window on a third-world sweatshop skank."

***

The goateed man with a penchant for positive camera angles and the lion's share of a recently cashed fifteen-thousand-dollar paycheck, chatted with the off-duty stewardess at Club Iota in Arlington. A local acoustic husband-and-wife team was packing up their guitars after an early weeknight show that had the bar half-full. The bartender cleaned glasses and hit the remote control for the small TV in the corner of the enclosed drink-mixing workspace. With the TV news in one ear, the man with the goatee tried his best to impress the stewardess, his goal to say whatever it took to get her down the street and into the bedroom of his new condo.

With the stewardess playing coy, the cameraman looked at the news on the TV and spoke involuntarily. "Look at this asshole."

"Who?" the stewardess asked.

"Senator Day. I filmed a documentary for him last month." So what if it wasn't a full-fledged documentary. No one was there to call bullshit on him.

The stewardess warmed up considerably and put her hand on the cameraman's knee. They both watched the story and the bartender turned up the sound.

The cameraman chuckled.

"What are you laughing at?" the stewardess asked, her arm moving to his shoulder.

"It's just fitting. You have Senator Day defending himself against an Asian Rights Group a month after going to Asia to film a documentary on Human Rights and Overseas Labor."

"Why is that funny?"

"Honey, that's between me, him, and the rest of the poor souls at the Ritz he kept up all night."

The cameraman asked for the check and pointed to the stewardess to indicate he was covering her bill as well. "You want to see a copy of the documentary? I live right down the street. I have the whole thing on DVD," he said getting off his stool.

"Okay. But just the documentary. Nothing else."

"Of course," the cameraman replied, the muscles in the corner of his mouth fighting to suppress a smile.

Chapter 17

The ride from Logan Airport to Boston's North End was a manageable twenty minutes. Before "The Big Dig," a construction project aimed at putting the city's freeways underground, the city was a rush-hour maze with no way out. But with the completion of the most expensive engineering project ever undertaken by man, Boston had once again become a charming big city. The streets were less crowded, the air was cleaner, the city quieter. Sure, Beantown was one major underground accident away from a total transportation hose-up, but for now the Big Dig was finally showing results after years of budget overruns and broken promises. The senator looked at the skyline of Boston, deep in thought. Home. It has its advantages.

A few blocks northeast of Faneuil Hall and Quincy Market lies the North End, Boston's version of Little Italy. In a city dominated by Irish immigrants, the Italians, backed with guns and pasta, had made their niche. Small Italian shops lined Hanover Street and pockmarked the surrounding neighborhoods. Mom and Pop establishments sold everything from cannoli to ice cream, pasta to seafood, wine to cheese. English was optional, and you got a discount if the owner knew your family or liked your face. Two blocks away, the North Church marked the edge of the cultural enclave and the beginning of Paul Revere's famous "the British are coming" gallop through Boston and the history books.

As the senator drove past the statue of Paul Revere, he thought about the luxury of having advanced warning. He needed a Paul Revere. Someone to tell him when he was being ambushed. *One if by land, two if by sea, three if you are being blackmailed by an unscrupulous sweatshop owner.*

The Gelodini family had occupied the corner of Hanover and

Prince Streets since the first barrel of tea was thrown overboard into Boston Harbor to protest British-imposed taxes. The Gelodinis came to the country carrying a few suitcases of clothes and a proud lineage of carpenters and bricklayers. Hard workers with big appetites to go with even bigger personalities. The love of food and the propensity for engaging conversation was the impetus for a change to the Gelodinis's chosen profession. For four generations the hammers and spades had been gathering dust as antiques in the attic, the family tools replaced with spatulas and pasta makers.

Michael Gelodini, a short Italian with a harsh Sicilian-rooted Bostonian accent, gave the senator a firm handshake and led him down a narrow hall and up a flight of stairs to a private dining room in the back of the restaurant.

"Your guest is waiting," said the current patriarch of the Gelodini family.

"Thank you," the senator replied.

"I will be taking care of you personally, Senator. Shall I get you a bottle of wine?"

"Please. A decent red."

"We have a nice 1999 Chianti Classico."

"Perfect."

The senator entered the room and Michael Gelodini disappeared. The senator's guest was seated at one end of table, facing the door. It was a habit that had kept him alive on more than one occasion. Some lessons are learned the hard way, and the scar across the middle of the guest's neck illustrated the point.

"Senator."

"DiMarco, I assume," the senator replied.

"Yes. And that is the first and last time you will address me by name." His dark soulless eyes combined with his black hair and the scar on his neck to give the impression that the inside of the man matched the intimidating exterior.

Neither man moved to extend the other a handshake. The senator, eyeing a man he would only meet once, pulled out a chair and sat down, sitting diagonally across the table from his guest.

"Nice restaurant. I don't make it to the North End much. I'm from Southie," DiMarco said proudly.

"An Italian from Southie."

"There are plenty of true bloods in Southie. Somebody has to keep tabs on the Irish. You know we have Italian restaurants in Southie, too. Good ones."

The senator smiled. He liked people from Boston. "This place is discreet without being dangerous, physically or politically. I'm a United States Senator. I can't risk being seen getting out of a car in Southie or Jamaica Plain or Roxbury. Here, if someone happens to see me, no one will think twice."

"Whatever. You're picking up the check."

Finding DiMarco had taken the senator exactly one phone call to his father. Edward Day III had provided his son, through DNA, with the brains, the looks, and the inherent instinct to survive at all costs. He shared his son's ambition. He wanted nothing more than to be the father of the President. If his son would only learn how to use a condom.

"Where can I find the individuals in question?" DiMarco asked over a steaming plate of mussels on the table.

"Saipan."

"Just where the hell is that?"

The senator gave DiMarco a brief geography lesson. Vincent Di-Marco listened and nodded.

"You have pictures of these acquaintances of yours?"

"No," the senator lied. He sure as hell wasn't about to hand over the pictures he did have.

DiMarco, dark eyes staring at the senator, thought for a moment. "One hundred thousand before I start. Another one hundred thousand when the job is done. Plus fifty thousand for expenses." He pulled a piece of paper from his pocket. "I deal in cash, and I don't start until I receive the first payment. This is the address where you can deliver the money. There is a door on the second floor in the back. Someone will answer. Here is a phone number where you can reach me. Don't use my name. I am the only one who will answer at that number, so you don't have to go asking for me. If I don't answer, don't leave a message. If I need to contact you, I will do so from a public phone or I will use an untraceable prepaid phone."

"Agreed," the senator answered. "It will take me a couple of days to get the cash."

"Fine. Like I said, I will be waiting. Once I receive the payment, I will start. When I finish, I will contact you and you will deliver the second payment to another address I will identify later."

"Fine."

"Now what can you tell me about your acquaintances?"

The senator liked the sound of the word "acquaintance." "My first acquaintance is a man by the name of Lee Chang, owner of a sweatshop operating under the name Chang Industries. My second acquaintance is a girl named Wei Ling who works at the sweatshop." The senator pointed to an address from a corner of his old itinerary to the island. "Here's the address of the sweatshop—it should be easy to find. Saipan is not a big island."

"Well, nothing is as easy as it sounds. I'll have to do some surveillance and pick my spot. It'll take a week. Maybe less, maybe more."

"The sooner, the better."

"Any preference?"

"What do you mean?"

"There are a lot of ways to get injured in this world. I mean, I'll take what I can get as far as the opportunity goes, but I try to accommodate my client's request."

Senator Day looked around the empty private dining room as if he expected the FBI to come busting through the door. "I'm not sure what you are saying," the senator answered coyly. "But if I had a choice of how *I* would like to die, *I* would prefer it be an accident."

"I'll see what I can do. I think I can rule out the use of a firearm. I'm not about to fly to some foreign country with a gun in my bag."

"It's not a foreign country. Saipan is a U.S. territory."

"Well, just the same. Taking a gun on an airplane, even a gun with a proper license, is not in our best interest." DiMarco didn't bother telling the senator that he preferred knives. They did the job, left fewer clues if you took the weapon with you, and they were silent. Every musician has their favorite instrument and DiMarco's were stainless steel, heavily weighted, razor sharp blades made by an old codger in Toledo, Spain.

The senator nodded and said nothing.

Mr. Gelodini entered with a fresh basket of bread and filled the senator's wine glass. Vincent DiMarco stood and straightened his jacket.

"Michael, my guest can't stay for dinner. Would you please see him out?"

"Certainly, sir. Will the senator still be dining with us this evening?"

"Yes, I will."

"Very well."

Michael Gelodini led Vincent DiMarco through the kitchen and out the side door to an alley beside the restaurant. The metal door shut and darkness surrounded DiMarco like a comfortable jacket. With quarter of a million dollars on his income horizon, DiMarco looked down the alley in both directions. To the left he could see the lights of Hanover Street silhouetting patrons as they shuffled down the sidewalk. DiMarco turned away from the light and vanished into the night.

Chapter 18

Marilyn opened her eyes as the morning sun peaked through a crack in the curtains. For the third night in a row, she had spent more time staring at the dark ceiling than she had at the back of her eyelids. The fax that had poured into the office earlier in the week had forced her to reflect on the last twenty years of her life, something she had managed to avoid through self-therapy and good old-fashioned medication. Admitting that she was the cause of Jake's parent's divorce, combined with the plight of a seamstress named Wei Ling, sent her tail-spinning into a level of depression she hadn't visited in years. She rolled over, got out of bed in her nightgown, and downed two Valium and a Zoloft with her morning espresso.

An hour later, she grabbed a seat on the crowded Metro and cautiously circled job possibilities from the employment page, looking over her shoulder as she rode the subway six stops on the red line. At the office, she made travel plans, took phone calls, and shifted around a never-ending carousel of meetings and appointments, dinners, and lunches. She brewed coffee for her boss as soon as she knew he was on the floor and served it with one spoonful of real sugar, stirred well. But for the first time in her life, she was looking at other job alternatives, scanning the opportunities available to a forty-five-year-old secretary with no educational background.

Reeling from guilt, she asked Jake to lunch—an offer which he politely declined. Marilyn's third offer to buy him a drink after work was finally, grudgingly, accepted. She didn't want to leave anything unsaid. She didn't want Jake to have any questions about the past. He was going to be burdened for life by the truth she had already spilled. She was going to apologize again, try to explain the unexplainable, and act like an adult for once in her life, even if it killed her.

Jake got out of a late evening meeting, a conference call with an Indonesian firm looking to import a new generator for an offshore, wind-power venture. He had prolonged the meeting as long as he could by peppering the international team with an inordinate number of questions. In the back of his mind, he hoped Marilyn wouldn't be waiting when he finished. Luck wasn't on his side.

The waiter led Jake and Marilyn to a two-seater booth in a shaded corner of The Dark Room, an appropriately named hole in the basement of an old office building five blocks from Winthrop Enterprises.

The waiter gave the young man and the older woman the usual look. Boy toys for the city's wealthy and lonely wives were an old sport, and a few establishments in Georgetown survived on such clientele alone.

Marilyn grabbed the red menu with the gold edge and flipped to the cocktails. Jake, uncomfortable, looked around the bar.

"Your friend Al is a little out there."

"He can help."

"He said he would, but not without giving me the first degree."

"He is a very smart man. Don't let the mental breakdown fool you."

"Did you know the guy used to work in intelligence?"

"I know he worked for the government."

"And my father?"

"You need to ask Al about that. I wasn't involved."

"What's his story?

"It's a long one."

"I don't have to be anywhere for a couple of hours," Jake responded, kinder than he needed to be.

"He lost his wife and son a few years back."

"How?"

"Remember the Air Egypt flight that crashed off the coast of Nantucket twenty-five minutes after take-off?"

"Sure I remember. They suspect the pilot nose-dived the plane into the sea intentionally."

"It gives me chills just thinking about it."

"His family was on the plane?"

"Yes," Marilyn said fading away momentarily. "His wife was a Japanese lady named Miyuki. From the pictures I have seen, she was quite beautiful. And their son was just adorable. An eight-year-old Indiana Jones. Loved archeology. After the accident, Al moved out of his family's house in Bethesda. There were just too many faces staring at him as he walked the halls, too many voices calling to him from the corners of the rooms. Too many memories. His brother moved into the house and Al moved into my apartment complex. I recognized him from meetings with your father years before, and we became friends. As it turns out, his move to the apartment was only a first step toward reclusion. One day he decided he had had enough. He left his apartment, fully furnished, and moved out to live on the streets. I used to come by and check on him, bring him clothes and food. So did his brother. But after a while he refused to accept things. Said he was getting by just fine and that there were plenty of others who needed help worse than he did."

"Pretty drastic."

"There was more to it than just a plane crash. He was supposed to be on the plane. He was called back to the office on his way to the airport. He put his wife and son on the plane by themselves and was going to catch a flight out the next morning. He was planning to take his son to see the Pyramids."

"Jesus," Jake said.

"Yeah, he felt responsible. Guilt does things to people that are hard to explain."

***

Chow Ying smoked his almond-flavored cigarettes and sipped his Tsingtao beer, close enough to smell Marilyn's Liz Claiborne perfume. He hummed a traditional Chinese song he had heard the old man who ran the hotel sing the night before. Between verses, he listened to the conversation over his shoulder. The woman cried twice, for reasons God only knew. Chow Ying couldn't care less. He was there for one purpose, to get closer to Peter Winthrop.

"So what did Al say?" Marilyn asked as she finished her third apology in as many drinks, changing the subject back to a more comfortable and less personal topic.

"He said he would look into it. Told me to come back in a couple of days."

"I am sure he will help."

"We shall see," Jake replied. "The whole thing is crazy."

Chow Ying leaned back to hear the near-whispers of the two behind him. When the young man started ranting emphatically about helping a pregnant girl in Saipan, Chow Ying's eyes bulged and he almost blew a load of beer on the table. The fun-loving, wise-cracking, opera-singing Chinese mountain swallowed his beer, threw his cigarette into the ashtray still lit, and flipped the switch on his mental mood to business mode. And the only business Chow Ying had on this trip to the States was filling coffins. He had everything but the price of the casket picked out for the two behind him.

The waiter handed the check to Jake who paid for drinks against Marilyn's weak protest. Employment did have its advantages, even if it was employment for your father under growing suspicion. He folded a fifty in the leather bound receipt holder and left it in the middle of the table.

Jake walked with Marilyn until the subway station was across the street. He said good-bye at the light and raised his hand to flag a cab. Kate was supposed to meet him at his apartment at eleven after her shift of riding ambulances, a part-time job perfecting her emergency medical skills. The thought of Kate, perhaps still dressed in her doctor-like scrubs, was all the reason he needed to get home, and pronto. Their relationship was still torrid. They tore each other's clothes off every chance they got, and he now had enough shirts and ties at her house to get to work without looking like he'd slept in the gutter.

Jake unsuccessfully tried to hail two cabs before the third one, a handicap-accessible, Red Top minivan, stopped. Chow Ying was twenty yards away, peering into the reflection of the closed window fronts. He bought time by acting as if he were making a withdrawal at the ATM. He watched Jake get into the cab, and eyed Marilyn as she stood on the corner waiting for the light to change.

They were splitting up.

The light moved from red to green as Jake shut the sliding door on the cab. Marilyn stepped off the curb and the heel on her red Nine West shoes caught in the gutter grate, snapping like a twig. Miraculously, the heel remained attached to the shoe, dangling by a strip of leather.

Jake watched out the back window of the cab as Marilyn limped her way across the street. The taxi driver cleared his throat and waited for directions from his fare. As Jake turned his head away from Marilyn and back toward the driver, he looked directly into the eyes of Chow Ying just outside the cab window. No more than ten feet away, Chow Ying stared at Jake with an intent that went beyond any casual glare. The eye lock lasted until Jake gave the driver his address and the cab pulled away from the curb and headed down the street.

Marilyn limped her way to the Metro station, trying to walk with her weight forward on the balls of her feet. Chow Ying turned his attention from the cab, looked over at Marilyn, and smiled. Women are the same everywhere, he thought. Fashion over function. Any man would have just ripped the dangling heel off. Marilyn, single and heading downhill toward fifty, wiggled her body as if she were having spasms, all in an effort to hide the broken heel. It was an act wasted on an empty sidewalk.

The McPherson Square Metro entrance disappears under the corner of a nameless glass and concrete office building with the roman letters MCXI written over the front door. Chow Ying, almost salivating, followed Marilyn across the street, closing on his prey. He looked in both directions as Marilyn approached the subway station entrance and then saw his opportunity. He took two large steps forward and as Marilyn turned to step onto the escalator, he shoved his hand under her armpit and sent her body upward and outward. Gravity did the rest. She bounced hard once on the moving steel stairs with a gruesome thud. Her body continued down in a mass of flailing arms and legs, the movement of the escalator keeping her in motion until the stairs flattened out two hundred feet below. The D.C. subway system boasts some of the longest escalators in the world, and Marilyn hit more than half of the three hundred steps on her way down. Her body lay at the bottom, the contents of her pocketbook and the dislodged broken left heel of her shoe spinning at the edge of the escalator like a boat caught in circular rapids near a dam.

***

The call to the rescue squad came two minutes after Marilyn's body reached its resting place. It took the genius station manager behind the security glass another full minute to make his way across the tile floor and push the emergency stop button on the escalator. Marilyn's body was a medical school extra-credit project. Gross cuts mixed with deep gashes. Blood pooled on the floor and on the stairs of the escalator, creating a shiny, sticky ooze. Marilyn would never walk again. Never breathe. Never move.

Detective Earl Wallace said goodnight to his wife on his cell phone and took his foot off the accelerator. His wife of thirty years wasn't going to wait up, and he was in no hurry to play matchmaker between the living room sofa and his backside. One hand on the wheel of his black unmarked police cruiser, he fished in his shirt pocket for a cigarette, found his favorite vice, and shoved it between his lips.

Detective Wallace had seen it all in his twenty-two years on the force. From the gangland slayings of the projects that were a weekend ritual, to the white-collar company employee who tried to kill his co-workers with doses of poison sprinkled on the powdered donuts. On any given night, Detective Wallace knew he would see the worst side of society, the dark side most people prefer to think exists only in movies and TV dramas. After a bad night, the real miracle came the next morning—when he woke up, got dressed, and prepared for another day of the same.

His first case in the homicide and robbery division set the tone for a career that he lived, breathed, and somehow loved. They say the first kill is the hardest for soldiers, and Wallace was sure he would take to the grave the image of the victim in his first case.

Twenty-two years later, the case was as fresh as yesterday. At first, no one had noticed the sleeping passenger in the back seat. For two hours the double-door white Metrobus made its scheduled stops along Route 2B. At some point during an otherwise lovely autumn afternoon, an elderly passenger made his way up the aisle of the bus and whispered in the driver's ear. The driver pulled over, walked to the back of the bus, and then turned to make a brief announcement. The uniformed driver spoke softly in an attempt to keep everyone calm. When he finished explaining the situation, the passengers flew from their seats and clawed their way off the vehicle, one on top of another. It was the natural human reaction to riding with a corpse.

Detective Wallace arrived on the scene, made his way to the back of the bus, and swallowed hard at the painful expression frozen on the dead man's face. An empty garbage bag lay crumpled at the feet of the slumping young man.

Wallace searched the body for evidence and identification. There were no visible wounds to the man's face or chest. The driver's license in the wallet indicated the victim was only twenty-seven, youthful for a heart attack, but not impossibly young. Wallace patted down the body one last time and pulled out an identification badge from the victim's shirt pocket that nearly made his own heart stop. According to the laminated blue ID with the victim's photograph, the dead young man worked in the reptile house of the Washington Zoo. Detective Wallace, relying on intuition as much as real detective work, radioed to the dispatcher who in turn called the dead man's employer. When Wallace heard the dispatcher's response, he jumped off the floor of the bus and climbed on the top of the seats to the vehicle's rear exit.

Two Russell's vipers, stolen from the zoo earlier in the day by the employee, had chosen the local transportation system to make their escape. The Russell's vipers—referred to by Vietnam vets as "two-step" snakes due to the fact that once bitten, the victim took two steps and died—had sunk their fangs into the hand of their captor when he opened the bag to check on them. The young man died without the courtesy of his allotted two paces.

It was a manhunt the likes of which had never been seen in the downtown area of a major city. A small family of Mongoose was released near the bus, as if the snake-killing rodent hunted its prey like a bloodhound. Poisons and traps were thrown around like rice at a wedding. In the end, the snakes were never found. To this day, Earl Wallace looked around his tiny back yard before letting his grandchildren run free. Twenty-two years and forty pounds ago. His short curly black hair was now heavy with gray, giving the detective a distinguished look to his black features. Twenty-two years.

Cigarette in his mouth, he patted down his shirt and swerved as he ran his hand on the floor and in the crack of the passenger seat searching for a lighter. The radio crackled and Earl Wallace tuned in, catching every word of the seemingly secret language of police radio dispatchers. The radio ended with a statement that even the Sesame Street crowd could comprehend. "Police requested at McPherson Metro station. Body discovered."

Earl Wallace snatched the unlit cigarette from his mouth and threw it out the window. The Metro station was two blocks ahead.

***

Two marked squad cars stopped beside Wallace as he pulled his increasingly heavy frame from the seat. Wallace paused at the top of the escalator and looked down at the scene below. He shook his head and walked down the stairs, his knees creaking the creak of an old athlete with new arthritis. The Metro Transit Authorities arrived ten minutes later and joined the EMTs as they made their way down the long escalators that were still powered off.

"Does Metro Transit want this? It's your jurisdiction if you call it," Detective Wallace asked the two Metro Police officers who had yet to approach the body. Wallace already knew the answer. When it came to dead bodies, the Metro Transit Police deferred to the D.C. Police. The city cops had more "stiff" experience.

"It's all yours, detective," came the reply.

Detective Wallace nodded and forced his heavy frame down on his painful knees and got to work.

The emergency personnel took up official positions at official distances around the scene. Detective Wallace gathered Marilyn's personal belongings and put them into separate plastic bags. He grabbed the broken shoe and the heel that had hung from the bottom of the hooker-red footwear by a strip of leather. He looked at the break in the heel and rubbed it with his fingers through latex gloves.

He looked up at the escalator and the steep angle at which it dove underground.

"If I had to guess, I would say that she broke a heel and then fell," Detective Wallace said, based purely on the evidence. "Or lost her balance as she broke her heel and then fell."

"No chance that the heel broke during her fall?" a white Metro Transit officer asked out of curiosity, as if the detective had all the answers.

"Maybe. Maybe she just lost her balance. But looking at the shoe, one thing is certain. If she had been walking on the broken heel it would have been scratched or embedded with grime. The break is very clean," Wallace said, putting the shoe into a plastic bag, the heel into another.

Both officers looked up at the looming staircase and the long tunnel to the lights of the street above. "Ouch," the white officer said. "A true fashion victim," he added with the type of police humor that was a prerequisite to get fellow officers through the reality of the job.

Detective Wallace didn't reply to the comment. He was still on the job. He asked the commuter who found the body a few questions, got his name and number, and then released him. He dragged his former-college-football-star body up the escalator stairs and checked the top of the landing for clues. Seemingly a mile below, the uniformed police entourage watched as the body was put on a stretcher. Detective Wallace stayed until the crime scene was officially closed. He took one last look down the stairs, rubbed his chin, and went back to the police station to fill out the paperwork for an accidental death.

***

Chow Ying, refreshed from the kill, walked the fifteen blocks to his home-away-from-home at the Peking Palace in Chinatown. The old man who ran the hotel was watching an old circa Seventies black and white TV. When Chow Ying walked in, the TV went off.

"Mahjong?" the old man asked, inviting Chow Ying into his living room at the back of the house-turned-hotel.

"And beer?" the old man added with a gappy smile.

Chow Ying, as politely as he could, asked him if he had anything stronger.

The old man nodded, walked to the kitchen, and pulled out a bottle of label-less liquor from a cabinet.

"Are you sure your wife won't mind?" Chow Ying asked as the host poured a glass of the nameless high-octane brew for each of them.

"No. It's almost midnight. She has been asleep for hours. And at our age, she isn't waiting up for a roll in the hay," the old man said with a straight face.

"I suppose not," Chow Ying answered, not knowing what else to say.

The hotel owner broke into a laugh that only old men can produce—old men who have seen things, been there, lived it. Three hours of drinking and mahjong later, the old man pushed a pillow under the head of the sleeping giant and covered him with a blanket. The sofa was empty, but Chow Ying was too heavy to move. The old man would have needed a forklift to get him off the floor.

"Sleep well, *nian qing ren*," the old man said, using a Chinese term of endearment meaning 'young man.'

In the morning, the old man's wife stepped over Chow Ying on her way to make breakfast. She left the house on errands before the Mountain of Shanghai awoke, and by the time she returned, he was back in his room sleeping off the effects of the old man's gasoline in a bottle.

***

On her fourteenth day of confinement, Wei Ling took the situation into her own hands. After her morning tears—which accompanied the realization that sleep was only a temporary break from reality—her head cleared to an epiphany. Lee Chang wasn't going to help her. The doctor was never coming back. The compassion of the Chang servant who served her breakfast, lunch, and dinner began and ended with a smile. Peter Winthrop, the one man powerful enough to help her from her predicament, was a thousand miles away, either not knowing her predicament or not caring. It had been a week, maybe more, since Shi Shi Wong had paid her a visit. Her roommate had promised to come back to see her when she could, but Wei Ling knew the girls were in lockdown. No communication with the outside world. No TV. No radio. Just work. It happened occasionally, usually when one of the girls escaped the premises or took off on her company sponsored chaperone while on a trip in the city. The missing girls always showed up. There was no Chinese consulate on Saipan. There was nowhere to run. Sometimes the girls made it to the police, who turned them back over to Lee Chang, who in turn, donated to the monthly "police assistance" plan. Wei Ling was trapped. If she was going to get help, it was going to have to start with her.

Breakfast came and Wei Ling feigned a stomachache. She asked for something hot to drink. The Chang servant smiled, removed the food, and returned with a perfectly blended cup of green tea. Wei Ling thanked her and put the earthenware on the side table. Humans can survive three minutes without air, three days without water, and three weeks without food.

Wei Ling wasn't trying to kill herself, just the baby.

Chapter 19

The three feet of freedom that Wei Ling had were now gone. She was tied to the bed, shackled at both the wrist and ankles. Her left arm was in a makeshift splint, bones sandwiched so tightly between two small boards that the skin was pinched flat against the grain of the wood. The intravenous drip in her immobilized arm was pumping the good stuff, a mixture of medication and vitamins. Something to take the edge off and keep her healthy. The tube running down her nose provided fifteen hundred calories a day.

The doctor from Beijing who replaced the dead American doctor had the bedside manner of Joseph Mengele. The dead doctor, while a part-time puppet for Lee Chang, had a glimmer of humanity when you looked in his eyes. He did what he was paid to do, even when it was wrong, but he did it with compassion.

The new doctor was expressionless. He was fit, in his early sixties, and in Lee Chang's infirmary he was all business. His patients were nothing more than objects he tried to keep alive. It was hard to experiment on the dead.

The doctor had become interested in medicine when he learned his father was killed in a WWII Japanese torture camp known as Unit 731. Over the course of WWII, Unit 731 was a medical team that ran a concentration camp in Pingfan, China. The unit, with approval from the Japanese government, took great pleasure in torturing Chinese citizens through a dreadful mix of concoctions devised to incapacitate and humiliate. Chinese citizens with no military connection were placed in closed quarters while rodents infected with un-pleasantries ranging from the plague to measles ran roughshod over their naked bodies. Live dissections were performed on prisoners who were fed healthy diets before their death in order to measure more accurately the affect on a normal body. Limbs were frozen and then amputated, the victims still alive. Prisoners, known as "logs," were drained of their blood, one pint at a time, day after day, until there was nothing left. All in the name of science and medicine.

Unit 731 was not a war-era secret medical facility, but those responsible did escape prosecution. Unlike many Nazis who were hunted down for killing Jews, the members of the Japanese torture squad Unit 731 were granted clemency. Some of the "doctors" involved went on to distinguished careers in post-war Japan. Not a single person was prosecuted for crimes against humanity. In return for leniency, the U.S. merely requested translations of the nature of the tests conducted and the results of the experiments.

The doctor now standing in front of Wei Ling had become a monster through hatred. He learned how his father had been tortured and killed, and soon thereafter the doctor's train to a righteous life jumped the track. In his mind, he saw medicine as a way to seek revenge. The doctor studied medicine with an equal passion of learning how to heal and learning how to hurt. Learning how to heal made him rich. Learning how to hurt was a life-long hobby.

The doctor found as much pleasure in the study of medicine as he did in the control of people. With the right dosage of the right medicine, he could have the final say in who lived and who died. It was a decision he made with as much thought as he put into his lunch menu. He specialized in internal medicine and was a Beijing legend in the circles of herbal medicine, acupuncture, and acupressure. When the great C.F. Chang slipped in the bath and injured his shoulder, the old doctor became C.F. Chang's personal physician. Three weeks of acupuncture and firm pressure applied to very specific points on the bottom of the feet brought relief and eternal gratitude. C.F. Chang paid well and the doctor took to the life of serving semi-royalty like a pig to mud.

Wei Ling looked at the new doctor and saw darkness in his dead-fish eyes. There would be no talking with this one. They were both Chinese, but that was where their similarities began and ended. Rural Guangzhou and downtown Beijing were worlds apart.

Wei Ling's hunger strike had lasted exactly two days. When she refused to eat her fifth consecutive meal, the middle-aged servant brought in Lee Chang. The conversation was short and ended with: "You will have this baby."

Wei Ling didn't cry. She had moved beyond self-pity. She would not have the baby. It was a battle of wills and it was a fight Wei Ling believed she could win.

The intravenous line in Wei Ling's arm caused a dull ache, just short of real pain. She had been kicked, punched, slapped, and pushed into walls since her arrival in paradise. The needle was far less punishing. The psychological affect was the worst. Being tied down and having someone stick a tube up your nose and needles in your arm was just a rude reminder that they were in control of her body. The only control she had was her mind, and she had turned the corner toward mastering her will. The IV and feeding tube pumped a solution with enough vitamins and calories for a healthy person to live, and a little extra for the valuable bundle of joy being treated as a scientific experiment. The doctor warned her that if she didn't cooperate, an additional dose of sedation would be added to the mixture. Wei Ling needed her senses. Being doped-up wasn't in her best interest. So she played along. For now.

Chapter 20

The tears were flowing at the reception desk when Jake stepped out of the elevator. Mascara streaks painted the receptionist's cheeks, her blonde hair ruffled. Jake avoided eye contact, said "good morning," and didn't break pace as he blew past the emotionally charged Winthrop Enterprises employee. The receptionist was prone to outbursts, and it didn't take much to send her fragile psyche over the edge. A bad hair day. A run in her pantyhose. Jake had quickly learned not to ask.

The somber ambiance and solemn faces of the other Winthrop Enterprises employees told him the receptionist's tears weren't a simple case of running out of hair gel.

Jason McDonald, financial wizard with a receding hairline, broke the news to Jake. "Did you hear?"

"Hear what?"

"Marilyn passed away this weekend."

Jake's posture slumped, the invisible punch to the stomach taking his breath away. "How?"

"She had an accident on the elevator stairs at the Metro. Broken neck," Jason said, shaking his head.

Jake's legs almost buckled and he put one hand on the corner of the desk for support. Jason McDonald quickly pulled over a chair.

"When did this happen?" Jake asked in a hushed voice.

"Friday night."

"Good God."

The timeframe of Marilyn's death made Jake nauseous. His head filled with images of his mother on the sofa, each breath more shallow than the last until the one that never came. She went quietly, with a smile, her hand in Jake's. Being the last person to see someone alive was not a prize to be cherished.

"I'm sorry to be the one to tell you. You two seemed to have gotten close in your short time here," Jason said, running his hand across his expanding scalp, as if plowing his fingers through an imaginary mane.

"Yeah, I guess. We had a few things in common, as it turns out."

"Well, don't let it get you down. The office will be closing early tomorrow. There will be a service at a funeral home in Alexandria. Then her body is going to be flown back to Milwaukee on Wednesday for burial in a family plot. Her brother is stopping by the office later to pick up some personal items. Maybe you could say a few words, offer your condolences."

"Yeah, sure. I will." Jake agreed, still in a daze. "Is my father in?"

"Not yet. He has been running around trying to help with arrangements. She was his secretary for twenty-five years."

Don't remind me, Jake thought. "Thanks again, Jason."

"Sure thing. Sorry to be the bearer of bad tidings."

Jake found his office and moved his chair to stare out the window. He shed a single tear for Marilyn and wiped his face when he knew it was going to be the last.

The anti-abortionists were next on the list for the protest-of-the-week, and their numbers were growing in Franklin Park across the street. Jake stared out the window at several mothers holding posters that read "abortion is murder," their children beneath them in their strollers holding smaller versions of similar signs. There were men and women, the religious element, and the politically charged. Jake gazed out the window and his mind wandered. The girl in Saipan. His father forcing Marilyn to get an abortion at the same time his mother was pregnant with him. Madness.

The street vendors were doing a brisk morning business feeding the anti-abortionists donuts and coffee at a three-hundred percent mark-up. A muscle bound man with a ponytail and twin boys joined the line, his children pointing at everything on the menu. Jake paused and squinted at the figure in the park. Something clicked in the back of his mind and for the second time in ten minutes his stomach dropped. "Son of a bitch," he said to himself.

***

Jake peeked under the edge of the bridge before walking past Al's neighbors who waved to the only guest their neck of the woods had seen in months. In the winter, Social Services and various help-the-homeless non-profits stopped by when the temperature fell below freezing. When it dropped to the single digits, the space under the bridge was one of the prime spots for the city workers to find a frozen body. In the summer, no one cared. Few homeless died of heat exhaustion or exposure, especially among the "river rats" who lived near the banks of the Potomac. Relief was only a bucket of water away. Nasty, undrinkable water, but still useful enough to drop a body's core temperature a few degrees.

Jake disappeared from the sun into the damp atmosphere of Al Korgaokar's living room. Al was sitting in his wicker chair with his feet on a milk crate, his eyes closed behind dark sunglass, one arm of a broken pair of Ray Bans clinging to his left ear.

"Al?" Jake asked, not sure if he was asleep or not.

"Jake?" Al answered without opening his eyes.

"Yeah Al, it's me, Jake."

Al moved his feet from the crate and placed the heels of his boots on the ground. He flipped the sunglasses to the top of his head, exposing a pair of crystal-clear blue eyes. "Have a seat," he said, pushing the empty crate forward with his feet. The guest chair for the day.

Al turned to his right and pulled back the corner of an old tattered blue tarp he had fished out of the river since Jake's last visit. A new piece of furniture covering for the living room.

"Marilyn is dead," Jake said abruptly.

Al shot upright in his chair and his sunglasses fell off his head. "When?"

"Friday night. It was in Sunday's paper."

"What happened?" Al asked. He reached for his stack of newspapers from the weekend, not believing he missed any piece of published news.

"She fell down the escalator at the McPherson Square Metro station. That's the report anyway."

"What do you mean?" Al asked, pulling out Sunday's Metro section.

"I was with her on Friday. And I'm not really sure, but I think we were being watched. Followed. I don't know."

Al's eyes watered as he stared off into the distance. "Tell me *exactly* what happened. Details count."

"We went out for drinks after work and went our separate ways near the station. As I was getting into a taxi, I think someone was watching me. An Asian guy."

"That's it?"

Jake told Al about Marilyn crying in the office and the morning conversation that had ruined his appetite for the day and his taste for waffles for life. "There is a service for Marilyn tomorrow evening," Jake said with compassion. "I thought you might want to know."

"Thanks." Al rubbed the bridge of his nose with his forefinger and thumb. There was something there, something below the surface that Marilyn's death had stirred up.

"Did you go to the police?" Al asked.

"Not yet. I wasn't sure if I should. Like I said, I don't know if it was anything. I don't know if it was a coincidence, or if the guy was just zoned out on crack. But he was definitely looking at me. Gave me goose bumps."

Al thought in silence before speaking. "It was probably nothing. I know a lot of homeless guys who will stare you down for no reason."

"I guess that's the truth."

"You know that girl you are looking for?"

"Did you learn something?"

"She works for Chang Industries, but I think you already knew that."

"Yeah, I knew where she worked. I wanted to know if *you* could find out where she worked."

"Thanks for the show of confidence. Let me see if I can tell you something you didn't know. Chang Industries is a sweatshop for which Winthrop Enterprises serves as the middleman. A guy named Lee Chang runs the sweatshop. Call it whatever you want, but Chang Industries, as benign as the name sounds, is not a nice place."

"I haven't heard anything about either Lee Chang or Chang Industries at work."

Al thought it over. "What do you know about your father?"

"Not much, really. Why? Do you think Winthrop Enterprises has something to do with this?"

"Probably not. Your father is just a middleman. A very good one. Very savvy. He knows a lot of people."

"I'm not following you."

"All right. I'll give you an example. Let's say you have a product you need to have manufactured. You go to someone like your father, and he arranges for you to see different factories and facilities. You name the location."

"So he just sets up meetings and acts as the intermediary."

"Yes. And, depending on the deal, he gets a cut of the profits. He could even finance some of the deal for a bigger cut of the profits."

Al was still thinking about Marilyn, trying to put the seemingly unrelated pieces together while carrying on his current conversation.

"So what's the story with the Wei Ling girl?"

"She's in Saipan on a work visa. It was renewed this June. Good for a year. She's still in Saipan. No record of her leaving the island. On a personal note, she is twenty-three, five-foot-three, one hundred and ten pounds. She is from a small town in the Guangzhou province. No siblings, not surprising as China has a one-child policy unless you are wealthy enough to pay a steep fine for additional children. Blood type O."

"Now how do you know what blood type she has?"

"A magician never reveals his secrets."

"You said she hasn't left the island?"

"No. She is still there. Why do you ask?"

"My father said she went back to China."

"So your father is hiding something."

"Hiding a few things I imagine," Jake said. "Speaking of hiding, you said you would tell me about my father working as a spy for the CIA."

"A spy? Hell no, Jake. He wasn't employed by the CIA—he provided information to the CIA, via yours truly."

"You were a spy?"

"An Official Cover Operative."

"What the hell is an Official Cover Operative?"

"A CIA employee working under the safe umbrella and diplomatic immunity of the State Department. A perfectly legitimate spy, if there is such a thing."

"A spy who spends his whole life telling everyone that he works for the State Department."

"Not just telling everyone, actually working in the State Department, with State Department personnel. The only difference was that my boss was located at Langley."

"So if my father wasn't a spy..."

"He didn't work for the CIA, but he fed the CIA information, for money. A very subtle difference."

"I don't think my father needs the money."

"Jake the snake, when you're right, you're right. It wasn't a matter of money with your father."

"Then why did he do it?"

"For the chance to be a big shot. We are talking twenty some years ago. Your father had started Winthrop Enterprises and was traveling the globe making connections, signing deals and hobnobbing with the international elite."

"That's what he's doing now."

"Yes, but aaaaah, the world was a lot smaller twenty-five years ago. There weren't a lot of westerners running around Tokyo and Beijing. Your father stood out. A young, successful, globetrotting American businessman."

"I still don't see the connection with the CIA."

"Connection. Good choice of words. Your father was a connection."

"How?"

"We paid your father to report on what he saw in Tokyo and Beijing. Who was talking to whom about what business. Deals in the works, activities of interests. Protests, if there were any. Incidents of bribing. Whatever he could tell us."

"Wouldn't the CIA know all of this?

"Sure, well, some of it anyway. But it cost a lot of money to get intelligence through formal channels. Renting real estate, setting up front companies, implementing electronic surveillance, these things aren't free and believe it or not the CIA does have a budget. Paying American citizens to tell us what they know is cheap."

"So what did he tell you?"

"Your father was a good source of intelligence for a few years. He tipped us off to the sale of certain illegal hi-tech goods in Asia that we weren't aware of. Some technology that ended up in a North Korean sub that washed ashore in South Korea years later. You can learn a lot from drunken businessmen in Roppongi. Hell, you can even get their business cards."

"Okay," Jake said, stretching out the second syllable.

"But after a few years we suspected your father of fabrication. We compared a lot of the intelligence from your father, and people like him, with our own intelligence. It is a good checks-and-balances measure. We started to see large discrepancies in the information from your father and the intelligence generated by the CIA through other means."

"Are you saying my father was lying to the CIA? I find that hard to believe."

"Not lying...exaggerating. But we couldn't really prove it either. And even if we did, there was nothing the CIA could do. The CIA is not a law enforcement organization. We are actually an organization designed for the sole purpose of breaking the law, just not American law. Your father is an American, he wasn't selling U.S. secrets to anyone, he wasn't in the military or in a position to have sensitive military information, and he was gathering intelligence for us. It wasn't a matter of national security."

"What happened?"

"We told him his services were no longer needed and that we suspected some of the information he gave us had been inaccurate. We turned his name over to the FBI, to have his information added to a watchlist, and that was the end of my involvement with him. There was nothing else we could do."

"And that's it?"

"That's it."

"So you know my father?"

"I worked in Asia during the same period that your father supplied us information. I was the one who discovered the discrepancies. I was the one who arranged for him to be recruited."

"Recruited?"

"Yes. The recruitment was finalized in a sauna in Tokyo, after several less-than-chance meetings I had arranged."

"The sauna?"

"A great place to recruit. Everyone is naked and the temperature is hundred and thirty degrees Celsius. No one is going to be eavesdropping. No one is going to be wearing a wire. And although I have no concrete scientific evidence to back me up, I think the heat makes people more susceptible to influence."

"How much did you pay him?"

"Oh I don't remember exactly, and if I did I couldn't tell you. Off the record, we probably paid him a couple of thousand a month. He was usually debriefed in D.C. when he got back in the U.S. That's how I met Marilyn. She was always by his side. Always very pleasant."

"If my father no longer fed you information, why did you keep in touch with her?"

"Marilyn? Pure coincidence, really. After my family passed, I moved into Potomac Falls Condominiums. Marilyn was my neighbor."

The mystery around the great Peter Winthrop just got deeper. For Jake, life as an English teacher was looking more appealing every second. "What's our next move?" Jake asked, half-afraid of the answer.

"Jake, why do you want to help this Wei Ling?"

"Because it is the right thing to do."

Al, homeless cover operative, stuck out his dirty paw. Jake looked at Al's hand and then extended his own.

"Then you and I are going to be pals, Jake. Spike Lee hit the nail on the head. *Do the right thing.*"

"So what do we do?"

"You need to decide what you want to do, Jake. I just agreed to get you the information."

"You're not going to help?"

"I didn't say that. But you're leading this expedition." Al thought about Jake and the slim chance that someone was after his newest friend. "Let me give you my number," Al said, looking for a pen. "If you see anything strange, duck first, then give me a call and leave a message."

"And in the meantime?"

"What?" Al asked.

"What's our plan?"

"Jesus, Jake. Life doesn't just map itself out for you. Talk to your father again. See if he can't straighten it out. Tell him you know he is lying and force him to give you some evidence that will rest your soul. Tell him you know the girl is still on Saipan. Rattle his cage a little. Write your letter to whomever."

"So that's it?"

"For now, that's it. Feel free to come back anytime to visit. I'm usually around the Mall somewhere."

Chapter 21

Jake rang the doorbell to the rectory on the side of the church. He waited and hit the buzzer again before walking back down the narrow walkway to the front entrance. He pulled open the oversized doors and light poured into the dark vestibule, reflecting off the top of the newly shined pew backs. He dipped his middle finger into the holy water and kneeled briefly while crossing himself in the name of the Father, Son, and Holy Spirit. Amen.

A lone parishioner sat in the sea of pews, head down, heavy into prayer, trying to vanquish years of natural Catholic guilt. It was the first time Jake had been back to the church since his mother's funeral. He had been to Mass with Kate twice in the last month, both times at St. Nicholas in upper Northwest D.C. The nice part of town. But Jake wasn't coming to pray. He walked down the aisle to the front of the altar, knelt one more time, and took a left.

Jake knew the church as well as anyone, save for Father McKenna and Sister Ann, the padre he had known since birth and the nun whose age could be measured in the wrinkles of her face. Jake knew the smell of the candles, the sound of the organ. He could identify the squeaky back pew with his eyes closed. Baptism, first communion, confirmation, four weddings, his mother's funeral and three years as an altar boy. The church had long since lost the power of the silent spell it cast on most parishioners who showed up for an hour a week of spiritual due diligence.

Father McKenna was in the back room, straightening the small locker that held his collar when he slept. Jake knocked lightly on the open door, and Father McKenna turned toward his guest, arms open wide.

"How are you, Jake? I haven't seen you since the service."

"Yeah, I know Father, my apologies."

"Don't apologize to me… unless my sermons are the reason you stopped coming to Mass."

"No, that's not it."

"How are you, son? How is your family?"

"I'm doing okay. I moved a few weeks ago."

"I heard your mother's house sold."

Jake forgot how plugged-in the priest was to the local community. As a priest, Father McKenna knew about the births, the marriages, the deaths. He heard the dirt, the secrets, things he wished he didn't know, and everything in between.

"Yeah, the house sold without a hitch. I'm renting an apartment in Cleveland Park."

"Fabulous. Nice area. You know there is a church five blocks from the subway stop."

"Yes, I know," Jake said dipping his head in temporary shame. "And I have a new girlfriend."

"How's that going?"

"Great girl. Overbearing parents."

"More often than not, one goes with the other."

"Working at my father's office for the summer."

"Work is good."

"It's nice to be employed. Trying to get to know my father a little."

"I understand. That can be hard."

Jake turned serious, his brown hair and chiseled face stern. "I'm not here for an update, Father."

"I know, son. It's written in your gait. Your tone of voice. But niceties are called niceties for a reason." The priest sat down and motioned for Jake to do the same. "What's bothering you?"

"Well, I'm not sure."

The priest laughed at the child-like delivery of the statement. "Jake, I am a man of the cloth, but unfortunately that does not make me a mind reader."

"You knew my mother. Ever hear her mention a woman named Marilyn Ford?"

"Marilyn…?" Father McKenna said. He looked toward the ceiling trying to recall a face to go with the familiar name.

"She works for my father," Jake added. "She was my father's secretary."

"Marilyn Ford," the priest said, the weight of the woman's name heavy on his tongue. "Her last name threw me off a bit. Thought it was a trivia question there for a minute. Like Henry Ford's daughter or something. Yes, Marilyn, I know her."

"Did you ever meet her? She said she attended my parent's wedding."

"I don't remember her from the wedding, Jake. But I do vaguely know her from the church. She was a parishioner here years ago."

"She came to the same church as my mother and I? I don't remember her."

"Used to come to the early Mass if I remember correctly. Not sure your mother ever spoke to her. I don't recall them being friends."

Jake thought about his mother and Marilyn in a throwdown, hair-pulling fight outside the entrance to the pearly gates. Settling earthly scores with a heavenly catfight.

Father McKenna continued. "Haven't seen Marilyn in, gosh, five years. Maybe longer. Time just flies by," the priest said, stroking the bookmark that hung from the pressed pages of the Bible on the table.

"She passed away on Friday. Fell down an escalator at the Metro station. We had just had a few drinks at a bar near my father's office."

"I hadn't heard. Poor woman." Father McKenna closed his eyes and muttered something undistinguishable in Latin.

Definitely old school, Jake thought.

"No one contacted me about a service."

"There is a brief service at a funeral parlor in Alexandria. Her brother is flying her body back to Wisconsin on Wednesday."

"Does your trouble have to do with Marilyn?"

"Maybe. She and I had been doing a lot of talking lately. She told me some things I could have gone without knowing. Things involving her and my father. Not very flattering revelations if you know what I mean."

"I see," Father McKenna answered noncommittally. He had probably received both ends of the story in anonymous confessionals, but it was a million affairs ago. A billion sins by thousands of sinners.

"And on top of that, it seems that my father has managed to get some Asian girl pregnant and is refusing to help her."

"Sounds like life has been interesting."

"You have no idea."

"So how can I help you, son?"

"How would you feel, hypothetically speaking, if I helped someone get an abortion?"

"Hypothetically, you say?"

"Yes."

"Do you want me to answer that as a priest or as a friend?"

"Either," Jake said. "Or both."

"Well, as a priest, all I can say is that the Catholic Church has a very dim view of abortion. The fetus is a living human from the moment of conception. Undoubtedly this is not a new thought to you."

"No, Father. I understand the Church's position... What would you say as a friend?"

"Do you believe that God loves you?"

"Yes."

"Are you willing to believe that God loves you more than even your mother did?"

"I'm willing to believe it is possible."

"If your mother were alive, do you think she would still love you even if you did something she did not agree with?"

"Sure, she would."

"Then, as a friend, and not a priest, I believe God would also."

Jake sat quiet for a moment. "Thanks, Father."

"Sure, Jake."

Jake stood and the padre pushed himself out of his chair using his palm against the corner of the desk.

"Mass on Sunday is still at eight, ten, and twelve. I will be doing the ten o'clock service. Bring your new girlfriend."

"Nice sales pitch Father. I'll try to make it."

"Don't be a stranger," the priest said, patting Jake on the shoulder and going back to his menial daily tasks.

Jake stopped and looked at the priest as he walked out the door. It was the closest thing he was going to get to a spiritual green light.

***

Jake walked through the vestibule to the back of the church, past the lone sinner, rosary still in hand. He dipped his finger in the holy water again, made the sign of the cross, and followed the short hall to the right, past the bathroom and the water fountain. At the end of the hall, he stopped and looked through the glass window in the door. The "silent room" as it was called among the parishioners, was built for parents to take their restless children during Mass. It was constructed a hundred years after the main church was built, a niche carved out from a few rows of pews and an old coat closet. The large glass window on the far side of the room offered a distant view of the altar. Two speakers were perched in the corners of the wall so the parishioners could hear the Mass in progress. When the speaker was off, the room was dead quiet. A pay phone, a rapidly disappearing species of technology, hung on the wall in the close corner. Jake stepped over a pile of religious children's books and shook his pocket for loose change.

The maddening, bureaucratic world of the D.C. Police was a shock to Jake's system. His first call to headquarters was picked up by Tonya Freeman, a woman with three kids, as many ex-husbands, and a dislike for her job. She tried to transfer Jake's call and promptly disconnected him. Jake shoved another fifty cents in the phone and called back. On his second attempt, Tonya put down her coffee long enough to connect him to the First District. His second transfer was as difficult as the first and Jake found himself talking to Officer Charlesworth from traffic enforcement. Ten minutes after his journey had begun, Earl Wallace, the detective who filled out the accident report on Marilyn, picked up his phone.

"Detective Wallace."

"Good morning, detective."

"Good morning. How can I help you?"

"I wanted to ask a question about a recently deceased woman. Her name is Marilyn Ford and she died Friday night in an accident at the McPherson Metro station."

Detective Wallace started shuffling papers around his desk. "What did you say your name was again?"

Jake stalled. "I'd rather not say."

"Then may I ask if this is an anonymous tip?" It was an early stalemate and Jake realized he wasn't prepared for what he was doing.

Detective Wallace followed his instincts and didn't push. "Okay. How do you know the subject?"

Jake noted the word 'subject', not 'victim.' "We go to the same church," he answered. It was stretching the truth like spandex at a Weight Watchers meeting, but it was still technically true.

Earl Wallace switched gears and eased into the soft approach. "I'm sorry for your loss."

"Thanks for saying so. Detective, I'm curious as to the specifics of how she died."

Detective Wallace listened to Jake's voice, trying to imagine the person on the other end—his age, his race, his education level. "She fell down fifty yards of escalator stairs. Broken neck. It was a violent fall."

"So it was an accident?"

"Yes, as far as I know. Do you have something to tell me it wasn't?"

"No, I was just wondering. We got the news at the church and we were looking for answers."

"Well, could I get your number, just in case I need to speak with you."

"That's all right. I just wanted to know how she died. You have been helpful. Thanks for your time, detective." Jake hung up the phone as he finished the sentence. He felt sweat run down the inside of his arm. He looked out at the altar and the hanging crucifix, and crossed himself one more time for luck before dancing around the toys on the floor on his way out.

Detective Wallace hung up the old black phone on his desk and stared at the receiver, the noise of the office and its activities silenced by concentration. He picked the phone back up and punched nine for the police operator. "I need a trace on the call that just came in."

"Yes, detective. The phone is registered to St. Michael's Catholic Church. 2300 Pennsylvania Avenue."

Wallace jotted a quick sentence in his detective's notebook. The phone call was unusual. He pulled the file for the case from the out-basket on his desk and went over the evidence again just to be thorough. The accident scene report and the medical examiner's cursory exam results all pointed to a lady with a broken heel taking a spill down one mean-ass escalator. He held the folder in his hand and tried to put it back in his out-basket. His fingers wouldn't let it go. Something about the phone call stuck in his craw. Cases had been made and killers sent to prison from investigations that started with clues far more benign than a random phone call.

Maybe it was nothing. Maybe it was everything.

Detective Wallace placed a call to the morgue. His request for a full autopsy on the victim wasn't well received. The medical examiner's initial report was already on file. The body had been in the morgue since late Friday night and it was due to leave in a couple of hours. A full autopsy was time consuming and the current backlog of stiffs was long and growing. Two teenagers found beaten, stabbed, and shot in an alley on U Street. A three-car accident that claimed four lives including a mentally ill man who was trying to cross the street with a grocery cart full of junk. A young man dumped at the entrance to the hospital with no visible signs of illness or injury. And those were only the dead from Saturday afternoon. Two bodies had just been fished out of the Potomac and were on their way over.

Dr. Hahn handled the call. "I'll get to her later today, detective. Looking for anything in particular?"

"Anything suspicious, no matter how minute. Double-check for forensic evidence that may have been missed in the initial exam. Anything that would contradict an accidental death by serious fall."

The doctor read the clipboard. "Alcohol, Valium, and Zoloft followed by a fall down the stairs at the Metro station?"

"That's what we know."

"Ouch," the doctor said. "I will get back to you by this afternoon."

***

The unmarked cruiser stopped between two of the most confusing parking signs ever manufactured. By process of time slot elimination, it was legal to park between six p.m. and midnight, excluding holidays and snow emergencies. Detective Wallace shook his head at the sign, shut the door to his black unmarked cruiser and jogged, stomach bouncing, across two lanes of traffic.

In the pace of the big city, Marilyn Ford's demise was ancient history. Fewer than twelve hours after her fall, the escalators were back in full motion, people trampling over microscopic blood stains left in the cracks of the tiles, beyond the vision of human eyes. Three days later and half the commuters using the station had forgotten the incident ever occurred.

Detective Wallace tried to recreate the scene. He walked to the top of the escalator, looked down and then turned around. He scanned the urban surroundings from street level and walked down the sidewalk half a block in each direction. With the mid-morning foot traffic passing him, he leaned against the blue mailbox and removed his left shoe. He stuffed his sock into his left Rockport and walked back to the escalator, shoe in hand. To his surprise, the one-shoe-shuffle created a nice limp, a solid simulation of a lost heel on a woman's shoe. Lawyers and business-men gawked at the detective as he limped down the sidewalk on one bare foot. The detective, deep in concentration, was oblivious.

He turned at the corner of the building toward the subway station, still dragging his bare foot and trying not to step on anything sharp. At the top of the escalator he measured his balance. *A definite possibility*, he thought. He was sober, but he knew it wouldn't take much for someone with a few drinks and a couple of pills in them to lose their balance. And not only was he sober, but the good shoe he had on his right foot was flat and made for walking. No heels. Still barefoot, Detective Wallace rode to the bottom of the escalator, stopped, turned around and looked back up. "Man, oh man," he said aloud. Murder or accident, it was a hell of a way to go.

He slipped on his sock and shoe and approached the subway station attendant's booth.

He flashed his badge and spoke into the pass-through in the thick security glass. "You guys got any surveillance cameras at the street level?"

"Not that I know of," the attendant replied pointing at the monitors on the console in front of her. "We have one at each end of the platform, one right above your head for evidence against fare dodgers, and anoth-er near the ticket machines to prevent vandalism and theft."

"Does the one near the ticket machine have a view of the escalators?"

"No, it is on the far wall facing the machines head-on. When you buy tickets, your back faces it."

Detective Wallace bent over and tied his shoe.

"Does this have something to do with the accident Friday night?"

the station attendant asked.

"Yes."

"It happens you know."

"What's that?" Wallace asked.

"Falling down the stairs."

"Yeah, I know."

"I haven't had anyone die on my shift, but there are plenty of sprained ankles."

Detective Wallace was still thinking. "Thanks for your time," he said.

"Sure, detective."

Wallace stepped away from the station entrance and again looked down the street in both directions. He scratched his head and gave a dirty look to the delivery driver who pulled his truck a little too close to the pedestrians in the crosswalk. He stood on the corner, eyes darting, mind running through scenarios. As the world passed around him, he found what he was looking for. He was willing to put down his weekend horse track money that he was about to get his first real clue.

**

Detective Wallace fumbled with the VCR before putting his tail between his legs and asking the young detective for help.

"Detective Nguyen?"

"Yes, sir."

"Could you lend me a hand for a minute?"

"Sure, sergeant."

Detective Wallace led the younger, fitter man to the empty break-room.

"Do you know how to hook this thing up?" Wallace asked, pointing to the VCR and a TV on the table.

"Sir, there is a TV in the corner with a built-in VCR."

"I need two," Wallace answered flatly.

Detective Nguyen nodded and went to work. "Hooking these up are pretty basic—there are three cords: one red, one yellow, and one white. They go into the holes in the back of the TV with the same colors."

Detective Nguyen finished the procedure that any twelve year-old could do with their eyes shut and turned the TV on. "What are we watching, if you don't mind me asking?"

"Surveillance tapes," detective Wallace answered, popping the tape in the VCR.

"Want an extra set of eyes?"

"Grab a seat."

Both men lit cigarettes and eased into the metal breakroom chairs.

"I'm looking into the fatal accident at the Metro station Friday night. I got this security tape from Fleet Bank this morning. They have two cameras running twenty-four hours a day near their ATM at Fourteenth and Eye Street. One of the cameras is a close-up, focused within five feet of the ATM machine."

"A mugger camera."

"Exactly. The other camera is an overhead feed with a footprint that covers the entire corner. This is the surveillance from Friday, five minutes before the call to 911. I watched this one already, but I was interested in seeing the tapes simultaneously."

A couple strolled in front of the ATM, hand-in-hand, laughing like young lovers do, months before the incessant fighting and bickering sets in. A minute later an older gentleman walked by with a cane and a cigar.

Detective Wallace hit the fast-forward for a few seconds and then released the button. "Then two minutes pass and there is no one until this character appears."

"Big boy," Detective Nguyen said.

"And Asian." Detective Wallace added. As if on cue, Chow Ying turned his face toward the camera and held still for a full three seconds, his pony tail resting on his left shoulder.

Detective Wallace paused the VCR with Chow Ying's face front and center. He hit play on the remote control for the TV in the corner. "Then from the overhead surveillance you see who I assume to be Marilyn Ford stumble, cross the street, and limp to the sidewalk in the direction of the subway station."

Detective Wallace hit play on the TV on the table. "The Asian guy turns his back to the ATM, looks to his right for a moment at something just outside of the view of the camera, and then follows behind Marilyn. Both of them are out of sight once they go around the corner and under the building, but you can't argue that it seems a little suspicious."

"What are you thinking?"

"I don't know. You used to work the gangs, right?"

"Yeah…used to, when I was on street patrol before becoming a detective. When the Asian gangs started making their mark a few years ago, I was brought in to help. Everyone just figures it takes an Asian to know one. There aren't too many of us in the D.C. Police, in case you haven't noticed. We set up the Asian Liaison Unit before Chinatown got squeezed. Now, the Latino gangs have taken over most of the activity outside the heavy drug turf, which is still black. No offense, Sarge."

"None taken. You ever see this guy before?" Detective Wallace asked. He rewound the tape and froze it on the black-and-white, grainy shot of Chow Ying's face.

"Can't say that I have, but Christ, you can't miss him. What do you figure he goes, six-four, two-forty?"

"I would say that is about right, give or take a Big Mac."

"Sorry, I don't know him."

"That's all right. Let me know if you hear anything, will you?" Detective Wallace asked.

"Sure thing. If you want me to help you out, pound the pavement a little, just give me a shout. I would be happy to lend a hand. Or my Asian face. And I could use the overtime."

"Ah, the truth comes out," Wallace said, jokingly. "But you're on. I'll keep you in the loop. In the meantime keep your eyes peeled for a large Asian guy."

"Will do."

Chapter 22

Jake introduced himself to Marilyn's replacement when he came into the office. Three days in the whirl of Winthrop Enterprises and the new secretary was still over her head. Between a stack of notes on her desk, and a phone with three customers waiting to be transferred, Marilyn's replacement managed to squeak out a "good morning." Shelly Fink, a formerly out-of-work executive administrative assistant, was recommended by a business acquaintance of Peter Winthrop who trumpeted her as mildly competent and stunningly beautiful. It was a half-honest evaluation. Peter took Shelly in as a favor, and intended to keep her in the office until he could find a permanent replacement. In the meantime, all she really had to do was keep his schedule straight and look good. The latter came naturally. Her long brown hair stood out in an office with a heavy slant toward blondes, and her body put every secretary in the building to shame, even the knockouts two floors below in the youngest corporate law office in the city.

The invitation to after work business came through Shelly, delivered in a scratchy voice that bordered between sexy and emphysematous. "Jake, your father wants to know if you are interested in joining him for drinks after work? It is business related."

"What's today?"

"Thursday."

"Yeah, I guess. I was supposed to have dinner with my girlfriend, but she stood me up to go out with some friends. Tell him I'll go, but I don't plan on staying out too late."

"I'm sure he will be pleased."

"Yeah, well, who cares?" Jake said with a snap, his mind elsewhere. Shelly stopped her retreat long enough to look back at Jake, his hostile answer unappreciated. "Humph," she said on her way back to her desk.

***

Hasad Bakar got out of the cab and slipped his way through the crowded doorway of Club Mombasa, a funky, semi-techno bar with a smattering of jungle motif thrown in for the happy hour animals. Jake and his father were seated on adjacent chrome stools, Peter slugging his way through his second whiskey and water.

"I'm sorry I am late," Hasad said with a thick Turkish accent. He had a slightly high-pitched voice, as if his nuts were slowly being pinched. His voice was somewhere between a robot on speed and a Middle Eastern, New York taxi driver. "It is so good to see you again, Mr. Winthrop. So good."

"Hasad, this is my son, Jake," Peter said standing from his stool.

"Your son! Fabulous. Yes, he does look like you, now that you mention it."

Hasad and Jake shook hands as Peter finished off his glass and pushed it away.

"Well. What do you think?"

"Of what?" Peter asked.

"The club—Club Mombasa." Hasad spread his arms wide as he announced the name with a shrill. "My cousin is part-owner. He is doing very well. Very well. The club opened two months ago and already it is making good money. Very good money indeed. At the rate he is going, he should break even in the first six months. Very good for a restaurant."

Peter smiled. Like the great businessmen of the world, the Turks love their numbers.

"That's great," Peter answered.

"What do you think, Jake?"

"It's nice. A good place to hang out," Jake answered with the authority of a twenty-four-year-old. He knew his father hated it.

"Shall we have something to eat?"

Peter was here on business and he wasn't going to let some techno music, blue neon lights, and a plastic jungle on the patio stand in the way. "Sure, let's get a table," Peter said.

"Nothing but the best in the house," Hasad responded with pride, disappearing in search of his cousin.

"He seems interesting," Jake said, not searching for another adjective.

"He's an idiot," his father replied. "But he is a rich idiot, and the son of an even richer one."

"What does his family do?"

"A little bit of everything. His father is Onur Bakar, a shipping mogul worth at least nine zeroes."

"A billionaire. That's a lot of money. What does Hasad want?"

"I don't know. He wouldn't tell me. The last time I did business with him he was looking for four identical Hummers, outfitted with the usual son-of-a-billionaire security features—bulletproof glass, grenade-proof undercarriage, run-flat tires and of course a one-thousand-watt stereo system."

"Any money in exporting automobiles?" Jake asked out of earnest curiosity.

"There is money in everything, son. Generally I don't get involved in onesy, twosy type deals. But when a billionaire's son starts asking for upgraded Hummers, I tend to smell a profit."

"How much did you make?"

"Enough to buy my Porsche, and ten more just like it. All it took was a couple of phone calls. Never even saw the vehicles in person."

"Couldn't he just buy them himself?"

"Hell, son, most of the people I deal with could do it themselves. But the rich like to pick up a phone, make a call, and let that be that. You know when I first realized how much money you could make in business?"

"No, I don't think I have heard this one."

"About twenty-five years ago someone heard through the grapevine that I could set up a meeting with the president of the Bank of Shanghai. These days, for those in the right circles, it isn't that big of a deal. Twenty-five years ago, China was just opening its borders, just starting to allow businessmen and students to visit. Being able to reach out and touch the president of the Bank of Shanghai was not something to be taken lightly. Not knowing what I could charge, or should charge, I aimed for the stars. I told the client how difficult it would be, that it might take some time, etc. I asked for two hundred fifty thousand dollars. It took ten minutes to get the meeting. Ten minutes and two long distance calls to China. That is when I realized how easy it is to make money."

Before Jake could ask another question, Hasad came back to the bar.

"This way, this way. The best seat in the house…" Hasad said, leading Peter by the shoulder.

***

The doormen and bouncers at Camelot's, one of the city's few mainstream strip clubs, were as large as they were ornery. Two beasts guarded the door with scrutinizing eyes, and both took an immediate disliking to Hasad, who was past the threshold of legally drunk and claiming to be in dire need of a little American entertainment.

Jake found the Turk to be annoying, and hoped the doormen would see it in their hearts to deny entry to Hasad and send them all home while it was still relatively early. A hundred dollars and a promise of good behavior from Peter paved the way down the stairs into the subterranean club. The three men followed a short skirt with an attached bunny tail to a table in the back, directly across from one of the three stages. Hasad pulled out a sizeable money roll, peeled off a few hundred dollars in various donations, and slapped the stack of greenbacks on the table. "The girls are on me," he said proudly. "And later, if I am lucky, the girls will be *on* me."

Jake was suppressing the growing urge to punch Hasad in the face in the name of peace. Peter calmly ordered drinks from the waitress, his hand gently caressing her bare shoulder as she bent over. She crouched down to whisper the order back, giving him a full shot of cleavage. He stared. She smiled. Two professionals, neither aware of the other's skill level. A muscled bouncer teetered on a stool next to the stage, waiting for a patron to reach for an unguarded body part, an attempt to touch the untouchable. Tiny yellow track lights ringed the stage, highlighting the establishment's moneymakers in flashing strobes.

The drinks arrived and Peter continued his flirtation with the waitress who batted her eyes shamelessly. She smiled as she placed a bourbon on the rocks, a shot of tequila, and a bottled beer on the glass tabletop. Peter handed the beer to his son and pushed the shot glass to Hasad.

"Tequila, my favorite," Hasad said picking up his drink with two fingers and offering a toast. "To D.C., and Mr. Winthrop, the greatest tour guide in the city." Hasad threw his head back with vigor and the tequila disappeared down the hatch. Jake sipped his beer while Peter took a polite swallow of his bourbon.

Over the next hour, Hasad downed three more drinks and shoved miscellaneous amounts of cash into the g-strings of each dancer who came on stage to grind with the pole. He booed when a girl came out hiding her good bits with tassels, and Peter had to calm the stage-side bouncer with a slight hand gesture and a crisp bill.

"Mr. Winthrop, my friends and I have recently taken up hunting."

"*Now we get down to business*," Peter whispered to Jake.

Most of his foreign clients were the same. Dinner, drinks, entertainment, and then business. The order varied occasionally, the speed of progression differed by nationality, but a thousand nights on the town with a thousand customers had proven that the elements of the deal were the same. "What kind of hunting?" Jake asked.

"Well, anything we can shoot. Fox, lynx, bear, mountain goat."

"What do you use?"

"Shotguns, rifles, handguns. Most of them are illegal to own in Turkey, of course, but there are ways around that."

"How is that?" Jake asked.

"*Baksheesh*," Hasad answered.

"What?"

Peter interrupted. "*Baksheesh* is a word for bribery originally used in Persia, but its meaning is understood in a lot of locales from Turkey to Eastern Africa."

"Very good. Mr. Winthrop, you are right as usual," Hasad said patronizingly. He was putting on his Middle Eastern charm, and Jake quickly saw through the transparent act.

"So, you have taken up hunting?" Peter asked, pushing the conversation forward.

"Yes, hunting," Hasad answered, his voice trailing. "…And we are thinking about starting a night hunting club."

"Night hunting?" Peter asked, one eyebrow raised.

"Yes, night hunting. The fox and jackal are very sly, very difficult to shoot during the day. They are night creatures."

"Nocturnal," Jake said, cringing at the expression 'night creatures.'

"Yes, that is right. Nocturnal."

The reason for Hasad's visit to the U.S., the driving force behind the evening's festivities, the payoff for Peter Winthrop's patience, were all on the tip of Hasad's tongue.

"We are interested in, uh, hmmm, equipment that will allow us to hunt better in the dark."

"Night vision equipment?"

"Yes, night vision equipment."

Peter turned his attention to the twirling tassels and gyrating hips and took a sip of his drink.

"How many were you looking for?" he asked without looking at Hasad.

"A thousand."

"That is a very large hunting group, Hasad."

"Night hunting is becoming very popular Mr. Winthrop," Hasad answered with a smirk. "Very popular."

"It may take some time. That kind of equipment is hard to obtain."

"Yes, I know. I have been trying to get them for about a year."

"Does it matter where they are made?"

"I want U.S. military issue. Nothing but the best."

"That might be tough. And they won't be cheap."

"How much?"

"I don't know, but if I had to guess I would say at least five thousand dollars apiece. It really depends."

"Okay. Whatever the price."

"And legally, they can't be exported," Peter added for the benefit of his son. "I keep Winthrop Enterprises on the up-and-up."

Jake did the math in his head. A thousand goggles at five grand apiece came to five million dollars. The cash register drawer opened in his mind and he heard "cha-ching." Jake wasn't sure of the legality of the deal being discussed, but he was damn certain it was unethical. There may have been a thousand night hunters, but Jake knew they weren't hunting jackals, foxes, goats or anything else on four legs. The deal was shady at best, and wildly profitable. Five million dollars was a lot of money by any standard Jake could come up with.

Hasad, pig-in-slop happy with the possibility of a successful transaction, bought lap dances for everyone. In a back VIP room, Peter finished his hands-on experience and negotiated with the club owner. The owner refused the first, second, and third offer. But when the number hit the estimated price of a pair of military-grade night vision goggles , he caved. He pulled two willing girls off the stage rotation. Peter returned to the table with the women.

"Jake, could you escort the ladies out? Shawn, my driver, should be out front momentarily."

Hasad and Peter had a short conversation and paid the bill with a stack of money thrown on the table half counted.

Jake walked the ladies through the club, leaving the hormone-driven patrons wondering who he was. He stepped up the stairs from the basement level club, a lady clinging to each arm, and stumbled head first into the path of Kate and her friends who were walking down the sidewalk on their way to the movies. Kate took one look at Jake and the two strippers—the heels, the mesh stockings, one with a push up bra, one without a bra altogether.

"You son of a bitch," was all she said before slapping him. As Kate broke into a run, Hasad and Peter came up the stairs behind him.

"Now it's time for a little fun," Hasad said replacing Jake between the strippers. Jake put his hand on his cheek. Peter Winthrop smiled. Business.

***

Chow Ying boarded the bus from the West Falls Church Metro station heading toward McLean, Virginia. He was dressed in jeans and a dark button-up shirt, as incognito as a six-foot-four Chinese national can be entering the whitest zip code in the country. He got off the bus next to the Riggs Bank at the bustling intersection of Chain Bridge Road and Old Dominion Drive. He took one second to get his bearings and kept moving. McLean was not a town for gawking. He walked four blocks through the center of town, past a sushi restaurant named Tachibana and a small strip of retail stores catering to clients with more money than they could spend. An exotic grocery store with an exotic window display sold everything from rattlesnake meat to jellyfish. Next door, a boutique chocolatier offered chocolate-dipped strawberries made on the premises.

Chow Ying kept his eyes straight ahead and followed the edge of the road until the sidewalk gave way to a small path that led into Dolly Madison Park. Marching forward according to the map in his head, Chow Ying passed an elderly man walking a small dog and a blonde trophy housewife at the end of her evening jog. Chow Ying stopped for a moment on a footbridge spanning a small stream, looked at the water rushing through two large rocks, and continued over the bridge before turning left. He checked the direction of the road over his shoulder as the streetlights came on, the sun now beyond the horizon. He walked casually down the increasingly dark path, heading north, following the sound of the stream as it made its way toward the Potomac, still several miles away.

An hour later, Chow Ying stepped off the path and into the woods. It wasn't his first time off the path, but it was the first time with intention. Looking around, he pulled a small flashlight from his pocket. Power lines hidden in the darkness nearby provided a steady hum to the air. A dog barked in the distance as Chow Ying popped the end of the light into his mouth and held it between his teeth.

He reached into his back pocket and unfolded the map he had printed out from the computer terminal at the MLK Public Library between Chinatown and the old D.C. Civic Center. The printout was a hybrid map from an application a twelve-year-old boy in the library had referred to as Google Maps. The Asian kid with the bright backpack and skateboard had shown Chow Ying a thing or two, just to get the Mountain of Shanghai out of the way for the real computer users. Whatever magic the kid had performed, Chow Ying now had a satellite photo of his target blended together with a roadmap and local geographical features.

Chow Ying's eyes settled on the paper and he flipped the map ninety degrees in the ray of illumination. He checked the streets, the contour lines of the land, and the boundaries of the park. Feeling confident, he twisted the light until it went off. He rested in the dark for a moment, letting his eyes readjust to the night. The streetlights from a cul-de-sac on the hill in the distance, combined with his uncanny sense of direction, told him he was close.

The last mile was uphill and the progress through the pathless woods was slow. Trying to remain silent and move forward on uneven terrain in unknown territory was something for trained military and backwoods hunters. Chow Ying, born and raised on the streets of Beijing, was neither. With each stumble in the darkness he fought the urge to use his light. But he knew there would be nothing more suspicious than a lone beam of light in the woods behind ten million dollar homes.

At the top of the hill, Chow Ying stopped for a rest. He first put his hands on his knees and then succumbed to the urge to take a seat on a large rock protruding from the earth near the crest of the slope. He did his best to remove the twigs and leaves that had hitched a ride on his clothes and in his hair. He swiped at his body, having no idea if he was successful in his attempt to clean himself. He ran his fingers through his ponytail in a final effort to look civilized, to look like anything but a criminal.

Chow Ying checked the printout again and looked at the neighborhood. From the woods he saw the side view of a house with a massive fountain in the middle of the circular driveway and a small fishing pond complete with a tiny pier. It was the same house as in the satellite photo, the same house three doors down from the red circle on his map. Ten miles by subway, a twenty-minute bus ride, a dark hike through the woods, and Chow Ying found himself three houses away from his goal. Not bad for a guy from the city, he thought to himself.

He kept to the back of the property lines as he moved toward his target, his shape melting into the darkness, his feet bouncing slightly on the edge of perfectly manicured lawns. A direct view and bright lights from another neighbor forced him into the woods again and he snapped his way through fallen brush as he walked up another lot. Arriving, he stopped on the backside of a massive fence and ran his hands along the boards, looking up at the top of the eight-foot wooden structure that enclosed the yard.

He looked around at the shapes and shadows in the woods, and jumped once in an attempt to see over the top of the fence. He put his hands on the top of the wood and tugged, testing the structure for strength. Satisfied, he pulled himself up for a better look into the yard. Feet hanging, his frame suspended, Chow Ying peered over the fence. He looked left and right, and without returning his feet to the ground, flung his leg to the top of the fence and flipped his body over. The

Mountain of Shanghai landed with a resounding thud that came with two hundred thirty pounds of muscle hitting the earth according to Newton's magic formula.

The Mountain of Shanghai crouched in the corner of the yard, looking out past a Japanese garden, a gazebo, and a swimming pool with its soft blue water gently circulating on the surface. The large glass windows on the back of the home offered a dollhouse view into the life of the super rich and he felt a pang of envy.

He let the atmosphere of the yard surround him and realized the fence was a blessing in disguise. It eliminated the chance of being spotted by a nosey neighbor, or worse yet, a nosey neighbor with an itchy trigger finger. With the fence and the size of the yard, Chow Ying only had one thing to worry about: the eighteen-thousand-square-foot mansion directly in front of him. He fought the urge to sit, have a smoke, and enjoy the evening.

Standing from his crouch, he moved slowly toward the house for a better look, trying to blend into the night and the large Japanese garden. A light in the house stretched from the kitchen into a family room that had never held a family, the plasma TV on the wall large enough to watch from the pool. A faint light peeked through closed blinds in a window on the second floor.

Chow Ying wiped the sweat from his forehead and swiped at a mosquito buzzing in his ear. When his forward path was cut off by the screened gazebo, he veered left and paused at the small walkway that meandered through the garden. He crouched again, and scanned the house for details. His eyes caught a small open kitchen window, the curtains swaying gently in the breeze. He measured the size of the window with his eyes and quickly decided his large frame wouldn't fit without a crash course in contortion. He considered his options. He was starting to favor plan B: showing up during the day, posing as a delivery man, forcing his way into the house, and overpowering the hired help. Then he could wait for Peter to come home, do him quick and dirty in the foyer, and leave the neighborhood in one of the finest cars Winthrop money had bought.

Chow Ying wanted a little closer look. Just a glance into the house to see the floor layout, to make things easier. He stared at the path leading through the garden to the swimming pool and paused to listen to the chirp of summer crickets. Slowly he put his foot on the path, breathing heavily. He took five consecutive steps on the large white stones, and when he passed a pair of traditional Asian lanterns standing on posts, the garden illuminated and the spotlights attached to the corner of the house came to high-wattage life.

Chow Ying froze for a moment, not sure what had happened, and then dove to his left for cover. He scampered forward on all fours through the rocks to the edge of a small bridge overlooking a pool of carp. He tried to hug the ground, to become invisible.

Inside, Camille was putting the finishing touches on her toenails while watching the broadcast of a Mexican game show. The bright lights on the motion detectors forced Camille from the bed in her maid quarters on the second floor. She shuffled slowly to the window, trying to keep her toes extended upward, and looked out into the backyard through the blinds. Crouched underneath the edge of the bridge, Chow Ying held his breath. Minutes passed and the motion-activated lights finally switched off, casting the yard back into darkness. Chow Ying waited before slowly crawling back to the edge of the path. He had choices. Continue toward the house, go through the small fish pool stocked with carp, or go back the way he came and endure a second trip past the hidden laser eye that had illuminated the yard. It was an easy decision. The next move he made would bring the lights on again. He checked his watch and waited another twenty minutes before making a break for it. Five seconds after breaking into a run, his huge frame was lunging toward the top of the fence.

The second blast of lights sent Camille to the window again, this time with the phone in her hand and her finger on the speed dial for 911. Peter Winthrop had given her strict orders. When in doubt, call the police. Words of wisdom from a man with as many enemies as friends. Peter had built the fence and installed high-tech security for a reason. Camille scanned the yard carefully before putting the phone on the bed.

Just beyond the wall to the Winthrop fortress, Chow Ying writhed in agony. Between whispered curses he bit his forearm to distract himself from the pain emanating from his ankle. He tried to stand and cursed in Chinese. It was going to be a long night.

Chapter 23

Senate committees do not create legislation, but they do influence the law-making process. Their history was the history of the country itself. Sometime between the signing of the Declaration of Independence and the Louisiana Purchase, a group of U.S. Senators in a meeting room in Philadelphia realized they were being asked to craft law on every subject known to man; a rapidly growing list of possibilities in a rapidly growing country. Even the predecessors to the modern politician were apprehensive about spending time on issues that impacted something as impersonal as the general well-being of the country. "Self before voters before country" has long been the unofficial motto of the one hundred elected officials in the Senate and their four hundred thirty-five counterparts in the House. There was no sense in being an elected official if you couldn't give yourself a fighting chance at continuing life as one. And the only way to remain in office was to cater to your constituents. Or at the very least, give the impression you were. A thoughtful, patriotic senator with their eye on the national picture could work themselves right out of a job if they weren't careful. Faced with that possibility, committees were born.

Committees are part investigative, part research, part dog and pony show. They look at the issues, listen to the testimony of so-called experts, create experts where they don't exist, and discuss pending legislation ad nauseam. They have investigative powers, empowered by the executive branch and based on fear and manipulation. Armed with their rendition of the facts, they present their findings to the rest of the Senate for legislative consideration. As faulty as the process is, in two hundred years, no one has come up with anything better.

For a final time, Senator Day read the letter delivered to his office days before by an anonymous Asian figure. He needed the support of three specific senators on one hotly contested topic. He had a plan, and he straightened himself in the mirror before he left his office and walked down the hall. It was time for the marionette show to begin. Senator Day on stage, dancing and twirling under wires that, unbeknownst to the actor, were controlled by C.F. Chang. They were wires Senator Day was trying to cut. But until he knew the seamstress with his child was no longer a threat to his career, he was going to perform like a star in an off-Broadway dance musical. Costume, high kicks, and all.

Senator Grumman's voice was still rattling the crystal glass on his desk, small circular waves rippling across his morning orange juice. Grumman, the self-proclaimed great senator from the even greater state of Mississippi, thumped his Bible as hard as anyone on The Hill. His flock of staunch Republicans, from generations of staunch Republicans, followed the senator with blind faith. He got the votes because he ran with God as his running mate, and there are fewer things more important than that in Oxford or Jackson or Biloxi, and the hundreds of small towns in between.

And Grumman had charm. The kind of personal charm that God-fearing southern preachers had. Southern preachers, charlatans, and the occasional trial lawyer. Grumman was born in the most poverty-stricken county in Mississippi, appropriately named Quitman, a name which most of the male population mistook as a directive when it came to employment. For Senator Grumman, it was a fortunately unfortunate birthplace, and one he touted every chance he got. The fact that he wasn't really *from* Quitman was a tidbit of info Senator Grumman left out of the story. He didn't announce, especially during an election year, that his parents were only in Quitman for a spell to help raise funds and rebuild a church that had been wiped out by a tornado. A convincing politician from poor Quitman County was more appealing to the southern constituents than the truth—a former cotton plantation owner's grandchild. Grumman, graying hair, ever-present red suspenders, and adorner of an ostentatious set of gold cufflinks in the shape of a crucifix with Jesus on them, was a growing figure on the Hill. And he believed that the Good Lord had blessed him with a position to bless himself.

"Senator Grumman," Senator Day said, entering Grumman's office with his hand extended.

"Senator Day. How is the wife?"

"She is fine. Just fine."

"And the soon-to-be-baby?"

"Both are well. Thank you for asking."

"Have a seat, please," Grumman said, slowly finding his. "How can I help you, Senator?"

"I wanted to talk politics for a minute."

"Hell, asking me to talk politics is like asking a fat man to talk about food. Shoot," Grumman said with a heavy Southern drawl, his bushy eyebrows moving as much as his mouth.

"As you know, the Special Committee is due to give its recommendation to the Senate on overseas job flight and an international minimum wage."

"Yes, Senator, I am aware of the upcoming need for a decision."

Senator Day laid his best idea on the table with confidence. "Well as Chairman of the Special Committee, I can propose that the recommendation be made in a variety of formats."

"Yes, Senator Day, as Chairman, that is within your rights. But you know senators don't like venturing too far from the standard mark-up process."

"Yes, of course. Everyone likes the mark-up process. Everyone gets to have their say, common language is agreed upon in a document that is incomprehensible to the average person, and no one can be held accountable for their opinion because one is never individually voiced. Together, we all write up a nice bill-recommendation to the Senate, and there is no ill-will."

"That's just the way things are done."

"Most of the time. But for the Special Committee on Overseas Labor we are going to have a vote. Twelve committee members. Everyone on record."

"Fine with me, Senator. It's only a committee vote. It's only a recommendation. Any proposal we agree to will have to pass the Senate as a whole no matter how the vote goes."

"Yes, Senator Grumman it does. And with that in mind, I would like to discuss your view on the direction of the committee."

"No offense Senator. I know you are the Chair, but Overseas Labor is one of the ugliest topics to rear its head on the Hill this session."

"There are a lot of committees vying for that title," Senator Day answered. Both senators laughed at the inside joke, a joke that would have cost them ten thousand votes apiece if anyone were listening.

"So what about it?"

"I understand, to the best of my knowledge, the committee is leaning toward blocking an international minimum wage system for multinational companies doing business in certain foreign countries. I certainly know how I'm going to vote, and I have a pretty good idea how the rest of the group will fall out."

"A minimum wage is about the only move we have to stop American companies from sending every damn job we have to China and India. We are heading down a slippery slope here in the U.S. We are eliminating jobs Americans need. Good Americans. Let me pose a question, Senator."

"Please."

"What percent of Americans go to college?"

"Nearly twenty-five percent."

"So some seventy-five percent do not have college degrees."

"That's the math."

"This seventy-five percent is the working class. The garbage men, the security guards at the mall, the factory workers."

"Yes, sir. They are."

"There are over three hundred factories in the state of Mississippi, making everything from ladders to furniture to rebuilt diesel engines. Three hundred factories, ten thousand jobs, supporting fifty thousand men, women, and children. That is a lot of mouths to feed, Senator Day."

"Yes sir, it is."

"With that in mind, what did you come here to discuss?"

"A vote in favor of support for overseas labor. A vote against an international minimum wage would be, to put it as plainly as I can, in my best interest."

"Senator, I know you support overseas labor. I know you have manufacturing constituents with overseas interests. But things in the Northeast aren't the same as the concerns of the Deep South. Mississippi is not sitting on Harvard or M.I.T. Mississippi doesn't have a major U.S. city within its borders. It does not have one of the largest ports in the

U.S. It does not have a thriving financial district. Manufacturing is all Mississippi has left. Hell, it's all we ever had. Except for cotton."

Senator Day waited for the initial storm clouds to blow over. On Capitol Hill, waiting was a profession in itself. In a world of talkers, a conversation was never dead.

"You're also on the Education Reform Committee aren't you?" Senator Grumman asked.

"Yes, sir."

"You believe in the 'No Child Left Behind' movement, don't you?"

"Yes, actually I do."

"How about the 'No State Left Behind' movement?"

"I'm sorry?"

"Mississippi ranks forty-seventh in education. We have been asking for additional education funding for years and we haven't received one Indian Head nickel. Did you know there are only six public schools in the whole state of Mississippi where students can access the internet? Six schools."

"I was not aware of that."

"How many schools in Massachusetts have internet-access?"

"I'm not sure of the exact number."

"More than six?"

"Yes, I'm sure it is more than six." Senator Day gave his first offer in the negotiation. "I will see to it that you get approval for the education funds your state is requesting."

"That's good…for starters," Senator Grumman said, looking out the window, hiding his smile. Sensing a fish on the line, the senator from Mississippi set the hook and started reeling. He spilled his tears over state roads, and the need for a larger chunk of federal funds for Mississippi asphalt.

"I'll see what I can do."

"Well then, I guess there is only one thing left."

"What's that, Senator Grumman?"

"What are you going to do for *me*?"

Senator Day read between the thick dark lines. Another check, another payoff. A personal endorsement to the re-elect Senator Grumman fund, available for immediate withdrawal. Senator Grumman pulled out a cigar as Senator Day left his office. Orange juice and a Cuban, the breakfast of champions. He had reason to celebrate. Senator Day had just guaranteed the great senator his re-election.

One vote down, two to go.

The Rupp Building was the oldest office facility still in use by members of the U.S. Senate, standing two doors down from the U.S. Supreme Court with its impressive staircase and soaring Roman columns. The Supreme Court blocked the morning sun, casting an a.m. shadow of righteousness that appropriately stopped at the foot of the Rupp Building and Senator Al Wooten's office on its east side.

Senator Al Wooten, ex-college basketball player and Oxford scholar, was the tallest official in the Senate. He was also on a permanent vacation and wasn't afraid to let everyone outside of his constituents know it. He was in his first term, planned on a second one, and as long as he played it cool, he figured he would set a record for Senate tenure. He had reached the apex of his career. He had no ambition to go further. Why should he? He knew life couldn't get any better, and he was willing to do anything to remain where he was. Six years was a long time between elections. He had four more years of R&R ahead of him. With good health, good luck, and good weather, he would be shooting par at Congressional by the start of his next term.

Senator Wooten was a man of many words, and not afraid to use each and every one of them. The gregarious senator showed up for votes on the Senate floor without fail. He made sure to give his two cents on whatever the issue was, just to be on record, proof to his constituents that he was hard at work. What no one knew was that Senator Wooten pushed the electronic vote button at his assigned seat in the capitol with the randomness of a roulette wheel. Less for the really important issues, the ones that affected him directly, he let lady luck form public policy.

He had developed numerous voting systems, all equally lacking in political acumen. Who cared how he voted? How many constituents actually follow the votes of their senators and congressman on a daily basis?

Exactly.

Senator Wooten's favorite vote-deciding factor was the number of guests in the far section of the visitor's balcony. An even number of visitors earned a "no" vote. An odd number ensured a "yes." The Anti-Deforestation Bill, and millions of century-old hardwoods, had passed by a single vote, thanks to the elderly gentleman with the cane who returned from the bathroom just as the senator was ready to lower his thumb.

The fact that Senator Wooten didn't care how he voted didn't mean he underestimated the value of a vote. Senator Day came to find out how much it would cost for the senator to put down the flip of the coin for the Special Committee on Overseas Labor.

Senator Day walked into Senator Wooten's office and announced himself. "He is waiting for you," Senator Wooten's middle-aged secretary answered, her wire-frame glasses hanging around her neck by a silver chain.

The opening conversation was a rerun of the one he had just had with Senator Grumman. Senator Day forced his way through the niceties with a smile, as if it had been years since anyone had asked him about his life, his wife, or his upcoming child. He explained the vote at the upcoming Senate committee, and Senator Wooten understood.

"So you want me to change my opinion and vote against an international minimum wage," Senator Wooten asked, cutting to the chase after five minutes of heavy hints and innuendo.

"Well Senator, I'm never sure what anyone's opinion really is until I see how they vote, so I can't say whether I'm trying to change yours."

"Senator Day, it wouldn't get me very far if I told you I was ready to go along with a vote in favor of a bill that would lead to more overseas job flight. You're here for a reason. If I tell you I was ready to vote in favor of overseas labor, what would that get me? Votes aren't free, Senator. So for the sake of progressing this conversation to a mutually beneficial conclusion, let's assume I am voting against overseas labor. Let's assume I am in favor of an international minimum wage for U.S. firms doing business overseas. Let's assume I believe legislation is the only thing that will drive jobs back to the U.S."

"Overseas labor is not a popular topic these days. Your assumptions merely confirmed my suspicion on your position."

"No, overseas labor is not a popular drum to beat in the current political environment. But I don't let public opinion interfere with business either. Constituents just aren't privy to all the information that we as senators have at our disposal. I believe I was elected to make educated decisions for my constituents. Whether they realize it or not."

"Thank you for your honesty, Senator."

"You invest in real estate?"

"Dabble a bit."

"You ever heard of Wellfleet Bay?"

Senator Day perked up. "Of course. It's a wildlife sanctuary on Cape Cod. Some of the most pristine land in my home state. A thousand acres of marsh and woodland, surrounded by spotless beaches. When I was a child, my grandfather took me clamming and fishing off the banks of Wellfleet Bay. Who knows, if God blesses me with a healthy son, maybe I can take him there someday."

"Yes, Senator Day. It is beautiful land. Pristine, as you say."

"Do you fish, Senator Wooten?"

"No, I don't even like the taste. But I do like real estate, Senator Day. I do like real estate. They just aren't making any more earth, and the law of supply and demand is being driven by an ever-increasing population and a finite supply of land."

"Never have truer words been spoken."

"Just north of Eastman on the Cape's west coast is a ten acre plot of land I have interest in. Only problem is that the land lies adjacent to a remote corner of the Wellfleet Bay sanctuary. No sense in buying the land if I can't develop it…"

Senator Day cringed as Senator Wooten described the plot of land with surveyor-like detail—information gleaned from online photos. Senator Wooten did love real estate. And he had spent the previous afternoon searching Massachusetts for a prime investment opportunity stalled by politics.

The two politicians drank coffee as Senator Wooten showed that he did indeed know the value of a vote. And if Senator Day could clear an inside tract to ten acres of idyllic real estate, he figured he could make a few million just divvying up the land and re-selling it.

"I'll be watching how you vote," Senator Day said, leaving the office.

"And I will be checking your progress on my land," Senator Wooten responded.

As Senator Day stepped into the afternoon air, the ulcer in his stomach bubbled. The combination of coffee on an empty stomach, and days of heavy liquor on a belly of coffee, burned a hole through the senator's stomach lining like hot grease poured into a plastic cup. He doubled over, eyes watering, and dug in his pocket for some ibuprofen, the finishing touch on the toxic waste in his gut.

One more vote and he could go home and say hi to his wife. Dana had the evening off, and his wife would be asleep by nine. He could drink himself silly in the privacy of his own home.

The last vote came at the hands of Andrew Thomas, senator from Montana, and virtual no name on The Hill. Senator Thomas was the youngest senator by three years, and Senator Day thought he still had enough seniority and slick-Willie, over-the-top charm to impress the new kid on the block. Especially a kid from Montana, home to a population of ten people per square mile.

Senator Day danced and kicked, sang and spun. For thirty minutes he felt up the young senator, fondled his beliefs, trying to manipulate the boy from Montana without giving any ground himself. He had done enough damage for one day. He had already written a check for a vote, an impeachable offense, and agreed to soil his childhood fishing ground with construction run-off and human waste. His charity was running thin.

Senator Thomas put on his innocent face, cherub cheeks fleshy under a mop of brown hair. He smiled the same smile that had won him the election and waited for Senator Day to run out of hot air.

"I'll give you the vote," Senator Thomas said flatly.

"That is a good decision, son," Senator Day responded with visible relief. The senior senator stood and stuck out his hand for a deal-sealing shake.

As Andrew Thomas rose from his seat to stick out his hand, he stopped. "And in return I'm just going to slip you right into my pocket. I'm going to save you for a rainy day, Senator Day. And when the day comes and I say 'jump,' I fully expect your answer to be 'how high?'"

Senator Day flinched and then nodded silently as Senator Thomas withdrew his hand without a shake. The boy knew his way around the political minefield. Senator Day took note to keep an eye on this kid. Someday, he might need a young man with his politically savvy, self-promotion, and survival techniques.

Senator Day left the office, promising to make good on his promise, and thinking about DiMarco. He was waiting for the word that the job had been done. Then life would be back to normal. Back to his wife, his new child, his undeniable political right to act like a senator without any distraction or repercussions.

Chapter 24

The line to the entrance of the Spy Museum snaked down Eighth Street toward Chinatown and the Verizon Center. Chow Ying stood near the front of the triple-wide crowd sucking the sweet coating off the Advil pills in his mouth before swallowing the remains. The Mountain of Shanghai, his foot bandaged and throbbing, mixed with the tourists, rubbing shoulders with a smattering of intelligence buffs and ex-spook types waiting for a chance to admire the best display human ingenuity had to offer.

It was his third day off from surveillance. Hobbling on one leg was no way to try to kill a man. He had no idea if his ankle was broken or not, and he wasn't going to the doctor to find out. Ice, compression, and elevation were the self-prescribed treatment for the dark blue bruises on the oversized appendage. As soon as he could get his foot back in his shoe, he would be back in business.

Besides, Peter Winthrop had proven to be a hard target. He didn't come to the office with the same strict regularity as the rest of the building. Chow Ying had come to recognize dozens of faces coming and going, but in a week of stakeouts he had seen Peter get out of his black sedan-for-hire, enter the building, and move quickly into the lobby exactly one time. He had waited until midnight for him to exit the building, but the man he had met in Saipan over a month ago never showed his face. There were reasons. There was a private parking garage under the building and another exit facing the street around the corner. It was a lot of ground for one person to cover. It was impossible on one leg.

But Chow Ying had notched one hit under his belt in just over a week in the capital. And it had been a thing of beauty. No gun, no knife. No piano wire around the neck, no pillow over the face. And no suspicion. There was nothing on the news about a killer loose on the street, and there was nothing in the paper beyond a brief mention of an accident and the normal obituary. He now needed a plan to get both father and son, and when they joined their secretary underground, he could work on executing his long-term survival strategy.

He still carried the gun Mr. Wu had given him in New York in the back of his pants, his shirt pulled over it. But as a tool of an assassin, the gun had its drawbacks. He had never test fired the .38 caliber weapon, and with a loose pistol grip he couldn't be sure of its accuracy. He had wondered why Mr. Wu hadn't at least provided a new gun, perhaps one with a silencer, but deep down he knew the answer. Mr. Wu didn't expect Chow Ying to live that long. When C.F. Chang sends you on a mission to the U.S. and threatens to take your passport, contributing to a retirement account is a waste of good money.

As easy as it sounded, walking up behind Peter Winthrop and his son, if he could get them together, and blowing their brains out on the K Street sidewalk, would bring an immediate and intense police response. He knew from experience that you could stab someone on a crowded street and keep walking before anyone noticed. It was done everyday in prison by inmates with shivs. But fire a gun and mayhem would follow. Guns are noisy, and a prominent businessman murdered in the midst of gunfire on the sidewalk would draw attention. Without a major distraction to give him a chance for escape, opening fire on a public street was his last option.

Chow Ying stood behind the crowd control barrier on the sidewalk and thought about other concerns. Men are more difficult to kill. They fight more, cause a bigger scene, take longer to die. He didn't take any particular pleasure in killing women, but he had to admit they were easier to hunt, easier to kill. Taking out two men, one of who could identify him on sight, was going to be difficult. If he killed just one, the other would be suspicious. Two deaths in the same office over the span of a week would have everyone jumpy. Including the D.C. Police. Chow Ying needed to get them together. He was working through several scenarios in his head, all of them ending with a dash to the airport for the next plane out. With ten thousand in cash, he had enough money to run. Not far or long, but enough to get a head start.

The Spy Museum was a field day. He laid his fifteen bucks on the counter, got his ticket, and entered the new museum as giddy as a school-boy. He breezed by the cryptology section and the biographies and busts of the most infamous names in the history of espionage. Agents, double agents, and triple agents. Heroes and traitors. He absorbed every word of the Israeli, Chinese, and Russian espionage sections. When Chow Ying entered the room named "Assassins and Tools of the Trade," he slowed to a snail's pace. He didn't want to miss a thing.

Chapter 25

Kate curled up on the canopy bed and took turns outlining the flowers on the wallpaper with her finger and staring out the window of her old bedroom in the Sorrentino mansion. It had been four days since Jake had walked out of a known topless joint with a stripper in each arm. For Kate, the image was still as fresh as the wound. But love, passion, and the loss of both made four days seem like four months. Her cell phone now rang every hour on the hour, down from the fifteen-minute intervals Jake called at the first day after his untimely exit. She kept the black Motorola within reach, and at one o'clock she checked the incoming call number on the small display screen. Jake had stopped leaving messages when her voice-mail became full, but he knew she was checking the phone display. All he needed was one chance to explain himself, to lay on a little charm. He had the truth on his side. He had apologized to the answering machine for acts not done, for causing images of dastardly deeds. In his heart, Jake didn't believe he was wrong, but he knew if he wanted to see Kate again, he would at least have to admit that he wasn't entirely right. It was a compromise, the key to relationships. Or so he heard. More flowers, chocolate, and a little poetry were all on deck as backup.

Kate was planning to mope around for a week and participate in a little shopping therapy with her mother on her father's credit. Staying at her parents's didn't affect her daily routine—riding ambulances out of the McLean Gardens station as an EMT four days a week, studying her medical books over coffee in the morning just to keep sharp. Three months was a long time for the soon-to-be-fourth-year medical student to retain the name and disposition of every muscle, bone, tendon, symptom, and illness she had memorized over the last three years. Her drive was remarkable, given the need not to have one at all. Riding ambulances, reviewing old medical books, and hanging out with Jake had been her plan for the summer. There was just something about him that she liked. It was everything.

James "Jimmy" Sorrentino was in the business of breaking impasses. The go-between, mediator, arbiter, and problem-solver. Real estate, construction, and waste removal were still his bread and butter, measurable businesses that kept him legitimate. They certainly looked better on the tax forms to the IRS than "self-employed problem-solver."

Jimmy Sorrentino had been around the block and had the mental and physical scars to prove it. But like Sampson and Superman, he did have a weakness. And for the tough guy from Providence, Rhode Island, the chink in his armor came in the form of a five-foot-five beautiful brunette named Katherine Elizabeth, his only child, and more importantly, his only daughter. Seventy hours ago Kate had once again taken up residence at the Sorrentino house, spending most of the day moping and shedding the occasional tear. Neither of these bothered Jimmy. But the combination of mother and daughter was like a flame and an open gas valve. His daughter's presence emboldened his wife, turning her from upper-crust housewife into professional nag. He couldn't reach for a drink, or smoke his thirty-dollar cigars without someone telling him that he was killing himself.

Mr. Sorrentino gave Kate until the weekend to straighten herself out. She was twenty-six, not a teenager, and he had bought her a condo two years ago in the name of peace and quiet. He would be damned if Kate was going to live at his house again, energizing his wife to run her nails down his psychological chalkboard, *and* pay thirty-five hundred dollars a month for a condo to boot.

It wasn't the money, it was the principle. A man of principle up against two women.

With his daughter and wife at the kitchen table, Jimmy Sorrentino gave them the rules for living under his roof.

"Kate, you have until the weekend to mope around this house. Then you are going back to your apartment."

"Don't listen to him honey, you are welcome to stay as long as you like," Mrs. Sorrentino added with daggers in her eyes.

"Ignore your mother. This is my house and these are my rules. You come down with an illness, you can stay. You are in an accident, you can stay. You let me sell your condo in the city, you can move back in. But I will be goddamned if I paid a half a million dollars for a condo so you can sit around my house, tag-teaming me."

"This is your flesh and blood here," Mrs. Sorrentino said. "Don't listen to him, sweetie. He's full of hot air."

"Cynthia, don't test me," Jimmy Sorrentino said to his wife with authority.

"Blowhard," his wife responded over her shoulder.

Cynthia Sorrentino grabbed her keys off the kitchen counter and turned toward Kate. "Let's go shopping, sweetheart. Let him calm down a bit."

Jimmy Sorrentino had the last word. "Kate, I told you that kid was no good. Just because he's Catholic doesn't mean he's Italian."

James Sorrentino continued talking to himself and cursing for five minutes after the ladies left. He felt better. A man has to posture once in a while. Beat the chest. Show them he was still the boss.

God, he hoped his daughter would get out of the house soon.

***

Vincent DiMarco had blown the first professional hit of his life and lived to tell about it. It had been a decade and a half since he stepped off the plane in Miami with nothing but a name, an address, and an order. It would have taken ten minutes to confirm the address, to make sure he was whacking the right guy, but it was ten minutes he didn't feel like wasting. The hit went down within an hour of his plane touching down, and DiMarco was back in Boston before dinner, treating himself to lobster tail.

The hit was easy and as an extra bonus, he was able to follow an old DiMarco credo that stated the better you were, the closer you could get to your victim. A young Vincent DiMarco had done just that. He had walked across the back yard to the dark-haired Italian man tending to his garden and had used the cord from the clothesline to finish the job. His wife of forty years found him three hours later, discolored, dangling, and dead.

The following morning Vincent grabbed a *Miami Herald* newspaper from a newsstand on the corner of Harvard Square that carried every major paper in the country. Paper under his arm, he headed for a diner down the street, away from the rich kids. He sipped his black coffee and flipped to the metro news section to read the details of his handiwork with pride. The death of a mistaken, innocent man didn't haunt him as persistently as those who hired him for the failed hit did. On Mother's Day in 1995, the payback came as he sat down to have dinner with his mom at a posh restaurant in Back Bay. The blood had spurted from his neck with enough force to cover two walls, the ceiling, and his mother. When he arrived at the hospital, he had lost sixty percent of his blood. But he lived, and he had learned a valuable lesson. A little patience and a little planning could make life simple.

Vincent DiMarco blended in with the Saipan locals like a white accountant in a rural Louisiana soul-food restaurant. What his harsh Boston accent didn't give away, his natural brash attitude did. Things were slow on Saipan, and the ruffian-for-hire was anything but. With beach attire, the scar on his neck was less noticeable than the tattoo on his left arm. The skin art had been a spur of the moment impulse, a Christmas day decision that would last the rest of his life. In a dingy tattoo parlor, he had narrowed down the selection to two choices—a detailed picture of St. Nick, or a ghoulish rendition of the Grim Reaper. The sickle that now crowned the top of his arm, just above the red hat with a white ball hanging on the end, showed he wasn't above compromise.

The son of an Italian father and South African mother, DiMarco traveled extensively before he could walk. Since his fifth birthday, when his Dad had taken him to see the family in the old country, he hadn't set foot outside of the continental United States. Until his meeting with the senator, he had never heard of Saipan. Three days after arriving on the sunny island, he found himself not wanting to leave.

He kept a low profile, eating at the cheap restaurants with tourist crowds and high customer turnover. He tried to avoid going to the same place more than once, but the pretty waitress at the Limbo, a dive with character and the largest shrimp he had ever seen, changed all that.

Unlike his Chinese counterpart on the other side of the world, DiMarco didn't have a face to go with his mark. He didn't have the benefit of a close-up encounter with the people he was coming to kill. No picture, no useful description.

When the cobwebs of jetlag finally cleared his mind, he drove down to the front of Chang Industries and played the lost tourist routine for all it was worth. A beach hat, sunglasses, a crazy Hawaiian shirt, and an unfolded map hid the scars, the tattoos, the camera, and the knives. He drove past Chang Industries twice in an unsuccessful attempt to circle the property and realized the map that came with the rental car was worthless. The single road leading to Chang Industries, and the guard booth at the gate, meant Vincent DiMarco was going to need an alternate entrance.

Still in tourist disguise, he pulled into the gravel parking lot of Saipan's official visitor's center and studied their wall of pamphlets and tourist attraction discounts. Whale watching and deep-sea fishing excursions. Go-cart racing. Scuba schools. He grabbed a newly published map of the island and smuggled out as many brochures as he could hold, the one-man staff too busy discussing local news and gossip on the phone to offer assistance. DiMarco pushed the door open with his butt and walked out of the wood-shingled building with enough material to teach a college course on the island. He spent the afternoon on the bed in his dingy hotel room, sucking down Marlboros and checking out the maps and brochures through the smoke until his head hurt from reading.

He couldn't help but think he should have charged more money for the job. The senator had failed to mention that the targets were locked away behind a fence with razor wire, with at least one guard covering the only entrance. He needed a back way into Chang Industries. The two hundred fifty thousand dollars that was sitting in a safe in an old car garage in Southie bolstered his patience, a virtue he had learned to appreciate. It was as critical to survival as never sitting with your back to the door, not even when you're having lunch with your own mother.

Chapter 26

The cleaning crew bantered back and forth in Spanish with a thick El Salvadorian accent. It was after eleven and on the top floor of the building that housed Winthrop Enterprises, Jake was the only native English speaker. A handful of lawyers burned the midnight oil on the floors below—writing their briefs, imposing their legal opinions on paper. It was good work if you could get it—forming legal policy, protecting the rights of the wrongly accused, or the wrongs of the rightly protected, and charging five hundred dollars an hour.

With far less focus on the legal ramifications of what he was doing, Jake stuck the pointy end of the letter opener in the keyhole of Marilyn's old desk. With one quick turn of the wrist, the drawer popped open, and Jake joined the ranks of petty thieves. With a vacuum humming in the background, Jake fumbled through Marilyn's old desk, pushing the new receptionist's personal minefield of cosmetics out of the way until he found the janitor-size key ring. He grabbed the keys and sent the bell attached to the silver ring singing its familiar ding, ding, ding. Two members of the cleaning crew looked up. The younger female in cleaning overalls continued to stare at Jake while wiping the glass wall between the work area and the breakroom.

Jake grabbed the wad of metal, a mix of stainless steel and brass that opened everything from the bathroom to Peter's personal liquor cabinet. He weaved his way through the office, over yellow extension cords and past cleaning carts, and stopped near the emergency staircase. He fumbled through his newly found source of power and jammed a key with a small label reading "files" into the lock. He entered the room, flicked the lights, and shut the door behind him.

The room was a massive cave of information, the walls lined with rows of shelves and stacks of boxes. With real estate leasing for a thousand dollars a square foot, the on-site filing room was costing a mint. Sparkling filing cabinets stood near the closest wall, and Jake started shoving keys into the locks as fast as he could. Each key was marked with a word or initials, clues to an indecipherable code that Marilyn took with her to her grave. He tried the key labeled "f.c." guessing it was "filing cabinets," but got nowhere. He tried his trusty letter opener again, but the drawers didn't budge. He dug through boxes and came up for air forty minutes later with a handful of legitimate looking invoices. "Shit," he said to himself.

He emerged from the filing cabinets ten before midnight and went to his office to see if Kate had broken down, forgiven him, and called. As he flipped through the key ring, checking his voicemail with the phone wedged between his ear and his shoulder, the newly printed key label with the initials "J.O." caught his attention. *J.O.*, Jake said to himself. *Jake's office*. He got up, walked across his ridiculously large office, and put the key in his door. The lock opened with a smooth click.

Jake sat down, put his right leg on the desk, and donned his decryption hat. He shifted through the set of keys reading labels aloud.

"F.D…" "Front door," Jake muttered, taking a shot in the dark.

"L.B…" "Ladies bathroom," Jake whispered.

"W.O.T…" "Waste of time", he chuckled.

"P.O…" "Peter's office," Jake said, catching himself.

"Peter's office," he said again, his feet already in motion.

At the entrance to his father's office he glanced at the remnants of the cleaning crew, turned his attention to the knob, and unlocked the door with as much I-have-every-right-to-do-this demeanor as he could.

He turned the small banker's light on his father's desk, and the green-stained-glass shade cast a pleasant hue into the room, the reflection from the bulb shining off the brass stem of the lamp. Jake opened the main drawer of his father's desk without a key. He yanked the other drawers in order, none of which were locked. Jake didn't take his father to be paranoid, and the open drawers were evidence that he was right. Paranoia and over-the-top confidence didn't go well together.

Jake didn't know what he was looking for, but knew he would recognize it when he saw it. He walked around his father's office like a thief casing a job—eyeing the walls, the photos, the shelves. Jake opened the towering custom-made cabinet on the far wall, beyond the leather sofa and table, near the private restroom. A stash of top-shelf alcohol used to replenish the bar on the far side of the room filled the upper cabinet. At the bottom of the bookcase was a smaller cabinet door. Jake took one look at the keyhole in the door, an octagonal shaped ring lock, and started sifting through the key ring in his hand. With another set of dings, Jake tried the only key on the ring that could possibly open the lock, and gave it a twist.

The key opened the door to intrigue and heartbreak. The front half of the drawer was business, the back half lined with folders of information labeled as personal. He flipped through both sets of files, three dozen in all, and stopped at the file named Chang Industries. There was information on Lee Chang, his father, his brothers. Schools attended. Positions held. Birthdays, favorite foods, vices of choice. Golf handicaps. Names of wives, kids, lovers.

Jake ran his finger along the top of the folders and his head spun when he read the tag labeled "Jake Patrick."

"What the hell?" he said to himself, as he opened the file and read his dossier.

***

The security guard's fluttering eyelids touched intermittently, flirting with sleep. The sound of the floor buffers were just loud enough to ward off a full onslaught of REM. Reina, the Spanish queen, wiped the last window on the revolving door with a final sweep of her hand. She stepped back to admire her handiwork and jumped at the face staring back at her through the window. She quickly moved aside and Peter Winthrop walked in the front door.

"Good evening Mr. Winthrop," the security guard said, trying to snap out of his daze. "Late evening tonight, sir?"

"Yes, I just flew in from Rio. Been back and forth three times in two weeks."

"I've always wanted to go to Rio. Big celebrations in the street with beautiful girls in little bikinis."

"You know, some of them even wear clothes," Peter said, busting the security guard's chops.

"I believe your son is working late, too. I didn't see him leave yet. Nice kid, likes to talk."

"He's still here, you say?"

"Haven't seen him leave."

"Not sure that means too much," Peter responded, stabbing at the guard's propensity to nap. The security guard looked nervous.

"Thanks," Peter said, ending his goodwill break at the security guard's counter.

"Goodnight, Mr. Winthrop."

***

Reina hightailed it to the bank of elevators as soon as she realized Peter Winthrop was the face on the other side of her just-cleaned window. She stopped at the passenger elevators and pushed the buttons to send them to the top floor. Then she boarded the service elevator and headed up.

Reina, cousin to Peter Winthrop's domestic help, flew out of the service elevator on the top floor as the CEO pressed the button for the passenger elevator from the first-floor lobby. He waited for a minute before cursing the cleaning crew. He turned toward the guard, now fully awake, and yelled. "How many times do I have to tell you to keep the cleaning crew in the service elevator?"

"Yes, Mr. Winthrop, I will remind them. It isn't like they forget. They just ignore the rules."

On the top floor, Reina stretched her short gait and jogged to the office on the far side of the floor. She knocked, grabbed the knob to Peter Winthrop's office, and pushed the door open. Jake jumped, and his pulse skyrocketed.

"Jake, your father just arrived in the building. He's on his way up. I thought you should know."

Jake looked up, completely confused, and calmly thanked the cleaning woman whom he had never spoken to. Then tried not to wet himself.

He grabbed two folders of interest, threw the rest back into the filing cabinet, gave the scene a one second look-over, and ran back to the safety of his office.

***

Jake held his head down at his desk, the haphazard spread of papers and folders under his nose evidence of someone hard at work. Peter finished cursing halfway through the ride up and calmed as he entered his domain. He headed straight for Jake's corner office.

"You're here late."

"Hey," Jake answered. "How was the trip to South America?"

"Good. Looks like I may be able to work out a deal with a Brazilian chemical company to import some Japanese cosmetics. Should be painless and profitable."

Jake put on airs of naivety. It was easy. His father barely took the time to get to know anyone but himself, unless there was money in it.

"The Japanese and Brazilians?"

"Sure. Brazil has the largest Japanese immigrant community in the world. They have close ties."

"I didn't know that," Jake said treading water while trying to avoid the riptide he had created. "On the topic of world trade, I have been working with the International Group on getting the night vision goggles for Hasad. I had a few questions that I didn't feel comfortable asking them and wanted to ask you directly."

"Sure," Peter said, finding the corner of the desk with his butt.

"Isn't the exportation of night vision goggles illegal?"

"Didn't you hear me tell Hasad that Winthrop Enterprises wouldn't be involved in illegal exporting?"

"Come on, Dad. I mean, Hasad lives in Turkey, everyone knows that is where they were going."

"Son, I make it a habit not to acknowledge that I know where they are going. I'm simply buying them and selling them to an interested third party. What they do with them is their decision."

Peter didn't bother enlightening his son on the best way around export control—transportation on military cargo planes paid for by Uncle Sam himself.

"Couldn't that be trouble?"

"Okay. Let's say these night vision goggles do go to Turkey. Then what? Let's say Hasad uses them to hunt Kurds along the border with

Iraq. Jake, these guys have been killing each other for thousands of years, and short of a nuclear war, they will be killing each other for a thousand more. The goggles will not change that."

"But it is illegal. You could go to jail."

"First and foremost, I don't export illegal goods. But hypothetically speaking, if I did, let's look at the risks. There are one hundred sixty federal agents assigned to the entire U.S. in the Bureau's Office of Export Controls. Do you have any idea how many companies export goods in a given year? Thousands. Do you know how many more people have exporting licenses? Thousands more. If these federal agents investigate ten percent of all suspicious exports, they are having a banner year."

"It's still the government. They are still federal agents."

"Son. One hundred sixty agents. That tells you the government is not serious about it."

A long pause followed.

"Do you know how much money the Bureau of Export Controls levied in fines last year?"

"No idea, but I am guessing you know."

"Thousands of companies exporting hundreds of thousands of goods... and the amount of all federal fines levied totaled $1.4 million. Peanuts. Son, I could afford to pay that with cash laying around in my money market. That is $1.4 million for the entire country. All illegal export fines. For one year. If someone wanted to export illegal goods, the cost of doing business is low."

"The cost of doing business?"

"Like the tobacco industry. They pay hundreds of millions in tobacco-related class-action lawsuit settlements. But they make billions. Subtract a few hundred million from a few billion and you still end up with one big number, son. The cost of doing business."

"How about going to jail?"

"Jail? Wouldn't happen. You know how many people these one hundred sixty export control agents put behind bars last year? One, Jake. One. One poor guy in Florida who was stupid enough to try and export shoulder-fired missiles. And they wouldn't have caught this guy if he hadn't initially applied for a license to export them and been denied. Then they were watching him. He was stupid and careless, and that is why he was caught. Your odds of hitting the nightly pick-three lottery drawing are better than getting arrested by the federal agents of the Office of Export Controls."

"The cost of doing business," Jake imitated.

"A payoff-risk analysis," Peter answered.

"How can you be so confident, Dad?"

"Because I have been buying and selling everything from air conditioners to underwear for over twenty-five years."

"What about the FBI?"

"The FBI? The FBI couldn't catch a cold in a Siberian hospital. The FBI only gets involved with the Office of Export Controls in cases of Terrorism and Espionage. And since 9/11, this country is overwhelmingly concerned with what is coming in to this country, not in what is leaving it."

"So you cover your bases…"

"Jake, let me walk you through the deal with Hasad. It'll be a good hands-on experience. I will show you the ropes myself."

"Sure, Dad. First thing tomorrow."

"Can't do it tomorrow, son. I have a golf tournament. The day after tomorrow."

"Deal," Jake said, not sure if his Dad was playing the same game he was, or if his father knew his son was playing at all.

"Any chance I can borrow a car?" Jake asked, pushing the envelope. "I need to put mine in the shop for a few days."

"You feeling responsible?"

"Always," Jake answered. What he didn't want to be called was irresponsible by a man who was the definition of the word. He deserved more than that. Eighteen months of dragging his mother to the hospital. A year of making every meal, doing all the cleaning, all the shopping. Six months of carrying his mother to the bathtub, bathing her, giving her medication. Responsibility was something he understood more deeply than his father ever would.

"Stop by the house and Camille will have the keys to the Porsche ready."

"Your new car?" Jake asked, feeling a fleeting twinge of guilt. "Dad I can't."

"Sure you can, Jake. Just remember it has about three hundred fifty more horsepower than your Subaru."

"Okay. I'll be careful."

"Atta boy."

As Jake walked out, his father smiled. He could control anyone, but his son was easy. His son was just like him. As the elevator doors began to shut and Jake turned to press the button, the unmistakable sound of a particular bell attached to a particular key ring still in Jake's pocket let out a "ding." For a split second that lasted entirely too long, Jake's eyes met his father's.

Chapter 27

Camille answered the door with a smile, and Jake fell back into immediate infatuation. There was just something about his father's domestic help. A spiritual connection that transcended current circumstances. Before Jake could ask, Camille reached into the pocket of her blue apron and produced the keys to the one hundred thirty-one thousand dollar automobile.

"I believe you have come for these?"

"Thank you," Jake said as Camille placed the keys in his hand. "How have you been?"

"I'm good, Jake. How about you? How's work with your father?"

"Work with my father?" Jake asked pensively. "Something tells me you already know the answer to that question."

"I don't know what you mean, Jake."

"In that case, I guess there is no reason to tell Reina thank you."

"Like I said, Jake, I don't know what you're referring to," Camille repeated.

Both knew the conversation Jake wanted to have wasn't going to take place. He smiled. Camille smiled. And with a silent understanding, Jake stepped off the porch. "I'll open the garage door for you," Camille said, as Jake walked down the stone path in front of the house.

Jake sat in the car, still safely parked in the garage. He rubbed his hand across the top arc of the wheel, depressed the clutch, and ran through the gears of his father's candy-apple-red Porsche 911 Turbo convertible. He turned the key in the ignition with a mix of excitement and trepidation, and the four hundred forty-four horsepower engine came to life. Jake felt the vibrations rumbling through the seat and immediately understood German automotive engineering. With wheels still frozen to the pavement, one thing was already clear—the beast was built for business.

He eased the car into reverse and down the driveway. The large ceramic brakes were powerful, and the sudden grip of the brake pads on the rotor pushed his skull into the headrest at the end of the driveway. Definitely not the Subaru, he thought. Jake chugged out of his father's neighborhood in first gear, the engine purring, begging for more.

Jake toured the winding roads near Georgetown Pike and cruised the quiet streets of Great Falls that were a dime a dozen among the woods that overlooked the Potomac on the Virginia side. At the entrance ramp to the GW Parkway, Jake needlessly checked the blind spot over his left shoulder, and punched it. The difference between a decade-old, four-banger station wagon with all wheel drive and a German sports car was measured by Jake's white-knuckled grip on the wheel. He hit fifty before shifting out of second and passed eighty-five with the turbo kicking in. A hundred and ten was fast enough to scare him for the day, and he settled into the traffic at an uninspiring seventy mph in a car that cost more money than he had made thus far in his life. He turned the radio up, looked for someone to impress, and kept pace with the lower forms of automotive life.

He zipped across the Key Bridge against the evening rush hour traffic, thousands of cars straining to ooze out of the city on every available road. He made one trip down M Street and turned a few heads at a safe, almost-stalling speed of twenty-five. Just another young entrepreneur, lawyer, or son of a diplomat showing his worth. He turned toward home. One stop and then it was off to see Kate. Enough was enough. He missed her. He needed to tell her the truth. What better way to make a lasting impression than in a Porsche, he thought. It should have been the car company's advertising slogan.

Jake turned left just beyond the fire station and drove by the sparsely populated parking lot on the far side of the three-story brick structure. Kate's Lexus was there, next to the lone picnic table where they had had lunch weeks before. Jake was tired of calling, tired of leaving messages, tired of thinking that he had lost his girlfriend because of an annoying Turk named Hasad and his ambition with two strippers. Kate may not have wanted to see him, but he was giving her no choice.

A block from one of the main traffic arteries, the fire station stood in relative isolation. A string of small shops lined the street across from the station, next to a library that had been slated for destruction in favor of a more modern, more audacious building to store books. Jake paused at the stop sign, took a last look around for other cars or pedestrians, and hit the accelerator. The car lunged forward and picked up speed until the thirty-six hundred pounds of moving metal was halted by the laws of physics.

The eight-man fire-and-rescue team inside the station sat down for dinner for the third time. A two-alarm house fire had interrupted their first attempt at a hot meal. An octogenarian with a system full of Viagra and a twenty-three-year-old wife kept them away from their plates for a second time, as normal dinner hours for the rest of the world flew by.

The unique sound of crunching, twisting metal is rarely heard by fire and rescue personnel. They deal with the aftermath—the bloody faces, the missing limbs, the unidentifiable remains in an unidentifiable car. The accident scenes they knew were filled with screams of hysteria and cries of pain.

With the crash in their front yard, the firehouse sprang into action. There was no need for anyone to call 911. No need for a dispatcher to give them the address. The accident had come to them. As the professional men and women of the life support and rescue team prepared for work, the question on everyone's mind was whether or not to get in the truck. The fifteen-foot doors to the station opened and the rescue team poured out across the driveway to the concrete utility pole. The candy-apple-red Porsche was still a Porsche, but its status as a legal street racer was going to depend on a very good mechanic.

Kate's supervisor, the resident expert on accident extraction, reached the driver's side first. He surveyed the damage to the inside of the car and calculated the possible injuries and potential exit strategies. The steering wheel rested within inches of the victim's chest. The deflated remains of the car's airbag hung like an unrolled condom in the space between. Another airbag dangled from the ceiling above the door. Hidden beneath the encroaching dashboard, the condition of the victim's legs was unknown. He flashed his ever-ready penlight into the eyes of the victim and gauged his alertness. The victim looked back with lids wide open.

Orders filled the air. Crow bar, neck brace, stretcher. The twenty-five-foot rescue squad vehicle finally rolled from its parking bay and stopped at the end of the station's driveway, setting a record for the fastest response time in regional rescue history. The head of rescue looked at the victim and scratched his head. The accident was a two on a ten scale. He had pulled far more endangered victims out of far more mangled pieces of metal.

Kate was on autopilot. After more than a hundred accident scenes, the car half-enclosed around the concrete pole at the end of the drive was nothing more than scenery. Irrelevant background information. Kate, her basic rescue kit in hand, headed around the rear of the car. She approached the driver's side door, looked in and spewed words her mother didn't know were in her daughter's vernacular.

She didn't bother with the latex gloves—she had exchanged more bodily fluid with the man behind the wheel than she cared to admit. The victim's pupils were normal, his pulse was strong. The extraction team peeled the driver's door back like the top on a tuna can. They removed the victim and placed him on the stretcher. Kate moved over Jake and checked for injuries. She unbuttoned his oxford shirt like she had so many times in the past months, passion now substituted with professionalism. She opened the shirt and cursed again. The head of rescue looked over at the victim.

"What the hell is that?"

"It's a note."

Across his Jake's chest, in dark indelible ink, were the words "I am innocent. Let me explain."

"Kate, you want to tell me what this is about?"

"Do I have to? It seems pretty obvious to me."

Jake smiled.

"You're an asshole," Kate said quietly.

"Sometimes it takes an insane act by a sane person to prove a point."

Kate tried not to laugh, but a smile formed on her face. Her words were being thrown back at her in the most ridiculous of circumstances.

"You can let me off the stretcher. I'm fine," Jake said as he was rolled toward the ambulance.

"Sorry, Jake. You're going to the hospital whether you like it or not. And I wouldn't be surprised if they keep you for psychiatric observation."

"How's the car?"

"I take it that was your father's?"

"Yes. My first time in a Porsche. The power got away from me."

"Don't bullshit me, Jake."

"That's my story and I'm sticking to it. Is it drivable?"

"No," Kate answered looking at the wreck. "How pissed is he going to be?"

"He'll get over it."

***

Peter went straight from the bar in the clubhouse to the hospital. Jake was in the recovery room, the healthiest patient in the D.C. metro area. He had endured the cursory exam, a standard chest and neck x-ray, and a stern consultation from a young District-licensed psychiatrist who determined Jake to be as mentally sound as anyone he met in his line of work. In fact, his last patient of the day was in better mental health than most of his stressed-out medical colleagues.

Jake flipped through the outdated *Sports Illustrated* magazine for the fourth time, having already burned through three issues of *Reader's Digest*. Peter met the nurse at the recovery room door, her station a single white table with a chair on wheels.

Dressed in his favorite golfing shorts and shirt, accentuated with a healthy tan, Peter performed his first fatherly duty in twenty years. "My name is Peter Winthrop. I am here to pick up my son, Jake Patrick."

The nurse didn't get out of her seat. "Last bed on the right, next to the window."

Peter walked past the curtains that divided the eight-bed room and stuck his head around the corner.

"Jake?"

"Dad."

"How are you, son?"

"I'm fine. Caught a little airbag in the face, but nothing's hurt except my pride."

"And the car?"

"It may need a little work," Jake said, putting on his best look of shame.

"You know, I was on a six-month waiting list for that car," Peter said, switching concerns.

Jake didn't know if his father knew about the note on his chest, and he wasn't about to volunteer that small detail. He kept up the charade as he got out of bed, and stood. "Dad, I'm sorry about the car. You were right. It was a little more power than I was ready for. I should have been more careful."

"I'm disappointed, son."

Peter was disappointed, and not just because he would be without his favorite toy for a while. He was disappointed for another reason. In the midst of the standard hospital formaldehyde scent, he smelled bullshit. The same bullshit he was famous for shoveling. This time it was coming from his son.

He hoped he was wrong.

Chapter 28

The old apartment was an orchestra of creaks and squeaks, groans and moans. The steps, the banister, the doors, the windows, all kept rhythm. The pipes to the sink, shower, and toilet hit all the high notes in various pitch. When the infamous D.C. summer thunderstorms blew in during the late afternoon and early evening, the whole building rattled and rolled. Jake had been there a month, and had yet to sleep uninterrupted until morning. Even when Kate wasn't there and he didn't have an excuse for being up half the night. There were hundreds of haunted jaunts in D.C., a winding trail of supernatural leftovers through the city, and Jake accepted that his building should have been an official tour stop.

Sex usually put him to sleep the moment his head hit the pillow, but between the thunderstorm raging outside and the noise from his apartment inside, he was wide awake. Post-sex dry mouth led him to the refrigerator where he quickly changed focus from thirst to hunger and choked down two pieces of cold pizza while standing barefoot in the kitchen in his underwear. He washed the pepperoni slice down with milk, straight from the carton, as usual. By the time Jake returned to the bedroom, Kate had taken the pole position on visiting Mr. Sandman. The remote control sat on his pillow, a considerate gesture from someone who was too busy studying how to save lives to watch TV.

Jake turned on the late news, the last edition of headlines for the day in a town with a neverending supply of new ones. Local news focused on the planned development of the Anacostia River front, a filthy stretch of land on the banks of water so polluted, one could do a Jesus impersonation on the cans and dead bodies floating on the surface. The second news story was even worse, and Jake cringed as he listened to the report on the re-entry of an infamous former D.C. mayor into the political fray—a man who once went to jail after being caught smoking crack on an FBI sting video. Framed by a hooker, the former mayor had won his second term, after serving his prison sentence, with the election slogan of "The Bitch Set Me Up."

And D.C. wondered why it had problems.

The local news broadcast switched over to Rock Johnson, exposé reporter extraordinaire, on camera in front of the Senate Hart Building. He was flanked by a small but vocal crowd, screaming improvised chants and pumping homemade signs into the air. When Senator Day's face flashed onto the corner of the screen, Jake inched up the volume. Kate, slipping toward sleep, moved closer to him, her head now resting on the edge of his thigh. Jake stroked her hair and turned the volume up one more notch.

The news clip started with glorious views of the surroundings—palm trees swaying in the breeze, seagulls floating in a cloudless sky. It wasn't until ten seconds into the report that Jake sat up at attention and adjusted the volume yet higher. Standing against a wall, just off-center from Senator Day, was one Peter Winthrop—tall, broad, and smiling like the politician he was with. The camera moved around to another view of the building, followed by excerpts of video taken during a quick tour of the inside and the facilities. Jake was mesmerized. Lee Chang, the face from the file Jake had stolen from his father's office, was shown shaking hands with Senator Day and good ol' Dad. Next to Lee Chang, crystal clear, was another Asian man whom Jake immediately recognized. Jake's pulse jumped and his mouth went dry again, this time from panic. The eyes, the ponytail, the sheer size of the man.

Jake almost choked on the desert in his throat. "Holy shit, holy shit, holy shit," he rasped.

"Nice language, Jake," Kate murmured through closed eyes.

"Sorry," Jake said, followed by a much cleaner "Dear God."

"What is it?" Kate asked, picking up her head and staring at her panicking boyfriend.

"You don't want to know."

"What is it?" Kate asked again. "You're freaking me out."

"Kate, I think I may be in real trouble."

***

The break-room in the First District was the oldest room in a building of old rooms. Brownish tiles that were once white ran four feet up the wall. The original plaster walls bulged and cracked, a relief map without a designated region. The sink in the corner dripped water steadily, and the a/c unit in the window screeched when it ran. If you wanted to have a conversation in the break-room during the summer, lip-reading skills didn't hurt.

Detective Wallace and Detective Nguyen sat around the wooden table in the middle of the room. Wallace, the big-bellied detective with an infectious laugh, smoked a cigarette, tipping his ashes into the small ashtray that rested on a tabletop with so many scratches it looked like it had been caught in a cat stampede. Detective Nguyen, bored by an incredibly slow week, drank a bottle of water, a rare break from the coffee that kept him alive during the graveyard shift.

"A quick game of five card?" Detective Wallace asked, blowing a cloud of used nicotine, tobacco, and tar across the room in the smoke-free building.

"What are we playing for?" Nguyen asked.

"A gentleman's bet. Gambling on the premises is against policy. You know that," Detective Wallace answered, taking another drag from his menthol to conceal his laughter.

"Right, no betting unless the captain is at the table."

"You young guys catch on quick."

The senior detective slid the deck toward Nguyen who shuffled the cards without protesting. Detective Wallace flipped the channel to the news and tuned in to the local stories. He picked up his hand of cards, looked at the two aces and pair of jacks, and wished he had money in the pot. He glanced back at the TV at the end of the next news story and for a brief second, he stopped breathing. Detective Nguyen watched the cigarette droop from Earl Wallace's mouth, and he wrenched his neck around to see a picture of Rock Johnson in front of the Hart Senate Building.

"Forget the game and grab your keys," Detective Wallace said, throwing his two pair on the table.

Detective Nguyen looked at the cards, and then back up at the TV.

"Taking me on a date Sergeant?"

"Yes, and you're driving. Meet me in front of the building. I'll be down in a minute. I gotta make a phone call."

***

The D.C. affiliate for the ABC network, WJLA-TV, is housed in the old *USA Today* building in Rosslyn. The twin glass towers stand on the Virginia side of the Potomac River and are regular recipients of unintended near misses with airplanes landing at Reagan National Airport. Restricted flight patterns over the capital city make the approach at Reagan National one of the trickiest in the nation, and the *USA Today* buildings are the highlight of the pilot's dexterity test. Planes bank left and right as they follow the Potomac, the flight path a slalom course a stone's throw from CIA headquarters, the White House, and the Pentagon. Passengers with window seats were known to get close enough to read the computer screen on the reporters' desks.

Earl Wallace and Detective Nguyen showed their badges to the security guard and walked to the TV studio and broadcast production facilities on the second floor of the building. A middle-aged production manager in jeans introduced herself as Crystal and showed the detectives to the newly appointed "news technology room." Crystal, a redhead with curly locks down to her shoulders, introduced a young, wire-thin intern wearing an old Metallica t-shirt that looked like it was held together by nothing short of magic.

"This is T.J.," Crystal said. "He can help you with whatever you need. If you would excuse me detectives, I have to go. News is coming across the wire on a potential terrorist incident in Kuala Lumpur. It looks like I'll be up all night."

"Thank you," Detective Wallace said to the departing woman's back. He turned toward T.J., who was happy to be helping with official police business.

"What do you have for us?" Detective Wallace asked.

"This is the story you asked to see," T.J. said, holding the tape in his left hand as if to impress his guests, before shoving it into the machine. "What part are you interested in?"

"The final picture. The one with the senator and a group of people in front of some building."

T.J. forwarded the tape and pressed stop.

"Go back a couple of frames. Can you do that?"

"This bad boy can define a standard video tape to fifty frames per second. It can also make a perfect digital copy of a two-hour movie in fifteen seconds. It is the best piece of machinery I have had the privilege to work with."

"So can you show me what I need to see?"

"Sure." T.J. pushed a button, dragged a small handle to the left and smiled. "There you go."

"Perfect."

Detective Nguyen took one look at the screen and realized the reason behind Detective Wallace's desire for the sudden date.

"Take a look at that guy. Does he look familiar?" Wallace asked with a serious look on his face. He knew the question was rhetorical.

"The big Asian guy from the Fleet Bank ATM."

"Yeah."

"Who are the other guys?" Wallace asked. T.J. picked up a note that came with the tape and its untimely, premature circulation. He scanned the handwritten note, words scribbled horribly across the paper at an angle.

"From what I can decipher from this note, this is the rundown. The guy on the left is Senator Day's aide. The man next to the senator is a businessman by the name of Peter Winthrop. The man on the other side of the senator is a man named Lee Chang. He is the owner of the manufacturing facility in Saipan where the piece was filmed. Next to him on the far side is one of Lee Chang's assistants. The 'big Asian guy,' as you referred to him. No name given."

"How much did you guys pay for this tape?"

"None that I know of, but I'm a just a techie intern. They don't let me have control of the checkbook, if you know what I mean. I work here for the cool toys and late hours."

Detective Wallace let it go. "Can you zoom-in on the face of the big guy and print a picture of it?"

"Sure."

"Can we get a copy of the tape?"

"I already made you one. I didn't figure you were coming over to spend your evening with me."

"Could you also print a picture of the screen with the entire group—the senator, the businessman, the aides, everyone?"

"Consider it done," T.J. answered. His fingers jumped to life and moved around the million-dollar equipment like a star player from the video game generation.

"What are you thinking?" Detective Nguyen asked.

"I'm not exactly sure yet, but I do have an idea."

The detectives thanked the gracious intern and left the building past the now-empty security booth.

"Where to, boss?" asked Detective Nguyen, behind the wheel.

"Taco Bell and then back to the station."

***

Earl Wallace pulled out the original file for Marilyn Ford and put it on his desk. Detective Nguyen watched the wheels of his mentor's mind chug through the evidence.

"Humor me for a minute?" Detective Wallace asked without taking his eyes off the file.

"Shoot."

"Ask me questions about the dead lady and see where it takes us."

"With pleasure. What's her name?"

"Marilyn Ford."

"Age?"

"Forty-six."

"Marital Status?"

"Single. Never married."

"Address?"

Earl Wallace looked down and read the answer.

"Phone number?"

Once again he read the number off the information sheet.

"Occupation?"

"Secretary."

"Place of employment?"

Detective Wallace looked down again at the sheet of paper. "Winthrop Enterprises."

The two detectives locked eyes.

"What was the name of the American businessman in the news clip?

Detective Nguyen checked his notes. "Peter Winthrop."

Momentary silence fell on the two as the evidence clicked. "Winthrop Enterprises," they said in unison.

"I'll be damned," Wallace added. He looked at the clock on the wall. "You better get home and get a few hours of sleep. Tomorrow we start knocking on doors. Early."

Chapter 29

The doctor used both hands to roll Wei Ling's small frame and lost the first knuckle of his middle finger in the rotting flesh of a festering bedsore. Wei Ling's scream could be heard on the sweatshop floor over the machinery and the cursing foreman. Upstairs, the blood-curdling wail pierced Lee Chang and he knocked a small plate of orange slices off his lap onto his morning paper. The prolonged agony ringing in the air propelled Lee Chang downstairs to the infirmary. He needed to check on his most-prized possession.

"How is she?" Lee Chang asked, out of breath, meeting the doctor in the main room of the infirmary.

"We need to move her," the doctor said plainly, digging through his black bag of medicinal goodies on the desk.

"Why. Is she ill?"

"No. But she has been restricted for a long time."

"You said she could be fed through the nose tube," Lee Chang said hastily.

"She can. But you aren't trying to keep *her* alive. It's the child your father wants."

"I told you to give her enough food through the tubes to feed both. It can't be that difficult."

"Her appetite is not my concern. Even if we stop feeding her through the tube, her hunger strike is not likely to kill the baby...without killing her. But there are other concerns. The feeding tube is causing breathing difficulties and irritation. The body's natural reaction to having a tube where one isn't needed. Wei Ling also has bed sores. Serious ones."

"Bedsores?" Lee Chang asked.

"Bedsores. Rotting flesh. They can form in less than a week of immobility, and Wei Ling has been tied up longer than that."

"Are they dangerous?"

"Not as dangerous as pneumonia which can take root in half that time, with the right conditions, in the right environment," the doctor said, thinking aloud. "But, yes, bedsores can be dangerous."

"I've never heard of them."

"They usually afflict patients in comas and victims of paralysis, but even a broken leg on an elderly person can prove immobilizing enough to develop them."

"What's the treatment?"

"With all the modern medicine and medical techniques available, flipping the immobilized patient twice an hour, twenty-four hours a day, is still the best prevention. Wei Ling has been on her backside for ten days, give or take. I added antibiotics to the IV drip, but there is no guarantee the infected sores won't get worse. If this happens and she starts to run a fever, we could have trouble. Pregnancy is a fragile thing. Even when there are no signs of complications, it can be precarious for both mother and child. But we are talking about a woman who can't move about freely, who is refusing to eat, and who is being fed through a tube. This puts stress on both the mother and the fetus. While self-forced starvation alone is not likely to cause a miscarriage, her body could reject the fetus in an act of self-preservation under a combination of circumstances. The body works in mysterious ways."

"Doctor, you were hired by my family to keep her alive."

"Yes, and I can keep her alive, but not here. Not under these conditions. Not in a storage closet. I need to move her back to Beijing. Put her in a hospital where we can keep her well and provide around-the-clock care. Your father can arrange it."

"I will call and discuss it with my father."

"Please. Time is of the essence."

Lee Chang walked across the infirmary and peaked in the storage room. Wei Ling looked over at the partially open door. "Let me out of here, you bastard," she said in a surprisingly strong voice.

***

Lee Chang wasn't sending Wei Ling to Beijing or anywhere else for that matter. She was his guarantee back to a real life. If he sent her back to China, he would be sending back his leverage, and with it, all hope that his father would find it in his heart to bring him back into a position of power within the family. He needed Wei Ling. He needed the senator's baby. The doctor wasn't going to take her away.

Lee Chang spent the morning trying to find a medical bed on the island that allowed the patient to be rotated like a pig on a spit. The hospital in Garapan had two such beds. Both were occupied and they weren't for sale. The nearest medical supply company, in Guam, could have one delivered in a week. Lee Chang thanked the medical supplier with surliness, ordered the three thousand dollar bed, and looked for other options in the meantime. He stared out the back of his apartment at the warehouses and piles of discarded fabric spools. *Maybe I could make a bed*, he thought. As Lee Chang considered an infirmary improvement project, the doctor downstairs drained the pus from Wei Ling's bedsores.

***

Lee Chang called his father and ran through the week's impressive numbers. Output had never been higher. It was amazing what a workforce under lockdown and pulsating with fear could do. Lee polished over the deterioration of Wei Ling's condition and ignored the medical opinion of the old doctor his father had sent to keep her alive. According to Lee Chang, all was well.

C.F. Chang finished the conversation as he had every call since finding out about the pregnancy—"keep that girl healthy"—and then hung up.

Lee Chang put down the receiver and bounded down the stairs.

The doctor was sliding into his white rental van when Lee Chang approached.

"I spoke with my father."

"What did he say?"

"He agreed with me. For now, moving the girl to Beijing is too risky. Besides, it will take time to arrange for her to stay at a hospital without raising suspicion."

"I understand," the doctor said, fully aware of the lie. C.F. Chang, the family laoban, could arrange for the girl to stay at a hospital with a wave of his hand. The doctor knew to be careful around Lee Chang. Slyness and mental instability were a dangerous combination.

The doctor stuck to his schedule until his evening visit to Chang Industries. When Wei Ling's blood pressure started to rise unexpectedly, the doctor knew it was time to act. From the phone in the infirmary, the doctor called C.F. Chang directly, speaking in a whisper.

"We need to move the girl back to Beijing."

"Why? What's the problem?"

"I thought your son explained it to you," the doctor asked, expectant of the answer that was forthcoming.

"No, he didn't."

"I was under the impression that he had," the doctor reiterated intentionally so there was no mistake.

"Tell me why you want to move the girl."

The doctor ran through Wei Ling's condition and the risks, the dangers associated with infection being at the top of the list. The discussion on the fragility of a fetus made C.F. Chang uneasy. He understood the doctor's request perfectly.

"I will arrange things with the hospital and with immigration at the Beijing airport. It shouldn't take more than a day or two. Feel free to sedate her for the trip. Do whatever it takes, doctor. If you need to take measures that will only guarantee the long-term survival of the baby, I fully understand. I want to see this child playing with my own grandchildren one day."

***

Earl Wallace thrashed on top of the sheets until his wife hit him with her pillow and told him to either quit his epileptic flip-flopping or follow the well-worn path to the sofa. He tried to lie still for another hour, stood, and slipped on his pants.

The answers to the questions in his head could wait until morning. Detective Wallace couldn't.

***

Wallace rang the doorbell three times before a light came on in the rectory. There was shuffling on the other side of the door, the usual routine of the drowsy awoken in the dead of night. Any time someone answered the door on the first ring in the middle of the night, sirens went off in Wallace's head. With the exception of strippers, call girls, drug dealers, and pimps—and of course detectives—the rest of the world slept at night. His mother always told him that nothing good happened between midnight and six. After twenty-two years on the force, he knew his mother was right.

Father McKenna opened the door, exposing his bare toes through the end of his leather slippers. He looked surprisingly dapper in an Irish-supporting green bathrobe with gold trim. "May I help you?"

"Good evening. I am sorry to disturb you at such a late hour."

"I believe it is more early than late," Father McKenna answered, neither perturbed nor trying to be funny.

"I guess you're right, my apologies. My name is Detective Earl Wallace with the First District."

"Good morning, Detective. Father Thomas McKenna. Please come in."

"Thank you."

Detective Wallace followed the Padre to the small living area in the rectory. The leather sofa was worn, a place where life, death, marriage, and baptism were discussed daily. Father McKenna turned on a small standing lamp near a statue of St. Joseph, and fumbled through the kitchen drawers just beyond the living area.

Detective Wallace walked around the quiet rectory and stopped to read a framed document on the wall titled "Desiderata."

Go placidly amid the noise and haste, and remember what peace there may be in silence.

As far as possible without surrender be on good terms with all persons. Speak your truth quietly and clearly; and listen to others, even the dull and ignorant; they too have their story.

Avoid loud and aggressive persons, they are vexations to

the spirit. If you compare yourself with others, you may become vain and bitter; for always there will be greater and lesser persons than yourself. Enjoy your achievements as well as your plans.

Keep interested in your career, however humble; it is a real possession in the changing fortunes of time. Exercise caution in your business affairs; for the world is full of trickery. But let this not blind you to what virtue there is; many persons strive for high ideals; and everywhere life is full of heroism.

Be yourself. Especially, do not feign affection. Neither be cynical about love; for in the face of all aridity and disenchantment it is as perennial as the grass.

Take kindly the counsel of the years, gracefully surrendering the things of youth. Nurture strength of spirit to shield you in sudden misfortune. But do not distress yourself with imaginings. Many fears are born of fatigue and loneliness. Beyond a wholesome discipline, be gentle with yourself.

You are a child of the universe, no less than the trees and the stars; you have a right to be here. And whether or not it is clear to you, no doubt the universe is unfolding as it should.

Therefore be at peace with God, whatever you conceive Him to be, and whatever your labors and aspirations, in the noisy confusion of life keep peace with your soul.

With all its sham, drudgery and broken dreams, it is still a beautiful world.

Be cheerful.

Strive to be happy.

The words were hypnotic and therapeutic. Detective Wallace finished reading and started at the beginning again before Father McKenna interrupted the most religious experience the detective had had since a child had fallen, before his very eyes, four floors from an apartment balcony, bounced once, and landed unharmed.

"How do you take it?"

"I'm sorry?" Wallace said, his trance broken.

"How do you take your coffee, detective?"

"Black is fine, Father."

Father McKenna joined the detective in the living area, balancing two cups of coffee that were filled to the brim.

"That is a very inspiring piece," Detective Wallace said, nodding to the framed document on the wall.

"Yes, it is."

"Where is it from? I don't recognize it."

"There's a lot of mystery behind it. It gained notoriety under the misconception that it was penned by a saint in the eighteen hundreds. In fact, it was written much later, by a common layman. Common except for the skill to be able to write something that people put on their walls. Something that people fold up and put in their wallets."

"It is inspirational," Wallace said, stressing the middle word.

"Yes it is." Father McKenna stirred his coffee and set the cup down. "How can I help you, detective?"

"I had some questions about a possible parishioner. Do you know a Marilyn Ford?"

Father McKenna paused for a split second. "Yes, I knew her. She was not a regular, if you will, but I knew her."

"Do you know all of your parishioners who aren't regulars?"

"No, not all. We have a few lapsed Catholics who are on their forth or fifth relapses. I don't know them all, but I did know Marilyn. I understand she passed away last week. Very tragic."

"Yes, very tragic. Did you perform a ceremony for her?"

"No. I believe her brother flew her body back to Wisconsin rather hastily."

"What do you know about the circumstances surrounding her death?"

"Just what I have heard."

"Which is?"

"That she had an accident in a Metro station involving the escalator."

"That's it?"

"That is all. Yes."

"Well, Father, we have reason to believe that you may be able to help us determine if she was a victim of foul play. On the morning of the sixteenth, I received a call from this rectory inquiring about the official filing status and the cause of death in the case of Marilyn Ford."

"And you suspect me?"

"God no, Father," Wallace said before catching himself. "I mean, no Father. But maybe one of your parishioners's guilty conscience got to them. Maybe they came in for confession, cleansed their souls, and then made a call from a phone here on the premises."

"Detective, the confessional is not a place to start an investigation. I wouldn't tell you anything, even if I could. Those are acts of contrition between man and God."

Wallace saw the dead-end sign in his mind and slammed on the brakes. "I understand, Father. Could I ask if you saw or heard anything suspicious last Monday morning? Any strangers around the church? Anything at all?"

"Not that I recall. But the days here blend into one another more easily than the defined lives of the masses. Services in the morning, visits to the ill during the day. Dinner and evening prayers. Sunday is really the only day where I have what most people would call a 'normal routine.'"

Detective Wallace opened the envelope in his left hand and pulled out the photo of Chow Ying from the surveillance tape. "Father, have you ever seen this man in church?"

Father McKenna adjusted the glasses resting on the bridge of his nose. He took a long look at the photo. "No detective. I think I would remember him."

Both men picked up their coffee cups. Father McKenna sipped the steaming coffee off the surface of his cup with puckered lips. Detective Wallace, with years of hot-coffee-induced asbestos on his tongue and throat, gulped down half the cup.

"Could I see the phone or phones with this number?" Detective

Wallace asked, showing the priest a page from the small detective note tablet that was an extension of his right arm and constant breast-pocket companion.

"That is the number for the public phone in the back of the church."

"Could I see it?"

"I can show it to you on the way out, if you like."

"Trying to get rid of me, Father?"

"No detective, not at all. But it is early. Is there something else I can do for you?"

"Would it be possible to get a list of current parishioners?"

"Absolutely," Father McKenna said standing and keeping his bathrobe closed with his left hand. "If you wait here, it should only take a minute or two."

"Sure Father," Wallace answered, starting to re-read the well-crafted verse on the wall.

Father McKenna came back with a simple stack of stapled white paper. Fifteen hundred names, listed alphabetically.

"Here you are, detective."

"Thank you, Father. And if you would show me the phone, I will get out of your hair."

Father McKenna led Wallace through the back halls of the rectory, past the altar, and down the aisle.

"The phone is just beyond the bathroom, in the room on the right. You can let yourself out the front door when you are done. The door is always open," said Father McKenna, pointing down the hall.

"I will. Thanks, Father," Detective Wallace said, producing a business card and handing it to the head of the church. "If you think of anything that may be useful, please give me a call."

"Of course, detective. Good luck with getting the answers you are looking for."

***

Nguyen walked up behind Wallace as the older detective dozed in his seat, his neck swaying back and forth like a flagpole in alternating winds. Nguyen tapped him on the shoulder and Wallace shook violently in his chair, his hand catching the corner of the desk, narrowly avoiding an incident that would have resulted in a daylong ribbing from colleagues.

"Nice recovery," Nguyen said with disappointment. "Been in long, Sarge?"

"Couldn't sleep. Got up early and went to speak with the priest at St. Michael's this morning. He doesn't know anything."

"Are you sure?"

"Yeah, he's a priest. The call came from the public phone in the back of the church. It's accessible to anyone. It's down a little hall in the back of the church in one of those play rooms for kids. One of those soundproof rooms where parents can take their crying kids so they don't disturb the service."

"You don't think the call was from someone who just happened to be walking by?"

"Not likely. I mean, would you look at a church and think 'Hey, this is a good place to make a call?'"

"Not unless I was a parishioner and knew the phone was there."

"Right."

"So you think it was a parishioner who made the call?"

"Probably."

"How many in the congregation?"

"According to the list the priest gave me, there are officially over fifteen hundred on the registry. Probably another thousand not on the list who come irregularly and could know about the phone."

"That is a lot of pavement to pound."

"Yes it is, Detective. And before going down that street, I was thinking about checking Marilyn's former company."

"I'm driving, I assume?" Nguyen asked.

"Until further notice."

"Yes, sir."

Chapter 30

Al's legs dangled over the edge of the Potomac's retaining wall, the water rushing by five feet below, a dangerous current lurking beneath the surface. Jake stepped under the bridge into the now familiar respite from the heat. The smell of urine was strong. Empty wine bottles with screw-off lids littered the embankment near Al's neighbor's designated area. Jake scrunched his nose as he walked by, two bare feet protruding from a worn dark purple blanket.

"Jake, my friend. I knew you would be stopping by today," Al said before his visitor got too close.

Jake looked in the same direction that Al stared, the Kennedy Center and the Whitehurst Freeway dominating the skyline, the morning sun bouncing off the water in the distance. Eight-man sculling teams raced down the edge of Roosevelt Island, oars cutting through the water in perfect unison.

"Oh, yeah? Why's that, Al?"

"Your problem hit the front page. Go grab those papers from the chair in the living room, if you don't mind," Al asked still staring off into the distance.

Jake tried to force a smile as he walked up the sloped dirt. *The living room...*

Jake dropped the papers on the concrete wall next to Al, flopped his butt down, and hung his feet over the edge, shoes still on. Al shuffled through the first paper on the top of the stack.

Jake reached into his backpack and pulled out a bag. "I brought you lunch, if you want it. An eight-inch sub with everything... an apple, a banana, and some milk."

"Sounds very nutritious. You'll make a great mom someday."

"If you don't want it, just say so. I'll eat it myself."

Al reached for the bag and put it on the other side of his body. "I'll make sure it goes to someone who can use it."

"That's what I thought," Jake said.

Al flipped through pages like a speed-reader on cocaine. Jake noticed the variety of the day's newspapers. The stack was thick. Everything from the *Wall Street Journal* to *Barron's* to the *Financial Times*. Al peeled off page after page and handed them to Jake.

"Take a look at the articles on the pages I dog-eared. Tell me what you see."

Jake opened the first page, started to fidget, and moved to the next paper. The same photo, taken a few frames later than the first.

Jake looked at Al. "I know all about the photo. The story ran on the news last night."

Al gave Jake a serious look, his mouth closed, his eyes focused. "This isn't what I would classify as a positive development."

Jake looked at the picture of his father and Senator Day, shaking hands with Lee Chang. All three men were identified in the photo caption.

"I'm not sure exactly, but there is something you need to know. You can't really see this clearly, but on TV they had a closer picture. That's the big Asian guy I think I saw the night Marilyn was killed."

"Are you sure it was him?"

"Not one hundred percent, but sure enough that if I see him again I'm going to be running in the opposite direction before I start asking questions."

Al fell into a deep silence, all of the life, the craziness, gone from his personality. He was somewhere else, and Jake waited for him to return.

"Senator Day," Al said with open disdain.

"What about him?"

"It's not good, Jake."

"I had dinner with Senator Day a month ago. He was harmless. Arrogant and full of hot air, but harmless."

"You had dinner with Senator Day? The senator from Massachusetts?"

"Yes. It was my first day working at my father's office. I guess he was trying to impress me."

"I'm sorry to hear that, Jake."

"What, that my father was trying to impress me?"

"No, that you had dinner with the senator. Just as I was beginning to like you, I find out you've been sharing your table with vermin."

"What are you getting at?"

"I'll tell you about the harmless Senator Day," Al hissed, pausing slightly before continuing. "The plane that killed my wife and son, Egyptian Air Flight 990, took off from New York at 1:20 a.m. on October 31, 1999. The plane flew for thirty-one minutes and vanished from radar sixty miles south of Nantucket Island, off the coast of Massachusetts. As usual, there was a large-scale investigation headed up by the NTSB, the FAA…the usual suspects. Lack of physical evidence made determining the cause of the crash difficult. The debris of the 747 was scattered across some fifty square miles of ocean. Two hundred and seventeen lives reduced to pieces of foam, plastic, and seat cushions bobbing on the water," Al said, fading out, his voice cracking.

"Of course, given my former employer, I was able to lean on a few people and get a little more information than the general public could get. There were complications with the investigation. The little black boxes were eventually retrieved via a robotic arm on an unmanned minisub. Contrary to popular belief, information from the data recorders can be hit-or-miss, and in some cases the black boxes are worthless. In the crash of Egyptian Flight 990, the data was too good. All evidence pointed to a plane that was mechanically sound. There was no history of failed hydraulics or engine problems, and a recent scheduled maintenance showed a perfectly fit aircraft.

"The crux of the crash was the voice recordings from the cockpit, and it wasn't until these were studied that real problems began. Two minutes of tape from some crazy-ass, co-pilot-in-training quoting the Koran and rambling on about Allah. There were all kinds of procedural inconsistencies, starting with the pilot leaving the co-pilot behind the controls in the first hour of flight. When the plane started dipping erratically, the pilot fought his way back to the cockpit and tried to regain control of the aircraft, battling the structural limitations of the airplane and the physics of an aircraft in a steep dive. All the evidence needed for the investigation was there, on the tape, in words."

Jake looked at Al as he continued to tell the story, tears rolling down his cheeks, his voice quivering.

"Well the Egyptians start screaming foul, claiming the cockpit recordings were inconclusive and that by portraying the Egyptian Air pilots as kamikaze, suicidal maniacs, it would damage the mainstay of their economy—tourism. Given the political nature of the claims, a special Senate inquiry team was formed to gather additional, impartial information from a clusterfuck of agencies and individuals. The FBI Anti-Terrorist Task Force, the FAA, NTSB, the Airlines Pilot associations, Boeing, Airbus. Anyone and everyone who knew anything about aircraft, or the two million parts that go into one, was paraded through the Capitol in front of the Senate inquiry."

"I think I see where this is heading."

"I guess you can. The inquiry team was headed by one 'harmless' senator from Massachusetts. The plane had crashed in his backyard, and with that individual piece of luck, Senator Day was nominated as the Senate point man for the investigation. The whole affair was anything but a picnic. Surviving family members were going toe-to-toe with the airplane manufacturers, the airlines, and the Egyptian government. Senator Day, avoiding decision and repercussions that could come from making the wrong one, simply drowned the proceedings with testimony, knowing the longer he could stall the proceeding, the less public interest there would be. Twenty months later, with the Egyptian government still protesting loudly, the official initial finding of the NTSB was thrown out in favor of a much more politically-correct finding of 'inconclusive.' I'm sure Senator Day got honorary Egyptian citizenship and a free lifetime pass to the Pyramids."

"I'm sorry, Al."

"Yeah. Everyone is sorry," Al responded with half the volume in his voice. "You know, I was able to pull a few strings and listen to an unedited version of the cockpit recording. The man plunged the plane into the ocean, pure and simple. And Senator Day sold out the Americans onboard that flight to appease the Egyptians."

"Did you ever meet him?"

"Senator Day? No, never met him face-to-face. He was too much of a coward."

Jake tried to say something else, but the words failed him, inaudible breaths escaping his mouth.

Al wiped his cheeks and both men watched the water rush by. "If

Senator Day is involved with this girl and your father, then you are in very deep indeed. He's a powerful man, even among senators who are generally power heavyweights."

"What are you thinking?"

"I hope you're wrong about the guy in the photo."

"Why? What does this have to do with me? This guy in the picture doesn't know me from Adam. This news story is in every major paper between here and Boston, but it was filmed over a month ago. Six weeks ago I was burying my mother and I hadn't seen my father in six years."

Al had already done the math in his head. "Don't bet on your anonymity. It's a small world." He leaned back and rested on his hands, his double-jointed elbows fully extended.

"Did Marilyn ever mention the senator?"

"No." Jake thought about the question. "Why?"

"Those newspapers articles represent a second explanation for the current situation," Al said, trying to draw Jake toward his own conclusion. "Your father, Marilyn, the senator, the Asian guy…a pregnant girl."

"I don't follow you."

"Two American men in Saipan, one pregnant girl," Al hinted.

Jake choked up. "The girl is pregnant with the senator's child," he said, the air rushing from his lungs in a moment of self-enlightenment. His face felt flush, his head light.

"Congratulations, you are smarter than you look after all."

Jake took a trip into the same pensive darkness Al had just visited. "I should've figured it out as soon as I saw the fax," he said. "That was around the same time we went out for dinner with the senator. I should have known."

"It's water under the bridge now, Jake," Al said gesturing to the bridge above and the water below. Jake didn't laugh. Al ran his fingers through his reddish brown hair, and threw his head back with a sigh. "Besides, I don't think it matters."

"What do you mean?"

"When did you get that fax from Wei Ling?"

"Ten days ago."

Al took a deep breath. "She is probably dead already."

"Dead?"

"If she isn't dead, she is locked away somewhere beyond your reach.

Beyond the reach of American law, the power of righteousness, civil liberties, all that good stuff."

"So what are you telling me?"

"I'm telling you it may be too late."

"Too late to help the girl, or too late to find out what is going on between the senator, my father, the girl, and this guy in the picture?"

"Jake, I'm going to spell it out for you very clearly. Be careful. For the next couple of days, be careful. If I were you, I would stay away from your girlfriend. Keep your head down for a while. Vary your routine. And you may want to tell your father what you know. He could be in danger."

"My father is out of town until the end of the week."

"Well, eventually he is coming back and unless you want to bury both your parents in one summer, you might want to warn him. Assuming he doesn't already know."

"Al, you're officially scaring the shit out of me."

"Good."

"Good for whom?"

"Fear is a good emotion. It creates alertness."

"I'm going to have to disagree with you. Fear sucks, Al."

"It can be good…" Al said thinking. "Who knows, today might turn out to be one of the best days of your life."

"Not unless we get a quick turnaround. The day is young and it's going downhill fast."

"You're missing the point. Some people wait their whole lives for a day like today. A day where they learn they have the chance to be an honest-to-goodness, balls-to-the-wall, hero."

Jake shook his head. "Maybe this hero is going to slip into his apartment, grab his sleeping bag, and join you right here at the Potomac View Retreat."

"My door is always open."

***

Jake left and Al dug through a plastic bag he kept on the shelf in the rafters under the bridge. He pulled out an old pair of running shoes, the treads almost completely bare in the path his foot followed as it hit the ground on the heel and rolled forward.

He slipped on the shoes with their bright yellow reflective trim and reached down to tie the laces. With the grace and lightness of a ballerina, Al propelled himself down the shore of the river. He passed the Jefferson Memorial at a six-mile-a-minute pace, and kicked it up a notch when he headed over the Fourteenth Street Bridge.

It was redemption time. It was time to join the world of the living.

Chapter 31

Detective Wallace walked into the lobby of the swanky office building on K Street with Detective Nguyen in tow. The pit stop at the security booth by the detectives in worn slacks and dated sports coats was a formality. Rent-a-cops weren't prone to giving the police a hard time. Sooner or later they would need their help dealing with real crime—a pickpocket on the premises, vandals breaking a window, workers stealing office equipment. The rent-a-cops were there to look like the police from a distance, and to call the real boys-in-blue when the situation got out of control.

"We're looking for Winthrop Enterprises," Wallace said, flashing his badge and looking for professional courtesy.

The black guard, a man in his early twenties with long whiskers on his chin, smiled and pointed toward the elevator, looking down his arm and past his finger like the barrel on a rifle. "Take the elevator to the top floor."

Detectives Wallace and Nguyen were the only people in the elevator without a shine on their shoes and a briefcase in hand. The presence of the detectives kept the morning elevator banter to a minimum. Lawyers can smell outsiders from a hundred yards in high winds, much less in the confines of an elevator. Three floors and eight departed lawyers later, the police's recently-formed detective tandem had the elevator to themselves on the ride to the top floor.

The detectives stepped into Peter Winthrop's kingdom and the receptionist gave her standard greeting. "Welcome to Winthrop Enterprises. How can I help you?"

Two long steps from the elevator and the detectives were at the counter under the Winthrop Enterprises sign, the silver wording gleaming with recently shined letters.

"Good morning. My name is Earl Wallace and I am a detective with the D.C. Metropolitan Police Force. This is my partner, Detective Nguyen."

The receptionist turned serious, an almost forced demeanor. "May I see your badges, please?"

Detective Wallace gave Nguyen a subtle glance before both men reached into their respective jacket pockets and pulled their shields.

"Thank you, detectives."

"We are conducting an investigation and want to have a word with Peter Winthrop," Detective Wallace answered with an equally serious tone.

"I'm sorry, detective but Mr. Winthrop is not available. He is out of town on business."

"When will he be back?"

"I believe he is in Prague until tomorrow and is making a stopover in London on his way back. Although I am not his secretary, I am pretty sure he is due back by the end of the week."

Wallace didn't like the receptionist. "Would you mind if I asked you a few questions?"

"Me?"

"It will only take a minute."

The receptionist looked around, turning her neck slightly and glancing out of the corners of her eyes.

"About Marilyn Ford," Wallace added.

The mere mention of Marilyn's name brought moisture to the receptionist's eyes. She waved her hand in front of her face as if to dry any tears before they formed. Wallace looked at Detective Nguyen with one eyebrow raised. Wallace pulled out his notebook, ready to scribble.

"She was a wonderful woman," the receptionist said, whimpering.

"Was she well-liked around here?"

"Yes, very. She'd been around Winthrop Enterprises before there was a Winthrop Enterprises. She was the president's secretary for over two decades. She could be nosey, but what middle-aged, forty-something-year-old woman isn't?"

Detective Nguyen butted in, "Nosey about what?"

"Nosey about the usual. Employees's lives in general. Who was working on what, who was cheating on their wives, you know, the usual."

"Before Marilyn's death, did you notice anything unusual with 'the usual?'"

"Not really. Not to me at least."

"Boyfriend?" Detective Wallace asked, knowing that over fifty percent of all homicides against women are perpetrated by the man they share their bed with.

"Not that I know of," the receptionist answered, now with an emotionless face that would have taken the pot at any Texas Hold'em tournament.

Detective Wallace handed the receptionist a picture of Chow Ying taken from the ATM camera. "Have you seen this man before?"

The receptionist leaned close, stared hard at the picture for few seconds and then looked up. "No. He doesn't look familiar."

Wallace wrote something in his notepad and ripped out the small sheet of paper when he finished. He placed the paper and the photograph on the marble reception counter. "Could you see to it that Peter Winthrop gets this picture and this note? It is important."

"Yes, I will make sure he gets it."

"And here is my business card. Please, have him call me."

"I will let him know you visited."

"Thank you."

"You're welcome, detectives."

***

Back in the wood paneled elevators, Nguyen waited for the doors to shut and then asked, "What did you think?"

Wallace pulled at his waistline and looked at the open page of the notebook in his left hand. "Seemed like a suspicious office. Never had a receptionist ask to see my badge before, have you?"

"Can't say I have. And she seemed to be a little emotional. Her tears came at the drop of a hat and vanished just as fast."

"Almost like she was acting. Did you notice that a lot of people in the office were staring at us?"

"Not really."

"Another ten years on the force and you will. Either way it looks like we have to wait a few days. But if Mr. Winthrop isn't available, there are some things we can do in the meantime."

"Starting with?"

"Shake the branches of the Winthrop fruit tree a little and see if anything interesting falls out."

Chapter 32

The trip to the mechanic had fixed one problem, and Jake's car no longer stalled. A few loose wires and a cracked distributor cap were diagnosed as the culprits, and the bill totaled forty dollars for the parts and a stinging three hundred for labor. The trail of blue smoke now coming from the tailpipe indicated even bigger problems were on the horizon. The telltale cloud of burning oil followed Jake's Subaru like a tail, zigging when he zigged, zagging when he zagged.

Jake came to a crawl at the stop sign at Macomb Street and Connecticut Avenue. He could see his apartment, but getting to the parking lot of the old brick building was going to require three left turns on consecutive one-way streets. Jake checked his mirrors, not sure if he should be on the lookout for a six-foot-four mass of Chinese muscle coming at him with a samurai sword down the double yellow lines.

His conversation with Al had scared him. Stuck in traffic as the sun finished setting, Jake ran through scenarios for his father, a senator, and a girl named Wei Ling.

He pulled into the small strip of private parking spaces behind his building and prayed for an open one. He worked his car into the sliver of asphalt next to the massive green dumpster, leaving just enough room to slide out the driver's side door. Another two inches of waistline and he would have needed a Crisco lube job to get by. He got out of the car, face-to-face with the stench of rotting garbage. He stuck his forearm into his nose and shimmied by without getting his shirt dirty.

As darkness fell over the city, Chow Ying smiled at his target's timing. He marveled at his own patience. From a bench in the stamp-size excuse for a park across the street, Chow Ying watched Jake pull his car into the lot. The Mountain of Shanghai threw his newspaper in the trashcan and crossed the residential street with a slight limp. The situation was as good as it gets. The police would think it was a robbery gone bad. Another good kid killed by a violent element of the city—violence so ingrained in the city's youth that neither prison nor the potential for an early funeral were deterrents. As Jake slipped from his car, Chow Ying closed in with slow measured movements. With thirty yards to go, Chow Ying's strides became longer and his hobble more noticeable. A brief crunch of gravel under his foot gave him momentary pause.

Jake, head down, shifted through his keys as he approached the first floor security door in the back of the building. Chow Ying looked around one last time for witnesses, in final preparation to pounce. The kid didn't stand a chance, ankle injury or not.

Jake pushed his way into the apartment and a giant hand crashed down on his shoulder from the shadows of the hall, the force spinning him around, slamming the security door open.

"Jake Patrick."

"Jesus," Jake said, looking up. It took a second to recognize the intruder. "Tony. You scared the shit out of me," Jake said, panting. The Castello brothers stood at both sides of Tony. Together, Jake's visitors stood shoulder-to-shoulder in the hall, blocking the passageway, stuffing the corridor from the mailboxes to the recycling room door.

Looking into the doorway from the outside, Chow Ying froze and then slowly retreated into the shadows near the building. He didn't take his eyes off the scene in the hall.

"Mr. Sorrentino is requesting your presence for dinner."

"Has Mr. Sorrentino ever heard of using the phone?"

"I just do as I am told."

"How did you get into the building?"

"You don't think a locked door would keep us out, do you?"

Jake thought about the question and considered it a moot point. If the three goons in front of him wanted to get into an apartment building, they would find a way. Window. Door. Trash chute. "Well, I can't make it this evening. I'm kind of busy," Jake said, still trembling.

"I can appreciate your busy schedule, Jake, but I don't care. Mr. Sorrentino pays my bills and he is asking me to offer you a ride, to have a civil meal together. Do me a favor and make it easy."

"Don't threaten me, Tony." Jake's adrenaline startled both himself and his unwelcome guests. Verbalizing the fact that he wasn't going to be a patsy for Tony or Mr. Sorrentino gave him a boost of confidence. Fear may indeed be a good emotion, he thought.

"Jake..."

"I'll tell you what Tony. I need to get something from my apartment. Then I'll go. But not because I have to. I'll go because I like Kate."

***

Chow Ying lurked outside the back door of the building as Jake and the trio of Mediterranean bloodlines firmly shut the door to the building and disappeared. Seconds from the kill and the prey had gotten away. There was nothing to do but wait. From the park across the street, Chow Ying watched the movement in Jake's bedroom window. Ten minutes later, the lights in Jake's apartment flicked off, and Chow Ying focused on the back door to the apartment. It was wasted energy. When Tony and the Castello brothers appeared with Jake wedged between them, Chow Ying cursed. The college-aged kid, surrounded by seasoned hard-asses, made Chow Ying think. The Mountain of Shanghai watched Jake get into the back seat of the car parked illegally on the main street and wondered if perhaps this kid had bigger problems than he did.

***

Jake sat on a bar stool and watched his three guardian angels play nine ball with skill and language that could only have been perfected in a pool hall. And not one of those pool places in Bethesda or Ballston where yuppies come to pick up chicks and scratch the velvet with the rental cues. No, Jake's current company used their cues to shoot serious pool, and, he imagined, crack the occasional skull.

Given the circumstances, the basement of the Sorrentino palace seemed like a safe place. If there was a large Asian on the loose in the city with ill intentions, he wasn't likely to be paying a visit to the Sorrentino residence. Jake's present company was only marginally better. They cursed and threw money at each other, taunted and shoved. Jake cringed at the guns, the handles of pistols hanging from shoulder holsters and protruding from waistbands. He prayed the guns would stay holstered. Jake was sure the crowd didn't practice NRA-approved firearm safety.

His guards weren't happy with their assignment and Jake knew it. They offered him a drink and pointed to the bathroom in the hall. "Don't go wandering past the bathroom. We understand each other?" Tony said.

"Yes," Jake answered, completing the longest conversation he had had since he had gotten in the car. Jake excused himself to the bathroom under the watchful glare of six eyes. He turned on the bathroom fan and lights before shutting the door. Then he pulled out his cell phone and made a call. *Bring in the cavalry*, he thought.

An hour passed and the bets on each game increased with every round. The pile of cash currently on the bar totaled six hundred and change, and the extracurricular violence was getting worse with every missed shot. After scratching on the eight ball, Tony grabbed the older Castello brother, put him in a headlock, and pulled out his revolver just for show.

The door upstairs slammed and Jake jumped in his seat. James "Jimmy" Sorrentino's feet on the stairs brought the room to attention. The owner of the house entered the room, looking as if he were the only one who hadn't had a stressful day. His suit was perfectly tailored, his gait strong and youthful. His face was stern, commanding the respect of the room.

"Gentleman, if you would excuse us?" Mr. Sorrentino said to the hustlers.

The part-time pool sharks left, leaving their money on the bar, next to a loaded pistol that the older Castello brother had yanked from his pants. Tony gave Jake a long glare as he passed.

When the room was quiet, Mr. Sorrentino stared at Jake down his formidable, double curved nose, evidence of too many fights to remember.

"Jake, I'm going to be honest with you."

"Please."

"I don't like you."

Jake smirked with fear. "I'm not sure how to reply to that, sir."

"I've been keeping tabs on you for a week or so, since our little problem."

"What problem is that?"

"The little problem with the strippers."

It all became clear to Jake—Tony, the intimidation, the offer for dinner. "Mr. Sorrentino, I wasn't with those strippers. As I explained to Kate, I was there with my father and one of his clients…"

"I heard the story, Jake. Boys will be boys, I understand this. I have been married for thirty years to the most beautiful woman I ever laid eyes on…but I understand that men have needs."

"Mr. Sorrentino, I wasn't *with* the strippers."

"But you were coming out of a strip club with them."

"Yes, but that's not the whole story."

"Maybe, maybe. Like I said, I've been watching you. Watching you on your way to work, watching you on your way home. To my surprise, you seem to be on the up-and-up. No other strippers. No other girl-friends. No heavy nights on the town. Pretty amazing considering your age."

"I'm older on the inside," Jake said trying to lighten the mood.

Jimmy Sorrentino didn't take the bait. "I sent my guys to get you today for a couple of reasons. First and foremost, I wanted to clear the air between you and me, man-to-man, face-to-face."

More man-to-man bullshit, Jake thought. The conversation of feeding his balls to the dogs was still fresh in his mind. "Sir, you could have called and asked me to see you. There was no need to send over three guys to harass me."

"Yes, I suppose I could have," Jimmy answered, simultaneously dismissing the statement as ludicrous. "The second reason I wanted to see you this evening was to ask you to stop seeing my daughter."

"Stop seeing Kate?"

"Yes. Don't break her heart, just remove yourself from her life slowly. Stop calling so often. Just fade away."

"Why?"

"Because I love her, and I don't want her around you."

"Mr. Sorrentino…"

"Jake. Put yourself in my shoes. Explain why I should support you as my daughter's significant other. I'm a man of great understanding. If you can help me understand, maybe we can get past this little problem."

Jake tried not to laugh. If there was one thing Mr. Sorrentino had shown, it was that he was anything but understanding.

"Go ahead and explain why I should continue to let you see my daughter. Take your time Jake. I am a patient man."

Jake excused himself for a second trip to the bathroom. He threw water on his face and let the drips run down his neck. *What have you gotten yourself into?* he asked himself in the mirror. She is just a girl. There are a million other fish in the sea. A million other fish with far more hospitable fathers. *She is just a girl,* he said to himself again. *She is just a girl…*

Jake walked back into pool room. Mr. Sorrentino was behind the bar sifting through bottles. Two empty shot glasses sat on the counter. Jimmy turned and filled the glasses with bourbon.

"So Jake, do we have an agreement?"

Jake looked down the counter at the gun next to the pile of money that Tony and the Castello brothers had left behind.

"Sir, with all due respect, I need to think it over."

"Okay, Jake. Okay. You think about it. Like I said, I'm a patient man. But I do expect an answer, and I do expect a handshake."

"Let me think about it," Jake repeated.

Mr. Sorrentino pushed one of the glasses toward Jake. "To making the right decision," he said raising the other glass.

"Salute," Jake answered, throwing back the drink with one swallow.

Kate's voice echoed down the stairwell as she ran down the flight of steps. Jake stood from his stool and Mr. Sorrentino gave him a management-busting teamster glare.

"Oh, Jake," Kate said through forming tears.

He embraced her, closed his eyes, and inhaled her perfume. Mr. Sorrentino looked at Jake's arms around Kate, hers tight around his neck. Jimmy sneered and cleared his throat, bringing the Hallmark Moment to a sudden end. His little girl could do so much better than this, he thought. And she would. As per the impending agreement. Just as soon as Jake came to his senses and dumped her. For his own good.

"Dad, how could you?" Kate asked. "Quit interfering in my life."

"We'll discuss it later," Jimmy said to his daughter.

"I would like to leave now," Jake said, safely in the company of his girlfriend. "And I need a ride," he added.

"I'll give you one," Kate answered.

"No, you won't. Tony and the guys will."

"Then I am going too," she said.

Chapter 33

Tony stopped the car near the south end of the Mall, and Jake said goodnight to Kate and the three goons. He had thought long and hard about Al's advice. *Be careful. Watch your back. Vary your routine. Stay away from your girlfriend. Lay low.* There was one way to do all of the above.

With a light breeze coming off the water hitting his perspiration-drenched shirt, Jake unfurled his sleeping bag and shivered for the first time since March. The flattest terrain he could find was still mountainous compared to his mattress, and Jake knew he was in for a long night. The addition of scrap cardboard boxes did little to absorb the undulations of the ground beneath his spine. Jake "princess-and-the-pea" Patrick flopped around until Al couldn't take anymore. "What is your problem? Haven't you ever been camping?"

"Not recently."

"Well the earth's composition hasn't changed much since the last time you went, this much I am sure of."

"I just can't get comfortable."

"I know, and as a result, neither can I."

Jake sat up and crossed his legs. He looked out at the Kennedy Center, the top of the white marble structure adorned with lights like the jewels on a crown. Al looked over at the silhouette of Jake's head. "Do you know what used to be there before they built the Kennedy Center?"

"Swamp," Jake answered with definitiveness.

"Good guess, but wrong. It used to be the Foggy Bottom Brewery. Founded by a German immigrant named Christian Heurich who died in the 1940s at the ripe old age of one hundred two. The beer is rumored to have preserved him quite well, and on his deathbed he was said to have looked younger than his eldest son. The brewery shut down during prohibition, but it came back to life when it was repealed."

"Must have been an interesting period in history. A country full of drinkers trying to find an illegal drink."

"Yeah, illegal is always more profitable than legal, all things being equal."

Jake paused at Al's statement. "Speaking of illegal, I've got a question for you."

"Shoot," Al answered. It was dark enough that Jake couldn't really see Al. He was hidden in the shadows, stuffed in the corner of his worldly possessions.

"Hypothetically speaking, how could someone export illegal goods for years without being caught?"

"Well, it's not as clear cut as you think. Look at the mob. Investigations into the mob went on for decades and some of them didn't yield any prosecutable information. And I'm sure during those investigations the mob was still making money. It wasn't until the mid-nineties when mafia members started ratting out one another that the FBI made real progress bringing the mob to justice. Up until that point, it was just faster to wait for mobsters to kill each other than to build a case against them."

"And if they're not the mob?"

"Are we talking about a crime that the FBI knows was committed, or investigating the possibility of illegal acts without a defined crime?" Al asked.

"The latter, I guess. Or the possibility of a crime at all."

"Does this have something to do with your father?"

"Maybe."

"Your father is very clever Jake. Very clever, very well connected."

"How about wiretapping, informants, all that good stuff?"

"Wiretapping an American citizen is a myth, Jake. I mean from a technical perspective, it's easy. Nothing could be easier. But even the FBI can't just slap a wiretap on your phone. They need a reason. A good reason. And if you are an upstanding American citizen with political pull, they need a really good reason. They need to have a defined period of time to use the wiretap, and it needs to be for the express purpose of a defined investigation. They need to document this and prove that traditional forms of investigation and surveillance have failed before they can wiretap. Then they need a judge who will look at the case and grant the wiretap. On top of that, wiretaps are granted for specific phone numbers. So if a company has a hundred lines, the investigative authority needs to specify which line they want to tap, and why. And if you have a suspect who changes phone lines regularly, the authorities will always be playing catch-up."

"Not like on TV. Sounds like it is a miracle they ever catch anyone."

"Proactively, yes. Reactively, the FBI is good. That is what they were designed for. I mean if you leave a footprint behind at the scene of a federal crime, chances are good the FBI will catch you. But if you ask them to prevent a crime, well, they don't have manuals for that."

"So, theoretically, is there any way to avoid a wiretap if the FBI has proof against you?"

"There are some things you can do. Have well-connected lawyers, preferably a few who have personal relationships with federal judges. Buy the clerk at the federal courthouse…"

"Buy the clerk?"

"Yes, every wiretap has to be approved by a judge and filed with the court. The clerk will handle the actual filing of the documentation."

"How does that help you?"

"If you have the clerk on your payroll, you will know the FBI has tapped your phones, and for how long. Then all you have to do is modify your behavior until the wiretap expires. Repeat this exercise a few times and it will get harder to find a judge to approve future wiretaps."

"So the clerk is like a last minute warning system."

"Exactly. But the Golden Rule still applies."

"The Golden Rule?"

"Don't use the phone, fax or computer for illegal transactions. Keep it all face-to-face."

Jake thought about the strip club and the evening with Hasad. No one was going to be wiretapping in a basement filled with loud music and gyrating naked women. Jake paused and listened to the cars rumble over the bridge, their suspension softening the bumps from the seams in the concrete above.

"Jake, I assume that you have some dirt on your father?"

"Yes and no, I guess. Nothing definite."

"That's an easy call, Jake. Call the FBI and tell them what you know. Help the FBI investigate your father and Winthrop Enterprises."

"I guess I'm still hoping it isn't true, that my father is just posturing."

"You're a piece of work, Jake. You're interested in saving a girl you don't know because it is the right thing to do, but you aren't willing to help the FBI even though it is also the right thing to do. Sounds like a moral dilemma to me."

"It's different with the girl. She is an innocent victim. I'm not."

"And neither is your father."

"I guess it goes deeper than that. If I admit that my father is involved in sweatshops, illegal exports, whatever, then I have to admit that I potentially have the same genetic tendencies."

"You need to look beyond yourself, Jake. This isn't just about you." Al shut his eyes and then opened them again. "The decision to report your father is a decision that you have to make. If you go to the authorities to have your father put in prison, you can probably forget about any inheritance," Al joked.

"Not sure I'd get anything anyway. Not after I wrapped his favorite toy around a telephone pole."

Al continued. "The girl is a separate problem. A bigger problem. A political problem."

"What do you mean?"

"Well, when it comes to third world populations, America sees lower life forms without seeing the human side."

"That's a broad generalization."

"I'm not talking about you and me, Jake. I'm talking about America, from a policy-making standpoint. From a policy standpoint the U.S. government supports this. We allow jobs to go overseas, particularly in the manufacturing area, for what? The U.S. government claims it's better for everyone. U.S. companies lower their costs and foreign workers receive an increase in pay from a penny an hour, to a dollar a day."

"I don't see where this is going."

"The problem is that before these companies decide to close their plants in the U.S., they are paying their American workers minimum wage—six or seven bucks per hour. The U.S. government doesn't see anything wrong with paying foreign workers a dollar for a full day of labor. These are American companies exploiting people."

"I don't know if I would call it exploitation."

"Jesus, Jake, maybe you are like your father. It is racial exploitation. Is there any place in the world where American companies are exploiting the white race? Anywhere?"

"I guess not."

"Of course not. But if these companies are exploiting the less fortunate in Latin America, Asia, India or Africa, it is fine."

"But the workers are better off. They are making more money."

"The average salary of the average worker in these locations is low because they are employed by domestic companies, which in most developing countries are corrupt and inefficient. They pay their workers crap because they make crap, goods you couldn't sell at a yard sale. American companies can afford to pay these workers a lot more than they do. Hell, these American companies aren't looking for cheap labor—they are looking for free labor. If America and its companies wanted to make a difference in these people's lives, pay them a couple of dollars an hour. See what it will do to the standard of living. Don't insult these people with what equates to an increase in hay rations for human donkeys. When it comes to American companies, American policy is the most racist machine on the face of the earth."

"I don't know," Jake said.

"Jake, what is the greatest manmade tragedy you can remember, outside of war?"

"9/11."

"Fair answer. And how many people died?"

"Just under three thousand, give or take. I'm not sure of the final number."

"Three thousand innocent people."

"That's a lot."

"You ever hear of a place called Bhopal?"

"Yeah, it's in India."

"What is it famous for?"

"Some gas leak."

"Very good. Not many people your age have ever heard of Bhopal. Union Carbide built a plant in India in the early eighties claiming they were going to bring jobs to a city teeming with potential. A year later, a chemical leak occurred in a densely populated area. Any idea how many people died in Bhopal?"

"A thousand?" Jake guessed.

"Twenty thousand, though the official number is up for debate and always will be. Union Carbide was built a couple of miles from the central train station in the middle of the city. Between the plant and the train station was one of the largest squatters' villages in India. When the gas leaked from the facilities, it crept over the squatters and smothered them while they slept. There was no way to accurately count the bodies. Internal estimates at the State Department, from people on site, put the number at close to twenty thousand. That is seven World Trade Centers. Put another way, imagine one hundred loaded 747s crashing in a single night. A U.S. company killed twenty thousand people and no one can remember it today. Why?"

"Because they were Indian."

"Exactly. They weren't people. Hell, they weren't even numbers. At least numbers get counted. These people were inconsequential nothings. And that is what is wrong with American policy."

"The world is screwed up."

"Yes it is. And that is the political level, which spills over into the personal level. Mail-order brides, prostitution, pornography, sex tours. These are all the same, all exploitation. Asia is the center. The conduct of companies and individuals, backed by policy or no policy, perpetuates looking at these foreigners as objects, not people. That is the end result. And Chang Industries, your father, Senator Day, they are a combination of all of these. A sweatshop using their employees as labor, selling them out as prostitutes at night. They are the scum on the inside of the outhouse shit-tank, Jake."

Heavy silence fell on the two.

"So what do I do?"

"I have an idea. But it is going to take a little luck and a lot of guts."

When Al finished telling Jake his plan, one thing was clear. They were going to need help. Jake's first thought was his friends. Friends who were currently in Europe, bouncing around Prague, Budapest, and Rome. Jake needed help, and for the love of God, only one thing came to mind.

"Try to get some sleep, Jake," Al said, interrupting his visitor's introspection. "You're going to need it."

"Why do you say that?"

"Well, if you manage to save this girl, things are likely to get hot around here."

"You mean if *we* manage to save this girl."

"Jake, I would love to go with you, but I don't fly. Not yet. I'm crossing one bridge at a time, and that one is a little longer than I am ready for."

"Al, you can't leave this all to me."

"I'll do everything I can, but getting on an airplane isn't on the list."

"If we do this thing, how long will it take you to organize it?"

"Couple of days."

Jake felt like hiding, but he already was. He was under a bridge, sleeping with the homeless. He had one idea and admitted to himself that it wasn't a good one. "Maybe I'll bring some people with me. Some muscle," Jake said, trying to convince himself he wasn't crazy.

"You have muscle, Jake? You didn't tell me that you have muscle," Al said, ribbing his friend.

"You know how you said fear is a good emotion?"

"Yes."

"Well I am tingling with it."

"Just remember, Jake. If you want to take on a senator, don't whisper it. Yell it from the tree tops."

With that thought, Jake got up from his uncomfortable sleeping nest and walked out from under the bridge. He waited for his cell phone to connect and when three bars indicated ample signal strength, he made the call.

Mr. Sorrentino was in bed with his wife. After apologizing profusely for the late call, Jake spoke nervously. "Mr. Sorrentino, I will agree to stop seeing Kate…"

"I knew you would come to your senses and see it my way," Mr. Sorrentino said before Jake finished.

Jake started over. "I will agree to stop seeing Kate on one condition…"

Chapter 34

Nguyen rode shotgun as Wallace drove the car through Chinatown. A picture of Chow Ying rested on Detective Nguyen's lap. He took intermittent glances at the photo on his thighs and looked at the faces on the street. Beyond the stereotypes, there was truth to the fact that Nguyen could look at another Asian and tell where they were from. As an Asian, he simply had an advantage in identifying and recognizing other Asians. Slight differences in the shape of the face distinguished the features of Northern Asians from their distant evolutionary kin in the south. The shape of the eyes was a second indicator of origin. And if facial features weren't a dead giveaway, clothes and hairstyles were.

"I don't like Chinatown," Detective Wallace said, behind the wheel for the first time since unofficially partnering with Nguyen. "It smells."

"What do you mean it smells? Just what smell is that, Sergeant?"

"It smells like Chinese food. Fish. Whatever. It just stinks."

"Be thankful it's not 'Koreatown.' Talk about a smell that will knock your socks off."

"My wife would warn against knocking my socks off, but that's a different kind of stench altogether."

"Could have gone all year without knowing that."

Wallace turned the cruiser north, crawling past a new restaurant on the corner called Wok n' Roll. The line snaked out the door, past a Beijing-style basement bodega. Two floors above, a sign for the now-defunct D.C. Police Asian Liaison Unit hung on the wall, the lettering faded by the sun. Wallace nodded toward the building and Nguyen grunted an acknowledgement as he continued checking the faces of a group of Asians strolling in the crosswalk.

Wallace began giving Nguyen an unsolicited lesson in local law enforcement history. "You know, Chinatown used to be a lot wilder. When I first started, the police came down here for the occasional late night raid. They had mini-casinos on the tops of some of these restaurants. Four or five dozen Chinese guys would be in there—betting, throwing money on the table, screaming. It was like a Kung Fu movie from Hong Kong, without Bruce Lee. No one spoke English. Most were illegal. There was always a pile of drugs in the room. Heroin being smoked in some back corner. Yeah, Chinatown was definitely not a place to park your car in the evening ten, fifteen years ago. Now look at it—it's becoming yuppie-central faster than you can order a bowl of egg drop soup."

"And you still think it stinks?"

Detective Wallace rolled down the window and took a left by the markets and restaurants on H Street. He inhaled through his nose and stuck the spear of agitation just a little deeper into Nguyen's side. "You don't smell that?"

Nguyen took a deep breath. "Smells just like my apartment."

"Then it looks like I'll be the one inviting you over for dinner. My wife can cook. Ribs and okra. The scent of the South."

The good-natured banter ended as Wallace stepped on the parking brake and the two detectives got out of the car. They walked past the Capital City Brewery and turned right on Sixth Street.

Wallace crossed between two double-parked delivery trucks as Nguyen began working the crowd on his side of the pavement. The market was alive with activity. The summer sun melted the ice bins, slowing bringing fish, clams, and squid to the surface. Wallace spoke with the vendors, smiled, and showed contrived interest in the funkiness-from-the-sea his Asian neighbors considered food. He stopped at a tray of sea cucumbers and gagged, forcing his breakfast back down. He dry-heaved a second time as the moving squid shot black ink on its Styrofoam container. Throwing small talk aside, Wallace pulled the picture of Chow Ying and started drilling passers-by on the person in the photo. He got a dozen negatives responses and twice as many blank stares.

At the end of the small string of temporary fish stalls, Wallace stopped and looked back at the street market scene. He would never understand how the local supermarket wasn't good enough. He turned into the open door of a small boutique and announced his presence. An elderly Chinese woman answered from the back of the store, a cloth-ier no bigger than a late-seventies station wagon. Wallace flashed his identification, and then the picture of Chow Ying at the sub-five-foot octogenarian. A younger woman popped her head between two hanging pieces of cloth in the doorway in the rear of the store, a sleeping baby strapped to her back. The elderly woman waved her hand at her grand-daughter and looked at the picture.

"Have you seen this man?" Wallace asked, looking around.

The old woman didn't bat an eye. "Yes, I have seen him."

Wallace snapped to attention, surprised by the answer and its im-mediate delivery in near-perfect English. "Are you sure?"

"Yes. My hearing is not so good, but there is nothing wrong with my eyes," the old woman said spryly.

Detective Wallace stepped to the door, rolled his tongue in his mouth, and blasted a whistle across the street to Nguyen.

"I saw him in the window," the old woman continued. "About a week ago. It was early in the morning, before we were open. He looked at something in the display window and walked off. I only saw his face, and I only saw him once. Right there, next to the mannequin."

Both detectives looked toward the window and the mannequin. A bright red dress rode up the mannequin's legs, her face painted with a thick layer of poorly applied cosmetics in ghastly colors. "Looks like a hooker," Nguyen said under his breath. Wallace suppressed his normal belly-shaking laugh.

Detective Wallace eyed the display window and noted the position of the mannequin and its pose on the raised floor near the window. "Where in the window did you see his face?" Wallace asked. The old woman stood at the small counter, the picture of Chow Ying resting on the wood surface next to the calculator that served as her register.

"I was standing here, changing the roll of paper on the calculator, getting ready to open. His face was right over the mannequin's shoulder. To the left." She took Wallace by the arm and steered him to where she had stood, changing places with the detective with a quick little step.

Detective Nguyen looked at Detective Wallace and read his mind. "May I?"

"Please."

Nguyen went outside and peered into the window. From the inside of the store, Detective Wallace and the old woman gave directions. *More to the left, a little closer to the window. A little higher. A little higher…*

Nguyen stood on his tiptoes and pushed himself as high as he could, leaving handprints on the glass. Wallace watched the old woman as she smiled at Nguyen's antics in the storefront window. With Nguyen's face just over the mannequin's shoulder, the old woman held up the picture of Chow Ying.

"Perfect. Just like that," she announced confidently.

"Thank you," Detective Wallace said removing a card from his pocket. "If you see him around, will you give me a call?"

"Is he dangerous?"

"No, we just want to talk to him," Wallace said. There was no sense in spooking the woman with a sudden urge to tell the truth. He had no idea if the man was dangerous or not. Detective Wallace exited the store as Nguyen was coming back in.

"Nice work, Stretch. How tall are you?"

"Five ten on a good day."

"How tall on your toes?"

"Six-two, maybe six-three."

"Give the guy that the woman saw another inch and we are looking at someone who could be our guy."

"She's awfully old to be a witness."

"Now why are you trying to ruin the only good lead we have had on this guy?"

"'Good', in this case, is a pretty subjective word, Sarge."

***

The three concentric circles they did around Chinatown led them to the Peking Palace, between Sixth and Fifth Streets. It was a transitional block where the Asian elements approached the long-standing housing projects, a quarter mile from a new loft apartment building whose own-er was rolling the dice on finding younger, wealthier tenants.

"Let's check this place out," Nguyen said, pointing to the large brick building that had once been residence to a dozen tenants.

"What is it?" Wallace asked.

Nguyen pointed to the Chinese characters in the window of the old building now known as the Peking Palace. "I think it says hotel," Nguyen said, squinting at the sign as if that would translate the mix of vertical and horizontal brush strokes into a more palatable form of written communication. "Then again, my reading is rusty and it may actually say 'baby pandas for sale.'"

"You read Chinese?"

"Vietnam used Chinese characters right through the twentieth century. They stopped using them officially in 1918. But I picked up a few characters here and there. My grandfather was a professor. He used to bribe me to study. I guess it is a good thing for us that I liked candy."

"Someday, someone needs to explain to me how twenty-six letters in an alphabet isn't enough."

"After you, detective," Nguyen said, opening the door.

Stepping into the Peking Palace was like stepping into 1950 colonial Asia. There was no air conditioning on the first floor and the humidity made the mid-nineties outside seem refreshing by comparison. The air was thick, stirred slightly by the underpowered ceiling fan. Wallace walked to the old counter and smacked his hand on the silver bell.

"You don't see those bells too often," Nguyen said.

"You don't see places like this hotel at all. Everything is sixty years old, including the dust." Wallace tugged at his collar and his tie. "And could it be any hotter in here?"

The door opened in the back of the housing complex turned hotel, and the old man walked forward at his normal glacial pace. The Asian senior citizen stepped behind a portable screen wall, weaved behind the counter, and approached the detectives from the front.

"You do the talking," Wallace whispered as the man stepped forward.

"How can I help you?" the owner asked.

"We are with the D.C. Metropolitan Police. We want to ask a few questions," Nguyen said, following orders and taking the lead on the questioning.

"The police?"

"Yes."

"We don't see many police around here."

"That's a good thing," Nguyen answered.

"Yes, I guess it is."

Detective Nguyen, face-to-face with an equally sweaty old man in white boxers and a tank top, cut to the chase. He pulled the photo from his hand beneath the counter and showed it to the hotel owner. Detective Wallace, a step back and to the left, concentrated on the reaction that flashed across the old man's face.

"Have you seen this man?" Nguyen asked.

The old man took one brief look and dug around under the counter for his glasses. He put the black-frame reading specials on his nose and gave the photo a long thoughtful stare. He raised his eyes upward slowly until they met Nguyen's. "No, officer, I have never seen him before."

"Are you sure? Take a good look. The ponytail, the defined face. He is big."

The old man played along, and looked harder at the picture, pinching his lower lip between his thumb and forefinger. "No, he doesn't look familiar to me, but I'm getting old, my memory isn't what it used to be."

"Okay. Thank you for your time," Detective Wallace interrupted. "If you see him around, please give us a call."

The abrupt end to the conversation caught Nguyen off guard. He was still pulling his business card out of his shirt pocket when the door shut behind Wallace as he exited the hotel. Nguyen fumbled with his card, dropped it on the counter, and followed Wallace's lead out the door.

Earl Wallace pulled out a cigarette as Nguyen came down the stairs from the front of the hotel. "That was a bit rushed," Nguyen said. "The old man...."

"The old man knows more than he is letting on," Wallace said confidently. "But we got all the information we are going to get from him."

"What makes you say that?"

"Gut reaction. Always trust your gut. Here on the street it may be the only friend you have," Wallace said, enjoying the role of teacher. There was something about being a mentor. It was more fun than actually having a partner.

"Why didn't we put his feet to the fire a little?" Nguyen asked.

"Didn't want to spook him."

"But you wanted to spook Peter Winthrop by leaving him with a copy of the photo?"

"Different fish, different bait."

"I guess."

"Well, I guess this means a stakeout. I'll betcha fifty bucks the big guy shows up here tonight."

"I'd love to keep you company, but I have a date tonight, Sergeant. Been planned for a month. It's my last chance with this girl."

"You young guys have no loyalty to the job."

"I'll stop by later and see how you're doing."

"Bring your date along. She'll be impressed. Nothing turns a girl on faster than a policeman at work. The consummate professional on a stakeout—belt undone, shoes off, zipper cracked."

"Better yet, call your wife and we'll double date," Nguyen answered, getting better at his comebacks.

"Fine. I'll drop you off at the station, get some coffee, and find a spot to look inconspicuous. As inconspicuous as an overweight black man can look in Chinatown."

Earl Wallace headed back to the station with his partner. He sighed the sigh of a big man with a bad back and bad eating habits. Stakeouts were for cases with evidence. Cases with strong leads. Right now, the case against the large Chinese guy in the picture didn't even qualify as a case. But his gut told him it was worth sitting in a car for a night. Agitating his hemorrhoids, spilling fast food all over himself, farting enough to make himself sick—with no one to share in the fun.

**

The old man in the hotel watched the detectives from the living room lobby of the old brick building. His favorite tenant, his newfound drinking buddy, and the temporary replacement for his long-lost son was being sought by the police. There had to be a mix up. Something easily explained. Chow Ying helped carry in the groceries, watched TV with him and his wife, had played card games with his grandchildren when they stopped by over the weekend. The old man refused to believe that Chow Ying was justly wanted for any crime. Chow Ying was an angel. He was polite, jovial, and kind.

Right up until it was time to kill.

One characteristic did not preclude the other. They were all traits of the same man. It is a misconception by people that somehow inconsistency of character is dishonest. A chameleon is a chameleon and the only consistency is its ability to change colors. People with similar traits are considered liars and deceitful. Chow Ying was honest with himself, and that was more than most people could say.

The old man kept an eye out front and waited patiently in the lobby, sipping tea, watering and pruning his plants, and reading the local Chinese paper. His favorite tenant limped down the stairs from an afternoon slumber, ready for another attempt to track down Peter Winthrop. After a dozen unsuccessful mornings, Chow Ying was changing his schedule for the singular purpose of accommodating the kill. Lions in the safari don't count on gazelles wandering by their den at lunchtime, and neither would he. A little after-hours hunt was the order of the day.

"Do you need anything while I am out?" Chow Ying asked his new family in the making.

"No, we're fine. Thank you for asking. Will you be late tonight?"

"No, I shouldn't be too late," Chow Ying said. "Unless I get lucky," he finished, with a slap on the old man's shoulder.

The old man thought his favorite guest was talking about women. Chow Ying was thinking far more sinister thoughts. The old man watched in slow motion as Chow Ying shuffled on his sore ankle toward the front door, steps from the outside world and the watchful eyes of the detective now parked four doors down. Chow Ying put his hand on the doorknob, turned it, and yanked the door open. The inward momentum of the door abruptly halted and the door slammed shut. Startled, Chow Ying looked down at the old crooked digits protruding from the toeless shoe wedged securely against the base of the door and the floor.

"Maybe you should start using the back door. It seems you have a few complications with your stateside visit," the old man said, before whispering the Chinese word for "police" and tilting his head in the direction of the outside.

Chow Ying looked at the old man and nodded in appreciation. "Thank you, I'll only be here a couple of more days, and then I will be gone. I won't cause you any trouble."

The owner's apartment in the back of the hotel was dark, the sun blocked by buildings and heavy venetian blinds. The old man moved slowly, Chow Ying following as he limped through the dimly-lit room— the evening drinking parlor and gambling den. In the last two nights, the old man had taken over three hundred dollars of Chow Ying's cash, a few lucky aces and the well-timed mahjong tile the coupe de grace. But the Mountain of Shanghai didn't protest too loudly. It was C.F. Chang's money anyway.

The door to the furnace closet at the end of the hall opened with a screech. The old water heater kept the room next to the kitchen warm in the winter, unbearable in the summer. Cockroach hotels lined the edge of the floor. A mousetrap was baited and waiting for one of Mickey's relatives. A conglomeration of mops, brooms, and cleaning equipment stood in the corner. As Chow Ying peered over the old man's head, the hotel owner reached into a mass of cobwebs and pulled out a key ring with a single key. The edge of a rifle stock peaked from the side of a broken piece of mirror, its barrel nuzzled against an old ironing board.

The old man blew at the dust clinging to the key, wiped it once against the side of his shorts, and handed it to Chow Ying. "This opens the back door. Take the alley to the right."

"Thank you," Chow Ying said again.

Even cold-blooded killers needed a little love.

***

It was three a.m. when Nguyen knocked on the driver's side window of the unmarked car. It wasn't until he tapped on the glass with his sizeable ring that Detective Wallace, sound asleep, jerked awake in the front bench seat. Nguyen laughed as Wallace thrashed his arms, hit the horn, and flailed even more. Cursing, Wallace rubbed his eyes. He pointed for Nguyen to get into the passenger seat.

"Son of a bitch."

"You really ought to get that looked at."

"What?"

"Sleeping on the job. Second time this week."

"Sleeping on the job my ass," Wallace answered, insulted.

"Okay, Sarge. Whatever you say. Any luck?"

"None. Not a single person has entered or exited that door this evening. Not one."

"While you were watching, anyway?" Nguyen said, smirking. "How many hotels in D.C. don't have patrons in the summer?"

"At least one."

"Looks like someone is still awake in a room on the third floor," Nguyen said looking up.

"I hadn't noticed."

"Uh-hmm," Nguyen said, looking up through the windshield. "Could be our Asian guy is up there right now."

"Or it could be a hotel guest watching porn."

"With the lights on?"

"Sure, why not?"

"Wallace, no one is going to be up at three in the morning, watching porn, with the lights on."

"How long you been working in this city?"

"Four-and-a-half years. But I have only been a detective for a year."

"Well, I'll tell you from firsthand experience that there are people in this city who would watch porn at three in the morning with the lights on. And whether you want to believe it or not, there are people who would watch porn and pleasure themselves in DuPont Circle in the middle of a sunny Saturday afternoon."

"Nice image. Are you ready to go home and get a few hours sleep?" Nguyen asked. "I'll keep an eye on things."

"We've got a big day tomorrow."

"Why's that?"

"We're going to the Capitol. Time to rub elbows with the bigwigs."

Chapter 35

"You have a stack of mail on your desk, and I have a list of people who called while you were gone."

"Give me twenty minutes," Peter said to Marilyn's replacement as he passed by without stopping.

The master of his domain missed his former secretary. His emotions went beyond their personal history, their years of working together. Peter loved Marilyn for one reason above all others—she was the only person he had ever met who was as anal as he was. She would have never left a pile of mail on his desk. The mail would have been filtered, sorted, labeled, and stacked in order of importance. Peter realized it was going to take years of training before he had another Marilyn. And if he was going to have to train one, they might as well be young and beautiful. The clock was ticking on Shelly, the replacement executive assistant.

Peter found his chair and leaned back, the comfortable crinkle of handcrafted leather coinciding with a morning yawn. He listened to his voicemail, took some notes, and checked the calendar in his Euro-style day planner.

"I almost forgot this," Shelly said, barging into the room unannounced. She handed the picture to Peter, who stared at the intruder with disdain. He was just starting his morning routine and didn't like to be interrupted until he was done. He dismissed Shelly with a flick of the wrist and read the note attached to the picture. He stared at the picture of Chow Ying, an unforgettable figure from the not-so-distant past, and read the small digital signature across the bottom of the photo that stated the time, date, and location of the shot. He rubbed the bridge of his nose and perused the details on the police-issued business card. The connection was lost on him. Why in God's name would a D.C. Police detective provide him with a photo of Chow Ying? And why was Chow Ying standing in front of an ATM two blocks away from Winthrop Enterprises?

Peter stewed for a few minutes before yelling out the door. "When was this picture dropped off?"

"Sometime earlier this week," the receptionist answered.

"*No shit*," he said to himself. Of course it was earlier this week.

"You're fired," he half-shouted, not sure if he meant it.

Peter did what any irrational person would do in his position. He started worrying about himself. He didn't believe in coincidences. The only rule to coincidences was that there weren't any.

"Mr. Chang, please," Peter said, his ear on the phone, his eyes on the clock on the wall, his mind calculating the local time in Beijing.

"Mr. Chang has retired to his quarters for the night."

"Please, wake him up. Tell him it is Peter Winthrop. Tell him it's important."

Peter tapped his sterling silver pencil on a pad of paper while he waited. "Mr. Winthrop," C.F. Chang said with a surprisingly spry voice for someone who had supposedly been in bed.

"Mr. Chang. Sorry to disturb you so late."

"Not a problem, not a problem. If one wants to play on the international scene, one has to make certain accommodations for the time difference."

"True. Very true. And how are things on the international scene, Mr. Chang?

"Good."

"Working the angles as always?"

"Of course," C.F Chang answered with a pretentious laugh.

"Would Chow Ying be one of your angles?" Peter asked, taking off the gloves.

"Chow Ying? I'm not sure I understand, Mr. Winthrop."

"Sure you do. Chow Ying is here in D.C. Please don't insult my intelligence by telling me you didn't know. A man of power like yourself. A man in your position."

"Thank you for the compliment, but I still don't know what you are referring to. I was under the impression that Chow Ying was in Saipan."

"Well, he's not. He is right here in D.C. And do you know how I know this?"

"Mr. Winthrop, I am afraid that..."

"The D.C Police left a picture of Chow Ying with my receptionist, Mr. Chang. The D.C. Metropolitan Police."

The words sunk into C.F. Chang like a needle slipping into the side of a balloon. Images of walking into the Oval Office and shaking hands with his close personal friend, President Day, started to fade. C.F. Chang had no idea how Chow Ying had ended up in a police photo. But as a long-term asset, Chow Ying's value had reached complete depreciation.

"Chow Ying works for my son, Mr. Winthrop..."

"Very well, then. I will leave you with this thought. I hope, for your sake, that Chow Ying is here on vacation, Mr. Chang."

"Mr. Winthrop. Your American bravado is surprising. You are so well cultured. So worldly. You should know better."

"Mr. Chang, fuck 'cultured.'"

"Let us not lose our professional decorum," C.F. Chang said. "But if we are going to be rude, I will leave you with a thought of my own. Don't ever threaten me, Mr. Winthrop. Ever."

Peter wasn't through. "In our last conversation I spoke of a particular employee that I was trying to locate."

"As I recall."

"Well, I believe this particular employee may put you in the position to have the undivided attention of a certain member of the U.S. Senate."

"Mr. Winthrop, as you know, I pay a lot of money to have the attention of a lot of members of Congress. It is good business. Campaign contributions and lobbying are the only forms of bribery your country allows."

Peter inhaled audibly through his nose. "Let me ask the question another way. How many other employees do you have working for you that are currently carrying the child of a U.S. Senator?"

C.F. Chang almost dropped the phone.

"Would holding the unborn child of a U.S. Senator for ransom be legal as well?"

C.F. Chang forced a transparent laugh. "I'm sorry, but I don't know what you are talking about, Mr. Winthrop."

"I'm going to make this very easy on you. I want in. I don't care about the girl. But having a senator in *our pockets*, particularly one with the ambition to do so much more, could be very beneficial for business. I'm thinking about a silent partnership—Chang Industries and Winthrop Enterprises, pulling the puppet strings on one U.S. Senator. One could argue that there is a lot of money to be made."

"Yes, well, just the same, I'm afraid your proposal is based on inaccurate information. Someone has misled you. You have reached conclusions on Senator Day that just aren't true."

"I'm sorry to hear that, Mr. Chang."

Both men were afraid of the other. In a city where he had congressmen on speed dial, Peter Winthrop could squeeze C.F. Chang's political veins. With equal ease, C.F. Chang could put a stranglehold on Winthrop Enterprises in Asia. It was a fight neither man wanted. C.F. Chang knew he was caught. Peter knew that C.F. Chang could make Wei Ling disappear with a snap of his fingers. If both men held their positions, it was a stalemate.

Until Chow Ying completed his task.

"Good night, Mr. Chang."

"Have a good day, Mr. Winthrop."

***

Peter called out to his secretary, who was still at her post, ignoring the verbal offer for her walking papers. "Is Jake in yet?" he asked as she popped her head into the room.

"No, he said he was taking a few days off. Something to do with getting ready for school."

"Nice of you to tell me."

"There is a sticky note to this effect in the pile of mail and messages on your desk."

Peter moved the mound of paper around, sneering at the communication gumbo. "You and I need to talk about how to run an office."

He dug for his cell phone and punched the autodial key for Jake's number. C.F. Chang was up to no good. Peter sure as hell knew that Chow Ying hadn't suddenly taken the urge to travel the globe. It was a game of chess, and Peter called his son to check on one of his pieces.

***

The ringing phone in his pocket startled him. Chow Ying put his plate of fried eggs on the table, fork tumbling onto the floor. He arched his frame on the sofa, couldn't get his hand in his pocket, and stood.

"Hello," he answered in standard Chinese.

"Chow Ying."

The Mountain of Shanghai immediately recognized the voice.

"Laoban."

"You should have completed your job by now."

"There have been complications."

"I don't want to hear about your complications."

"Mr. Winthrop is a hard target to reach. He travels, works in a secure building, has a driver. He's never alone. He lives in a secure neighborhood. Very remote. I don't have a car and I can't rent one without creating a paper trail."

"Take a taxi."

"Take a taxi to commit a murder? The police would have no problem finding me."

"They already have."

C.F. Chang explained what he knew. Chow Ying had nothing to say in his defense. He thought about mentioning his ankle but knew it would get him nowhere.

"If you don't finish what I have asked you to do, a paper trail will be the least of your worries."

"Laoban. I will complete the job. But it will take time."

"What about Peter Winthrop's son?"

"He is an easier target. I almost had him the other night, but the job was interrupted. I haven't seen him since. It takes time to stake out two people."

"Very disappointing, Chow Ying. Perhaps I do need to get someone else on the job."

"No, Laoban. I will handle it. But this is not Beijing. Things are different."

"You are running out of time and I am running out of patience," C.F. Chang said sternly. C.F. Chang looked down at the paper on his desk and read the itinerary he had paid good money to get his hands on. "I am going to help you, Chow Ying. I want you to write down every word of what I am about to tell you."

"Yes," Chow Ying answered, grabbing a pen and an empty paper bag to write on.

"I'm going to give you precise directions and I expect them to be followed precisely," C.F. Chang commanded. C.F. Chang explained what needed to be done and finished with a final bit of non-negotiable advice. "If you fail, there will be no second chance. The next time I am forced to call you, it will be too late."

Chow Ying answered to a dead phone line that he understood.

Chapter 36

Wallace walked into the station, greeted the staff sergeant on duty, and bee-lined it for the coffee pot. He filled up, and turned around to a grinning Nguyen.

"You gotta stop sneaking up on me. You're going to give me a heart attack for Christ's sake."

"He has a son," Nguyen reported, smiling ear-to-ear. "And I wasn't sneaking up on you."

"Who has a son?"

"Peter Winthrop," Nguyen answered, looking at the paper in his hand. "His son is named Jake Patrick, raised by his mother after his parents's divorce. The mother legally changed her name back to her maiden name after the split, and she switched the son's name as well."

"Where is the son and why is he important?"

"Well, I was thinking about the phone in the church. How you said it was in the back, down a hall. It would be tough for someone to see it if they didn't know it was there."

"Right."

"Well, I went back to the list of parishioners that the priest gave us."

"Let me guess, you found a 'Jake Patrick' on the list…"

"No, but there was a Susan Patrick on the list. Forty-six-years-old. Recently deceased. Mother of one Jake Patrick and ex-wife of one Peter Winthrop. I ran a background check on Peter Winthrop, found out he had previously been married, and went back to the list of parishioner's from there."

"So the son was the one that called."

"It's as good a guess as any."

"Well, after we visit the senator, let's find our good friend Jake. He has some explaining to do."

Chapter 37

The countdown clock to the vote on the Senate Special Committee for Overseas Labor ticked past the eleventh-hour mark. The demands of a week of ass kissing and trading votes for his future had taken their toll. The embroiled Senator Day sat in his office, reading the letter from C.F. Chang for the twentieth time. He stood from his chair with a stooped posture, like a boxer slowly rising from the stool in the corner, barely supported by wobbling legs. All he had to do was make it to the middle of the ring to hear the decision.

The senator had been battered in round one by the AWARE group and their vigor for protesting and newly found love affair with media attention. Their Alamo would always be the moment Senator Day detained fifty-plus Asian Americans in the hall of the Senate Building for no other reason than they were Asian. The group continued to stake out prime real estate near the Capitol and showed no signs of going quietly. Kazu Ito had given them a reason to come to D.C. Senator Day had given them a reason to stay.

Round two was a flurry of combinations to the head and body. The senator had been mugged by his colleagues, his political pockets picked clean. He had no idea Senator Wooten and Senator Grumman had such criminal tendencies. They were like prison guards who took advantage of their position with the inmates. And Senator Day had been the one wearing orange pajamas.

The middle rounds were waves of sharp jabs—personal injury with heavy bruising. His pregnant wife was vacillating between an emotional breakdown and demonic possession. His liver hurt, a dull ache between the eight and ninth ribs on the right side. To make matters worse, it was Dana's time of the month and for the last week he hadn't been able to shine the top of his desk with the back of her blouse.

The final round was the newscast and the questions surrounding the sweatshop. It was a punch the senator didn't see coming. Sure the senator knew the tape was out there, but it wasn't his intention to have it playing on the evening news, not with a pregnant sweatshop girl holding his future in her womb.

For the committee, the senator had done everything he could. He bought the votes he needed to buy. He knew his unseen master would be watching. Every committee recommendation was posted in the morning edition of a dozen Capitol Hill news rags and on twice as many congress-monitoring websites. His performance would be measured with perfect accuracy. Selling constituents down the river for a chance to win them back wasn't a new sport. It was congress at work.

Despite it all, the senator was still there. Everyone had taken their shots and he was still standing. All he needed was one call from DiMarco, and his life was back on track. He somehow managed an arrogant smirk.

But there was one more punch coming at the senator's head, a good old-fashioned haymaker, and no one was there to tell him to duck.

***

The cars snaked in single file, each one stopping at the temporary stop signs erected amidst the sea of jersey walls. Detectives Wallace and Nguyen flashed their badges to the Capitol Police officers who manned the roadblock with a level of seriousness rarely displayed by government employees. The one-way streets near the Capitol and its surrounding buildings were already a tourist's nightmare, and when the national terrorist warning level hit orange, roads started shutting down, sealing off the end of the maze where the cheese was stored.

"Streets around here open and close like a stripper's blouse," Detective Wallace said, easing on the accelerator.

"That's the world we live in. Someone finds a few computer disks in a terrorist safe house in Pakistan, and the next thing you know you can't drive your car around the block."

The detectives pulled into the back lot of the Hart Senate Building, showed their badges again, and approached the entrance to the building and the main security booth. A courtesy nod from the man behind the glass let the officers bypass the line of constituents waiting to be frisked on their way to see their duly elected public officials.

"I've never been in here before," Nguyen said, embarrassed.

"It's just another building. I was here for a day about seven years ago. Some woman took a dive off the balcony in the atrium. Made a nasty mess on the marble floor."

"Suicide?"

"It appeared that way. The woman was from Arkansas somewhere. Came to see her senator complaining about carcinogens in the water near her house. Twelve people in her neighborhood had come down with a rare form of leukemia, including her son."

"A cancer cluster."

"Yes. She had been blown off by everyone—her local politicians, the EPA, and finally her state senators."

"I guess she got the last word in."

"That she did. But I bet the blood on the floor was easier to clean than whatever was making people sick in her neighborhood."

Nguyen approached the end of the hall and stopped at the foot of the stairs. "Can you make it to the third floor, old man?"

"'Old man' my ass. Keep moving," Wallace responded. If he were by himself, he damn sure would have taken the elevator.

Wallace breathed hard with every step. The name of every state in the union was carved in the walls of the stairway, a star at the beginning and ending of each name. Nguyen ran his fingers across them as he ascended.

"Taxation without representation," Nguyen said.

"What?"

"Taxation without representation. One of the tenets this country went to war over. Two hundred and some years later and we are still being taxed without representation here in D.C."

"I guess," Wallace answered.

"You don't agree?"

"I don't really care. Having a senator doesn't mean the citizens of D.C. would pay less taxes. Hell, we would probably end up paying more taxes. I figure if you are that hell-bent on having a senator, move to Maryland or Virginia. No senator has ever saved a state, and they sure as hell wouldn't save the District."

The detectives stopped at the brown door with the Massachusetts state seal plastered on the lower third panel. A glass window with black writing further indicated they had arrived at their destination.

"After you," Nguyen said, right hand extended.

Dana and the senator's bowtie-wearing page were standing at the main desk, banging on the side of the computer monitor when the detectives came in.

"Good morning."

"Good morning, how may I help you?" Dana asked, looking up with her hands still on the desk, offering a nice cleavage shot to the D.C. detectives.

Wallace forced himself to stay focused on her blue eyes. "We are detectives with the D.C. Police, First District. We would like to have a word with the senator."

"And what is this in reference to?" Doug the Page said, before Dana could interject her mindlessness.

"We think the senator may have information that could help with an ongoing investigation."

"Are you saying the senator has been the victim of a crime?"

"No, we are not saying that."

"Is the senator a suspect in an ongoing investigation? If he is, I assure you he will want legal representation present before answering any questions," the sniveling page pontificated. After the AWARE fiasco, the page had endured a long lecture on how to protect the senator from unwanted guests. The page tried to sound tough, tried to flex his legalese. Detective Wallace was unfazed.

"It is nothing of that nature. It will only take a minute."

The page looked at the detectives as if considering the career impact of the request. "I'll see if the senator is available."

"Thank you."

***

The senator's head pounded and he gave his temples a brief massage with his index fingers. The detectives came through the door and the senator sprang to life. "Please, please come in, detectives." Handshakes and introductions followed, and the detectives accepted seats in matching high back chairs at the senator's beckoning.

The detectives glanced around the room from their seats, and Senator Day let the spell from the magic of the room cast down on his visitors. The detectives were unaffected by the room, the senator, the aura of the building, and the view from the perch overlooking the Mall.

"Senator, if I may be so bold as to get straight down to business," Wallace said.

"Please."

"We understand you made a recent trip to Saipan with a man named Peter Winthrop."

"Peter. Yes. We went in May. The second week in May, I believe."

Wallace scribbled in his little spiral notebook. "How was the trip?"

"Great. Beautiful island. Wonderful people."

"Did you have any trouble? Anything out of the ordinary happen?"

At the mere mention of trouble on the island, the senator started to sweat beneath his shirt. A combination of frayed nerves and his body's desire to expel last evening's alcohol. He thought about the girl with his child. Everything about the trip to the island was trouble. The senator tried to clear Wei Ling's face from his mind and focus on the room, on the detectives.

"No, nothing out of the ordinary. It was a quick trip. In and out in thirty-six hours." The senator fidgeted in his chair before continuing. "Well, actually we did have one small incident..."

"My chief-of-staff had a waterskiing mishap. He has been out of the office on medical leave. Started with ACL reconstructive surgery and has moved on to a staph infection. He has been helping out as best he can via phone, but this is Washington, and out of sight is out of mind. It has been crazy here without him."

"How large is your staff?"

"Thirty in total. But ten of those are in the office in Boston. There are twelve here full-time in the Senate Building. The rest are in a two-room office off Independence Avenue, south of the Capitol. Space is limited here on The Hill. I have a speech writer and communications group on one side of the suite, and on the other side are a few legislative assistants so nothing falls through the cracks."

Detective Wallace produced the photo of the six men in front of

Chang Industries. "Do you recognize the man on the right?"

"I don't remember his name, but he works for Lee Chang, the owner of the factory we visited. I called him the 'Mountain of Shanghai' because of his size."

"The Mountain of Shanghai?" Nguyen repeated.

"What did he do for this guy...this Lee Chang?" Wallace asked.

"I guess he's Lee Chang's right-hand man. Drives, handles employee relations."

"Does he speak English?" Nguyen asked.

"Yes, quite well. Speaks with a slight British accent on some words, which I thought was odd."

"Do you know anything else about him?"

"No, why?"

"Any idea why he may be in D.C.?"

"None. Is he?"

"We have reason to believe he is in the city."

"And what do you guys want with him?"

"We want to ask him a few questions."

"Well, I don't know what he is doing here. He could be here on business. Have you spoken with Peter Winthrop? He could probably tell you more about him."

"We have contacted Mr. Winthrop and he was out of town. He is still on our list of people to speak with."

"I can make a few calls and see if I can't get his name for you."

"That would be great, sir," Nguyen answered.

"I'm sorry I couldn't be of further help," the senator said, rising from his chair hoping the detectives would take the hint.

"Thank you for your time. If you think of anything else about this individual, please give us a call."

"I will," Senator Day said. "Could I keep this picture, detective? Maybe it will jog my memory."

"It's all yours."

Senator Day showed his guest through the door and past Dana and the page. It was obvious the senator's helpers had been straining to hear the conversation in the inner office chamber. With the guests safely in the confines of the elevator on their way to the first floor, the senator looked at the picture of Chow Ying and called Dana and the page into his office.

"Is the man on the right the same man who dropped the envelope off last week, before our little encounter with the AWARE group?"

"No," the page answered.

"Are you sure?" the senator asked again.

"Yes, sir. I am sure. The man who dropped the envelope off for you last week was average size. This guy is huge. I definitely would have remembered him."

"You'd better be right. I have taken all the surprises I can handle for one term."

The page took the insult to heart. Then he tried to be helpful. "By the way, sir. Rumor has it that the AWARE group is going to keep protesting right through the week. Just so you know."

"Thanks, Doug. That is just wonderful fucking news."

***

Detective Wallace flashed his badge to the departing mailman who held the door open for the two officers. Inside, Wallace stopped in the small landing at the front of the building, looked up the stairs, and then back at Nguyen. With a completely straight face Wallace asked, "No elevator? I already went up one flight of stairs today."

"Sarge, you need an exercise program," Nguyen answered, sliding by his partner and starting upward.

"I already have one," Wallace answered, head down as he lifted each leg.

"What exercise program is that?"

"Trying to avoid my wife."

"How's it going?"

"It's tough. She has pretty good aim throwing things around the house, and I'm not as quick as I used to be. She's angry because I've gained two pounds a year, for twenty-some years. She claims she doesn't remember hearing 'for fatter, for thinner' in our wedding vows."

"Two pounds a year?"

"Like clockwork."

"Slow and steady, heh?" Nguyen said, with perfect respiration, legs moving in an easy tempo.

"That's my motto."

The stairs broke a moment of silence, creaking in pain as Wallace followed in the younger detective's wake. Nguyen reached the fourth floor and looked back down at Wallace. The twenty-two-year veteran with a growing waistline was grasping the banister in an effort to both pull himself up and prevent himself from falling back.

"The exercise program starts next year, with my New Year's Resolution," Wallace managed through a thick cough.

"It's July."

"I know. Remember what I said, 'slow and steady.' I don't like rushing things."

Nguyen knocked on the door with three hard thuds. A few seconds passed before Wallace tried his special if-you-knock-loud-enough-someone-will-answer-even-if-they-are-not-home technique.

"I'm coming," a voice said, agitated. *The Wallace Theory* proved correct again. He smiled at Nguyen who shook his head at the immature, albeit effective, approach of his mentor. Wallace pounded once more for good measure.

"I said I was coming, you don't have to be such an asshole," the voice said as it approached the foyer.

Robert Plant Everett, bong smoker extraordinaire and son of the self-proclaimed biggest Led Zeppelin fan ever, opened his apartment door and a visible cloud of smoke billowed out. Wallace and Nguyen turned and stared in disbelief at the lifelong student peering out through the haze. Door open, it registered in Robert's rusted cerebrum that the visitors were pounding on his neighbor's apartment. "Jake isn't home," Robert said, with long stretched syllables, a common speech impediment of a daily toker.

"Do you know where we can reach him?" Wallace asked, taking a step toward the neighbor's door.

"That depends. What do you want him for?" Robert asked, eyes bouncing slowly from Wallace to Nguyen and back to Wallace. A mix of smells, none of which were appealing, poured from the apartment. A lava lamp cast a slowly flickering shadow that nudged against the doorframe. Nguyen stepped to the other side of Wallace and peeked into the stoner's paradise. It was impossible to tell whether the twice-baked neighbor kept a bowl burning in his apartment or whether the smell was just "cannabis cling," smoke impregnated into the neighbor from years of abuse.

Wallace pulled out his badge and shoved it in Robert's face. The quick flash of the shield was too fast for the veteran stoner, and Robert's brain tried to process what his eyes had just seen.

Wallace didn't wait for a reply. "Where is he?" the detective asked.

"Where is who?" Robert asked.

"Jake Patrick. Apartment 4-A," Wallace answered.

"He's not home."

"We already covered this ground, bright eyes. Where is he?"

"He said he was going to be away for a few days. Said he had something to take care of."

"Where did he go?"

"Out of town, I guess."

"When did he leave?" Nguyen asked, perturbed.

"What day is it?"

"Monday."

"Then he left yesterday," Robert said, trying to sound straight.

"When will he be back?"

"Wednesday, I think. He gave me his fish bowl and asked me to feed his fish while he was gone."

"You two friends?"

"Nahhhhh. But Jake seems like an all right dude. For someone who doesn't really party," Robert added, once again no longer conscious of his audience's profession.

Wallace looked at Nguyen. *Let it go, just let it go*, he thought, hoping Nguyen would read his mind.

***

Vincent DiMarco watched the white van turn left at the end of the road leading to Chang Industries, followed by the rumbling of two, five-ton trucks, shaking the ground, stirring up a cloud of dirt and bugs. DiMarco's rental car was littered with surveillance mainstays: binoculars, grease-stained fast food bags, an assortment of coffee cups and soft drink cans. He was a man of habits, and in the hours he spent on surveillance, DiMarco drank his caffeine, chewed his gum, and smoked his cigarettes—all with equal passion.

He sweated through three shirts a day, and the smell of perspiration and bad food in the car was growing rancid. Worse still, DiMarco was becoming immune to his own funkiness. He had briefly visited the stage where he could smell himself and he knew he stunk. He was now at the point where he knew he reeked, but smelled nothing. It was all downhill from there. He could step in a pile of fresh dung and it wouldn't affect him in the least. The population of indigenous flies was enjoying the Wop from Boston like a rotten-flesh buffet.

The small park with a semi-unobstructed view of Chang Industries was one of three famous suicide spots on Saipan. During WWII, when the Japanese knew that the U.S. offensive on the island wasn't going to end with the honor of victory, the cliffs earned the nickname that has haunted them for half a century.

Facing impending doom, ruthless Japanese soldiers convinced the local population that the Americans would torture, rape, pillage, and burn. Believing that a certain and most unpleasant end was at hand, the island's population—a mix of Pacific Islanders with a history of Spanish, German, and Japanese colonization—started throwing themselves from the top of what are now called "suicide cliffs." When the bodies stopped raining and the waves below washed away the crimson evidence, twenty thousand islanders had killed themselves. Those residents who had resisted suicide of their own volition were simply thrown off the cliffs by the Japanese military. By comparison, twenty-four thousand Japanese soldiers and three thousand American G.I.s had died in the weeklong battle for the island.

DiMarco stood and for the hundredth time read the landmark sign identifying the cliffs and their infamy. He threw away his coffee cup in the green basket trashcan that buzzed with two-winged activity and looked over the edge of the cliffs with an extended neck.

Surveillance was boring but necessary, and the isolation of the cliffs was perfect for staying low. The oppressive heat kept most tourists at the beach, away from the scorching sun. And when the odd tourist or history buff did infringe on his activities, DiMarco got out of his car and headed down the narrow trail that lead to an even smaller scenic overlook. The trail was narrow and treacherous enough to scare a billy goat, much less beachcomber tourists in flip-flops. A ten-minute walk by DiMarco was usually enough time for the crowds to move on.

Now armed with a photocopied picture of Lee Chang liberated from the circulation stack at the local library, DiMarco kept his eyes glued to the back end of his binoculars. On his fifth day of surveillance, the Bostonian from Southie realized Lee Chang wasn't coming out, and even if he did, he certainly wasn't coming out with the girl. He had noted the two guards on duty during the day, and the team of four that patrolled the lot at night. The girls who worked in the factory walked from the building on the left in the morning, and returned at night. There was little else to see, with one exception. For the fifth day in a row, he watched the white van arrive, the driver retreating into the smallest building on the company grounds. The van and its driver left an hour later. It was a routine repeated three times a day—morning, noon, and night.

DiMarco stood by his car and felt the breeze on his face. He shooed away a persistent horsefly that attacked by stealth, twice making a getaway with a small bit of flesh. DiMarco slapped his leg and missed his target, never taking his eyes off the facilities. *Maybe I just found my way in,* he thought.

Chapter 38

DiMarco followed the white van into town, blending in easily with the island traffic in his rented American two-door. The Chernobyl-red sunburn on his driver's side window left arm was his biggest risk to being spotted.

The van obeyed the speed limit and signaled when turning. DiMarco kept pace. Years of driving in Boston—a mix of Indianapolis raceway and demolition derby, with extra points for nastiness to your fellow commuter—made driving on the island almost boring.

DiMarco followed the van to the Seaside Breeze Resort, an establishment neither grand enough for a resort nor close enough to the ocean to be seaside. The garbage cans in front of the hotel were full from the tourists who walked down the main drag, launching trash missiles in the hotel's direction. At night the empty beer bottles, thrown by teenage gangs with nothing better to do, rained down. The pool was empty, a green sheen on the remnants of water resting on the bottom. The pink paint on the balconies of the hotel peeled, begging for a new coat. The van pulled into the parking lot, past a set of palm trees with dangling brown leaves, its roots no longer able to find an ample water supply.

The doctor pulled his van into the small parking lot wedged between the hotel and the moped rental shop and miniature golf course next door. DiMarco found a space near the back of the lot that allowed him to keep one eye on the empty pool, the other on the white van. He took a walk around the lot to stretch his back, peeked into the back of the van as casually as he could, and walked across the street for more fast food. The stakeout continued, only the location had changed. Tonight the bucket seat would be his mattress.

The doctor strolled out the front door of the hotel at six-thirty.

DiMarco, already up for an hour with back pain, stood from the park bench on the side of the hotel near the pool, leaving his two-day-old newspaper on the table and throwing his half-eaten honey bun in the grass for the already circling seagulls.

The doctor pulled the handle on his van, the door sliding smoothly back on its rollers. He threw his little black bag on the back seat, shut the door, and rolled down the manual window. The knife on the side of the doctor's neck snapped him awake much quicker than the black cup of Hawaiian coffee and shower he had already had.

The doctor looked at DiMarco out of the corner of his eye, the knife touching his skin a fraction of an inch from his jugular. "What do you want?"

"If you do exactly as I say, you will live. If you don't, you won't. Those are the rules. The only thing keeping you alive is that I am not interested in you."

"Take my wallet and the car."

"I'm not interested in money."

"What do you want then?"

"You are on a need-to-know basis."

"I think you're making a mistake. I'm just a doctor. It is my job to help people. Take the car and my wallet. I won't call the police."

"Well, doctor, if you are in the business of helping people, then you're perfect. You're going to help both of us. I have told you the rules. You can take them or leave them."

"That's not really much of an option."

"I was hoping you would see it that way."

DiMarco slid the side door open and switched knife hands, the blade now touching the skin at the base of the doctor's skull. All Di-Marco had to do was grab the doctor's head, pull it back, insert the knife and scramble his brains. The doctor, fully aware of the anatomical danger, kept his hands on the wheel as instructed.

"Where are we going?"

"According to my schedule, you have to be at Chang Industries by seven. Let's get moving."

The white van slowed as it approached the gate to the sweatshop. DiMarco pulled the doctor's black medical bag onto his lap. Still sitting behind the doctor in the back seat, DiMarco spoke with an eerie calm.

"Tell them I am a fellow doctor from the local hospital. And if I hear you speak a single word of anything other than English, it will be the last words that ever leave your mouth."

The doctor never had the chance to scream for help. The two day-time guards waved the van through without even a cursory inspection, too busy with their conversation to be distracted by the doctor and his clockwork routine.

"Pull up close to the building. Closer than you usually do."

"You have been watching me."

"Of course. I *am* a professional," DiMarco said with pride.

The doctor did as he was told, pulling the van near the door in a dirt spot between the infirmary and the building that housed the sweatshop floor. "Get out slowly."

The doctor took his orders. DiMarco followed him into the infirmary, knife at the doctor's back. The Bostonian shut the infirmary door behind them and checked the room, keeping the doctor in front of him as he moved from corner to corner, from the door to the bathroom. The doctor played along, trying to give the impression of a lamb to the slaughter.

"Now what?"

DiMarco walked to the last door in the room and rattled the knob of the locked storage closet.

"I need to meet with Lee Chang."

"He's not home."

"The man doesn't leave. If he did, I wouldn't have gone through all this effort to come to see him."

"Wouldn't it have been easier to just make an appointment with him?"

"If I wanted to meet him, yes. If I wanted to kill him, no," DiMarco said into the doctor's ear.

"Kill Lee Chang?" the doctor said aloud.

"Yes, and if you don't keep your mouth shut, you'll be first."

DiMarco moved closer, one hand on the doctor's shoulder, the knife still at the base of the doctor's skull, only flesh between metal and the brain stem.

"Call him," DiMarco said.

The Chinese doctor moved slowly toward the wall and pressed the intercom button near the door. The speaker crackled.

"Lee. Could you come down to the infirmary for a moment, please?"

"I'll be down in just a minute, doctor."

DiMarco pulled the doctor to the corner of the room and pulled out a second knife, a heavily weighted, perfectly balanced Spanish piece of steel that DiMarco used with the precision of a surgeon. DiMarco stood by the door, behind the doctor, a knife in each hand. He looked up at the ceiling as Lee Chang's footsteps made their way across the second floor and down a flight of stairs.

As promised, a minute after being called on the intercom, Lee Chang entered the room and the door shut behind him. Lee Chang looked around the room, and as he turned to the corner over his left shoulder, the kid from Southie kicked the inside of Lee Chang's knee. A quiet snap accompanied the tearing of ligaments. It was DiMarco's signature move—years of practice told him that an injured knee took the fight out of most people.

"Lee Chang?" DiMarco asked, moving the doctor and himself to the middle of the room. DiMarco tried to determine if the face of the man in pain on the floor was the same one he had seen in the local paper.

Lee, sprawled on the tiles, grabbed his knee and grunted through the agony.

"Yes," Lee Chang answered. "And you'll never make it off this island alive."

DiMarco raised his arm and flicked his wrist with a powerful follow-through. Five inches of steel stuck in Lee Chang's neck, blood spilling on the tile floor like a broken liquor barrel in a prohibition raid. Lee Chang looked up at DiMarco and tried to speak. Only gargles escaped. Lee Chang's hands moved from his knee to his neck as he choked on the blood that flooded his throat. DiMarco, and the doctor in his grasp, watched as Lee Chang bled out—choking and spitting blood.

"Nothing personal," DiMarco said into his dying eyes.

DiMarco had the doctor's attention.

"Now what?" the doctor asked. "You said you would let me live."

"I will, but I'm not finished yet. I'm looking for a girl. Her name is Wei Ling. You deliver her and I will keep my end of the deal," DiMarco lied. "Call the work building and have her sent over."

"I can't do that. I'm just a doctor here. The foreman only takes orders from Lee Chang."

DiMarco cut the side of the doctor's neck and blood trickled down. A flesh wound for compliance, which the doctor quickly understood.

The doctor moved slowly, never turning around, keeping the distance between himself and DiMarco constant. He sidestepped Lee Chang on the floor and moved slowly toward the storage room. With each deliberate move of his feet, the doctor measured the movement of the killer on his shoulder. The doctor wasn't afraid. He wasn't rattled by the Boston accent, the scar, the tattoo, or the knives.

"I need to get a key out of my pocket," the doctor said.

"Do it slowly."

The doctor twisted the key in the lock and pushed open the door. Wei Ling shook her shackled hand and muffled something inaudible through her taped mouth.

The doctor's demeanor didn't change. DiMarco had done him a favor by killing Lee Chang. It was something he was going to have to do anyway. A father can only be embarrassed by his son so many times. Whether DiMarco knew it or not, the doctor had allowed him to kill Lee Chang. Lee Chang's death was one that wouldn't be on the doctor's conscience, on the outside chance that the practicing atheist found himself standing in line to chat with St. Peter.

Wei Ling was different.

"Now may I leave?" the doctor asked again.

"Not yet," DiMarco said, pushing the doctor into the room in front of him. "Is your name Wei Ling?" DiMarco asked looking at the girl with the taped mouth, the IV in her arm, the shackles on her wrists and ankles.

Believing that DiMarco was a savior coming to rescue her, Wei ling nodded vigorously, shaking her hands and arms, rattling the metal that held her in place.

The split second DiMarco stepped toward the girl and moved the knife off the doctor's neck was the last mistake of his professional life. The doctor reached up, grabbed DiMarco's knife-wielding hand, and jammed his powerful fingers into a precise location on the underside of DiMarco's right wrist. The nerves in the muscles that controlled his metacarpals flexed, and the knife fell to the floor. Another finger to the side of the neck and DiMarco crumpled to the floor.

The doctor quickly went to business with a series of pressure point holds that DiMarco wished he knew. With Wei Ling watching in horror, the doctor placed one hand on the side of DiMarco's throat and applied a second finger to the side of his neck under his ear. The tough guy from Southie lost consciousness without a whimper.

The doctor moved swiftly, wrapping Wei Ling's already taped mouth with enough medical adhesive to re-attach a missing limb. He rummaged through the medicine cabinet and filled the needle with an elephant-sized dose of potassium. He dragged DiMarco's body into the main room of the infirmary and injected the full contents of the syringe into the unconscious man's leg, shoving the needle into the upper thigh and the major artery that ran straight into the heart. He waited three minutes, checked for a pulse, and made the medical determination that DiMarco was dead. The poison would baffle the police for a while. An unnamed Caucasian stabs a local businessman then falls dead of a heart attack. It would take days to figure out what happened.

Wei Ling watched with tears running down her cheeks, her mouth so tightly covered that the muscles in her face couldn't move. The doctor prepared to move Wei Ling. He couldn't have police milling about the premises with a girl tied to the bed. The police, as understanding and appreciative as they were to Chang Industries and the family, would not overlook a girl gagged and chained to a bed.

Not with two dead men on the floor.

Wei Ling was going back to her mother country. The doctor picked up the phone and called C.F. Chang. "We are coming home. Get me on a charter flight out. Have people at the airport in Beijing. This afternoon."

"It is done," Laoban answered. "And my son?"

"As you ordered."

The doctor filled a clean syringe with Seconal, walked up to Wei Ling, and delivered a measured dose in her moving arm. Just enough to knock her out until they were on the plane, safely in the air over international waters. Once back in China, he could do anything he wanted with her, as long as the baby was born healthy.

The doctor went to the bathroom and put an adhesive bandage on the small present he had received from DiMarco, the blood from the cut on his neck already beginning to dry on the edges. He went back to the murder scene, opened the drawer in the desk, and pulled out Wei Ling's file and passport. He put the file in his medical bag and flipped open her passport. There were two stamps on the first page and a valid work visa for the U.S. Just a Chinese citizen going home before her visa ends.

***

The Saipan Police questioned every non-seamstress employee on duty, and started contacting the long list of guards who had worked for Lee Chang in the past. No one came forth with any clues as to the identity of the dead white man on the infirmary floor next to Lee Chang. The girls were locked in their rooms while the police questioned the foremen and guards, employees untrained and unskilled in any form of security other than keeping a hundred girls in line.

Police Captain Marco Talua arrived as the bodies were removed from the premises. Saipan's only official coroner vehicle, used by its only coroner, carried Lee Chang in its long rear section. The dead American with a scar on his neck and a tattoo of the grim reaper dressed as Santa Claus rode in an ambulance, covered in the obligatory white sheet. Captain Talua walked over to the soon-to-be transported bodies and took a look at their faces.

Looking at Lee Chang, the captain bowed his head for a moment of silence. He stared at the white American, forewent any visible indication of prayer, and gave the nod for the bodies to be moved. He turned toward the facilities of Chang Industries and stopped one of his officers on the scene.

"Did anyone question the girls?"

"No, sir. Not yet. All indications are that they were at work. They couldn't have seen anything."

"No surprise, I guess."

"No sir, I guess not. Do you want to question them? It could take all night to do it right."

"If it takes all night, it takes all night. They may not have had the opportunity to do any killing here today, but every last one of them had the motive."

"I'll get the foreman. He should be able to lead us around."

"Fine. I'm going to take a look at the crime scene. Come find me."

"Yes, sir."

Captain Talua stepped into the infirmary and looked at Lee Chang's coagulated blood on the tile floor. A crime scene investigator, who issued parking tickets during the week, milled about taking snapshots. He measured the distances between objects in the room and the locations of the now absent bodies. The quiet clicking of the camera shutter and flashes of light filled the room. The captain looked around at the empty beds in the infirmary, all perfectly made. He checked the bathroom, which was spotless and smelled of bleach. The room was sterile enough to host an organ transplant operation.

The crime scene investigator stepped from Wei Ling's former residence in the storage room and looked around for any obvious photo shots he may have missed. He had been there an hour already, snapping through two hundred shots with the bodies and another hundred after they had been removed.

"Good afternoon, Captain," the investigator said, finally speaking.

"Not for the two victims."

"Yes, sir."

"Give me the scoop. Tell me what I need to know."

"Two victims in the infirmary. One Caucasian, the other Asian, all signs indicating that it was Lee Chang, though I have never met him."

"I saw him in the body bag. It's him."

"Like I said, I never met him."

"What's in that room?" the captain asked, nodding in the direction of the storage room.

"It seems like a storage closet that has had a bed thrown in it. The room is pretty clean of evidence as far as the crime is concerned, less for the handcuffs. One bed, one side table, a trash can, a bed pan…."

"…handcuffs?"

"Yes, sir."

"I would say that's out of the ordinary. An empty infirmary and a bed in the storage closet with handcuffs."

"A worker who was being punished?" the investigator asked noncommittally.

"Possibly," the captain answered, suddenly concerned that he may have to explain the situation to someone outside of the comfort of his island.

"Where is the person who was in this room?"

"It looks like she left with the doctor."

"The doctor? I thought the doctor was pulled off the beach a few weeks ago."

"He was. A new doctor arrived from China sometime during the last week."

"Where is he now?"

"We don't exactly know. We're trying to locate him. He was staying at a hotel in Garapan City. No one really seems to know much about him."

"Has anybody notified next of kin for Lee Chang?"

"The housekeeper is upstairs. She made the call about thirty minutes ago."

"Did she see anything?"

"She claims she was upstairs working."

"Squeeze her a little. Make her cry if you have to. She knows something. Lee Chang wasn't changing any bedpans himself."

The captain thought as he looked around the crime scene. What a mess. As the crime scene investigator left the room, Captain Talua gave his parting remarks. "I have to check on something, but I want updates every thirty minutes. Phone, radio. Whatever."

"Yes, sir."

Chapter 39

With Jake in the passenger seat, Tony drove the SUV down the last hundred yards of road and came to a halt in front of the police barricade. Two squad cars were parked at an angle, head-to-head, blocking the road and the main entrance to Chang Industries under the auspice of checking passing vehicles. In the last hour, traffic had amounted to one delivery truck that was turned away and now Jake and his three burly guests. Tony looked at the police and his natural aversion to blue flashing lights made him squirm in his seat.

Jake looked at the looming fence with its roll of razor wire running along the top and his lips puckered slightly. The description of Chang facilities as a prison went far beyond proverbial. Tony eyed the fence through the windshield and had a flashback of a federal vacation he had endured in New Haven, Connecticut, for getting caught with an eighteen wheeler full of stolen cigarettes.

"Jake, maybe we should come back."

"It would be too suspicious. Besides, I didn't just fly halfway around the world to get cold feet. We are U.S. citizens on U.S. soil. We haven't broken any laws."

"Yet," Tony added. The Castello brothers sat expressionless in the back seat.

"We aren't going to break any laws, Tony. Chang Industries cannot keep us from meeting this girl. This is not a prison. She is here of her own free will. If she decides she wants to leave, we are here to assist." Jake held a folder in his hands with legal documents quoting every law that Lee Chang was breaking on U.S. soil, unlawful imprisonment at the top of the list. Tony and the Castello brothers were there purely as a show of force. A combined seven hundred pounds of persuasion.

Jake rolled down the passenger side window, nodding and smiling at the officer.

The elderly statesman of the Saipan Police Force was quick to try his rusty, ornery officer routine.

"Who are you?"

"Jake Patrick."

"What are you doing here?"

"We had an appointment to meet with Lee Chang. These gentlemen are my business associates. Here is the invitation and our itinerary."

Jake produced documents that would have made Lee Chang wonder if he had arranged the meeting himself. They were perfect forgeries, including an invitation on Chang Industries letterhead complete with the signature of the rapidly cooling Lee Chang.

"You are awfully young to be a businessman."

You are awfully old to be a police officer, Jake wanted to say, but stifled it. Instead, he went for "good genes."

"Well, Mr. Patrick you won't be doing any business here today. A serious crime has been committed on the premises. Turn your car around and get out of here."

Jake looked at the old officer who hadn't been on a crime scene in nearly a decade and then looked at the activity on the grounds of Chang Industries. As Al would have said, the police presence was not a "positive development."

"Sir. I can see you are busy, but it's urgent that I see Lee Chang."

"You'll have to come back."

"It's important," Jake said one more time.

"If it's important enough, you'll come back."

The officer's radio crackled and Tony jumped in his seat. Officer Moses cut off his radio and looked at Jake. "What are you waiting for? Move out."

Tony stared straight ahead and waited for the nod from Jake, who was changing mental gears. His call several weeks prior to the Saipan police had proven fruitless. The Saipan Police were in a position to lie without impunity and he would never know the difference. He, quite simply, didn't know if they were friend or foe.

The elderly officer gave him his answer. "Move your car or I'll have you arrested for obstruction of justice and interfering with a police investigation."

"Yes, sir," Jake replied, throwing in a "thank you" for added politeness.

Tony looked at the flashing police lights in his rearview mirror and felt better with every foot of distance he put between the car and the scene behind him.

"What now?"

"We go to the hotel and check in. I need to make a phone call," Jake said trying to keep some semblance of a plan. Al's words and the sight of Chang Industries bounced around in Jake's head. He tried to force them out. *The girl is probably already dead.* Al's comments didn't seem so melodramatic now. Maybe they had just left the murder scene.

As Tony drove, Jake read directions from a page he had printed off the hotel's website. After getting lost twice, they asked a middle-aged man out for a run to point them in the right direction. An hour after leaving Chang Industries and taking a tour of some of the finest Saipan residential neighborhoods, the SUV stopped in front of the hotel.

"This place is a dump," Tony said flatly as Jake got out of the vehicle.

"When you are paying the bill, you can choose the hotel," Jake answered.

Jake and the small team of pasta lovers approached the hotel's front desk. An unattractive island native with dark skin and shark teeth smiled over his wire-framed glasses as Jake placed one hand on the desk. "Welcome to The Dunes. How may I help you?"

"My name is Jake Patrick and we have a reservation for three rooms."

"Mr. Patrick, just one moment please." The front desk manager vanished behind a doorway and returned a few seconds later. "There is a message for you, Mr. Patrick. Please take a minute to read it before you check in. I was told it is important."

Jake read the message with a single glance. "Thanks," he said before turning to Tony. "Back in the car. Change in plans."

Tony took one long look at Jake and tilted his head toward the car. The Castello brothers started bitching and Tony put them in line. "The sooner we are done here, the sooner our lives get back to normal."

Chapter 40

"Please have a seat, detectives," Peter said with a powerful voice. "Can I get you something to drink? Coffee perhaps? My secretary Shelly makes a fine espresso. We have a machine right in the breakroom."

"I'm fine," Nguyen said.

"I would love an espresso," Wallace said, not missing the opportunity to create rapport. It was something Nguyen would learn with time on the job. If a person-of-interest in an investigation offers you a dish of fried crickets, you did your best to choke them down.

Peter went to the entrance of his office and gave the order to Shelly from the doorway. He found his seat at his desk and looked over at his guests.

"How can I help you this morning?" Peter asked, knowing damn well what the detectives wanted.

"We want to discuss the photograph we left with you last week."

"Ah, yes. The photograph. I apologize for not getting back to you sooner. I have been in and out of the country on business."

"That's what your receptionist told us," Wallace said.

"Have to work to pay the bills."

"Doesn't everyone?"

Detective Wallace pulled out a copy of the photo and placed it on the desk. No one needed to be reminded of the photo, but Wallace did it to measure Peter's reaction.

There wasn't one.

"I have the copy of the photo right here in my desk," Peter said.

"Mr. Winthrop, do you recognize the man in the photo?"

"Sure I do. He works for a business associate of mine. A garment manufacturing facility in Saipan."

"You wouldn't know his name would you?"

"Detective...?"

"Wallace."

"Detective Wallace. I only met the man once. He was a new employee. I don't remember his name. The man who runs the facility in Saipan is named Lee Chang. I can call him first thing in the morning, Saipan time."

"That would be helpful."

Detective Nguyen flipped to the page in his notebook from the detective's interview with the senator. "We met Senator Day last week. He referred to the man in the photo as the 'Mountain of Shanghai.' Does this ring a bell?"

"Yes, I do recall the senator gave the man a nickname. He has one for everybody. Unfortunately, his geography isn't so good. There are no mountains in Shanghai. It's a port city. Pretty flat."

Wallace ignored the comments. "Any idea why this man is in D.C.?"

"None. But he works for Lee Chang, and the Chang family has business interests around the world. Not unlike myself. He is probably in town on business, visiting some lobbyist on the K Street corridor."

"Mr. Winthrop. The night that picture was taken was the night your former secretary had her accident. That photo, as I explained on the note, was taken from an ATM across the street from the Metro station where she died."

"Are you saying this man had something to do with Marilyn's death?"

"That is why we are here. We were hoping you could answer that question," Detective Wallace said.

Peter didn't flinch.

"I thought her death was ruled an accident?" Peter asked. He spent enough time with lawyers to know how to ask his own questions.

"That was the original finding."

"Well, detectives, I have been doing business with Lee Chang and the Chang family for years. I assure you they are not interested in killing my secretary."

Wallace didn't have an answer for the seemingly simple statement.

"Do you know anyone who would want to harm your secretary? A boyfriend? Disgruntled employee?"

"Not that I'm aware of. She wasn't dating anyone recently that I know of. As for a disgruntled employee, we are one big happy family here at Winthrop Enterprises."

Shelly knocked on the edge of the doorframe and delivered the espresso to the desk for Detective Wallace.

"Are you familiar with St. Michael's Catholic Church?"

"I hope so. I was married there. As much as I would like to forget it."

"Are you a parishioner?"

"No, no. My ex-wife was. I was raised a Baptist. But my wife came from a strict Catholic family. It was a concession on my part. You have to pick your battles when it comes to marriage."

Detective Wallace smiled with understanding.

"So you haven't been to the church recently?"

"Not since my ex-wife's funeral."

"Let me ask another question."

"Please, that's why we're here."

"How well do you know your son?"

"Well enough. We haven't been as close over the years as I would have liked, but he has been working here this summer. He is a good kid."

"Your son works here?"

"Yes."

"Can we speak with him?"

"He's not in the office today. He has been out all week, getting ready for school to start next month. Registering for classes, whatever it is you have to do these days."

"We would like to speak with him as well. It's rather urgent."

"What does my son know about all this?"

"We don't know. We went to his apartment but his neighbor said he was out of town."

"Out of town?"

"That's what his neighbor said."

"News to me."

Wallace and Nguyen both scribbled in their notebooks.

"We have reason to believe your son may have been with your secretary the night she was killed."

"I thought it was an accident."

Wallace rephrased the sentence. "We have reason to believe your son was with your secretary the night she had her accident. The night she died."

"He might have been. They were co-workers. You don't suspect my son had anything to do with her death, do you? I thought you were suspicious of the man in the photo? Are you saying there are two suspects? Working together?"

Wallace felt like he was in the hot seat. "No sir. Your son is not a suspect. We would like to ask him a few questions about that night. Maybe he saw something that could help us get to the truth."

"I thought the medical examiner's office already got to the truth."

Wallace didn't like the way that line of questioning was going and changed topics. "Do you have a phone number for your son? A mobile phone number?"

"Sure, I can get that for you. Is there anything else I can help you with? I have to meet someone at the airport, and if I get going now, I should be right on time."

"No, that's it. If you think of anything that may help us, please contact either me or my partner here."

"Certainly. And if you need to reach me, here is my direct number. Either Shelly or I will answer the call. She will get you my son's phone number on the way out."

"His mobile phone number. We have his home number," Detective Nguyen said for clarification.

"Yes, she will provide you with whatever you want."

Detective Wallace checked his notes. "And we will be waiting for the name of the man in the photo."

"Yes, detective. I will get that to you as soon as possible."

***

Peter Winthrop picked Hasad up at Reagan National Airport with Shawn, his driver, behind the wheel. Shawn, dressed in his usual black suit with a white shirt and blue tie, put the bags in the trunk as Hasad gave Peter his over-the-top greeting. Handshake, half-hug, followed by another handshake.

"So good to see you again, Mr. Winthrop. So good."

"How was your flight?"

"Long. As you know. Istanbul to New York was non-stop. Zipped into Manhattan to visit a friend for lunch and caught the Delta shuttle here."

"Well, I hope you can survive for another hour or so."

"Where are we going?"

"Baltimore."

"I love Baltimore," Hasad said. "They have the best Hooters restaurant, right there on the harbor. Maybe we can stop there for a late dinner."

"I think we can work it into the schedule."

"Where is Jake?"

"He's not going to make it."

"That's too bad. I enjoyed our night out in D.C. on my last visit."

"So did Jake. He would be here but has been busy preparing for school. He's been out of the classroom for almost two years and said he needs to re-register, talk to some professors, see what classes he needs to take."

"I understand," Hasad answered, no longer listening.

Baltimore Harbor is home to the third largest port on the eastern seaboard after Newport News and Charleston. Its larger siblings accounted for most of the steel and commodities coming into the U.S., the continued strength of a hundred plus years of post-slave imports. Baltimore, in contrast, had a little bit of everything. Located at the foot of the Northeast Corridor, the container ships lined up five miles out for their turn to load and unload.

Life on the docks never stopped. A stench of dead fish and diesel fuel was as consistent as the flow of the brackish waters where the river met the bay. A massive conglomeration of warehouses, docks, and miles of cracked pavement—work went on twenty-four hours a day, performed by some of the hardest men ever put on God's green earth. U.S. Customs resided in the main facilities building on the west side of the complex, overlooking the forklifts that milled about like ants. Cranes swung back and forth, delivering cargo to the decks of ships that stood sixty feet out of the water. Pneumatic conveyors blew powdered goods from the ship hulls to waiting railcars at the far end of the yard.

The strip of warehouses and storage facilities that began near the water stretched as far as the unaided eye could see, running south like a retired couple from northern Michigan. Each building was an unofficial standard size—ninety feet by a hundred twenty. Each one was three stories, a sea of metal boxes holding priceless valuables and crates of worthless crap. Over the years the warehouses had yielded numerous front-page-worthy finds, including a stolen Picasso and a mummified family of five dating back to the Great Depression.

Warehouse 21-C was the third building down from the main access road that ran through the middle of the field of storage. Some of the smaller warehouses were divided into two multiple storage facilities, separated by a wall of plyboard and chicken wire, each side large enough for a full basketball court. Warehouse 21-C was undivided, Winthrop Enterprises its lone resident.

Dark clouds formed a front to the west as Shawn pulled into the Baltimore Harbor Warehouse and Storage facilities. A passkey combination started the gate in motion with a thud, followed by the silence of well-greased wheels on their tracks.

"Looks like storms are coming, sir."

"Yes it does. What's July in the D.C. area without a few afternoon boomers?"

"Yes, sir. Just letting you know the forecast."

"Thanks, Shawn," Peter said. "Pull the car over to the right."

The black sedan-for-hire parked next to a roll-up door on the warehouse across from number 21-C. On cue, the rain started falling in a light pitter-patter. Peter and his Turkish client got out of opposite sides of the car. Peter pointed in the direction of the warehouse with an open hand extending from the cuff of his suit. Hasad followed as the rain picked up in intensity, larger drops, cold to the touch.

"Is this your main warehouse?" Hasad asked, unable to keep silent, even when there was nothing to say.

"I don't own it. Winthrop Enterprises leases it on a semi-permanent basis."

Peter opened the side door with a key and a nudge from his right shoulder. The warehouse was pitch black and Peter fumbled his hand along the right side wall until he found the oversized power switch. With a pull on the lever, the floor of the warehouse illuminated.

Boxes filled the back half of the floor space, each box neatly labeled and stacked in separate piles, some twenty feet high. The concrete floor was swept and clean. A lone forklift was parked in the back, near an emergency exit with an intermittently flashing sign.

"What's in all the boxes?" Hasad asked.

"Let's see," Peter answered, walking among the stacks. He looked at the labels and started the tour. "I believe we have some Civil War memorabilia going to a collector in India. The collection includes a set of rare cavalier sabers, and a few cannon remains. Not a big shipment, but we are still finalizing some documentation before it can be exported. We keep most of our large shipments in another location. Heavy items that can't be moved as easily by forklift."

"Things like Hummers."

"Exactly. Your Hummers were retrofitted not too far from here."

"They are great vehicles."

"I am glad you enjoy them."

"I do, I do. My friends and I enjoy them very much."

***

Shawn looked through the window of the parked car, rain cascading down the windshield in sheets. He saw a figure in front of the car and hit the wipers. The swipe of rubber across the glass brought the leveled gun into perfect focus. The door was yanked open from the outside and Shawn looked out of the corner of his eye to see another gun—very real and very close.

"FBI. Don't move," Special Agent Ann Cahill said with glee. "Keep your hands on the wheel where I can see them." The agent had fire-red hair and a personality to match.

The rain on the roof of the warehouse drowned out the pounding of heavy feet, fit bodies weighed down by thick bulletproof vests and rifles. Two teams in standard cover formation closed in on the warehouse exits, one team going through the front door, another team with a door-ram coming in the back.

Inside the warehouse, Hasad was enjoying the conversation, marveling at the breadth of interest of Winthrop Enterprises' clients. It was Hasad's turn to grease the wheels of politeness. A little business before *his* business. The tour was winding down and Hasad knew the neatly stacked boxes near the large rolling door were his shipment. It was the only section of the warehouse Peter hadn't shown him. Hasad knew the American was saving the best for last.

The front door swung open a split second before the back door flew onto the floor, torn from its hinges.

"Don't move motherfucker," Agent John Tulloch screamed with six months of pent up anger. Six months of wasted time. Six months of the runaround. Six months of chasing leads that were nothing more than dead ends. Six months of putting up with his partner.

Peter Winthrop looked at Agent Tulloch, a five-foot-five Napoleon complex with a gun, and raised his hands. "Don't you move," Agent Tulloch repeated, dropping the vulgarity.

Hasad looked at Peter and put his arms straight up like a kid playing cops-and-robbers.

Federal Agents from the FBI and the Office of Export Controls swept the warehouse with guns drawn, each man covered by another as they made their way through the maze of boxes. Shouts of "clear," echoed through the air as every corner of the warehouse was secured. Agent Cahill joined her partner in the warehouse, hair dripping on her FBI windbreaker, her pants soaked. Agent Tulloch was quick to notice the positive effect the wet outfit had on the little beauty his partner did possess.

"Peter Winthrop, we are placing you under arrest for the purchase of controlled goods with the intent to export," Agent Cahill said, a large drop of water falling off her nose as she spoke.

"What goods would that be?" Peter asked.

"One thousand military-grade night vision goggles, for starters. They are illegal to own without a permit and they sure as hell are illegal to sell to foreign nationals."

Hasad visibly squirmed.

"Without a search warrant, this arrest, and anything confiscated during a search, is illegal and invalid in a court of law." Peter looked at the agents with the same smug smile he flashed when he last cleaned up at the high roller table in Vegas.

Agent Tulloch reached into his jacket, pulled out the warrant, and handed it to Peter. Peter quickly flipped the warrant to the back page and looked at the judge's signature. Elizabeth Rubin. "Elizabeth Rubin," he said quietly to himself, committing the name to memory.

"Something wrong, Peter?" Agent Cahill asked with sarcasm.

Peter shrugged his shoulders and ignored the agent's comment, focusing his thoughts forty miles south to the Nation's Capitol.

***

Peter and Hasad, now handcuffed, sat on the edge of the dirty desk near the door as the federal agents tore the warehouse and its contents to shreds. The cursing by the agents started immediately and didn't stop until the last box was on the floor, opened. Two hundred and fifty boxes labeled with night-vision goggle tags were reduced to cardboard scraps. Two hundred and fifty boxes filled with over a thousand household items ranging from tea kettles to cookie sheets. All bought at Walmart. All paid for with a Winthrop Enterprises corporate American Express card.

Agent Cahill stood next to the CEO and Hasad, working over the piece of gum in her mouth like a beaver on a log. Her face had passed flush half an hour ago and now teetered on the verge of white, drained by anger and embarrassment.

Agent Tulloch called Agent Cahill over, pulling her gently by the sleeve of her jacket, turning her back toward their suspects.

"There is nothing here. No goggles, no guns, nothing illegal. He has paperwork for everything in the warehouse. Nothing in the boxes labeled 'goggles' but a household clearance sale from Walmart—the price stickers still attached."

"How did he know?"

"I don't know. Maybe his son had second thoughts and let his old man know we were coming."

"But why?"

"Because he is his father."

On the other side of the room, Hasad looked confused. "Peter, what happened? Where are my hunting goggles?"

"They are due to arrive in Istanbul this evening," Peter said in a whisper.

But how? How did you know they were coming?"

"Because my son is just like his mother."

Chapter 41

The van lurched over the speed bump that marked the edge of Saipan International Airport property and the beginning of the parking lot for the small general aviation terminal on the south side of the runways. Inside the small terminal, two rows of seats sat twenty plastic molded chairs that hadn't been filled in a year since a U.S. military transport aircraft was forced to make an emergency landing after taking an albatross through the engine.

The general aviation terminal's Customs and Border Protection (CBP) staffed exactly one person who rotated shifts and split their time working at the main terminal where most of the action was. A young local woman with a nose ring and geeky demeanor was the only non-government staff, spending her time organizing and coordinating the half-dozen charter flights that landed and took off on any given afternoon. On days when the employees outnumbered the number of flights, the lone baggage handler took naps in the back room while the young lady at the counter openly studied accounting in her third attempt at passing the course online.

U.S. Customs and Border Protection, even on Saipan, was a serious bunch, and the doctor with the sedated Chinese girl in the wheelchair brought natural scrutiny. The lone CBP officer on duty in the general aviation terminal, a short man of nearly equal height and width, looked at both passports and then at the faces of the doctor and the girl. He checked the date on Wei Ling's U.S. work visa and then checked the doctor's visitor visa. He looked at the documents and the faces one more time and reached for a paper on his desk. He scanned the paper feverishly and then gestured with his hand toward the empty seats in the waiting area.

"Please have a seat."

"Is there a problem? I am a physician providing medical care for a sick patient."

"Doctor, have a seat and I will be right with you."

The doctor smelled trouble. He had traveled enough to know that either you get a stamp in your passport immediately, or you could be waiting as long as the authorities deemed necessary. And government bureaucracy could wait longer than any man.

"What are we waiting for? I have legal and medical documentation concerning this girl. I am her personal physician. She is a Chinese national, and I am taking her back to Beijing for medical care. Read the documents."

The stout CBP Officer, phone now in his ear, raised his hand and silenced the doctor with his palm. The officer with the girth of a large oak was following orders to the letter.

The doctor refused to sit down and stood with military line-up posture, exchanging glances with the CBP Officer who was getting agitated. The officer made no effort to hide his focus on Wei Ling. The girl's eyes were shut, her breathing heavy. She was dead to the world and, according to the doctor's schedule, at least an hour away from consciousness. The doctor grew nervous.

The plane hired by C.F. Chang was fueled and ready for takeoff. The emergency flight, hired on ninety minutes's notice, cost C.F. Chang twenty-five grand. The pilot, who stood to pocket most of that sum, waited in the plane for further instructions. He leaned back in the seat, checked the instruments and adjusted his sunglasses. When his sciatic nerve acted up, he came into to the terminal to check on his passengers. The doctor told him to wait, gave him a brief lesson in acupressure to alleviate the pain in his leg, and sent him back to the plane. "It will all be straightened out shortly," the doctor assured him.

"I'm getting paid either way," the pilot answered.

Forty minutes later, the doctor took a seat in a corner of the room, sulking over his detainment. He wheeled the still-sleeping Wei Ling to a spot beneath the television on the wall, and called C.F. Chang at fifteen-minute intervals.

The Chang family's political contacts jolted into action. A call to the Chinese Embassy in Washington was received and passed along the chain of command. The son of a senator hung in the balance, information that under other circumstances would have brought immediate intervention. The lines were clogged with lies and threats, the Chang political machine chugging down the track, cutting between what they could and couldn't say. Phone calls started trickling into the State Department's Chief Liaison Office for the Commonwealth of the Northern Mariana Island, Saipan. The man in charge looked at the ringing phone, checked the number on the display screen, and walked out the door.

***

Jake flew through the double doors first, Tony and the Castello brothers behind him, sweating as if they had been sprayed with a hose. The rushing bodies were like a tornado churning up the stale winds of inactivity in the small charter terminal. The stocky CBP Officer glanced at the new arrivals. Rush hour had just arrived.

"May I help you?" the young lady behind the counter asked, pushing her open textbook to the side.

"Yes," Jake answered, not sure what the follow-up should be.

"How may I help you?" the lady answered, trying to lead Jake into supplying useful information.

Jake checked out the room. He glanced around, looking directly at Wei Ling in the wheelchair and then at the doctor. Then he improvised. "We will be flying out in a couple of hours. Just wanted to check in."

"We don't really check in for charter flights, Mr. ....?"

"Jake Patrick."

Still on the phone behind the lady at the counter, the CBP Officer's eyes flinched. He nodded to the future bean counter and stepped toward Jake, his gold shield pinned through the white shirt of his uniform. Covering the phone in one hand, the cord stretched behind him, the CBP Officer offered Jake the same attitude and advice he had offered the doctor. "Yes, Mr. Patrick. Please have a seat. I'll be with you shortly."

Not knowing what to do, or what he was waiting for, Jake found a seat with his three bodyguards-for-hire. He looked at the doctor in the corner of the terminal who continually switched his attention between his phone and checking on the Asian girl in the wheelchair. Oblivious that the girl he had traveled halfway around the world to meet was sitting right in front of him, Jake shut his eyes, and said a small prayer. It was a prayer for guidance that was coming, but it wasn't from the man upstairs. It was from a man who wore old clothes, ate at soup kitchens, and read more newspapers than any person on earth.

***

The suit was the only buttoned linen blend on the island on a sizzling July day. The sleek, frameless glasses, with flip-up dark lens attachments, added an exclamation point to the attire. Tom Foti, dressed for a meeting, strolled into the general aviation terminal office and was on the CBP Officer before he turned around. "Where is he?"

"Are you the Liaison Officer?"

"Yes. Tom Foti. Chief of the Liaison Office for the Commonwealth of the Northern Mariana Islands, Saipan," he said, using a title that put most people to sleep before he could finish spitting it out. He placed the manila folder in his hand on the counter and shook hands with the CBP Officer.

"It is a pleasure to meet you face-to-face," the officer answered. "I received orders at the morning briefing directing me to contact you if either of these individuals showed up." The CBP Officer explained the situation to the newest member of guess-who's-in-the-charter terminal and slipped the paper to Tom Foti, who read the document with the dark lenses on his glasses still down.

"If you don't mind me asking, what does the State Department want with him?"

"I'm not at liberty to say."

"I'm just following orders, but technically he hasn't broken any law from the Department of Homeland Security's perspective. We at Customs and Border Protection have no legal reason to hold either of them."

"It isn't a matter of DHS or CBS jurisdiction."

"Sure. Sure. I just want to make it clear that there isn't a DHS violation. Both of them have valid visas."

"I understand that there is no DHS violation. The State Department is still interested in speaking with him. I assure you that CBP will not be held culpable in any way."

A look of relief washed over the officer's face. "Like I said, I am just following orders. The morning briefing asked for our cooperation."

"I appreciate it."

"He's all yours," the CBP Officer said gesturing toward the doctor before leaning into Tom and whispering. "Word to the wise…the old man is a little feisty".

Tom Foti walked up to the doctor, flipped the dark lenses on his glasses up, and introduced himself with his full title. With no partner to take the role of the good cop, he took his turn at the bad cop side of his routine.

"What's your name?"

"Martin Yu."

Tom Foti flashed a skeptical don't-try-to-bullshit-me look, and asked another question. "Real name?"

"Yu, Hao Kuang."

"Occupation?"

"Physician."

"Place of employment."

"Beijing."

"Do you work in a hospital?"

"No, I am a private physician."

"What are you doing here?"

"I am here on Saipan as the temporary physician for Chang Industries. I am taking an ill patient home on a charter flight."

"You are here on a tourist visa, not a work visa."

"I am here as a favor to the Chang Family. I am not being paid and therefore do not need a work visa." The doctor was confident in his reply. He was backed by a Chinese powerhouse. He had all the answers.

Tom Foti let the doctor know he wasn't some schmuck in a suit.

"Is the girl in the wheelchair your patient?"

"Yes she is."

"Do you realize it is illegal to take an incapacitated individual for international travel without documentation?"

"I have documentation," the doctor said smartly, pulling a folder from his bag. The medical folder was thick.

Tom Foti read through the top page in the folder. "You need documentation from a physician with a U.S. medical license. Saipan is a U.S.

territory. Your Chinese medical license is not valid here."

"You don't understand. This girl is very ill," the doctor said gravely. For the first time, real worry settled in. "She needs medical care that cannot be provided for her on the island. Chang Industries is paying for her well-being, and I am sure the Chang family would appreciate your understanding in this matter."

Tom Foti dragged the doctor by the arm into the isolation of the small Customs and Border Protection office. He shut the door behind him and scrolled the blinds open so he could see through the metal slats. Tom looked beyond the venetians, through the glass wall at the collection of oddities in the terminal. Then he spun and stared straight into the eyes of the doctor.

"Here is the deal, doctor. We are all going to wait until *your patient* wakes up, and then *I* am going to decide what needs to be done."

"You can't do that," the doctor said with without defeat.

"I can do anything I want, doctor. This is my corner of the world and I will see to it the law is followed as closely as I see fit. Go out there, sit down, and let's wait. If you administer any medicine to the young lady in the wheelchair, I will have you detained. Is that understood?"

"But she needs medical attention."

"I will have a doctor here in ten minutes."

***

Jake heard his name called from across the room. He stood, shrugged his shoulders at Tony and the Castello brothers, and made his way to the small office. The girl behind the counter had put away her accounting books for the day. It was obvious that something out of the ordinary was unfolding, and she wasn't about to miss it over the cost of goods sold or an income statement.

"My name is Tom Foti. Please have a seat, Jake."

The CBP office smelled putrid. The rotting scent of a confiscated durian invaded every corner of the room. Tom looked out the window over Jake's head. The Chinese doctor, the girl in the wheelchair, and a freshly arrived physician on call at the main terminal huddled in the corner. C.F. Chang's doctor watched as the physician on call, a doctor with a U.S. medical degree, checked Wei Ling's pulse, respiration, and blood pressure.

Tom opened the folder he had brought with him. "Jake, do you mind if I ask you a few questions?"

"Please," Jake said, the words coming out much more comfortably than he was feeling.

"Who is your favorite writer?"

"I'm sorry?" Jake asked, puzzled.

Tom checked his facts. "It says here you are an English Literature student. Is this not accurate?"

Jake looked at the Liaison Officer, his eyes wide. "It says what?"

"English Literature. American University."

Jake looked at Tom Foti in his suit and glasses with the dark lenses sticking straight out, and wondered what in God's name was going on. "I like Emerson."

"Emerson?"

"Of course Shakespeare is the most influential writer in the history of the English language, but it's basically unreadable to the average person. I like to read the thoughts of the great writers, not spend my time deciphering them."

"I'm partial to Shakespeare, actually," Tom said. "Classic Literature was my main area of study in school."

There was silence as they measured each other.

"What else do you know?" Jake asked. "You're the second person this month to have a file on me."

"You must be busy."

"I am now."

"I would say so," Tom added. "Born in Washington D.C., raised by your mother after your parents's divorce. Currently working for your father, Peter Winthrop, at a company with the same name. A medical degree from Georgetown University."

"A medical degree?" Jake asked.

"That's what it says here. I even have a copy of your diploma."

"Sir, I don't have a medical degree."

"You do today. And if that doctor out there starts asking questions about the girl in the wheelchair, just play along."

"Play along?"

"I had the doctor brought in for procedural reasons. He is on our side. He's American. But he may ask a few questions for show. If he does, say something that sounds medically viable. It makes a nice cover for the other ears in the room." Tom motioned toward the CBP Officer and the future accountant.

"Who is the girl in the wheelchair?" Jake asked.

"The girl you came to take back to Washington."

Jake's mouth opened and he stared out the glass wall of the office, the pieces of the puzzle falling into place. The message at the hotel desk. The CBP Officer at the charter terminal. Jake was just along for the ride.

Tom let Jake zone out for a minute before continuing.

"Her name is Wei Ling. As I understand it, she is the reason you are here." Tom Foti pushed the folder toward Jake, and the former summer help for Winthrop Enterprises flipped through the documents. They were perfect in their illegitimacy.

"So what do we do now?"

"We wait for the girl to tell us she wants to go to Washington. If she does, there is nothing to stop you from taking her with you."

"And if she doesn't?"

"Well, as much as I would like to help, that would be kidnapping."

"So we wait."

"We wait. The charter plane you came in on is fueled and standing by."

***

Captain Talua stepped from his police cruiser in front of the general aviation terminal and looked at the license plates for the two rental cars and at the government issued tags on the white four-door. He tugged his pants a fraction higher on his waist and put on his swagger. It was a full house in the charter terminal, and Captain Talua was the last card in the deck.

"May I help you?" the young lady behind the counter asked, her mind trying to place the familiar face. A flash of his badge pried open her memory. The vertically challenged CBP officer and the State Department representative stepped to the counter, one standing on each side of the girl in her chair.

"Captain Talua," the CBP Officer said with a smile. He knew the captain—all the CBP Officers did. Customs and Border Protection used the police facilities on occasion to hold uncooperative visa violators. "How are you today?"

"Not very well. Not very well at all," the captain said, looking at the waiting room and the hodgepodge collection of characters. "Quite a scene at one of the factories this morning. One murder and one suspicious death."

"Related?" Tom Foti asked, butting in. He assumed the captain of Saipan's police force recognized him.

The pitfalls of assumption.

"And you are?"

"Tom Foti, Chief of the Liaison Office for the Commonwealth of the Northern Mariana Islands, Saipan."

"The State Department."

"Yes, sir. We met last year when the president of the Philippines was in town for the weekend."

"Ah, yes. My apologies for not recognizing you," the captain said, looking at Tom's outfit as if that were the reason for his forgetfulness.

"Not at all. In your line of work, you meet a lot of people. You can't possibly remember them all."

"I guess I do," the captain answered, liking the excuse Tom Foti offered better than the run-of-the-mill "premature senility" comment he was ready to use.

"What brings you down here, Captain?"

"I'm looking for someone," Captain Talua said, glancing around the room. "A doctor who works at Chang Industries."

Tom Foti smiled, his white teeth stretching to the corner of his mouth. "Well Captain, it looks like it's your lucky day."

Captain Talua squinted perceptively. A hint of disbelief on his face. "You're kidding?"

"Right over there," Tom answered, gleefully pointing toward the corner as the doctor looked up.

"And the girl. Is she from Chang Industries?"

"Yes."

"I need to see her too. She might be a witness to a serious crime."

"The girl is incapacitated and under my supervision and care," Tom Foti said sternly. "She will not be questioned today, Captain. It's not a point up for negotiation."

"Mr. Foti, you have no jurisdiction over me."

"Perhaps you can step into the office for a moment," Tom said, still smiling. "We can discuss jurisdiction."

The office door shut and the CBP Officer and girl at the counter were miffed for being cut out of the juicy part of the conversation.

"Have a seat, captain."

"I'll stand."

"Captain. I have no jurisdiction over you. I have no authority to arrest or investigate anyone. But I can sure as hell bring a shit storm to your door. A cloud of investigation the likes of which you cannot even begin to imagine."

"Are you threatening me?"

"No. Not at all. But I would be interested in what the Department of Justice has to say about a police officer on a sweatshop owner's payroll."

"I need to speak with the girl. There was a murder at Chang Industries this afternoon and the girl may have been the only witness."

"What is an incapacitated girl from a sweatshop going to know about a murder?"

"You don't understand."

"No, you don't understand. If you need to question someone, start with the doctor. Ask him about the bandage on his neck. Do your job. Believe me, when this girl starts telling her story, I don't think you are going to want to have the questions streaming into your office. And I will make sure they do."

Captain Talua considered his options. On the off chance the man before him wasn't bluffing, he folded.

"Have a good day, Mr. Foti."

"And you, Captain."

The captain waited for two of his officers to arrive and lead the doctor away. As C.F. Chang's personal physician exited the door, his hands cuffed behind his back, he yelled out over his shoulder to Wei Ling in the wheelchair. "*You've got nowhere to run. C.F. Chang will find you.*"

***

It had been an hour since Wei Ling first opened her eyes—a brief visit to the conscious world before fading out seconds later. In the hour since her initial arousal, Tom and Jake took turns speaking softly to the girl in the wheelchair.

"Wei Ling?" Tom asked, sitting in a chair, their faces on the same level no more than a foot apart. "Wei Ling?" he asked again with the same soft tone. The thin Chinese sweatshop worker with the child of a senator in her womb looked at Tom and nodded ever so slightly.

"My name is Tom Foti and I work for the U.S. government. You are safe now. You have nothing to fear."

Wei Ling smiled a doped-up grin, hope radiating in her slowly clearing mind. Twenty minutes later, as she realized she was no longer captive, warm tears trickled down her cheeks. It was only a matter of time before the sedatives would wear off, and she would have to make a decision that would change her life forever.

Another hour passed as Jake paced the floor. Tom Foti went outside to talk on his incessantly ringing cell phone. Wei Ling opened her eyes and said, "water."

Jake jumped from his seat, raced across the charter terminal, and fetched a paper cone cup of spring water. He handed her the water, sat down, and introduced himself to Wei Ling with a handshake. Her hand was weak, clammy, her fingers calloused.

"My name is Jake. My father is Peter Winthrop."

Wei Ling looked at Jake with warm eyes. "I didn't know Peter had a son."

"There are a lot of things you don't know about him. There are a lot of things I don't know about him."

"He sent you to get me?" Wei Ling asked, groggily.

Jake paused. The question was a hopeful one. Jake didn't want to be breaking hearts and trashing dreams, however misguided. He certainly didn't want to be doing his father's dirty work, telling women things his father wasn't man enough to say himself. Jake swallowed and answered without elaborating. "No, my father didn't send me. I'm sorry."

"How did you know about me?"

"It is a long story. But I guess your friends were looking out for you."

Tom Foti came back into the room and interrupted. His jacket was off. The perspiration under his armpits dripped down to his elbows. "Jake, we need to get moving. There are some forces at work that can't be held at bay forever."

Jake nodded.

"Wei Ling, Jake needs to ask you a serious question. As a representative of the U.S. State Department, I assure you that you can answer freely. Either way, I am here to help you. Do you understand?"

"Yes."

Jake moved closer to Wei Ling and put his hand on the arm of her wheelchair. "Wei Ling. If you want, I would like to take you back to Washington, D.C. I will make sure you receive medical care from the best doctors."

"Can I stay here?"

"Yes, you can," Tom Foti answered. "If you want, you are welcome to stay here. Or I can arrange for you to go home."

Wei Ling thought about her parents in Guangzhou. "Why Washington?"

"The chance to save a thousand girls just like you," Jake answered.

Tears welled up in Wei Ling's eyes. Her mind played a mini-film of the two years she had been on the island. Five days off in two years. A hundred other girls just like her, locked up with no money, no power, no options.

"Then I will go."

***

The preparation for departure was short.

"Do you need anything, Wei Ling?" Tom asked as Jake, Wei Ling, Tony, and the Castello brothers prepared to exit the waiting room. Wei Ling refused to sit down in the wheelchair in which she had arrived. She had had enough immobility. Her healing bedsores hurt. Jake held her by one arm, guiding her steps toward the door.

"Can you call my parents?" Wei Ling asked.

"I can do that. What do you want me to tell them?" Tom Foti answered.

"Tell them don't worry."

"It's done."

Tom Foti watched Wei Ling shuffle out the door. "Hey Jake."

"Yeah."

"Say hi to Al for me."

"Sure. I will. And thank you."

"Do the right thing," Tom said, sounding suspiciously like Jake's homeless counterpart.

"Always," Jake answered.

Chapter 42

With the eastwardly jet stream pushing the Gulfstream G550 near-ly four hundred mph, and the outside temperature at twenty-five below zero, Wei Ling curled up into the reclined seat of the private aircraft. She slipped both hands under her head, something she hadn't been able to do for weeks, and dreamt the dreams of someone set free. Heavy breaths, followed by drool, followed by a light rhythmic snore.

Jake was buried in medical books, dog-earing pages, taking notes, slapping sticky notes on appropriate pages. He read every passage scrawled in Kate's handwriting on the cheat sheet she had given him. It was a crash course in pregnancy and neonatal care. Armed with a stethoscope, thermometer, and a blood pressure gauge, it was as close to practicing medicine as he was going to get. A doctor for the day, now complete with a fake diploma.

Jake looked at Wei Ling and felt relieved. Her face had good color, a basic indicator of proper health. At least according to his grandmother. The healthy hue was Jake's medical ace-in-the-hole. Sure Wei Ling was thin, but she wasn't play-her-ribs-like-a-xylophone thin. And if her spirit were any indication of her physical well being, the girl would be fine.

Tony, the heavy-hitting bone-breaker, looked at Jake with a hint of respect. A young kid who just went halfway around the world and, only God knows how, managed to pick up a girl who was ill. What had transpired in the airport was beyond Tony's comprehension. All he knew was that Sorrentino had ordered him and the Castello brothers to accompany this kid for a couple of days and see to it that he stayed out of trouble. Tony was following orders. But when he looked at Wei Ling in her chair, and then at Jake in his seat with a pile of books and paper, for a human moment Tony considered that perhaps he had missed the opportunity to do something with his life.

"She'll be all right, won't she?" he asked toward Jake, who was almost startled by the sudden question.

"I don't know, Tony," Jake answered, flipping through pages. "She should be fine through the flight. She has bedsores, which look pretty bad. Of course, I have nothing to compare it to other than a picture here in this book. She is also running a slight fever, which could be a sign of infection," Jake said checking his notes. "But the thing that worries me is her high blood pressure. One sixty over one twenty. According to the book, this could be the symptom of something called pre-eclampsia. This can lead to seizures and even death," Jake added with a serious tone that was at least partially contrived.

Tony nodded.

"Did you know that it is possible for pregnant women to have diabetes during their pregnancy? It's called 'gestational diabetes.'"

"I had no idea. Makes you thankful guys aren't the ones getting knocked up." And with that statement, Tony turned toward the window and shut his eyes.

The cabin of the plane was quiet, the flipping of pages, the hum of the ventilation system, and the occasional squeak of leather under Tony's heavy frame were the only sounds. Twenty-four hours without sleep, and Jake shut his eyes with a pull-out diagram of the female reproductive organs spread in his lap. Now that he had the girl, things were bound to get interesting. In a moment of pride, and with thoughts of a senator on his mind, Jake smiled. In five weeks, he had gone from a graduate student who had just buried his mother to a twenty-four-year-old with serious ambition. The latter was infinitely better than the former. In the fifth grade, his mother had dragged him to the Boy Scouts because she thought there were some skills her son needed to learn that she just couldn't teach him. Twenty-four years old and Jake Patrick, still a Boy Scout at heart, was about to bump bellies with a senator.

***

After refueling in Sapporo, Anchorage, and Denver, the private Gulfstream touched down and taxied to the general aviation terminal at the southeast end of Reagan National. Tony stepped off the twin-engine private jet first, his frame filling the small doorway, noticeable from the gate window nearly fifty yards away. Al and Kate, self-introduced in the lobby an hour before, stood side-by-side, their faces reflecting in the glass window.

"I can't believe it," Al said, giddy. "You have done it now, Korgaokar. Trouble with a capital 'T,'" he said out loud, using his own last name. "You've unzipped your fly and are about to piss on a spark plug."

"Trouble?" Kate asked, looking at Al with concern over his mental health.

"With a capital 'T'," he repeated. Al stared straight ahead, eyes fixed out the window.

With the intuition of a woman, Kate pressed for details. "What have you two done?"

Al didn't answer. He stood tall and smiled proudly like the father of a son who had just left the house on a date with the prom queen.

Jake walked Wei Ling down the stairs of the aircraft, and Al cherished the moment. With a strong breeze blowing her loose fitting clothes, Wei Ling stepped on the tarmac and looked out across the Potomac at the illuminated white dome of the Capitol Building in the distance. The center of power in the free world was lost on her. She was trusting a complete stranger, the son of someone who had thrown her to the wolves. All she knew was that being locked to a bed had changed a lot of things for her. *A chance to save a thousand girls just like her.* The words Jake had thrown out there meant everything.

Still smiling, Al looked at Kate. "I guess it doesn't matter now."

"What doesn't matter?" Kate answered. She had been waiting for an answer since Al had started talking to himself.

"You know the girl is pregnant," Al asked.

"Jake mentioned it."

"Did he tell you who the father is?"

"I figured it was his father," Kate said, trying to connect with Al, still waiting for the punch line.

"Are you familiar with Senator Day from Massachusetts?"

As soon as Al's words registered, Kate longed for the state of ignorance-is-bliss. "Don't tell me…"

"Right there on the tarmac. In the flesh evidence that will ruin a man's life."

"Oh my God," she whispered. Suddenly, it all made sense. The night on the bed with Jake and the news on TV, the secrecy over the last few weeks, the paranoid behavior—it was both clear and unbelievable. She didn't know if she liked Jake more or less than before. "Oh my God," she repeated, touching her lips lightly with the palm side of her fingers.

"I don't think God has anything to do with it...but I guess there is no harm in asking for His help. Though I'll be the first to tell you it hasn't done me much good."

"You shouldn't have let him go."

"Who?"

"Jake."

"He came to me."

"But you helped him."

"Yes, I got him the plane. I helped him on the other end through an old friend. And I'll do everything in my power to protect him."

Kate looked at Al, a handsome man in his late forties with weathered skin, reddish brown hair, and striking blue eyes. His suit fit perfectly, his shoes shined, his face shaven. Al was back among the living. Jake was in good hands.

Tony held open the door as Jake walked Wei Ling into the terminal. Kate pushed the terminal's wheelchair to the door but Wei Ling refused to sit down.

"Bedsores," Jake said, as if Wei Ling needed an excuse to stand. Kate gave Jake a hug and a peck on the cheek. "You and I need to talk," she said before turning to Wei Ling, taking the young Asian woman by the arm and offering her a bottle of water. She checked Wei Ling's pulse as Wei Ling stood at attention, her arm out.

Al stood tall, back straight, arms crossed, and waited for Jake's eyes to meet his. Jake gave him a head-to-toe once-over, smiling at the suit, the shave, the shoes and their shine. "You clean up well," Jake said.

"Just in time to get dirty again," Al responded. The ex-State Department CIA official cover operative stepped forward and shook Jake's hand, pounded a few pats in his back, and finished him off with a bear hug that lifted Jake off his feet.

"You did it."

"We did it."

"How is she?" Al asked with a sideways nod of the head in Wei Ling's direction.

"Ask her," Jake said.

Al stepped past Tony and the Castello brothers, who stood in their standard shoulder-to-shoulder, arms folded pose. Al gently touched Wei Ling on her shoulder. He looked her in the eyes and cleared his throat. "*Wo jiao Al.*" My name is Al. "*Ni gan jiao zen yang.*" How do you feel? *Lu tu shun li ma?*" How was the flight?"

Wei Ling's face lit up, her eyes bugging with appreciation and surprise. Nodding vigorously, Wei Ling answered that she was fine. Al struggled to dislodge the Chinese that had been collecting dust in the corner of his mind for a decade. He heard the words, slowly translated them, and remained a few seconds behind Wei Ling as she spoke. Tony and the Castello brothers stood there, staring, as if they were watching a foreign movie with live subtitles.

Kate finished her cursory standing medical exam on Wei Ling and tugged at Jake's hand. Jake was listening to Al, the bag with medical books in his left hand, the ear-ends of the stethoscope hanging out from the zipper.

"What's the prognosis, doctor?" Kate asked.

"She is running a fever. Blood pressure is one sixty over one twenty. Pulse is eighty-three."

"High blood pressure, huh?" Kate asked.

"What do you think? Pre-eclampsia?" Jake asked, showing off his newfound medical knowledge.

"It's not pre-eclampsia. That doesn't occur until well into the third trimester."

"She looks thin, I think."

"Thank you for the diagnosis."

Kate and Jake moved on to bedsores and antibiotics. Al conversed with Wei Ling in Chinese. Tony and the Castello brothers stood around like hired help at a cocktail party.

"Can we get out of here?" Tony asked, breaking up the arrival meeting. The Sorrentino clansman had no idea of the role he had played in the biggest news story of the summer. All he wanted was to get home, call one of his girlfriends, and hit the hay.

Al looked around at the small group. Laughing, still enthralling

Wei Ling with his very passable Chinese, he gave the orders. "Let's get the hell out of here. We don't need any unwanted attention."

***

C.F. Chang arrived on Saipan with an entourage of twenty. Lawyers, bodyguards, advisors, friends. His youngest son was dead and the formality of mourning was a prerequisite to moving on. It was also the perfect excuse. He had every right to raise a little hell. And it was all a show. He didn't care about his son or the doctor; they were inconsequential variables in his equation. He was looking for a girl, and he was not going home without answers.

Chapter 43

Al's brother limped up the narrow stairs from the basement, one hand on the small of his back, the other on the banister. In the monster-size kitchen, he pulled open the freezer door of the white Whirlpool, grabbed a bag of frozen broccoli and carrots, and pushed it against the bare skin of his back just above his pants line.

Don Korgaokar, a part-time computer programmer with far greater skills than ambition, was still trying to digest the fact that he would have to vacate his comfortable four-bedroom, all-brick colonial in Bethesda. With eviction by his brother looming, Don knew it had been a good run. He had milked the near-free housing for all it was worth. The house had been paid for long ago, the benefits of Al's overseas career where all expenses were covered by Uncle Sam, or "Uncle Sugar" as the Foggy Bottom Boys called him.

For a pittance, Don had lived in a beautiful home in one of the most desirable locales in the metro area. He mowed the grass in the summer, raked the leaves in the fall, and cleared the sidewalks when it snowed. He hired a maid service to come and clean once a month, a chore too daunting for a thirty-five-year-old child who skirted responsibility like a dry cleaner that breaks buttons. When Don had moved into the house, his brother had left him with only a few rules to follow. The house had to look respectable. The bills had to be paid on time. The master bedroom and Al's son's room were not to be touched. Everything else was negotiable. When it looked like Al's adventure on the street was becoming permanent, Don rented a storage facility for his brother's items and started transforming the house into something comfortable. He had a week to change it back.

Don arched his back slightly and pain streaked from his heels to his lower cheeks. He had been packing for two days, eviction to the basement only a temporary stop. He knew the next station on the gravy train express was out the door. He figured he had a week to find "steady employment," two words he had been avoiding since Clinton, the intern, the dress, and a cigar had hit the news.

He moved gingerly to the living room, frozen veggies still in place, and stopped at the sofa to survey the damage of the move-in-progress. The room-by-room musical chairs exercise was backbreaking. Stuff into the basement, more stuff out of the house, all the original items dragged back in. Don looked at the war zone of boxes and shoved a pair of ski gloves, which had never seen the slopes, into a box with a web of computer cords that couldn't be untangled. Cardboard boxes of dishes were neatly marked and stacked in the corner of the dining room, ready to be unpacked.

Twelve years younger than Al, Don's jeans, sneakers and t-shirt had a combined age that exceeded his own. Don, with his scruffy goatee and wisps of curly hair venturing over his ears, cracked open a beer and joined the discussion at the long dining room table. As he settled into his seat he realized it was time to move on. Find a steady girlfriend. Get married. Have a child.

Al, Jake, and Kate looked in Don's direction as he found his seat and gulped a mouthful of beer. "Just ignore me," he said, before taking another nip from his twelve-ounce companion. The conversation was getting interesting and he planned to stay until they kicked him out.

"What about the legal system?" Kate asked. "We could have a judge order the senator to provide a DNA sample."

Al shook his head slightly, showing both patience and prudence. "That could take months. Hell, with a senator stonewalling us, it could take years. Senator Day will pull together a team of man-eating lawyers, specialists in paternity suits, you name it."

"I know that my mother would roll over in her grave if she heard me say this, but Wei Ling wants to get rid of the baby and she deserves not to have to wait. So whatever we come up with, let's keep that in mind. I think she has been jerked around enough for one lifetime."

Upstairs, Wei Ling slept in the spare bedroom, the room's first visitor in six years. She had been in the U.S. for six hours and had managed to sleep five of them. Kate kept her vitals monitored, writing the numbers down in neat columns in a notebook. The fourth year medical student was ready to give the pregnant woman a clean bill of health.

"Well, we could have the abortion and save a tissue sample from the fetus to test later," Kate said, her eyes darting to the faces around the table.

"A tissue sample from the fetus?" Jake asked, his chiseled face contorted, looking like a rubber mask that had been left in the car window on a hot summer day.

Al's brother shared Jake's reaction and got up from the table. "And with that, I am officially grossed out," he said. He leaned against the frame of the entrance to the grand dining room and took another slug of his beer.

Kate muffled a giggle. "At any rate, she's going to need to gain her strength for a few days. She needs to eat. I can watch for a fever and continue to treat her bedsores. Just precautionary. She can have an abortion anytime really."

"So if we can't get a judge to order the senator to cooperate, and we have a deadline for the abortion, how do we get our hands on some senator DNA A.S.A.P.?" Jake asked, thinking out loud.

"Very carefully," Al answered.

"I'll get you his DNA," Don said, drawing stares from the table.

"Excuse my brother. He's drunk," Al said.

"This is only my second beer."

"Then excuse my brother. He's an idiot," Al said looking at Kate and Jake on the other side of the table ringed with eight chairs.

"Let's hear it," Jake said.

"Easy. Get some girls to go visit him in his office. Ask to have some pictures taken. Get the girls to sit on his lap, stroke his hair a little, and pluck a sample."

"Pluck a sample?" Jake said in disbelief. "The use of the word 'pluck' threatens the validity of the idea."

"Like I said, my brother is an idiot," Al repeated with the addition of a 'voila' hand gesture.

Jake's mind drifted back to the dinner he had had with the senator. The hot young senator's assistant. Wei Ling. The idea wasn't as crazy as it seemed. "We know the guy can't keep his hands off the women," Jake conceded, looking for support.

"I'll come up with a better plan," Al chimed. "I just need some time to think it through."

"I'll do it," Kate said.

"Do what?"

"Me and my girlfriends. We'll get you a senator hair. The poor guy won't know what hit him."

"The youth of America," Al said, shaking his head. "Am I the only person who sees the beauty in devising a well-constructed, intelligent plan? You can't just walk in and 'pluck' a senator's hair."

"Why not?" Kate asked.

Al stammered.

"Because he didn't think of it," Don answered. "My brother doesn't like any idea that didn't originate between his own ears."

"Either way, we have a couple of days," Jake said, bringing the room back to focus. "We can't make Wei Ling wait until we figure out what we're going to do."

"So I have a couple of days," Kate said, not looking for permission.

Al turned his palms upward in a weak sign of giving up. "You are all overlooking one fact. Even if we get a hair from the senator and perform the DNA test, we will still have to prove that the hair we tested was the senator's. Not to mention that it was illegally obtained. Once again, that will bring us back to a legal battle."

"So what do you have in mind, Al?"

Al ran his fingers through his newly cut hair. "Let me make a few calls."

***

Jake followed Kate up the carpeted stairs, turning left at the landing where pictures of Al's son and wife hung in matching wood picture frames. Kate passed the bathroom and stopped outside the partially closed bedroom door. She peeked in at Wei Ling and felt Jake's face on her neck, his lips moving slowly up her skin to her ear. Kate nuzzled back against him and Jake's heart skipped a beat.

For Jake's whole life, Uncle Steve had told him that every woman, no matter how perfect they may seem, has a major flaw. Unless Kate was hiding a deep, dark, yet-to-be-revealed deal-breaker, Jake surmised that

Kate's major flaw was her father. Maybe it was a flaw they shared. He pushed aside the image of Jimmy Sorrentino and squeezed Kate a little tighter until she purred quietly. With the exception of the little stripper faux pas, time with her had been the best six weeks of his life. The fact that they came after the worst eighteen months of his life only made it that much sweeter. Who knew, maybe when the smoke cleared and Mr. Sorrentino learned what Jake had done, he would reconsider the deal. Jake didn't know if it was an even trade, but he looked at the girl on the bed and wondered what he had done. Simply fading out of Kate's life was going to be easier said than done. He dug his nose deeper into her hair and inhaled. Maybe he could keep dating her on the sly. Mr. Sorrentino would never have to know.

***

Al walked in the door just before six a.m. Sweat stains darkened the neck and the back of his gray t-shirt. It had been a night without sleep, walking the streets, seeing people. He took off his dirty shoes at the door and treaded quietly through the main hall of his house. He entered the kitchen, turned on the light over the stove, and trained himself on a new coffee maker. It had been four years since he had made his own coffee, and he added one scoop of grounds to the filter for every two cups of coffee. The math hadn't changed during his time on the street, and five minutes later he poured in a splash of milk to a perfectly brewed cup.

Jake and Kate were asleep on the pull-out sofa bed in the living room. Al walked in with two cups of coffee and put them on the glass tabletop next to a thick picture book on the American West. He gently shook Jake, who rolled over and continued sleeping. Al shook him harder.

With his feet on the floor and his hand on a coffee mug, Jake yawned. "What time is it?"

"Six-fifteen."

"Early."

"You can sleep when it's over."

"When what's over?"

"The job we started." Al flung his chin in the direction of Kate who was still under the covers. "Wake her up and then have her wake up Wei

Ling."

"At this hour?"

"We have to be prepped and ready by eight."

"Ready for what?"

Al didn't answer the question. "And you're going to need a suit. See if my brother can dig up one you can borrow," he added on his way out of the room.

Chapter 44

The black sedan-for-hire with D.C. tags pulled in front of the Pe-king Palace and maneuvered itself into a parallel spot with an eight-point turn, leaving half-a-foot off both bumpers. The Asian driver in a black suit that matched the car and his jet black hair, set the vehicle in park, pulled the keys from the ignition, and put them under the seat. He reached into the glove compartment and checked the documents one last time before slipping them under the seat next to the keys. He got out of the car, looked around cautiously, and shut the door without locking it. He broke into a slow walk down the sidewalk, taking in the early morning neighborhood activities on his way to the active side of Chinatown. Five minutes later, he disappeared into the mix of similar faces and was gone.

The ringing silver cell phone on the side table woke Chow Ying from a peaceful sleep. He reached over and opened the flip phone. A voice on the other end of the line told him that the car he claimed he so desperately needed was parked out front. He was out of excuses.

Wearing only tan boxers, Chow Ying rolled out of bed and peeked out the window at the roof of the black sedan from his third floor room. "Shit," he said in English. He paced, made one lap around the room, and stopped again on the far side of the table near the window. He checked the note with the precise instructions C.F. Chang had given him over the phone five days before and shook his head.

Today was the day.

The water pressure from the shower head wasn't strong enough to knock pollen off a dandelion, and Chow Ying let the water run through his newly cut hair in the standing-room-only shower stall. The pony-tail he had worn with pride for ten years was now in the small plastic bathroom wastebasket. A few runaway strands of hair draped from the lip of the sink, next to an old pair of scissors that had been just sharp enough to do the job.

Back in the room, still dripping, Chow Ying pulled the suit from its plastic wrapping and held it up to the light that pushed its way through the window and its nicotine-stained curtains. For seventy-five dollars, the custom-made, single-breasted suit tailored in a shop in Chinatown was a thing of beauty. With the skill of a man who knew fabrics and sewing, he examined every stitch, felt the linen-wool mixture between his rough hands, appreciated the perfect crease in the slacks.

He dried himself and got dressed in a suit for the first time since a Chinese New Year celebration the year before. On his first try, he tied a beautiful double-Windsor knot on a red power tie he had bought for eight bucks. He posed in the hotel room for a few seconds and deemed himself to be one dashing gentleman. When he finished the one-man fashion show, he sat down at the small round table near the window and wrote a letter to the old man who ran the hotel. He counted out a thousand dollars, put it into the folded letter, and wedged the paper under the dirty ashtray. The money was more than enough to cover his bills.

Chow Ying felt a moment of loneliness in leaving his one room mansion. The old man had been the first person he could remember who liked him without wanting anything. The Mountain of Shanghai smoked a cigarette, wrote another letter, and slipped the remaining wad of cash into his inside breast pocket with his passport. He put the cell phone on top of the revolver at the bottom of the small bag he had gotten from Mr. Wu in New York at the beginning of his stateside journey. He took the key to the back door of the hotel and slapped it on the table next to the ashtray with his room key. Whatever the day held in store, he was permanently checking out from the comforts of his room at Peking Palace.

The back door to the hotel led to an alley behind Eighth Street, too narrow for the oversized city garbage trucks to reach the trashcans, much to the chagrin of D.C.'s finest sanitation engineers. Chow Ying walked down the alley for fifty yards, cut across a small residential street, and followed another alley into the back end of Chinatown proper. He hadn't seen the two policemen in their car for two days but he knew they were out there, moving their location, never parking in the same spot twice. He had seen the car giving Peking Palace the occasional drive-by from his dark hotel room window. Yes, they were out there somewhere. He felt it.

After wandering the neighborhood's less aesthetic side and checking for Johnny Law, Chow Ying approached the black sedan from the opposite direction, slipped behind the wheel as elegantly as someone the size of an NFL linebacker can do, and reached under the seat.

***

"Pull around the block," Wallace said to Nguyen. "We'll wait on the other end of the one-way street for him to come out."

"And then what?"

"And then we follow him."

"We have been waiting to get our hands on this guy for over a week, and now you want to follow him?"

"Something's fishy…and I'm not talking about the kind with scales in the market down the street. This guy has been lying low and now he has a car delivered to his doorstep? Something is wrong with this picture."

Chow Ying familiarized himself with the car as he rode around the block and then took a slow drive up the narrow alley behind the hotel. He looked over at the back door he had used a dozen times, and slammed on his brakes to avoid a scrawny calico cat that darted from a row of trash cans.

"Where do you think he's going?" Nguyen asked.

"I don't know, but he's being careful. Don't spook him. Go around the block again and we'll pick him up on the other side."

The unmarked police cruiser lurked five cars back in light morning traffic. Most of the commuters pouring into the city came from the north or south, with a few million additional cars trying to squeeze down Connecticut Avenue. Chinatown was not a major route and the detectives were thankful for the quick pace on the road. Slow traffic was the perfect way to blow a trail. The slower the traffic, the more time the suspect had to observe his environment. At five mph, drivers tend to look around, check out their neighbors, take a peek in their mirrors. Nguyen checked the speedometer. Thirty mph.

The black sedan headed in the direction of the Mall and Nguyen voiced the only thought he had, "I'd pay money to know where this guy is going."

"You and me both, partner. And I would love to know how in the hell this guy is behind the wheel of a for-hire sedan."

"Maybe he is a legitimate driver."

"My ass."

"It's possible. Maybe this guy has nothing to do with that woman who fell down the escalator."

"Why did he cut his hair?"

"It's hot as hell here in the summer. He was probably sweating his ass off."

"You know how long it takes to grow hair that long? Years, man, years. You don't cut that off unless you have a really good reason."

"Well, Wallace, there is one way to put an end to all this speculation. We are just a flick of the siren away from the answers to all of our questions."

"Not yet. Keep following him while I radio in."

Wallace reached for the radio as Nguyen hit a pothole large enough to engulf half of the front right wheel. Both officers nearly hit the roof as the suspension succumbed to the laws of physics, the decompression of the springs sending the car bouncing upward.

"Potholes in July," Wallace said, pressing the call button on the radio. He gave the information on the black for-hire sedan to the dispatcher who ran the plates while Wallace waited, eyes straight ahead.

Chow Ying jockeyed for position, changing lanes twice. He kept one eye on the road and one eye on his rearview mirror.

"It is registered to Capitol Chauffeurs, Sergeant," the radio chirped.

"Do you have a phone number?"

"Just a minute."

Wallace wrote the number in the notebook on his lap, the other hand holding the radio. He looked at the number he had just written and repeated it back to verify that he could read his own chicken scratch.

"That's it, detective. Anything else I can help you with?"

"No, that's all. Thanks."

"Have a good shift."

Wallace punched the phone number into his cell phone and

followed the black sedan with his eyes.

In the middle of the third ring, an elderly woman answered the phone for Capitol Chauffeurs, proudly announcing the name of the company, followed by her own, Regina.

"How are you this morning, Regina?"

"Just fine," she answered with the slightest hint of a southern twang.

"My name is Detective Wallace of the D.C. Metropolitan Police."

"Yes, detective. How can I help you?"

"I need information on one of your vehicles."

"Yes, detective. Our rates vary by the size of the car, but prices range from thirty to three hundred dollars an hour, with a three hour minimum."

"No, Regina, no. I'm not interested in renting a car. I'm interested in one of the cars owned by your company."

"I don't understand, detective," Regina said with more hints of her Alabama upbringing.

"Let me paint a picture for you. My partner and I are driving down Seventh Street right now, following a car that is registered to your company. I need you to tell me who is driving."

"Is he speeding?"

"No, Regina. The car is not speeding. If I give you the license plate can you tell me who's behind the wheel?"

"Is this some kind of prank?"

Regina was hard work. Her charming southern accent grew stronger, as did her natural propensity to avoid the question without trying.

"Regina. Let me give you my badge number and you can call the D.C. police to verify that I am, indeed, a detective."

Regina took a sip of her morning glass of sweet tea without ice.

"Hmmmmm…" she said, drawing the sound out for a few seconds.

Wallace turned toward Nguyen and covered the small holes on his mobile phone. "This woman is killing me."

"That's fine, detective. I won't need to call your station."

"Let me give you the license plate number," Wallace said, reading the tag number quickly.

"Could you hold a minute? I need to check the paperwork."

"Hurry."

Chow Ying pulled further ahead and Nguyen switched lanes trying to close the gap. He reached over and hit Wallace's shoulder as the black sedan drove through the intersection with the green light thirty yards ahead.

"You lose him and you're fired," Wallace barked.

The police cruiser reached the intersection just as a marked car, sirens blaring, blocked both lanes of traffic. Nguyen hit the brakes and the horn simultaneously. A uniformed officer hurried out of his car and held out his arm in the universal traffic cop hand gesture for stop.

"What the hell?" Wallace said, pulling at the handle of the passenger door, phone pressed to his ear. Walking toward the officer, Wallace reached for his badge and held it straight out as more wailing sirens approached. The detective with more than two decades on the streets of D.C. looked up at the oncoming entourage and cursed.

The stretch limousine was sandwiched between four dark SUVs, blue lights flashing from the dash behind the thick bulletproof glass. Six additional patrol cars buzzed around the limo. On the front corners of the limousine stood two small flags—blue, white, and red in three vertical stripes of equal size. The car drove by quickly, the flags rippling in the air with a crisp snap, snap, snap. Wallace shook his head at the uniformed officer and got back in the car, phone still in his hand.

On the far side of the intersection, Chow Ying heard the sirens. He didn't wait to see if he was their target. He used the turn lane to pass three vehicles, and stomped on the accelerator at the next signal as it turned yellow. By the time he focused his vision in the rearview mirror, the flashing lights from the security entourage were almost out of sight.

Wallace jumped back in the cruiser. "That better be someone important."

"French Ambassador."

"France?"

"The flags were French."

"Goddamn French. If it weren't for the U.S. of A, they would be speaking German and eating bratwurst in Paris right now."

"You hate everyone Wallace."

"Not everyone. But I make a special exception for the French."

Wallace yelled into the phone waiting for Regina to get back on the line. Time stood still. "The second they are out of the way, get this car moving."

With the French entourage tearing down the street, the police cruiser on intersection duty pulled away as quickly as it had appeared.

Traffic moved forward toward the now red light and Nguyen tried to pass on the right.

"Do we hit the sirens?" Nguyen asked, adrenaline pumping.

Before Wallace could answer, Regina was back on the phone.

"Detective Wallace?"

"Yes, Regina."

"Sorry to keep you waiting."

"Talk to me, Regina," he said, his voice rising.

"The car with the license plate you gave me is not scheduled to be on the road today. It should be in the maintenance lot in Rockville, Maryland. Time for the car's sixty thousand mile servicing."

"Can you call someone at the service lot and confirm the car is where it is supposed to be?"

"I did. No one is answering the phone."

"I'm going to give you my number. Let me know when you reach them."

Chow Ying hit a string of green lights and by the time Wallace hung up the phone with Regina, the trailing unmarked car was a mile away. As the for-hire approached the Capitol Building and the government offices that surrounded the jewel of D.C., the black sedan was as inconspicuous as a yellow cab in Manhattan.

"What do we do?" Nguyen asked, panicking. "I think we lost him."

Wallace looked around like his head was on a swivel. There were three black for-hire sedans within a hundred yards, two of them heading in the opposite direction and another pulled over to the curb, a short Hispanic driver unloading his passenger.

"Goddamnit," he said, picking up the radio. "This is Detective Wallace. I need to issue a BOLO on a black for-hire sedan, last seen in District one, heading south."

Wallace panted his way through the car's tag number and the dispatcher echoed the letters and numbers. "Charlie, Papa, Four..."

Wallace finished his command to police dispatch. "Do not approach or stop this vehicle. I need the location reported back to me ASAP."

Wallace threw the radio handset at the dash, cursed a string of vulgarities that would make a Hell's Angel member proud, and then reached over with his hand to hit the siren. The short blast of chirps and screams from the car was enough to clear a path through the intersection.

"Now let's find this fucking guy."

Chapter 45

A block from the Capitol and three hundred yards from Union Station and the train tracks that marked the beginning of the neglected northeast side of the city, the Russell Senate Building was the smallest legislation-making structure on The Hill. Erected in 1909, the Russell building had witnessed its share of historical moments—from the investigation into the sinking of the Titanic, to the Watergate hearing, to the Teapot Dome investigation that resulted in the country's first senator-turned-convict.

The Senate Special Committee on Overseas Labor met on the first floor of the Russell Senate Building. As a special committee, and thus temporary in nature, Overseas Labor didn't have its own chamber. Senator Day and the rest of the Overseas Labor Specialists were forced to share use of the Foreign Relations Committee's vestibule—a picturesque legislative room adorned with grand traditional ornamentation that was duplicated in fifty similar chambers around Capitol Hill. A wood-paneled wall climbed three stories to the ceiling above, creating an impressive backdrop for the committee chairman and his cronies to flex their legislative muscles.

The conclusion of a committee hearing was showtime for the senators involved. Final comments ranged from passionate to downright emotional. Every senator thrived on knowing they would have a chance to speak and, God willing, influence the law. At the very least, they would show their specialization of the topic at hand, self-defined brilliance gleaned from reading a few excerpts of investigations and research done by others. The glamorous lunches prepared for the final day of committee testimony did as much as anything to pack the house. After months of investigation and testimony, the committee's recommendation to the

Senate was the final word before the feast and backslapping.

At eight-thirty, the chamber doors opened. The fruit plates brimmed in a colorful display of berries and melons, next to large trays of muffins mixed with a variety of pastries. Coffee, regular and decaf, served in real china, held its position on a smaller table next to the cream and sugar. Food for the kings while the commoners, who paid for it all, lined up at Starbucks.

The press filed in first, a half-dozen reporters representing an equal number of papers that included *The Post* and the Reverend Moon-owned *Washington Times*. The reporters were young, still-hungry new-hires who were blown off bigger stories and took whatever assignment came down the pike. They prepared their position in the unofficial press section, the first row on the right-hand side of the committee chamber. Notebooks were already pulled, pens in hand. Hand-held recorders were checked and double-checked. A three-person camera crew from C-SPAN set up their tripod and microphone on the opposite side of the room. It was standard operating procedure. Every committee meeting was filmed, every word transcribed, every opinion saved as a small piece of history. A warehouse in Silver Spring now held thousands of videos and boxes of verbatim transcripts and, with senators showing no signs of embracing brevity, they would be looking for a larger storage facility before the next presidential election.

At five before nine, the twelve senators on the Overseas Labor Committee strolled in, shaking hands, waving, winking. Lobbyists and lawyers, wearing suits from the same shelves of the same stores in Georgetown, filled half of the one hundred seats in the chamber. Those who were on the final list to testify had seating preference at the long table directly in front of the committee. Behind them, the first row was shoulder-to-shoulder with CEOs, human rights activists, PhDs from think tanks and universities that dotted the city. It was a who's who on International Labor, a list developed and edited ten times over, depending on who was taking what legal bribe.

Senator Day found his throne in the middle of the raised row of chairs. From their perch five feet in the air, the committee members had an indisputable psychological advantage. Physically looking down on witnesses as they testified gave the committee power. It didn't matter if those testifying had PhDs from Harvard or Yale. Everyone who wasn't a senator on the committee was a pissant. Their speeches would be heard, their testimony noted. And then the senators would mold legislation as they saw fit. Senator Day looked over at Senators Wooten, Thomas, and Grumman. In turn, all three senators returned the chairman's glance and silently acknowledged their prescribed agreement.

At precisely nine o'clock Senator Day reached to his right, raised his hand, and lowered the gavel with an authoritative bang.

***

Minutes after the siren parade in his rearview mirror, Chow Ying took two laps around the four-lane circle in front of Union Station to be sure he wasn't followed. On his third pass, Chow Ying slowed his car and pulled over in the pick-up lane among a mixture of taxis and similar black sedans. He reached for the envelope from beneath the seat and dumped it upside down on the passenger seat next to him. With his right hand he spread out the contents of the envelope, picking up the chauffeur license with his own picture and a phony name. The DMV-authorized license was beyond legal reproach, complete with the requisite holographic security image and magnetic strip. He read the forged company paperwork for the car he was driving, fondled a Senate-issued VIP parking permit, and glanced at the bonded-paper sign with "Senator Day" printed on it with a quality laser printer. He put the chauffeur license in his shirt pocket and picked up the lone remaining gift from C.F Chang, a piece of white office paper. He read the detailed instructions, an elaboration of the ones he had received on the phone. The instructions were neatly typed, without a single spelling error. Trust wasn't C.F Chang's strong suit.

Senate Special Committee Hearing on Overseas Labor. Thursday July 18th. The Russell Senate Building. Peter Winthrop is scheduled to testify. Senator Day will also be present. Avoid being seen. Peter Winthrop has a reservation with his chauffeur company, a car will be waiting for him in the parking lot. A Senate parking permit and valid chauffeur license is needed to enter the lot. The Capitol Police may sweep the car for explosives. A body search is typically not done at this time. You will be searched if you enter the building.

Chow Ying started the car and headed east. He did one lap around Stanton Park, came down Constitution and turned the for-hire sedan right on Second Street. With the appropriate trepidation, he slowed the car to a crawl as he approached the Capitol Police barricade. His gun was wedged as far under the seat as it would go, ten grand and a passport in his breast pocket. If anything went wrong, he would make the afternoon news.

Chow Ying smiled and rolled down the window. "I am here to pick up Senator Day at the conclusion of the Senate Special Committee on Overseas Labor." He handed the officer his chauffeur license and Senate parking permit. The overweight black Capitol police officer looked at the license and the Senate-issued parking pass. The officer peered at Chow Ying over his stretched waistline, checked the face on the identification a second time, and then handed the license back to its owner. Chow Ying held his breath.

"You can park anywhere in the back lot next to Union Station Plaza. Do not keep your car running, and there is no loitering outside the vehicle. Make sure the parking permit is on display and visible on the rearview mirror."

"Yes, sir," Chow Ying answered.

"Please open the trunk."

Chow Ying took another deep breath and fumbled along the inside of the driver door until he found the lever for the trunk release. The lid of the trunk rose slowly as the officer put his hand on the back fender. Another officer, and former Marine by all appearances, started moving forward from Chow Ying's blind spot, running a mirror along the ground, checking the underside of the car for explosives. When he finished, he slapped on the passenger window. "Open the doors, please."

Chow Ying tightened his sphincter as his mind turned toward the gun under his seat. He pushed the urge to panic aside and hit the door lock release. The officer opened the front and rear passenger doors. He looked at the spotless interior and yelled over the still open trunk to his partner. "He's good to go."

The black officer shut the trunk and hit the top of the roof twice, sending the most dangerous man in the city right into the Senate living room. The fact that the Capitol and D.C. Police fall under different jurisdictions, under different edicts, with different dispatch systems was a security flaw that would have heads rolling by the end of the day.

The open-air parking lot on the far side of the Russell Senate Building held a hundred cars. A handful of mid-sized sedans with outlandishly bland colors stood out in the sea of black for-hires. Chow Ying pulled into a spot in the middle row, and put the car into park.

He read the instructions from C.F. Chang one last time, the information memorized. He folded the note and put it in his breast pocket next to his passport and money. He placed the sign for Senator Day on the dashboard, and hung the parking permit from the rearview mirror. He removed the gun, and with the firearm between his thighs, he checked the cylinder and confirmed that its six occupants were all accounted for. He leaned forward and stuffed the revolver into the back of his pants. He checked the car a final time before getting out slowly and looking around.

He walked across the lot between the black stretch sedans, reading the signs displayed on the dash of identical cars. J. Storm, CEO Asian Strategies, Ltd.; Senator Grimm, Ohio; Senator Albritton, Oregon; M. Higgins, CEO Republic Outfitters. The last car in the first row read P. Winthrop, CEO. Chow Ying got chills. C.F. Chang was a man who could get his hands on very accurate information. He had led Chow Ying to the spot, given him a car, and given him a time to make the kill. Now it was up to him. The only thing clear to Chow Ying was there would be no more excuses.

Chow Ying stopped at the pedestrian entrance to the parking lot and took in his surroundings. In his head he diagramed a potential getaway map. The outline of Union Station was duly noted, three hundred yards to the north. He could see the top of the Capitol in the opposite direction down the tree-lined street. He checked out the people on their way to work, and looked down at his own red tie. He couldn't complain about his outfit. He fit right in. Shuffling his feet with his eyes on his environment, Chow Ying bumped shoulders with a Capitol police officer who had the unenviable assignment of patrolling the sidewalk between the Russell Senate Building and Union Station.

The officer flashed a watch-what-you-are-doing glare, and the

Mountain of Shanghai turned on his morning charm. "Excuse me, officer. Do you know where I can get a cup of coffee?" The officer held his stare on the well-dressed driver coming out of the VIP parking lot and answered. "Most of the drivers wait down the street at the L.O.C. Café. One block down, turn left just past the Justice Building."

"Thank you," Chow Ying said.

"Have a good morning," the officer said, turning to continue his two blocks up, two blocks down foot patrol.

Chow Ying checked his watch. He was right on schedule.

***

Al pulled the seven-year-old white Dodge Caravan up the curb to an empty meter spot. Jake got out first and pulled open the sliding side door. He offered his hand to Kate, who stepped out rear end first. Al came around the front of the car and shoved a pocketful of change into the meter. All three helped Wei Ling from the van—hands on her arms, grasping her wrists, on her shoulder. Her eyes were wide, her first steps uneasy.

"Are you sure you are okay?" Jake asked.

"I'm fine," she said, subtly shaking Jake's arm from its position on hers. "I can walk," she added with conviction. Jake removed his arm and raised his hands.

Al checked his watch and looked across the street at the Mall and the fountain in front of the Capitol Building. It was quiet. He looked down at his watch again and shook his wrist.

"Is everything all right?" Jake asked.

Al turned his neck and looked east toward the Washington Monument. "They're late," he said.

"Who's late?"

"Reinforcements," Al answered.

"What reinforcements?"

Al didn't answer the question. "Let's go."

***

Detectives Wallace and Nguyen drove around the city blocks near the Capitol, chasing black for-hire sedans that were as plentiful as beads at a Mardi Gras parade. They had received two possible sightings of the car over the radio and both had turned up negative. It was now approaching thirty minutes of radio silence. *Thirty minutes*, Wallace thought. *Our guy could be in Annapolis by now.* Wallace's disappointment penetrated the stale air in the car and Nguyen kept quiet, following orders as they came. *Turn right, go straight. Pull over...*

Nguyen stopped the car in a no parking zone next to the Department of Transportation. Wallace smacked on the back of his soft pack cigarettes until one popped out. Nguyen offered him his Zippo lighter as a peace pipe for losing their suspect.

Wallace spoke through heavy drags and clouds of exhaling smoke. "Let's think about this for a minute. What do we know about this case? We have a dead girl, who may or may not have been killed. We have a suspect in the city driving a for-hire sedan that is not supposed to be on the road today. We have a videotape that shows the suspect with the only two Washington D.C. connections we can come up with. One of them is Senator Day, who I believe doesn't know what the suspect is doing here. The other is Peter Winthrop, a businessman who gives me an uneasy feeling. What am I missing?"

"The son, who was with the only victim in this case, and who we have been unable to talk to."

"Yeah, the son. So we have three possible connections between our suspect and Washington D.C."

"Still doesn't help us find our driver," Nguyen said.

"Let's start over."

"Start over?"

"After we found the videotape, what did we do?"

"Started knocking on doors. Started asking questions."

"So we ask them again."

"I don't follow you."

Wallace opened his little notebook and flipped through the pages backwards. He folded down the top corner of one page, and turned three more pages.

"Got your cell phone?" Detective Wallace asked.

"Always," Nguyen answered, pulling the black phone from his jacket pocket.

"You call Senator Day's office and I'll touch base with our friend Peter Winthrop."

"And ask what?"

"Do routine follow-up. Ask the same questions we asked before. See if the senator is available for another face-to-face. Maybe something has jogged his memory. I will check back and see if Peter Winthrop has the name of our suspect yet. He should have had it yesterday."

Detective Wallace called Winthrop Enterprises, bypassing the front desk and dialing directly into Shelly's desk. Peter's personal secretary answered with her normal perkiness.

As Wallace spoke, a broad smile broke across his face, breaking the curse of the morning's failed tail. He hung up the phone and waited for Nguyen to finish his conversation with Senator Day's office. When Nguyen snapped his black phone shut, Wallace jumped in.

"You're not going to believe where Peter Winthrop is this morning."

"At the Senate Committee Hearing on Overseas Labor?" Nguyen answered proudly.

"You're shitting me."

"Am I right?"

"Fucking A, you're right. Russell Senate Building. Corner of First and Constitution."

"You think we'll find our big Asian there?"

"If we don't, I'm buying dinner."

"Deal."

Chapter 46

Detective Nguyen pushed his way through a small crowd near the curb and took the marble stairs two at a time. Detective Wallace felt spry, went for two steps, and came up with a twinge in his hamstring. Nguyen pulled the brown wooden door open and waved his hand in a circular motion, cheering his partner to finish the climb to the main entrance of the Russell Building.

The Capitol Police security detail manning the entrance to the building was busy with a family of tourists from New York. Five backpacks chugged down the conveyor of the baggage screening equipment. A hand wand was being used on the eldest son, a high school kid with multiple holes in each ear. As the eldest son dealt with the scrutiny that comes with dressing like a punk, his two siblings ribbed him from the safe side of the metal detector in heavy Brooklyn accents. "Do a cavity search," the middle son suggested, his father responding with a smack to the back of his head.

The Capitol Police didn't pay any attention to the two hundred and forty pound detective until Wallace pulled his badge and announced his arrival.

"Detective Wallace, D.C. Metropolitan Police. We need the room for the Senate Committee in International Labor."

"Overseas Labor," Nguyen corrected.

The security officer on the far side of the metal detector picked his clipboard off his stool and scanned the map.

"They are in the Foreign Relations Committee Room, first floor, opposite side of the building. Take the hall to the right and follow it around."

Wallace and Nguyen set the detector off as they walked through, and then shuffled sideways through the gauntlet course constructed by the family from New York and their bags, cameras, tourist pamphlets, and water bottles.

Wallace turned back toward the door as he rounded the corner on the hall. "Have you seen a large Asian guy come through this morning? A big guy, six-four or so. Wearing a suit."

"No, sir. Not that I remember."

"Make sure everyone gets searched on their way in," Wallace said turning back around. "And if a large Asian tries to come through, stop him and come find me."

***

Peter Winthrop, Senate-approved expert on International Business, was in the middle of summarizing his testimony. He was called by the honorable Senator Day himself, the last voice of reason after a spring and summer of opinions from every expert who had one. It didn't matter that most of the votes had already been bought, borrowed, or stolen. The CEOs that lined the first row had paid millions, Ben Franklins channeled through lobbyists and anonymous contributions to re-election campaigns. They had watched the progress of the committee for six months, their livelihoods and the price of their companies' stock hanging in the balance. Neither an act of God nor a speech from Peter Winthrop would change things now.

It didn't matter to the man on the Senate committee floor. Peter flew among the clouds as he described the lives of those overseas who benefitted from corporate America's charity. Charity in the shape of the Blata shoe factory in suburban Jakarta and the Top Knit garment manufacturing outside Ho Chi Minh.

As Detectives Wallace and Nguyen entered the chamber and squeezed into the back row of seats, Peter pontificated on the brief history of job internationalization. He started with the maquiladoras, factories just over the Rio Grande that were the original benefactors of job flight. He quoted the improved corporate performance of those companies and the value of their successful internationalization, particularly the rise in stock prices, the real creation of wealth.

Peter acknowledged the "shift in employment demographics," but didn't elaborate on the aftermath of the maquiladoras. There was no need to dwell on the indisputable fact that once these jobs went south of the border, they just kept on running.

When the labor exodus had begun, the only ones screaming had been the constituents of Kentucky, Ohio, and other places where blue collar was the only collar available. At the time, who cared? No one did. Mainstream America didn't start to panic until they called technical support for their Dell laptops and found themselves talking to Rajiv in Mumbai, who identified himself as "George." These were service-level jobs. White collar jobs. Not ivory-tower white, but white nonetheless. This was the beginning of a crisis. The public wasn't bright enough to know that the service jobs were dependent upon the manufacturing jobs. But they were bright enough to start screaming.

Peter Winthrop moved into a set of poignant rhetorical questions. Were the jobs being transferred any worse than jobs being displaced by robots or new manufacturing processes? He stressed the leaps up the social ladder that foreign workers had made. He painted a portrait of huts in Southeast Asia with running water, electricity, well-shingled roofs, and even the occasional satellite dish. All thanks to U.S. corporate charity. Setting a minimum wage for American firms overseas would put an end to the dreams of millions in the third world. The answer wasn't a minimum wage. The answer was better training for better jobs for American workers.

Peter Winthrop was high. Showmen are showmen, until the last bow has been taken, the curtains have shut, and the hook has dragged them off stage. And even then, a true showman would crawl back in front of the audience for an encore. Peter was the poster child for show, and he didn't really care if he was the dog or the pony. He was on the Senate Committee floor, bullshitting among the kings of bullshit, bending the ear of the pundits, and putting on a show with his usual Winthrop charm. It was every cocktail party and business schmooze meeting he had ever been to, all rolled into one. The CEO audience nodded vigorously, agreeing with Winthrop scripture as if Moses had brought down his speech from Mount Sinai.

"This guy is something else," Nguyen said.

"Yeah, he can really sling it."

Nguyen stood slightly and lifted his head to peek around the room.

"Don't see our Chinese friend."

"Me either. How many exits we got?"

Both men looked around and Nguyen answered first. "Three. Two main doors on both sides in the back. An exit on the far wall in the corner."

"That's what I count too."

"What do you think?"

"My gut tells me we are in the right place. Our guy is here somewhere. I am sure of it."

***

Fifty yards away through the thick walls of the Russell Senate Building, Chow Ying lit the end of his new cigarette with the burning ashes of his dying one. He had finished off his carton of almond-flavored Chinese domestic smokes a week ago and was moving his habit down a list of major American brands. He was counting on the two packs of Camels he had in his pocket to take him through dinner.

The map in his head was complete, a drop-down list of potential escape routes programmed in his mind. If X occurs, then Y. If Y happens, then Z. If X, Y, and Z unfold, start shooting. Chow Ying ran his thick finger along the top of the jersey wall near the Senate parking lot and crossed the street. He measured his steps to the front of the Russell building, counting each stride without succumbing to the natural urge to look down.

When he reached one hundred fifty-eight paces, he found himself at the bottom of the stairs leading to the main entrance. He memorized the measurements and then tested himself. A quarter mile to the Union Station subway station. One hundred fifty-eight yards to the parking lot. Three hundred yards to the nearest cargo train tracks. Then he converted the distance to time. Four hundred yards in a minute with a good ankle. One hundred fifty yards in twenty seconds. The cargo tracks in half a minute. One security booth stood between the Russell Building and the entrance to the Senate VIP parking lot, its lone occupant a wafer-thin officer approaching mandatory retirement. If it came down to it, Chow Ying, bad ankle and all, would run him over like an All Black winger against a team of Cub Scouts. He added another second to his getaway route.

As tricky as his escape would be, the stakeout was proving harder. He needed to be near the main entrance of the Russell Building. He needed to avoid arousing suspicion. He needed to wait, potentially for hours, and be ready, potentially within seconds. He couldn't go into the building because of the gun, and he couldn't lie down and take a nap on the front stairs either. His options were limited. He could wait in the car and hope that he saw his man coming out of the building from some two hundred yards away. Or he could become a professional loiterer.

He took his third trip around the block, down the street, and back to the front of the building. He imagined the Russell building security looking down at him, measuring him, making a sketch of his face and re-tasking the security cameras to reach the stairs of the building. The reality was that security was too lazy and ill-trained to do anything other than search bags.

When the first chants came from down the street, Chow Ying wanted to run, to get away from the noise, to get away from the attention. But as the group and the screams got closer and more voluminous, Chow Ying froze. He looked at the approaching crowd and realized that Christmas had come early.

***

C.F. Chang had spent the day turning Chang Industries on its ear. Every girl had been interrogated under the watchful eyes of C.F. Chang's lawyers and Captain Talua. No one had seen Wei Ling in weeks. When C.F. Chang finished at Chang Industries, he started searching every hotel on the island from the Ritz Carlton to the string of dirty by-the-hour motels on the south shore. No one had seen the girl, and not even hundred dollar bills pulled from a thick money roll could change that. Wei Ling's trail grew cold at the airport. She had last been seen at the charter terminal by both Captain Talua and the doctor who was still in jail, being held without bail. Wei Ling had been left under the watchful eye of Tom Foti, State Department personnel. And then she had simply vanished. No flight records. No evidence.

Captain Talua pulled up to the front of the house in the cleanest police cruiser the Saipan Police Department had to offer. The sky was dark, the stars brilliant, and the strong wind from the south helped keep the bugs down and the crickets quiet. C.F. Chang looked up at the house and the low light that shined through the living room window of the small bungalow.

"Are you sure about this woman?" C.F Chang asked Captain Talua.

"She works in the general aviation terminal. She studies accounting most of the time. She may be able to tell you what happened to the girl you are looking for."

"Why would she talk to us?"

"Offer her a thousand dollars and she'll tell you. She's a dreamer."

"A dreamer?"

"Yes. There are two kinds on Saipan. Those who love it and don't ever want to leave, and those who dream of something more. This girl is a dreamer."

Ten minutes and fifteen hundred dollars later, C.F. Chang and Captain Talua walked out of the small one floor bungalow with the answer to their question. The Chinese girl had left with three American men on a charter flight heading for Washington D.C.

C.F. Chang cursed all the way back to the hotel. He had his fingers on speed dial and was punching buttons.

Chapter 47

"Thank you Mr. Winthrop," Senator Day said into the microphone after his final witness shined his way through twenty minutes of question and answer from the committee members.

The CEO and president of Winthrop Enterprises found his seat at the end of the testimony table, a large stretch of wood covered with a deep burgundy tablecloth that hung to the floor with frills on the hem. He reached for a glass of water as Senator Day covered the microphone and spoke quietly to the senator in the next seat.

The man in the new gray suit pulled the large door open and walked toward the front of the committee room. With perfect posture and an unquestionable professional presence, he approached the Capitol Police officer at the end of the rows of spectators. He reached into his breast pocket and handed the note to the officer, whispering in his ear. He pointed toward Senator Day and nodded. The officer carried the paper across the room and reached upward to deliver the priority letter to Senator Day in his chair. A short conference ensued with half of the committee rising from their seats and gathering around the Chairman.

The brief meeting adjourned and Senator Day spoke. "Ladies and gentlemen, we have one additional speaker today before we put this to a vote. Please step forward and identify yourself to the committee."

Al stepped past the officer and walked to the end of the testimony table. "My name is Al Korgaokar. I am a Foreign Affairs Officer for the State Department's Bureau of Economic and Business Affairs. Retired. As I have stated in the letter you hold, I want to testify as to the improvements I have seen overseas as a result of internationalization."

Al Korgaokar's presence snapped Peter to attention. Peter looked at the man he knew years ago and could see that Al's face hinted at years of hard existence. Peter took another sip of water as he watched Al move toward the center of the chamber. Peter knew that Al had seen him, and he thought it didn't matter. Washington was a small city when it came to politics, and Al Korgaokar testifying at a Senate Committee meeting merely caused Peter Winthrop to pause. It was an interesting coincidence. Nothing more.

Senator Day looked at Al. "Mr. Korgaokar. Testifying at a Senate Committee is a serious matter. Furthermore, protocol generally requires that we receive your written testimony in advance. Given your service to the country, we will allow you to testify, but this committee will also require a written statement as to your testimony."

"Fair enough, Senator. I will be brief."

The official Senate Bible carrier stepped from the side of the chamber and Al was sworn in—oath, lock, stock, and barrel.

Senator Day nodded at the conclusion of the formality and addressed Al directly. "Please sir, go ahead."

"As I mentioned, I spent twenty years serving my country with the State Department, primarily in Asia. I was stationed with the embassies in Japan, the Philippines, China, and Thailand. I have seen the impact that American corporations have had on the native population. I have seen lives changed."

Senator Day smiled. Nothing wrong with a cherry on top of Peter Winthrop's brilliant testimony. A tried-and-true American with first-hand experience supporting the senator's position.

The senator's grin lasted until Al's next sentence hit the audience, the press, and the history of the committee transcripts.

"And I have seen lives ruined."

Senator Day's posture snapped straight and his eyebrows shot upward. There were a few muffled gasps and one noticeable giggle from the committee audience. Peter Winthrop fought the urge to run from the room.

Wallace looked at Nguyen. "Now this is getting interesting."

"Sir?" Senator Day asked.

"You heard me correctly, Senator. Lives ruined. But today I am here to end the lies."

The doors opened in the back of the room and Jake walked in with Wei Ling on his arm. Senator Day took one look at the girl he had spent the night with in a threesome and stood from his seat. Then he came unglued. With high shrills and screams that bordered on unintelligible, the senator commanded the officer on duty to stop the intruders.

Al grabbed the microphone off the testimony table and spoke over the senator in a booming voice that echoed through the PA system. "Ladies and gentlemen, the woman you see entering the room works in a sweatshop in Saipan. And she is pregnant with Senator Day's child."

The audience collectively inhaled, gasping, falling silent for a spilt second before the decorum of the room officially shifted to the hysteria of an animal outbreak at the zoo.

"Holy shit," Wallace said to Nguyen, whose mouth opened wide enough to catch a tennis ball served at full speed.

Senator Day banged his gavel and screamed orders like Judge Judy with PMS. "Officer. I want these men arrested. This committee meeting is in recess. I want this man's testimony erased from public record." Then Senator Day pointed his finger directly at Peter Winthrop. "You son of a bitch. You and your goddamn son."

Peter looked over at his son and Wei Ling. He shook his head, opened his mouth, and for the first time in his adult life, was speechless. Jake looked over at his father, the first contact with him since going to the FBI. His father stared back with blood-pumping hatred.

The room turned into a sea of questions, waves of accusations crashing down every direction. The rookie reporters began yelling, cell phones in their ears, calling in the biggest story of their lives.

"What the hell just happened?" Nguyen asked.

"I don't know, but I think we found Peter Winthrop's son."

Senator Day climbed down the stairs from his noble perch and pushed his way through the rising crowd. Peter exited the back of the chamber from the far door. Al rounded up Jake and Wei Ling and pulled them out of the storm. Reporters and senators poured from the chamber behind them, a mass of commotion in their wake.

"Let's go," Wallace said to Nguyen. "Time to get the answers to our questions."

Chapter 48

The long main hall of the Russell Senate Building felt like a tunnel, tightening with every step. The walls breathed. Senator Day couldn't. His life was slipping through his hands. He picked up the already breakneck pace as if jogging away from the committee chamber was going to put distance between himself and his freefall from grace.

Senator Day needed air. He turned right towards the main entrance and descended down the marble stairs to the foyer, past the security booth on the left. The four guards on duty stopped their search-and-question routine and stared at the senator with disdain and disbelief. Good gossip traveled fast.

Senator Day pushed on the wooden doors, hoping to leave the madness behind him. He needed time to regroup, time to think. He needed air. With a single stride forward, the senator stepped from controlled unpleasantness into mass chaos.

The senator froze on the top stair of the Russell Senate Building and looked down into a hornet's nest. Hundreds of protestors, signs waving and bullhorns screaming, assaulted the senator's senses as he stumbled to the side of the granite staircase. The AWARE group's numbers had tripled overnight, their presence buoyed by over two hundred reinforcements from the city's finest homeless establishments. Standing at the bottom of the staircase, waving a large sign with one hand and yelling into a bullhorn with the other, was Kazu Ito's father. A look of fury on his face, he cheered the crowd on, screaming in the memory of his dead son and looking for an apology.

The noon sun combined forces with the multitude of lights from the news crews who were there en masse in response to an anonymous tip. A sea of microphones were shoved into the senator's personal space, and he stepped back, one hand covering his eyes, the other hand help-lessly trying to protect his body from intrusion. Behind him, the audi-ence from the Senate subcommittee squeezed through the doors onto the packed staircase.

The questions came in a flood of babble, a dozen at a time, and the senator tried to push forward past the first wave of cameras and lights. He reached the first landing of the stairs, his path blocked, bodies ev-erywhere. "Shit," was the first comment caught on tape.

The crowd filled the street, reaching thirty yards in either direction. The AWARE group, led by Kazu Ito's father and joined in delirious cel-ebration by several hundred of Al's closest friends, was extending their cause to support their suppressed Asian sisters toiling away in sweat-shops around the world.

Stuck like a herd of cattle in a slaughter chute, Senator Day knew silence wasn't the answer. It didn't matter what he said, but he knew he had to say something. He had lied on far less appropriate occasions than this. He shoved his way to the granite walls that encased the massive stairs of the Russell Building, pushed his way up two steps and floun-dered for his footing. He waved his hands to hush the media and the growing rebellion below.

Peter came out the door as Senator Day tried to quiet the crowd. Al stepped from the building next, Wei Ling sandwiched safely between himself and Jake, who brought up the rear. Detectives Wallace and Nguyen were in pursuit, flashing their badges at anything that moved as they forced their way to the exit. Through the door, Wallace pointed down the stairs at Jake and Wei Ling. Nguyen moved in.

The crowd quieted slowly, Senator Day's hands waving up and down, begging for silence. His lips moved first, his mouth opened in slow motion, and then he doubled over as blood sprayed from two new holes in his chest.

The echo of three rapid-fire gunshots was the start to a full scale riot. The media scattered, cameras rolling in every direction. Trees, the sun, stairs, and legs caught in shaky frames on film. Senator Day's body tumbled down half a flight of stairs before coming to rest on his right side, shoulder and head below his feet. The AWARE group and their homeless friends lost their urge to protest, bodies running in every di-rection. Among the madness, running with a pronounced limp, was a six-four Asian in a business suit.

Nguyen caught Jake from behind and pulled him to the side as Wallace pushed through. "Get inside," Wallace said, pulling Jake and Wei Ling by the arms as the Capitol Police poured from the Russell Building.

Al looked at Jake, who had Wei Ling in his grasp, and nodded. "You got her?"

"Yeah, Al. I got her."

Al jumped over two crouching reporters and joined the Capitol Police at the senator's side. Blood stained the white marble, a trail moving down the staircase like a broken Slinky.

The screams for 911 mixed with the overall hysteria in the air. Twenty seconds after the gunshots, the 911 emergency switchboard lit up like the Vegas Strip.

***

Chow Ying got on the Metro at Union Station and rode until New Carrollton, Maryland. He got off the train and took the pedestrian bridge over the subway tracks. He waited ten minutes and boarded the northbound Amtrak Metroliner. He found a seat in the back row next to the toilets and bought a ticket from the conductor as the train picked up speed leaving the station. He peeked inside his jacket pocket to check on his passport and his money. New York City was next on his list. After that, it was anyone's guess. Maybe San Francisco. Chow Ying pulled the phone from his pocket and checked for messages. Six in the last half hour. Chow Ying knew he was dead already. He had known it for weeks. When the gentle Mr. Wu had asked for his passport in New York, Chow Ying knew his time was short. He knew too much. C.F. Chang would never let him live. And if he wasn't going to live, then he was going to his grave knowing that he had taken away the one thing that C.F. Chang wanted. C.F. Chang had made the kill easy. Instructions, timeline, transportation, identity cover. All the authorities had to do now was find the car.

Chapter 49

Jake squinted as he came out of FBI headquarters. He rubbed his temples and the bridge of his nose before putting his hand up to shade his eyes from the sun. He looked at the trees that lined the street, and turned away from the sun's western position to admire a light blue sky. He inhaled deeply and took in a dose of smog and thick humidity. After forty hours of interrogation in dimly lit rooms without windows, nature's canvass was a pleasant shock to his system.

The white Dodge Caravan was parked at the corner, beyond the steel barrier that lifted vertically from its position flush with the pavement of the street. Al was leaning against the grill of the van, the seat of his jeans cleaning off a thin layer of dead bugs plastered to the flat front of the vehicle.

"Thanks for coming," Jake said, walking slowly, taking in the sights.

"I guess I was your one allotted phone call," Al said smiling.

"Yeah. When did you get out?"

"They questioned me for a few hours and let me go pretty quickly. The privilege of professional courtesy. That and the fact I still have a few friends around town. I tried to get you out sooner, Jake. I pulled every string I had and promised a few things I would have never been able to deliver."

"Thanks for trying."

"You okay?"

"I will be," Jake said confidently.

"Didn't know it was going to turn out the way it did."

"No shit. Neither did I."

"Senator Day getting shot wasn't in the plan."

"How is he? They mentioned inside that he was hanging in there."

"Well at least they didn't keep you completely in the dark."

"There were a couple of good guys in there. A lot of assholes, but a few nice people."

"Looks like Senator Day is going to make it. Chalk it up to the good doctors in D.C. having a lot of practice with gunshot wounds. He caught two shots in the chest. A third shot missed and hit a reporter in the leg. The senator is still in Intensive Care, but he's going to survive. Politically, he may not."

"I don't think either of us is sad about that."

Both men looked down the street toward the Mall.

"So what did they grill you on?" Al asked.

"Everything. Things about the Asian guy, my father, about Senator Day, about Wei Ling. They grilled me on Marilyn's death."

"What did you tell them?"

"I told the truth."

"The whole truth and nothing but the truth?"

"Most of it. Given that the senator had just been shot, they were most interested in what I knew about him. They wanted to know about the girl. What my father knew. They wanted to know why I turned my father over to the FBI for illegal exports, and how he thwarted their raid. They actually started accusing me of trying to blackmail the senator. Then they dropped that threat and moved on."

"There is a reason for that."

"They didn't give me one."

"The guy who shot the senator left a note in his car implicating the head of Chang Industries, a guy by the name of C.F. Chang. The note implicated him in the attempted murder of Senator Day with the intention of influencing the Overseas Labor Special Committee. The note also implicated him for the murder of an American doctor in Saipan. This C.F. Chang is a big fish, Jake."

"And the guy who fired the gun?"

"They haven't found him yet. They have him on tape getting on the Metro at Union Station. Whoever he is, he's got big balls. The guy admitted to being hired by a well-connected Chinese family to assassinate a U.S. senator. He won't get far. But he obviously didn't want to go down alone."

"I don't get it, Al."

"What's that?"

"If this guy came to the U.S. to kill the senator, then why did they keep Wei Ling captive? What's the point? Seems like a contradiction."

"I'm sure the FBI is asking that same question. Or if they aren't, they will be shortly."

"Where is Wei Ling?"

"She's fine. Kate is with her. Amnesty International is giving her the velvet glove treatment. She is staying at the Mayflower. We can stop by and see her anytime. Amnesty International is planning to make you their official Hero-of-the-Month."

"What about our sleight of hand in the charter terminal in Saipan?"

"Technically, we didn't break the law," Al said.

"We bent the hell out of it."

"Is that what you told them?"

"I told the truth. I told them I went to Saipan to see the girl and couldn't get into the sweatshop facilities. I told them that when I arrived at the general aviation terminal the girl was there. I asked her if she wanted to come to Washington and she made the decision to come to D.C. voluntarily. I told them I consulted with a State Department representative who happened to be at the airport at the time and that he told me I wasn't breaking any laws by bringing the girl back to D.C."

"That's pretty close to the truth."

"That is the truth. How could I have known any better? I'm just a student who wants to be an English teacher."

"Did you use that? It sounds rehearsed..."

Jake looked around. "You better believe I used it."

"That's not bad."

"Thanks. What do you think is going to happen to your friend in Saipan?"

"Technically he didn't break the law either. He lied, but he followed the letter of the law. Besides, it looks like he will come out of this smelling like a rose. He was on hand to pick up C.F Chang in Saipan. Our friend Tom may even end up with a medal pinned to his chest. Responsible for grabbing a suspect in the attempted assassination of a senator. And the beautiful thing is that we got him on U.S. soil. No red tape with extradition."

"We got lucky."

"Yes, we did."

Jake had beaten around the bush for as long as he could.

"And my father?"

"He's still in there. But he's not alone. He's got the A-Team of lawyers playing hardball. His political connections are rattling cages."

"What do you think is going to happen to him?"

"I don't know, Jake. I'm sure they are up his ass with a microscope as we speak. Travel history, phone calls, emails. They are probably still investigating you too."

"I didn't do anything. I told them everything I know."

"There may be some lingering questions about Marilyn. Those two detectives you met when the senator was shot know you were with her the night she died. They have you and the guy who shot the senator on the same tape near the scene where Marilyn died. They are still trying to put the pieces together. And they are under a lot of pressure. They are the only law enforcement officers in the city who were pursuing the guy who tried to kill a senator. They are going to need a good explanation for letting him slip by."

"Can't be guilty of something you didn't do. If they had a case against me, I would still be inside. Regardless."

"Yes, you would be."

"So where to?"

"I need something to eat. Been on orange crackers from the vending machine for over a day. Orange crackers and Coke. I need real food. Then we can check on Wei Ling."

"And Kate?" Al asked.

"What about her?"

"You plan on keeping that promise you made to her father?"

"Not sure yet, Al. But you know how I do like to keep my promises."

Al smiled as he got behind the wheel. "You've kept every one since I've met you."

About the Author

Mark Gilleo holds a graduate degree in international business from the University of South Carolina and an undergraduate degree in business from George Mason University. He enjoys traveling, hiking and biking. He speaks Japanese. A fourth-generation Washingtonian, he currently resides in the D.C. area. His first two novels were recognized as finalist and semifinalist, respectively, in the William Faulkner-Wisdom creative writing competition.

Made in the USA
Lexington, KY
29 September 2014